Berkley Prime Crime titles by Rhys Bowen

Royal Spyness Mysteries

HER ROYAL SPYNESS
A ROYAL PAIN
ROYAL FLUSH
ROYAL BLOOD
NAUGHTY IN NICE
THE TWELVE CLUES OF CHRISTMAS
HEIRS AND GRACES
QUEEN OF HEARTS
MALICE AT THE PALACE
CROWNED AND DANGEROUS
ON HER MAJESTY'S FRIGHTFULLY SECRET SERVICE
FOUR FUNERALS AND MAYBE A WEDDING

Constable Evans Mysteries

EVANS ABOVE
EVAN HELP US
EVANLY CHOIRS
EVAN AND ELLE
EVAN CAN WAIT
EVANS TO BETSY
EVAN ONLY KNOWS
EVAN'S GATE
EVAN BLESSED

Anthologies

A ROYAL THREESOME

Specials

MASKED BALL AT BROXLEY MANOR

Malice at the Palace

RHYS BOWEN

BERKLEY PRIME CRIME, NEW YORK

BERKLEY PRIME CRIME

An imprint of Penguin Random House LLC
375 Hudson Street, New York, New York 10014

MALICE AT THE PALACE

A Berkley Prime Crime Book / published by arrangement with the author

ISBN: 9780425260449

PUBLISHING HISTORY
Berkley Prime Crime hardcover edition / August 2015
Berkley Prime Crime mass-market edition / August 2016

PRINTED IN THE UNITED STATES OF AMERICA

Cover illustration by John Mattos.
Cover design by Rita Frangie.

Penguin
Random
House

This book is dedicated to Karen Mayers,
with thanks for her friendship, her support of authors
like me and her fantastic Giants tickets!
Love that seat behind home plate!

Thank you to all the fans of Lady Georgie
who write me such lovely letters
and come to my speaking events.

And thanks as always to my own Queens of Hearts:
my editor, Jackie Cantor, and my stellar agents
Meg Ruley and Christine Hogrebe.
You are my biggest champions.
I feel blessed every day that I work with you.
And not forgetting John who is my first reader
and whose many tweaks keep me humble!

Chapter 1

SUNDAY, OCTOBER 28, 1934
CLABON MEWS, LONDON S.W.7.

Weather outside: utterly bloody! Weather inside: cozy
   and warm.

Enjoying life for once, or would be if Darcy hadn't gone
   off somewhere secret again . . .

Why must he be so annoying!

By London standards, it was a dark and stormy night. Nothing like the wild gales that battered our castle in the Scottish Highlands, of course, but violent enough to make me glad I was safely indoors. Rain peppered the windows and drummed on the slates on the roof while a wild wind howled down the chimney. If I'd been at Castle Rannoch, where I grew up, the wind would also have sent icy drafts rushing down the corridors, making tapestries flap and billow out so that it was almost as unpleasant indoors as it was out. But on this particular night I lay listening to the storm feeling snug, warm, comfortable and very thankful that I wasn't at Castle

Rannoch. I was instead in my friend Belinda's mews cottage in Knightsbridge and enjoying every moment of it.

When I returned from America at the end of August—having been dragged there by my mother who was seeking a quickie divorce from one of her husbands—Mummy had immediately flitted away with the very briefest of good-byes as usual. She had abandoned her only child with monotonous regularity and barely a backward glance since that first time she bolted when I was two. But on this occasion she had actually demonstrated a spark of maternal feeling I hadn't known she possessed. As she left Brown's hotel she handed me a generous check. "Georgie, darling, I want you to know that I think you behaved splendidly in Hollywood," she said. "I simply couldn't have survived without you in that savage place."

I went pink and didn't quite know what to say as this was so out of character. "Golly, thanks awfully," I managed to mumble.

"I have to go back to Max in Germany, darling," she said, kissing me on the cheek, "but I don't want you to think I'm running out on you. You do know you are very welcome to come and stay whenever you want to."

"Thank you, but I don't think Berlin would be to my liking," I said. "Not since that horrible little Hitler chappie came into power. Too much shouting and strutting."

She gave that tinkling laugh that had delighted audiences across the world. "Oh, darling. Nobody takes him seriously. I mean, who could with a mustache like that. He once kissed my hand and it was like an encounter with a hedgehog. Max says he's good for German morale at the moment but he can't last."

"All the same, I'd rather stay in good old England for a while," I said. "That time in America was quite enough excitement for me."

"You don't mean to go home to Scotland?" she asked.

"Actually no," I said. "I'm not exactly welcome at Castle Rannoch these days, and Belinda told me I could use her London house while she stays on in Hollywood." I added,

"And now you've given me this check, I can actually afford to eat for a while."

A frown crossed that lovely face. "Darling, have there been times when you couldn't afford to eat?"

"Oodles of them. I once survived for a month on tea and baked beans."

"How disgusting. Really, Georgie, if you need something just ask. Max is revoltingly rich, you know. I could get him to make you an allowance, I'm sure."

"I can't live off Max's money, Mummy. Granddad wouldn't approve, for one thing. Not German money. You know how Granddad would hate that after your brother was killed in the war."

"One must learn to forgive and forget, as I keep telling your grandfather. And once we're married—well, it will be my money too, won't it?" She raised her hands excitedly. "You must come over for the wedding! You can be my maid of honor."

"Do you really intend to marry him?" I couldn't bring myself to look at her.

"It's what he wants, so I suppose the answer is yes. We'll just have to see, won't we? Well, I must be toddling off, darling, if I'm to catch the boat train. Take care of yourself and for God's sake let that gorgeous Darcy take you to bed as soon as possible. Virginity simply isn't fashionable or even acceptable after twenty."

And with that she was gone. I had moved into Belinda's lovely little London mews home and had enjoyed playing a lady of leisure for a while. The one aspect of my happiness that was lacking was that Darcy was off on another secret assignment and I had no idea when he'd return to London or how I could contact him. Really, he was the most infuriating man. I knew he did things that were often hush-hush (I suspected he might even occasionally work undercover for MI5) but an occasional postcard from Buenos Aires or Calcutta would have been nice.

A particularly violent gust of wind made the window frame rattle. I pulled the blankets up and curled into a little ball, enjoying the knowledge that I was safe and warm. The money that Mummy had given me wouldn't last forever, but I hoped at least I could stretch it out until after Christmas. If only I could find some kind of job, I could go on living here until Belinda came home—and who knew when that would be if she became a successful costume designer in Hollywood. But jobs didn't seem to exist for young women like me, trained only to snare a husband. I was even toying with the idea of applying for a temporary Christmas job at one of the department stores, if I didn't think that the news might leak back to my relatives and cause a stink.

And in case you're wondering why my relatives should care if I worked behind the counter in Selfridges or Gamages I should point out that they were not exactly your run-of-the-mill, ordinary people—they were the king and queen. My great-grandmother was Queen Victoria so I was half royal, expected to behave in a way that befitted my station without being given the means to do so. Jolly unfair, actually.

I pushed worrying thoughts aside. For the moment all was well. It had been remarkably peaceful, since my maid, Queenie, had been absent for the last few weeks. She had gone home to look after her mother, who had been hit by a tram while crossing Walthamtow High Street and broken her leg. But the leg had healed and Queenie was due to return to me any day now. I was anticipating it with mixed emotions since Queenie was the most utterly hopeless maid in the history of the universe. In fact I rather suspected that her family was urging her to hurry back to me, not because of any sense of duty but because they couldn't wait to get rid of her. I sighed, settled down and let my mind drift to more pleasant subjects. I was half asleep when I heard a noise that jerked me instantly awake again.

Over the noise of the wind and rain I had heard the distinct metallic click of a latch, followed by the sound of a door being opened. Somebody was coming into the house. I wondered if I had forgotten to lock the door before I went to bed, but I definitely remembered doing so. I was out of bed in a flash. Belinda's cottage was really tiny, with a flight of stairs leading up to the bedroom I was occupying, a bathroom and a minute maid's room. I looked around desperately. There was nowhere to hide if burglars had broken in. I examined the bed, but Belinda had piled boxes and trunks under it. The wardrobe was still full of her clothes. I wondered if perhaps I could tiptoe across the hall to the box room, or better yet the bathroom. Surely no burglar would think of looking in the bath?

I opened the door cautiously and was about to peer around it when I heard the sound of low voices in the hallway down below. Golly. More than one of them. I glanced back into the room to see if there was anything I might use as a weapon— but I didn't think the frail china table lamp would be much good, even if I could unplug it in time. Then I heard a laugh that I recognized. Belinda's laugh. She had come home unexpectedly and she was probably talking to the taxi driver who was carrying in her luggage. I was about to step out to greet her when I heard her say, "Toby, you are so naughty. Now stop that, at least until I have my gloves off."

"Can't wait, you delectable creature," said a deep man's voice. "I'm going to rip off all your clothes, throw you down on that bed and give you one hell of a good ravishing."

"You are certainly not going to rip anything," Belinda said, laughing again. "I happen to like my clothes. But you may undress me as quickly as you like."

"Good show," he said. "I've been dying to bed you since we first danced together on the ship. But too many watchful eyes. It was dashed clever of you to suggest coming back here rather than a hotel. A man in my position can't be too careful, don't you know."

Toby? I thought. Sir Toby Blenchley, cabinet minister? I had no time to consider this as they were now heading for the stairs. I stood behind that door in an agony of embarrassment and indecision. Surely she couldn't have forgotten that I was occupying her house, and thus her bedroom, could she? Did she really think it would be acceptable to roll in the hay with a cabinet minister while I was there? Where did she expect me to go while they were thus engaged? I sighed in exasperation. How typically Belinda.

I heard her giggle and say, "My, but you are impatient, aren't you?" as they came up the stairs. What on earth was I to do? Leap out on them and say, "Welcome home, Belinda, darling. Perhaps you had forgotten that you'd lent your house to your best friend?" Sir Toby wasn't in the first flush of youth. What if the surprise brought on a heart attack? On the other hand, there was now no way I could cross the upstairs landing to the maid's room, and I certainly didn't want to be trapped in there listening to their hijinks.

Then it was decided for me. Belinda ran up the rest of the stairs calling, "Come on then, last one into bed is a sissy!" She pushed open the bedroom door with full force, trapping me behind it. She had several robes hanging from the back of that door and these were now in my face. I heard the sounds of two people undressing hurriedly. Maybe if I kept quiet and didn't move he'd have his way with her and then go, I decided. Better still, maybe they'd both fall asleep and I could creep out and take refuge in the box room.

"God, you really are delectable," I heard him say. "Those neat little breasts. Enough to drive a man wild. Come here."

I heard bedsprings creak, a grunt, a sigh. Then something terrible happened. One of Belinda's robes was trimmed with feathers. And one of these feathers was now tickling my nose. To my horror I realized I was going to sneeze. I was pinned so tightly behind the door that it was hard for me to get my hand up to my nose. I managed it just in time and clamped my fingers over my nose and mouth. The noises on the bed were getting more violent and urgent. The sneeze was still lingering, waiting to come out the moment I let go. I willed it to go away but I had to breathe. And then, in spite of everything, it came out, a great big "A—choo," just at the moment when Belinda was moaning "Oh yes, oh yes."

It was amazing how quickly the room fell silent.

"What the devil was that?" Sir Toby asked.

"Someone's in the house." I heard the bed creak as Belinda got up.

"I thought you said there'd be nobody here."

"It must be my maid, although I didn't tell her I was coming home," Belinda said. "How could she have known? I'll go and see if she's sleeping in her room." Then she lowered her voice. "Don't go away, you big brute. I'll be back and we can continue from where we left off."

"I don't know about that," he said. "Not if your maid's in the house. Is she likely to gossip?"

"My maid is paid very well to close her eyes to anything that goes on in my bedroom," Belinda said. "You don't have to worry, Toby, I promise you. I'll just get my robe. . . ."

And she swung the door open. . . .

Chapter 2

It was fortunate that the storm outside was making such a racket or her scream would have been heard all the way to Victoria Station and maybe even across the Thames.

"Belinda, it's all right," I said, reaching out to touch her. "It's me. Georgie."

"Oh God." She was gasping now, her hand over her naked heart. "Georgie. Have you gone mad? What on earth are you doing hiding in my bedroom?"

"I'm sorry if I scared you, Belinda," I said. "I didn't intend to hide, but by the time I'd woken up and heard you coming up the stairs it was too late to do anything sensible. And you were the one who pushed the door open so hard, trapping me behind it."

Sir Toby was standing up beside the bed and had obviously just realized he was naked in the presence of a strange female. He grabbed a lace-trimmed, heart-shaped pillow and attempted to hold it over the important parts. He looked old and ridiculous and quite unlike the masterful, dapper man whose picture I had seen on newsreels and in magazines. "You know this person, Belinda?" he demanded. "Should we call the police?"

"Oh no, of course not," Belinda said. "She's my best friend—Georgiana Rannoch."

"Lady Georgiana, sister of the Duke of Rannoch?" Sir Toby said. "Good God. But what's she doing in your house? In your bedroom, for God's sake?"

"I've no idea, Toby."

I'd had enough. They were both looking at me with horror and suspicion as if I were a dangerous cornered animal. "Perhaps in the heat of passion you forgot that you invited me to stay in your house while you were away, Belinda," I said. "And you might have given me advance warning that you were coming back."

Belinda had taken down one of the robes and was in the process of trying to put it on. I noticed that her body was curvier than when we had shared a room as teenagers at a finishing school in Switzerland. No wonder men were so attracted to her.

"I remember mentioning that you could use my house," Belinda said as she successfully pulled on the robe and tied it at her waist, "but I'd no idea that you'd taken me up on it. You might have dropped me a note to tell me."

"Dropped you a note?" I was fully indignant now. "Belinda, I wrote you two letters. And since I didn't know where you'd be staying, I addressed one to you, care of Golden Pictures, and one, care of the Beverly Hills Hotel. Do you mean to tell me you didn't receive either of them?"

"Of course I didn't receive them. I never went back to Golden Pictures. It's been virtually shut down by Mr. Goldman's widow; at least all work is halted for now. And my budget certainly didn't run to the Beverly Hills Hotel."

Sir Toby cleared his throat. "Given the circumstances, Belinda, I think I should depart as rapidly as possible. So if you young ladies don't mind stepping outside while I get dressed . . ."

Belinda followed me out onto the landing. "Honestly, Georgie. You've spoiled everything."

She stood there, glaring at me while I squirmed in embarrassment.

"I'm sorry, but you did offer and I did write to tell you. And I'm not about to walk out into the storm at this hour so that you can finish your little tryst with a cabinet minister."

Sir Toby emerged, now looking more like himself in a dark suit and old school tie. "I'll just be toddling off home then, Belinda," he said. "I'm sure I'll pick up a cab on Knightsbridge. I'll see myself out."

Belinda followed him down the stairs. "Will I see you again soon?"

He cleared his throat in that annoying way that some men have. "I don't really think that would be wise . . . much as I'd like to. Can't afford to risk bringing scandal to the party, you know. Let's just put tonight behind us. Forget all about it."

And with that he grabbed his overcoat, opened the front door and stepped out into the storm.

I stood there at the top of the stairs, then came down slowly. We looked at each other in tense silence.

"Oh well, that's that, I suppose," Belinda said. "Is there anything to drink in the house?"

"I could make you a cup of tea, or I believe there is cocoa," I replied.

This made her burst into laughter. "God, Georgie, why do you have to be so damned pure and naïve all the time? When are you going to grow up and realize what life is all about and when people say they need a drink they mean a large whiskey, not bloody cocoa."

"I think you have Scotch in your drinks cabinet," I said. "And my life is very different from yours, Belinda. I don't bring cabinet ministers home for sex. As a matter of fact I don't bring anybody home for sex."

Belinda sighed. "You really are a cocoa type of person, Georgie. God, and I was looking forward to that. There is something about powerful men that really attracts me. And he was obviously good at it too. And now I'll never know. . . ."

Another awkward silence. "I've said I was sorry," I repeated. "I don't know what else to say. And you've used me often enough, including turning up out of the blue in Hollywood, so I do think you owe me the odd favor."

There was a long silence as she went down the stairs and over to the cabinet in the corner. I heard liquor slosh into a glass. Or rather two glasses. She came back up the stairs, holding out a half tumbler of whiskey for me. "Here, drink this. You need it as much as I do. And you're right. I did offer you my house and I have used you shamelessly on many occasions. Go on. Down the hatch."

I did as she commanded, feeling the fiery liquid going down my throat and spreading warmth throughout my body. I coughed and wiped my eyes. She laughed. "You must be the only Scot who can't take her whiskey," she said.

"I'm only a quarter Scottish," I said, managing a weak smile. "And I've never developed a taste for it."

"You and your bloody cocoa," she said, and she started to laugh again. "Oh well, I don't suppose it would have led anywhere. It was just one of those shipboard flings. And now he's gone home."

"Back to his wife, if I remember correctly," I said. "And wasn't he the one who gave that speech about the sanctity of the family and every proud Englishman being king of his own castle with his wife and children around him?"

She nodded. "He's a politician, Georgie. They say what people want to hear."

"Belinda, I think I did you a favor. You could have caused real trouble. You could have brought down the government."

"That might have been interesting," she said. "At least people would know who I was then. I'd be a celebrity."

"Of the wrong sort," I said. "No respectable household would invite you for dinner, in case you seduced their husbands."

"I suppose you're right as usual," she said. "It did cross my mind that it might be nice to be someone's mistress, taken care of, set up in a swank flat somewhere."

"With no security whatever, Belinda. Why not someone's wife? Your pedigree is as good as mine—well, almost."

"But I'm soiled goods, darling. No top-drawer family

wants their son to get hitched to someone like me. I'm clearly not a virgin, like you. I've a reputation now, and no fortune to go with it. And I'm stony-broke at the moment—no idea how I'm going to pay my maid and put food on the table, unless something good turns up."

"So Hollywood didn't work out for you, then?" I said. "You said that Mrs. Goldman shut down Golden Pictures, but what about all the other studios? Didn't any of them want a talented costume designer? You had terrific contacts, after all—you swam nude with Craig Hart."

Belinda frowned. "It seems there are too many talented people in Hollywood, fighting for too little work. And I didn't really feel comfortable over there. That sort of lifestyle wasn't for me. Too brash. Too artificial. Nobody means what they say. They talk big, make big promises and it's all fabrication."

"I'm sorry," I said. "I bet you'd have made a brilliant costume designer. You are very talented."

"Kind of you to say so, darling." She managed a weak smile.

"You have trained with Chanel, Belinda. And you're really good. You could easily start your own line over here. I know you could."

"I know I could too," she said, "except that it all takes money. I'd need premises, seamstresses, fabric . . . and remember what I found out before? Those who can afford good clothes want everything on credit. It's a constant fight to make them pay up."

I sighed this time. "It's not easy, is it? My mother gave me a nice check when she went back to Germany but it won't last forever. And now that you're home I'm not even sure where I'll go. Back to Scotland, with my sister-in-law telling me what a burden I am, I suppose."

Belinda put a hand on my shoulder. "I'd let you stay on here, but there's nowhere for you to sleep when my maid comes back. And it does rather cramp one's style having a friend asleep on a downstairs sofa."

"Of course I realize I can't stay on here," I said.

"But you have the family home on Belgrave Square," she said. "Oodles of bedrooms. What's wrong with that?"

"Nothing, except that Fig made it quite clear they couldn't afford to open it up just for me. Apparently even the small amount of coal I'd use to heat one bedroom is beyond their means."

"Your brother is really as hard up as that?" Belinda asked.

"His wife claims he is. Actually I think she's just naturally stingy, and she doesn't want any of their money spent on me. She's told me over and over that Binky's responsibility for me ended when I had my season. It's my fault that I haven't married well."

"Speaking of marriage . . ." She paused. "What news of Darcy? He's still in the picture, isn't he?"

"When he's around," I said. I stared out past her, at the white painted front door. "I haven't seen him in a while. You know Darcy. He shows up, it's heaven and then he goes again and I never know where he is or when he'll come back. He's the most infuriating man, Belinda. He doesn't even have a proper London address. He borrows friends' houses when they are out of town, sleeps on their couches. And half the time he can't tell me where he's going."

"Georgie, who does he actually work for when he takes these little jobs—do you know? Do you think it's something frightfully illegal, like drug running for gangsters?"

"Golly, I don't think so," I replied. "Some of the things he does do tend to be remarkably hush-hush. I think he takes almost any assignment he's offered, but mostly on the right side of the law." I looked around and lowered my voice, even though we were alone and the storm was raging. "In fact sometimes I think he might be employed as a spy by the government on occasion. He doesn't say and I don't ask. I know he's trying to make enough money so that we can get married. . . ."

"You're engaged, darling?" She grabbed my hands.

I felt my cheeks going red. "Well, sort of secretly. We can't announce an engagement until Darcy feels he can support me, and heaven knows when that might be. I've told him I wouldn't mind living in a little flat, but he's determined to do the thing properly."

"Of course he is." She was looking at me wistfully. "You're so lucky, Georgie. You've a wonderful future to look forward to with a terrific man who loves you."

This was so unlike Belinda that I turned to look at her. "Belinda—you'll meet the right chap, I know you will. You've got a brighter future than I because you're so talented."

"Dear Georgie." She reached out to hug me. "You're so nice. You deserve to be happy."

"Cheer up, Belinda. Everything will work out splendidly," I said. "You'll find a job, or your father will relent and give you some money . . . and aren't you set to inherit something from your grandmother?"

She made a face. "My grandmother will live to a hundred. She still walks three miles every morning and takes cold baths. And I'll get no money from my father as long as my evil stepmother is in the picture. No, darling, I'm afraid it's back to Crockford's for me if I'm to survive."

"Crockford's? The club, you mean? Do you really expect to make money gambling?"

"Actually I do rather well, darling," she said. "I play up the helpless and innocent young girl act—you know—first time at the tables and it's all so terribly confusing. Kind men usually put in my stake for me. So I never actually lose my own money and I win remarkably often. Of course, some of the men expect something in return. . . ." She managed a bright smile. "But enough gloom and doom. There is room enough in my bed for two and in the morning we'll make plans."

Chapter 3

**Dear Diary: Belinda came home unexpectedly last
night. Rather embarrassing, actually. Now I have no
idea where I'm going to go. I hate living like this,
relying on the kindness or pity or duty of others to
take me in. When will I ever have a place of my own?**

In the morning the storm had blown itself out. The world
was bathed in bright sunshine. I got out of bed and went
over to the window, savoring the morning quiet. The pavement below was littered with swaths of sodden leaves and
even small branches, bearing testimony to the violence of
the night's storm. Belinda sighed and muttered something
and I turned to look back at her. She was still sleeping bliss-
fully, looking remarkably innocent and angelic in sleep. I
stood there, staring down at her. Belinda was usually the
optimistic, opportunistic one, living rather well by her wits.
She'd had affairs with glamorous Italian counts and

Bulgarian royals. So it was quite unlike her to reveal a vulnerable side. I wondered if something had happened in Hollywood. . . .

Then I decided I should be more concerned about me. At least she had a place of her own to live. At least she didn't have royal family connections to live up to. I wondered where I'd go now. Would she expect me to move out immediately? In which case I'd have no choice but to take the next train back to Scotland. Oh golly, I thought. Castle Rannoch with winter coming, lashed by gales, gloomy beyond belief. I'd have to write to Fig to see if they'd have me, since it was now no longer my home. And if she said no . . . I turned away from the window, trying not to think about it. Mummy said I was welcome to stay in Germany, but I didn't fancy that either—not the way things seemed to be going there these days.

Either way, I'd have to start packing up my things. I'd need to collect Queenie from her parents' house, which would mean an excuse to visit Granddad. That thought made me smile. I'd been visiting my grandfather on a regular basis while I'd been in London. I suppose I should add that I'm talking about my mother's father, the retired Cockney policeman who lived in a semidetached with gnomes in the front garden, not the fierce Scottish duke who married a princess. The Scottish grandfather died before I was born, thank goodness, and it's said that his ghost still haunts the battlements of Castle Rannoch.

But my living grandfather was one of my favorite people. He always made me welcome, even though he had very little himself. Another thought crossed my mind: wouldn't it be lovely if I could stay with him for a while? I pictured waking to the smell of bacon cooking, sitting drinking tea in his tiny kitchen, chatting with him by the fire. I sighed. Unfortunately I knew this would be frowned upon. It had been made quite clear to me that it would create great embarrassment to the family if the newspapers got wind of it. Royal in Reduced Circumstances. Her Highness Eats

Down the Fish-and-Chip Shop. I could see the left-wing newspapers would have a field day.

Really my family was too tiresome. I couldn't take a job that might embarrass them. I couldn't stay with the one person who wanted my company. And yet they offered me no financial support. How on earth did they expect me to live? I knew the answer to that one immediately: I was expected to make the right sort of marriage to some half-mad, chinless European princeling—the sort who get assassinated with monotonous frequency. They had introduced me to a couple of candidates and I had turned them down, much to everyone's annoyance. But there are some lengths a girl won't go to to put a roof over her head.

There must be something I can do, I thought as I tiptoed downstairs and filled the kettle for tea. The trouble was that I wasn't trained for anything except how to behave in the correct social circles. And in these days of depression there were people with real qualifications who were lining up for jobs. I sighed as I made the tea. If only I'd inherited my mother's stunning looks, I could have followed her onto the stage. But alas I took after my father—tall, lanky, healthy Scottish outdoor looks.

I cheered myself with the thought of going to see Granddad and made boiled eggs and toast before I went to wake Belinda. She looked rather the worse for wear as she sat at the dining table, sipping her tea and nibbling on a piece of toast.

"I feel terrible turning you out now, darling," she said. "If only I had a spare room . . ."

"I know. It's quite all right," I said. "Don't worry, something will turn up. I'll go and retrieve Queenie and she can pack up my things and if worse comes to worst I can stay with my grandfather for a few days."

"I thought that was frowned upon by the family," Belinda said.

"It is, but they aren't exactly offering me an alternative, are they? I'll pick up a copy of *The Lady* when I go out. There must be some job I could do."

"Georgie, don't be silly. The *Lady* has advertisements for governesses and ladies' maids."

"And things like companions and social secretaries. Anything's better than Castle Rannoch."

"I agree with that. But feel free to sleep on my sofa until you find something. I don't want to turn you out into the storm."

I smiled. "In case you haven't noticed, it's a lovely sunny morning."

She glared blearily at the window. "Is it? I hadn't noticed." Then she turned back to me and smiled. "Sorry. You should know by now that I'm not at my best in the morning. I'll cheer up as the day goes on. And I'll be in top form by the time I go to Crockford's."

I thought about Belinda as I went upstairs to wash and dress. I had always envied her her confident worldliness, her savoir faire, her elegance and style. I had always thought if anyone knew how to survive, it was she. I put on my cashmere jumper—one of my mother's castoffs—and tartan skirt, topped it with my old Harris tweed overcoat, and out I went into the cold, crisp morning. I loved walking on days like this. At home in Scotland it would have been a perfect day for a ride through the heather, with my horse's breath coming like dragon's fire and the sound of his hooves echoing from the crags.

As I walked I began to feel more optimistic. Maybe Castle Rannoch wouldn't be that bad. I could go out riding and walking and play with my adorable nephew and niece. And even Fig couldn't object to my visiting for a week or so—long enough to scan the *Lady* and send out letters of application. After all, I had helped out at a house party last Christmas. Maybe I could do the same sort of thing this year. Lady Hawse-Gorzley would give me a good reference. Or I could perhaps be someone's social secretary. I might not be able to type properly but I could write a good letter and I did know the rules of polite society. Maybe someone newly rich would be tickled to have a secretary with royal connections who knew the ropes. And the family couldn't frown at that sort of job, out of London, away from the prying eyes of the press.

Then I had another encouraging thought. I could always go to stay with the Dowager Duchess of Eynsford. I had been a sort of companion cum social secretary to her, hadn't I? She had been grateful for my company earlier in the year and I was sure she'd welcome me back. Perhaps the young duke and his cousin had returned from Switzerland, in which case it might even be quite jolly. I strode out with renewed vigor along Pont Street. My head was so buzzing with ideas that I hardly noticed where I was walking. By the time I had to stop to cross Sloane Street, I realized I was in Belgravia, very close to our London home in Belgrave Square. I couldn't resist taking a look at it, although I had hardly ever stayed there as a child and it had never felt like home to me. I crossed and entered the quiet of Belgrave Square with its elegant white-fronted houses and the gardens in the middle, with trees standing stark and bare behind their iron railings.

Two nannies were walking their charges, talking together as they pushed prams. A maid was scrubbing a front step. A milkman was making a delivery, the bottles rattling as he carried them down to a service entrance. It was all so peaceful and domestic that I found myself staring up at Rannoch House with longing. It was in the middle of the north side of the square—the biggest and most imposing of the houses.

"I wish . . ." I heard myself saying out loud, but when I analyzed it, I didn't quite know what I wished. Probably that I had a place where I still belonged in the world. I was just about to walk past when the front door opened and none other than my brother, Binky, current Duke of Rannoch, came down the steps, adjusting the scarf at his neck as he came. He was about to walk past without noticing me but I stepped out in front of him.

"Hello, Binky," I said.

He stopped, startled, then blinked as if he thought he was

seeing a mirage. "Georgie. It's you. Blow me down. What a lovely surprise. We didn't know you were in town."

"I didn't expect you to be in town either," I said.

"We came down a couple of weeks ago," he said. "Fig's aunt just died and left her a nice little legacy, so we decided to have a central heating system put into Castle Rannoch. It can be beastly cold in winter, can't it? And little Adelaide gets such nasty croup. So while they're putting in boilers and pipes and things we decided to come down to London. We have to look for a governess for Podge anyway so it was really killing two birds with one stone. But enough of our boring lives—how about you? What have you been doing? The last we heard you were staying with the Duchess of Eynsford."

"A lot has happened since then," I said. A spasm of guilt passed through me that I should have written to my brother more often. Then I told myself that Fig would probably have burned the letters anyway. "But are you on your way to an appointment? I could come to visit when you have time and give you all my news, rather than standing here in the street freezing."

"Come in now, if you're not too busy," he said. "I was only going down to my club to read the morning papers and Fig would love to see you."

This later was completely untrue, I was sure, but I wasn't going to turn down the invitation. "I'd love to see everyone," I said. "It's been ages since I've seen Podge and Adelaide. Are you still calling her that, by the way? It doesn't seem the right sort of thing to call a baby."

"I call her Dumpling, because she has round chubby cheeks," Binky said, "but Fig doesn't like that and Nanny insists on calling children by their proper names. No baby talk and no nonsense."

"You have a new nanny?"

"Yes. Fig's idea, actually. She felt that our nanny was too old and too indulgent. So she pensioned her off. Must say I don't quite take to the new one. Too modern and efficient and worries about germs."

As we talked Binky went back up the steps and opened the front door. "Come in, Georgie."

I followed him into the foyer. Binky had hardly had time to close the door behind us when our butler, Hamilton, appeared with that uncanny sense that butlers have when someone is going in or out.

"Back so soon, Your Grace? I hope there is nothing amiss," he began, then he saw me and his face lit up in a most satisfying way. "Why, Lady Georgiana. What a pleasant surprise. It's been so long."

"How are you, Hamilton?" I said as he helped me out of my coat.

"As well as can be expected, my lady. Rheumatics, you know, and a lot of stairs in this house. Should I serve coffee in the morning room, Your Grace, or would her ladyship prefer a proper breakfast in the dining room? It hasn't been cleared away yet although I believe Her Grace had a tray sent up this morning."

"Jolly good kidneys this morning, Georgie. And you know what damn fine kedgeree Cook makes."

"Sounds lovely," I said. In an attempt to make my mother's check last as long as possible I had been living quite simply, apart from the occasional splurge of ready-made food from Harrods. And I didn't know how to cook kidneys.

"Go and help yourself," Binky said. "I'll let Fig know you're here and then I might join you for another round, although Fig complains I'm putting on a bit of weight around the middle." He patted his stomach, which was becoming a little like Father Christmas's.

"Should I have fresh coffee sent to the dining room, my lady?" Hamilton asked, hovering at the baize door that led down to the kitchen.

"That would be lovely, thank you, Hamilton," I said. "I'm sure I haven't forgotten my way to the dining room."

I started for the back of the house while Binky went up the stairs. I hadn't quite reached the dining room door when I heard a shrill voice say, "Here? Now? What does she want?"

"I don't think she wants anything, Fig," Binky's voice

answered. "We met on the pavement quite by chance and I invited her to come in, of course."

"Really, Binky, you are too tiresome," Fig's voice went on. "You don't think, do you? I am not even up and dressed. You should have told her to come back at a more suitable hour."

"Dash it all, Fig, she is my sister," Binky said. "This is her home."

"This is our home now, Binky. Your sister has been off for months, God knows where, making her own life—as well she should, since she's no longer your responsibility." A heavy sigh followed. "Well, go downstairs and entertain her and I suppose I'll have to get up. I was looking forward to a long lie-in with *Country Life* this morning too."

I tiptoed through to the dining room as Binky came down the stairs again.

"Fig will join us in a minute," he said, managing a bright smile. "Slept in late today, don't you know. But do go ahead and tuck in. I'm sure it's all still hot."

I did as I was told and sat down with a plate piled with kedgeree, kidneys, scrambled egg and bacon. It was a feast such as I hadn't had in a while and it made me wonder whether Fig's legacy had been big enough to have improved their standard of living. When I had last been at home at Castle Rannoch, Fig's catering had been decidedly on the mean side, to the point of replacing the Cooper's Oxford marmalade with Golden Shred.

Coffee was brought and I had almost cleaned my plate when I heard footsteps tapping down the hall and Fig came in. "Georgiana," she said in a clipped voice, "what a surprise. How lovely to see you." She looked older than when I had seen her last and permanent frown lines were beginning to show on her forehead. She'd never been a beauty but had once had that healthy if horsey look of country women, with a perfect complexion. Now she looked decidedly pasty faced and I felt renewed pity for Binky that he was stuck with someone like this for the rest of his life. If things went as planned I would have Darcy to look at across the break-fast table every morning—a far more desirable prospect.

Fig poured herself a cup of coffee then sat down across the table from me. "We didn't even know you were in town or we would have had you over for a meal. In fact we had no idea where you were, had we, Binky? Your brother was quite worried that he hadn't heard from you."

"The last we heard was when you went to stay with the Eynsfords," Binky said, "and there was that spot of bother, wasn't there? That unpleasant business with poor old Cedric."

"Georgiana does seem to attract unpleasant business," Fig said. "You've been abroad since you left the Eynsfords? We met the dowager duchess at Balmoral and she mentioned something along those lines."

"I went to America with my mother," I said.

"What on earth for? Is she looking for a rich American husband now?" Fig stirred her coffee fiercely.

"Oh I say, Fig, that's really a bit much," Binky interrupted.

"On the contrary. She went there to divorce one." I smiled at her sweetly. "She is planning to marry the industrialist Max von Strohheim."

"A German?" Fig frowned at my brother. "You hear that, Binky? Georgie's mother is going to marry a German. How people can forget the Great War so quickly I just do not understand."

"I don't suppose Georgie's mum's beau had much to do with the Great War," Binky said in his usual affable manner. I didn't like to say that I thought he had probably made a fortune in supplying arms. His industrial empire was certainly wide reaching. "So did you have a good time in America, Georgie? Were you there long?"

"Parts of it were lovely, thank you," I said. "The crossing on the *Berengaria*—"

"You hear that, Binky?" Fig interrupted. "She sailed on the *Berengaria*—the millionaires' ship, they call her. Something I'll never be able to do. Obviously I went wrong in life. I should have become an actress and had dalliances with all kinds of men, like Georgie's mother."

"You don't have the looks, old thing," Binky said kindly. "You have to admit that Georgie's mum is an absolute corker."

Fig went rather red and I tried not to choke on my coffee.

"She is little better than a high-class tart," Fig snapped.

"Steady on, old thing," Binky said. "Georgie's mum may have led a somewhat colorful life but she's a thoroughly decent sort. Really kind to me when she married Father. She was the only one who could see I was miserable at boarding school."

Fig saw that this battle wasn't going her way. "You were missed at Balmoral, Georgiana," she said. "The king and queen both commented on your absence. Quite put out that you weren't there."

"Oh, I'm sure my presence hardly made a difference," I said, secretly pleased that they even noticed I hadn't joined the house party this year.

"Quite put out," Fig repeated. "The king actually said to me, 'Where's young Georgiana, then? Had enough of putting up with us old fogies? Rather spend time with the bright young things, what?'"

"And the little princesses missed you too, Georgie," Binky said. "That Elizabeth is turning into a damned fine horse-woman. She said she was sorry you weren't there to go riding with her."

"It's probably not the wisest thing to snub the king and queen, Georgie," Fig said. "They are the heads of the family, after all. And you know how the queen absolutely expects one to show up at Balmoral."

That was true enough. It was hard to find any excuse good enough to get out of it. It was even reported that a certain member of the royal clan timed her pregnancies so that she could miss Balmoral biennially. Actually we Rannochs didn't mind it. We were used to freezing cold rooms and the piper waking everyone at dawn, not to mention the tartan wallpaper in the loo.

"We had a lovely time there this year, didn't we, Binky?" Fig drained her coffee and got up to help herself to a piece of toast.

"Oh rather," he agreed. "Of course, the weather wasn't too kind. Rained every bally day, actually. Missed every bird I shot at. Apart from that it was quite jolly. They've a new piper who plays at dawn."

"I'm sorry I had to miss it," I said with a straight face. I turned back to Fig. "So I hear you've come into a legacy, Fig, and you're having central heating put in."

"Only a small legacy," Fig said hurriedly. "My aunt lived very simply. No luxuries. She was very active in the Girl Guides until she died."

"And you're just down here until the new boiler is put in?"

"Actually we thought we might as well keep on here until the wedding," Binky said and got a warning frown from Fig.

"The wedding?" I asked.

"The royal wedding," Binky said.

"The Prince of Wales is finally going to buckle down and get married?" I asked in surprise.

"Not the Prince of Wales, although it's certainly taking long enough for him to select someone suitable to be a future queen," Fig said. "It's the younger son, Prince George, who is to marry next month."

I couldn't have been more surprised. "George?" It came out as a squeak. Prince George, the king's fourth son, was utterly charming and delightful and fun, but from all I'd heard (and seen on occasion) he had been rather a naughty boy. "So the king and queen are trying to rein him in."

"What do you mean, rein him in?" Fig asked.

"One has heard rumors . . ." I glanced at Binky but got no reaction, so I supposed that news didn't travel as far as Scotland or my relatives were so naïve that they weren't aware that behavior like George's went on.

"Come now, Georgiana. Even princes of the realm are allowed to have a little fun in their youth," Fig said. "As long as they do the right thing and marry well."

Personally I thought that posing naked wearing nothing but a Guardsman's bearskin and having an affair with Noel Coward were slightly more than "having a little fun." I'd once spotted him at a party where cocaine was being snorted. There were rumors also of affairs with highly unsuitable women.

"Who is he marrying?" I asked.

"Princess Marina of Greece," Binky said. "Danish royal family, you know. You've met her cousin Philip, haven't you? Very handsome. Nice boy. Good sportsman."

"And of course we've been invited to the wedding," Fig added with satisfaction. "Wouldn't miss it for the world, would we, Binky?"

"Oh no," Binky said. "Ripping good fun."

"I wonder if I'm invited," I said. "Is it to be a big affair?"

"Westminster Abbey," Fig said. "I wouldn't know if you've been included in the guest list. They have to draw the line somewhere."

Binky pulled up his chair a little closer to me. "So, Georgie, what are your plans now you've returned from America? Are you staying in London?"

"I was borrowing a friend's mews cottage," I said, "but she has returned home unexpectedly so I'm having to move out. I was thinking of coming up to Castle Rannoch while I look for a suitable job, but of course that's now out of the question. There is always my grandfather. . . ."

"The one in Essex?" Fig made it sound as if it were one of the outer circles of hell.

"Since the other one has been dead for many years the answer to that would be yes," I replied. "He's a perfectly charming person, just not—"

"Of our class," Fig cut in. "You can't seriously be thinking of living in Essex! What would the family say if they found out? I don't think they would appreciate the news that you were staying with a Cockney in Essex, Georgiana. However charming he is."

"Then do you have a better suggestion?" I asked.

"You must stay here," Binky said with great enthusiasm.

Fig's face was a picture. She opened her mouth, went to say something, closed it again. I couldn't resist answering hurriedly, "If you're really sure it wouldn't be inconvenient?"

"Inconvenient?" Binky said. "It's your home, Georgie, old bean. We'd love to have you—wouldn't we, Fig?"

There was a distinct pause before she managed a tight smile and said, "Of course we would. Absolutely love you to stay."

Chapter 4

I had to smile to myself as I left Rannoch House and headed for the Hyde Park Corner tube station. I had somewhere to stay for the immediate future. Now all I needed to do was to collect Queenie from her parents so that she could pack up my clothes and help me move in.

"Oh golly," I thought as reality dawned. That would really annoy Fig. She couldn't stand Queenie and had wanted me to sack her on numerous occasions. I found I was taking a perverse pleasure in knowing that both Queenie and I would be a source of irritation to Fig. Of course it wouldn't be for long, but if I was also invited to the wedding, then I'd have to stay until the end of November, by which time I should have secured some kind of job or invitation.

The train arrived and we plunged into darkness on our way to deepest Essex and my grandfather's house. His next-door neighbor was Queenie's great-aunt so she would know whether Queenie's mother had recovered sufficiently for me to drag Queenie away. My grandfather's house was on a quiet suburban street of lower-middle-class respectability. Each semidetached house had a small square of front garden blooming with roses and lavender in the summer but at this time of year looking sorry and bare. Granddad's front garden still looked cheerful since he had three brightly painted gnomes in the middle of his flower bed. I took a deep breath before I went up to the front door. I seemed to wait a long time before I heard a voice saying, "I'm coming. I'm coming."

The door was opened and Granddad stood there. To my surprise he was in his dressing gown and slippers. He looked at me with suspicion then his old wrinkled face broke into a broad grin.

"Well, swipe me," he said. "You're the last person I expected to see, my love. I thought it would be her from next door coming round with the stew she promised me. If I'd known you was coming I'd have spruced meself up a bit."

"You're not well?" I asked, kissing the stubble on his weathered cheek as he hugged me.

"Nothing serious. Just a touch of the old bronchitis. I get it something shocking when the weather's like this. But I'm on the mend now. Taking it easy like the doctor said and letting her next door take care of me. I must say she's a good sort, coming round with all manner of dishes to tempt me to eat again. But come on in. Don't just stand there. I'll put the kettle on and she baked a tasty Dundee cake the other day."

I followed him through to the kitchen, then perched on a wooden chair while he filled the kettle.

"I wish you'd told me you'd been ill, Granddad," I said. "I could have come to take care of you."

"Very kind of you, ducks, but like I said, it weren't nothing serious. Just a spot of the old trouble. These lungs have lived in the Smoke too long. Don't work proper no more."

"I wish I had a house in the country, then I'd take you to live with me," I said. "You're so much better in good country air."

"Don't you worry about me, my love." He patted my hand. "I've had a good innings. Can't complain."

I gripped his hand. He had always seemed so strong, so

chipper before. The ex-policeman who had tackled everything in his life. It was worrying to see him almost giving up. "Don't talk that way, Granddad. You've got to stay around for a long while yet. You have to come to my wedding and hold my first child."

"Either of those likely to happen any day now?" he asked with a cheeky smile. "That Darcy fellow still courting you?"

"Hardly courting me." I smiled. "And he's not around at the moment. But one day . . ."

"He's the right sort, that Darcy," Granddad said. "You stick with him and you'll do all right."

The kettle boiled and he put three scoops of tea into the pot before pouring on the boiling water.

"So what brings you down here today? Just come for a chat or was it something more?"

"I'm always happy to come for a chat," I said. "Seeing you always cheers me up, but actually I've come to reclaim Queenie and I find that I don't know her parents' address."

"You've come to take her back?" Granddad asked, then he gave a wheezing laugh that turned into a cough. "Blimey, ducks, that won't half be good news for her folks. Driving them up the pole, that's what she's been doing. Her own mum said she didn't know how Queenie didn't drive you round the blooming bend. Said you must be some sort of saint, she reckoned."

"So Queenie hasn't actually been that much of a help?" I inquired.

Granddad chuckled again. "You could say that. She tried to do the cooking and the gas cooker exploded. Then she knocked the fireguard onto her mum's broken leg. No, I think I can safely say that they'll want to kiss your feet for taking her away again."

"Poor old Queenie," I said. "She does seem to be rather disaster prone."

"And yet you're prepared to give her another go?"

"Oh, Granddad." I gave a sigh. "Who else would employ her? Besides, she is the only maid I can afford and most of the time she's better than nothing."

"Well, if you're really sure about this, she's next door with her great-aunt right now," he said. "Her great-aunt's been trying to teach her to cook—without too much success, so I hear. Her dad claims she'll poison the lot of them. Pity really, because her gran's a lovely cook. Here, try the cake."

He took the lid off a cake tin and cut a generous slice of Dundee cake. It was rich, moist and fruity and I ate with relish.

"Her grandmother is a good cook," I agreed. "I'm surprised she hasn't won you over with her cooking yet."

He grinned. "She's certainly tried hard enough, and dropped enough hints. But between you, me and the gatepost, I like things the way they are. She's there when I need her but she's not driving me round the bend with fussing over me too much. And if I ever married her, I'd be stuck with Queenie as another granddaughter. I don't think you'd want that, would you?"

"Oh crikey," I said. "Queenie as a relative would be a bit much. She doesn't do what I tell her now, when she's only my maid. If she were a fellow grandchild, she'd be impossible."

We laughed.

"So are you still at your friend's place in the snooty part of Knightsbridge?"

"I was until this morning," I said, and told him the story.

"You know you'd always be welcome to stay here," he said, "but your lot wouldn't like it."

"I know," I said. "But don't worry because things sorted themselves out rather well. My brother is in town and has invited me to stay. I gather there is to be a royal wedding so he and Fig are staying on in London for another month. By that time something may have turned up."

"Turned up? What sort of thing?"

I sighed and stared out past him into the row of identical back gardens with washing flapping on clotheslines in the stiff breeze. "I wish I knew. I'm always hoping I can find a job. I must be employable in some capacity. I'm sure I'd be a better lady's maid than Queenie."

He chuckled again. "I'm sure you would too, ducks."

I drained my cup of tea and finished my cake. "Oh well. I suppose I'd better go and face the inevitable and retrieve Queenie. My only consolation is that my sister-in-law is going to be livid when she finds that Queenie is coming back into her house." And I gave him a wicked grin.

Having given Granddad a good-bye kiss and promised to visit him again soon, I went to the house next door and rapped on the knocker. The door was opened fiercely and a face topped with hair curlers peeping from a scarf glared at me. "If you're another of them Jehovah's Witnesses telling me I'm going to hell, then I'll tell you where to put this . . ."

"Hello, Mrs. Huggins," I said.

She stopped and a look of utter horror crossed her face. She put her hand up to her mouth. "Blimey. Oh, your lady-ship. I'm so sorry. I didn't recognize you for a second there and them ruddy religious lot were here again yesterday. I don't know what they want from the likes of me. I ain't got no money to give them and that's what they're normally after, ain't it?" She made a gesture to smooth back her hair, then remembered she was wearing curlers, which clearly embarrassed her even further. "Here to see your granddad, are you, then? He's been a bit poorly the last few days, but I think he's on the mend. I'm just making him a good Irish stew and dumplings to build him up."

"Actually I believe Queenie is with you at the moment."

"She is, your ladyship. Helping me out in the kitchen, and turning into a lovely little cook too. It was ever so good of you to spare her to look after her poor mum. I suppose you want her back now?" There was a note of hope in her voice.

"That's right. If you think her mother is on the mend and you can spare her."

"Well, we have to let her go, don't we, your ladyship? After all, you are her proper employer and it wouldn't be right to make you have to look after yourself for longer than absolutely necessary. I expect it's been hard for you, trying to get on without her."

"I've managed, Mrs. Huggins," I said, "and if you really feel that her mother needs her longer, I'm sure I can survive—"

"Oh no, your ladyship," she cut in. "Right is right. Queenie needs to go back up west to you. No doubt about it. Come on in, ducks—I mean, your ladyship."

I could see where Queenie got it from. She had never learned to call me by my correct title. I stepped into a dingy hallway.

"Queenie!" Mrs. Huggins yelled in a voice that would do any sergeant major proud. "Come and see who's turned up for you then. Come all the way out here for yer. Missing yer, she was."

This was going a little far, but I didn't say anything as the kitchen door opened and Queenie came out. She was wearing the same outfit as the first time she came to be interviewed—a purple hand-knitted jumper that hugged her generous curves a little too tightly and a bright red skirt. Her face broke into a big smile when she saw me.

"Whatcher, miss," she said. "I ain't half glad to see you. Can't do without me no longer, eh?"

"Hello, Queenie," I said. "Nice to see you too."

"Well, I won't say I'm sorry to be leaving," she said. "I like my family all right, but they've run me off me bloody feet. It will be good to get back to a bit of peace and quiet with you."

"I've come to retrieve you because I need help packing all my things. We're moving out of the mews cottage."

Her moon face looked at me expectantly. "So are we off somewhere nice again? The Continent? America? You should have seen my neighbors' faces down our street when I told them I'd been to Hollywood. They wouldn't believe me, but I told them, 'You can ask Lady Georgiana, what's my mistress, then. And see her in the picture papers in Hollywood with her famous mum what's a film star.'"

"We're not going far this time. We'll be staying at Rannoch House for the next few weeks."

"By ourselves?"

"No. My brother and his family will be there with us."

"Bloody 'ell," she said. "We're moving in with your toffee-nosed sister-in-law?"

Whatever I thought of my sister-in-law it was not up to servants to criticize her. I had tried to impress this fact upon Queenie before, but like most things it went right over her head. "Queenie, remember I told you it wasn't your place to criticize your betters. I agree my sister-in-law is not the easiest person but if you did your job perfectly, she'd have nothing to criticize, would she?"

"She don't like me because I'm dead common," Queenie said.

"If you'd rather stay on here and keep looking after your mother, I'm sure I could do without a maid a little longer," I said.

"Oh no, your ladyship," Mrs. Huggins said before Queenie could reply. And she shoved Queenie in my direction. "She has to do her duty. Her place is looking after you. Ain't it, Queenie."

Queenie nodded. "That's right. So why are we kipping over at your brother's house, then? What was wrong with the mews place? I quite liked that. Cozy, it was."

"We're moving because Miss Belinda has returned unexpectedly."

"That's bloody annoying of 'er, ain't it? I thought for sure she'd like it in America. Find herself a rich American bloke."

"I thought so too, but she's home now and I have to move out. So go and get your things and meet me back at Miss Belinda's ready to pack up my trunk."

"Bob's yer uncle, miss," she said.

Chapter 5

Golly, I was right! Fig's face was positively puce when she saw Queenie. Loved it!

As I had predicted, Fig was frightfully put out when she saw Queenie struggling with the footman to carry my trunk up the stairs, especially as she was dressed in her ancient and moth-eaten fur coat and red felt hat that made her look like an oversized hedgehog with a flowerpot on its head.

"Don't tell me you still have that awful creature as your maid, Georgiana," Fig exclaimed in ringing tones, loudly enough for Queenie to hear. "Surely you could have found someone more suitable by now."

"I can't afford anyone more suitable, Fig," I said as the trunk disappeared onto the first-floor landing. "I am as completely penniless as you claim to be."

"If only you would do the right thing and marry well, Georgiana." She turned away from the stairs and headed for the drawing room. "Heaven knows the queen has tried to put suitable young men into your path, but you have seen fit to turn them down for some reason."

"If you're talking about Prince Siegfried . . ." I began.

She spun back to me. "I can't believe you turned down Prince Siegfried. He's an oldest son, Georgiana. He'll be a king someday."

"If the family isn't assassinated first," I said with a grin.

"It is hardly a laughing matter." Fig sank onto a sofa by the window, picking up a copy of *Horse and Hound* as if she already found me too boring to bother with. "You could have been a queen—far above the expectations of your lowly rank in royal circles."

"Siegfried was awful, Fig."

"I agree he was a little supercilious and arrogant," she said. "Not the sort of person one warms to instantly. But don't forget he has been raised and educated to rule. One expects that kind of behavior from European royals. After all, they still have peasants to rule over, don't they?"

"He prefers other men, Fig," I said.

"Lots of men prefer male company. They find women's conversation to be tedious."

"I'm not talking about conversation. I'm talking about the bedroom."

She looked up, frowning. "I beg your pardon?"

"He's a fairy. A pansy boy."

Her eyes shot open at this. "Good heavens. Are you sure? I mean, one hears about such things, I suppose, but one never thinks . . ."

"He told me that if I married him and produced an heir, he'd never bother me again. He'd turn a blind eye to my lovers and I'd turn a blind eye to his. A charming future, don't you think?"

Fig blinked rapidly. "Well, really. You were quite right to reject him in such circumstances. One does not expect that kind of deviant behavior in royal persons."

"Oh, I think that historically one finds it quite often in royal persons," I said. "Too much isolation and inbreeding." I grinned at her shocked face. I was going to mention Prince

George but swallowed back the words at the last second. I liked George. He was pleasant and fun. I shouldn't spread gossip about him, even if I had seen hints of his deviant behavior myself.

Fig was now shaking her head fiercely. "No, no. I can't believe that. Certainly not. Royal persons are raised to do their duty, Georgiana. Which you, even as a minor royal, should remember."

"My cousin David doesn't seem to be doing his," I said. "He's still dallying with a married American lady."

Fig frowned. "He will shape up when the time comes. He'll have to before his father dies. The country is counting on him." She looked up and wagged a finger at me. "Which gives me an idea, Georgiana. I think you should stay on in London for the wedding. I'll have Binky write to Their Majesties and make sure you receive an invitation to all the festivities. There will be a good sampling of foreign princelings and one of them must be good husband material. You must seize the moment, Georgiana. How old are you now— twenty-four? The bloom does start to fade, and I'm sure you don't want to face life as a lonely spinster nobody really wants in their home."

"Thank you for the confidence in me." I gave an uneasy laugh. "But don't worry. I promise not to dump myself upon you as a maiden aunt. And I do have a chap in mind, actually."

"Not that awful O'Mara person. Surely you are no longer pining after him?"

"He's not an O'Mara person. He is the son of an Irish peer and therefore one of us. He will be Lord Kilhenny one day."

"But that family is bankrupt, Georgiana. The father had to sell the castle and the racing stables, so I heard, and your young man has nothing to offer you. And one hears things about his reputation with women too. He'll be a bounder who breaks your heart, Georgie. You mark my words. Settle on someone steady and reliable, even if they are boring like Binky."

"Darcy may have lived a wild existence before he met me,"

I said, "but now he's working awfully hard so that he can provide for me someday. And I don't want to marry anyone else. I'm prepared to wait for Darcy, as long as it takes."

"While he is no doubt dallying with other women around the world." Fig smirked. "You are such an innocent, Georgiana. I'm only having this discussion for your own good."

"I'm sure you are," I said. "Now if you will excuse me, I'll go up to my room to make sure that Queenie is putting my clothes away properly. I may still have my old room, I hope?"

"There is no one else occupying it at present," she said.

"And then I must go up to the nursery and say hello to my nephew and niece."

"Young Podge is fond of you, you know. He asks after you."

"I've missed him. And Adelaide won't even know me."

"She's turning into rather a willful child," Fig said. "Absolutely refuses to come to her mother."

My opinion of Adelaide rose instantly. "Maybe she needs a little more loving and someone to play with her," I said. "It can be lonely in the nursery. I certainly found it so. But then I had a really kind nanny."

"Children need a strict routine and discipline. One must not be soft with them, Georgiana, as you will find when you have some of your own."

"I thought I was destined to be a lonely spinster with my bloom gone," I said with a grin as I headed for the drawing room door.

As I reached the first landing I jumped as the lavatory door to my right opened about an inch and a voice hissed, "*Pssst.* Is that you, miss?"

"Queenie?" I said, staring at the portion of her moon face visible through the crack in the door.

"Come in here, miss. Sharpish." She opened the door and almost dragged me inside.

"What are you doing in a family bathroom?" I demanded. "You know you are supposed to use the servants' facilities."

"Yes, well, I had to go in a hurry and they're all the way down in the basement," she said.

That was when I realized that my feet were decidedly damp. The floor had a good inch of water on it and more was slopping over the sides of the lavatory. "What in heaven's name?" I began.

"Sorry, miss. I had a bit of an accident," she said. "I finished me business, got up and pulled the chain, and the chain sort of flew up and knocked me hat off."

"Your hat?"

She gave me a sheepish grin. "I must have forgotten I still had it on. I was worrying about unpacking your clothes like you said and I took off me coat, but forgot about me 'at. Silly me, eh? And now it's got knocked down the loo."

I peered through the depths of murky water and spotted a bright hint of red poking out from the pipe. "It's still there. Have you tried getting it out?"

"I ain't putting my hand in there!" she exclaimed in horror. "It's full of you know what."

"Queenie, any minute now this water will soak through the floor and start dripping through the ceiling below. And if my sister-in-law sees it and finds out you've been using her lavatory, then I'm afraid you'll be sent packing—sharpish, as you would say."

"Well, what I am going to do?"

"Run downstairs. Ask for old towels for the floor and see if you can find something to hook out the hat."

"Then everyone will know it was me," she wailed.

"Queenie, I am not about to take the blame for flooding a lavatory for you," I said. "Now either you roll up your sleeve and pull that hat out yourself or you find something to do it with. Go on. Run. Before it's too late."

The best she could manage was a spirited waddle but she soon returned with towels and a poker. "I just said there had been a bit of an accident in her ladyship's bathroom," she said. "I didn't go into details."

A few minutes later the hat was retrieved—now a soggy mess of red felt.

"I don't think I'll ever get it back in shape, do you, miss?" Queenie said, holding it out mournfully.

"Queenie, you can't wear a hat that has been down the loo," I said in exasperation. "Throw it in the dustbin. Immediately. And finish drying the floor too. I've a good mind to send you back to your parents today."

"Accidents can happen to anyone, miss," she said. "Even you."

I sighed. Of course this was true. They happened to me. In moments of duress I had been known to be a trifle clumsy, shall we say. Only they happened rather more frequently to Queenie. Maybe we were destined for each other.

My nephew greeted me with touching enthusiasm, hugging me fiercely. Even my niece seemed pleased to see me, but that might just have been because I was preferable to Nanny, who was crisp, starchy and not the sort of person one warmed to. When I went into my bedroom, Queenie had unpacked my things without any serious mishaps and was very subdued, even calling me "my lady," which showed she was trying hard.

I settled into my old room and Binky wrote to the palace on my behalf. Everything seemed to be working out rather satisfactorily. What's more, Fig actually took *The Lady* so I curled up in an armchair and browsed through the latest copies of the magazine. There were plenty of advertisements for servants but precious little else. But now there was no rush to find a job. The wedding wasn't for another month. My brother might even decide to stay on in London for Christmas and by then, who knew what might have turned up?

I was amazed to receive a reply to Binky's letter the day after he sent it. It was addressed to me and, what's more, was written in the queen's own hand.

My dear Georgiana,

I was delighted to hear that you have now returned to London and will be here for my son's wedding. I understand you have been abroad until recently. My granddaughters certainly missed seeing you at Balmoral this year.

Perhaps you would be good enough to come to the palace tomorrow, if it's convenient. I must tour a factory in the morning and have lunch in their canteen, but I should be home in time for tea at four.

Your affectionate cousin,
Mary R.

The *R*, of course, meant *Regina*.

Fig came in as I was reading the letter.

"Something came from the palace, I hear," she said. "That was certainly rapid. They are able to fit you into the guest list then?"

"I don't know. The letter is from the queen. She wants me to come to tea tomorrow."

"Good heavens. From the queen herself? What could she possibly want to see you for?" She looked up as Binky joined us. "The queen has written to Georgiana," Fig said in clipped tones. "She's invited her to tea. We never get invited to tea at the palace, do we?"

"The queen is dashed fond of Georgie," Binky said. "One noticed that when Georgie didn't show up at Balmoral. She probably wants to hear all about her travels abroad."

Oh golly. I hoped not. I didn't want to have to tell someone like Queen Mary about the shenanigans that went on in Hollywood. She would not be amused, I was sure.

"You should do more to make our presence in London known, Binky," Fig said. "Then we might receive more invitations. We should get out more. Be more social. Go to nightclubs and dine where we are seen."

"All that takes money, old bean," Binky said. "Something we have precious little of. Unless there is some of your legacy left after the central heating?"

"Oh, I don't think there will be," Fig said hastily.

Chapter 6

WEDNESDAY, OCTOBER 31

**Tea with the queen today. Oh golly. Please don't let me
  spill anything or smash a priceless vase.**

The next day I started to prepare for tea with the queen the
minute luncheon was over. I agonized over what to wear.
One should wear a tea dress to tea and I didn't possess one.
I had a few stylish items of clothing, courtesy of my mother,
even though I had lost the best ones in a fire. Still, I was able
to look presentable in a cashmere cardigan and gray jersey
skirt she had bequeathed to me. I added a cream silk blouse
and my good pearls. Pearls always go down well with royals.
I was tempted to wear my mother's cast-off fur coat but it
was raining hard and I didn't want to look like a drowned
animal when I arrived at the palace.

It didn't matter how many times I had been to Buckingham Palace, I still found the experience frightening. Those
tall gilded iron gates and impossibly tall men guarding them
were horribly intimidating. I knew there were side entrances
into the palace from Buckingham Palace Road, but today I

found them locked so I was forced to approach the gates and then cross the forecourt, sensing all those eyes watching me and feeling incredibly dowdy and unroyal in my mack. That forecourt was designed to be crossed in a carriage or a Daimler, preferably wearing a tiara—the person, I mean, not the conveyance.

I managed to reach the door without tripping over my umbrella or having the wind blow it inside out. So far so good. A footman helped me out of my mack and took my umbrella before I was led up the stairs to the *piano nobile* (or noble floor), which was the part of the palace where the royal family lived. I breathed a sigh of relief when we did not turn in the direction of the Chinese Chippendale Room this time. One of the queen's favorite rooms, it was full of priceless Oriental antiques and I was always sure I'd knock over a Ming by mistake. Instead I was led to the right side of the house and the queen's small private sitting room, overlooking the side gardens.

The footman knocked, then opened the door. "Lady Georgiana, Your Majesty."

I stepped inside, carefully avoiding the footman's foot, which I'd tripped over once before. Either my clumsiness was improving or I was learning from my mistakes. The queen was sitting in an armchair by the fire. She held out a hand to me.

"Georgiana, my dear. What a beastly day out there. Come and get warm."

I took the hand and curtsied but didn't attempt to kiss her cheek, as my hair and face were rather wet and there was a tea tray on a low table that I didn't want to risk knocking over. "Thank you, ma'am," I said and took the seat she indicated in the armchair across from her. "How good to see you looking so well."

"I am in remarkably good health, thankfully," she said, "unlike the poor king, whose health is not the best. He has been failing since that bout of pneumonia, Georgiana. I worry about him."

"I'm sorry to hear that, ma'am."

"He missed you at Balmoral this year," she said, giving me an accusatory frown. "We all did."

I was clearly not going to live down my absence. "I was unfortunately in America with my mother in August."

"America. How interesting. Such a busy sort of place, I found. Everyone rushing around."

I nodded.

"Well, I'm very glad to find you are here now. Most fortuitous, as it happens. I've been searching my brain for the right person and of course you'd be perfect."

My heart beat a little faster. When the queen invited me to the palace for a chat, it wasn't ever a purely social occasion. She had little assignments for me, never easy, some barely legal, ranging from spying on her wayward son and his American lady friend to stealing back a missing antique.

"But first let's have some tea, shall we?" she said and poured a cup for me. I took it, noticing that it was not a grand royal tea table today, but just a simple tea with a plate of shortbread and some slices of Dundee cake similar to the one Mrs. Huggins had baked. I stifled a grin at the thought that Mrs. Huggins's cake might be better.

I accepted a piece of shortbread when offered and took a bite, but I was so tense about what the queen might be about to say that it felt like chalk in my mouth and I couldn't swallow it. Then luckily for me the door opened and the Prince of Wales came in.

"Ah, there you are, Mother," he said as he breezed into the room. "How was lunch in the factory canteen? Did you have cottage pie or rissoles as I predicted?"

"It was quite a passable roast beef, although the Yorkshire pudding left something to be desired," she said. "I'm having tea with Georgiana."

He looked across and noticed me in the other armchair. "What-ho, Georgie. Long time since we've seen you."

"Hello, sir," I said. I should point out that protocol demanded I address him as "sir" even though he was my cousin.

"She's been in America," the queen said.

"Actually I traveled on the *Berengaria* with a friend of

yours, sir," I said. Of course I was referring to Mrs. Simpson. We had been tablemates at the captain's table.

The prince cleared his throat and his mother said quickly, "I am hoping we can count on Georgiana to help us, David." She leaned closer to me. "Tell me, have you been to Kensington Palace?"

"I've walked past it when I've crossed the park, that's all, ma'am," I said.

"You may not know that it's divided into several apartments," the queen went on. "Queen Victoria's two remaining daughters live there—your dear grandmother's sisters. As well as two other royal ladies, your father's cousins."

Oh Lord. My heart sank. She had suggested once before that I might be a lady-in-waiting to an elderly female relative. I pictured holding the knitting wool and reading to her on long dark evenings. Still, at least it was in London.

"Mother, you can't send Georgie to the Aunt Heap," David said. "She'd die of boredom." He glanced across at me and gave me one of his charming smiles. The thought flashed through my mind how very nice he was, and I wondered why he would ever be attracted to a sharp and brittle woman like Mrs. Simpson.

"The Aunt Heap?" I met his eyes and saw the twinkle in them.

"You are always so flippant, David. It is about time you took life seriously and knuckled down to your responsibilities," the queen said. "Your brother Bertie has done his duty and produced two lovely little girls. Now your brother George is doing his duty and getting married to a charming princess. I told you there were still plenty to choose from."

"Don't let's start that again, Mother," David said. "I'm delighted my brother is doing his duty and I agree Marina is quite charming. Quite a looker, actually."

"Well? I'm sure we can come up with 'quite a looker' for you, if you'd only give us a chance. You have a delightful young second cousin here, for a start."

I blushed. David looked across at me and laughed. "That really would be cradle snatching and this family needs no more inbreeding, Mother." He paused. "Besides, she's taller than me. That would never do for a future king, would it?" He started to move away. "I must be off and leave you to your scheming. I'm going down to the Fort for a few days. Not sure when I'll be back, so don't count on me for dinner on Sunday."

"David, you are so infuriating sometimes. The dinner is to welcome Marina when she arrives. You should be there."

"I have things I have to take care of and might not be able to make it up to town in time. I'm sorry, but I can't leave people in the lurch. Besides, Marina might be so dazzled by me that she forgets about my brother." David chuckled. "I'm sure I won't be missed." He blew me a kiss and made a hasty exit. The queen looked at me and shook her head. "That boy is worrying his father to death," she said. "And what sort of king will he make?"

"I'm sure he'll do the job well when the time comes, ma'am," I said. "He's very kindhearted and he does care about the ordinary people."

"But he's becoming ever more obsessed with that woman," the queen said. "She has a hold over him. One hears she went to America to inquire about getting a divorce, you know. Ridiculous, really, because she and David can never marry. The country would never countenance a twice-married American as queen."

When I said nothing she went on, "I have told him if he makes a proper marriage he can keep that woman quietly as his mistress and nobody would mind too much."

I smiled. "I don't think she's the kind of person who can be kept quietly. She likes the limelight too much."

"That's the problem." The queen sighed. "But let's turn to more pleasant matters. I asked you about Kensington Palace because that's where we plan to house Princess Marina until her wedding. She'll be arriving at the end of the week and will have a little time to be introduced to London and our ways. And that's where you come in, Georgiana, dear. Marina's family were exiled from Greece when her uncle was deposed as King of the Hellenes. She has grown up in exile, living with various relatives, and even rather simply in an apartment in Paris, so one understands. The king and I were afraid that she might find London society overwhelming. We thought Marina might appreciate having someone her own age to help her settle in and to show her around London."

She looked at me questioningly. I nodded and waited for her to go on. "You would move into Kensington Palace as her companion. Familiarize her with English ways. Take her shopping and to the theater perhaps. Show her the best of what London has to offer."

I hesitated. She had asked me to host a visiting European princess once before, not seeming to understand that I had no money to host anyone and was living on baked beans myself. Now she wanted me to show a princess the best that London had to offer. But queens never touch money. In fact it was considered frightfully bad form to discuss money at all. But I knew I had to bring up the subject now if I wasn't to face the embarrassment of taking a princess to a theater for which I couldn't pay. I was trying to find a way to mention this tactfully when she said, "The master of house at Kensington, Major Beecham-Chuff, will be in charge of looking after Marina's needs until her wedding. I'll let him know you will be taking care of her and showing her around. Just ask him for what you need."

I presumed this meant monetarily and not just recommendations and reservations. And as for the major's name, I found out later that it was actually spelled Beauchamp-Chough. Yes, I know English is a strange language.

"I'll be happy to help Princess Marina settle in," I said.

"Splendid." She gave me an approving smile. "I knew I could always count on you. Such a steady girl. You have the family sense of duty, Georgiana. If only my son would marry someone like you."

And she sighed. Then she leaned closer to me again, although we were alone in the small sitting room. "And I'm going to ask another favor of you, Georgiana."

Oh golly, I thought. Now comes the difficult part. I held my breath.

"Like his older brother, my son George has not always been the wisest in his choice of friendships," she said. "But I understand that there may be rumors flying around that completely exaggerate his behavior. It is important that this marriage starts off on the right foot, so I would appreciate it if you could heartily refute any rumor Marina may have heard and reassure her on what a decent fellow he is. I can count on you, can't I?"

"Of course, ma'am," I said. So now I was expected to lie for my royal kin. Still, I reasoned, it was probably better that a sheltered girl like Marina not know the truth about her future husband's hijinks.

I WENT BACK to Rannoch House with a spring in my step. Not only was I to be invited to the wedding, I was to play an important part in welcoming the bride. I wouldn't have to endure Fig's barbs any longer and . . . I stopped, frozen on the pavement halfway up Constitution Hill. Oh crikey. I'd have to take Queenie to a palace. A palace full of princesses and with a master of house called Major Beauchamp-Chough. She'd already shown what havoc she could wreak in a normal house, with no royalty present and no priceless antiques around every corner. It was hard enough for me, who tends to be a little clumsy at times, but Queenie was far worse. She really was a walking disaster. And yet I couldn't arrive at a palace with no lady's maid. I'd have to make it quite clear to her that she must never leave my suite. If I had her meals sent up on a tray maybe we'd be all right.

Fig and Binky were sitting by the drawing room fire when I returned. Podge was with them, sitting beside his mother and showing her a drawing he had made, while Binky had Adelaide on his knee and was bouncing her while Nanny hovered protectively near the doorway.

"There you are, Georgiana." Fig looked up. "So how was tea at the palace?" She almost spat out the last word.

"The cake wasn't quite as good as the one I had at my grandfather's," I said with a smile.

"Was anybody else present? Was it a large tea party?"

"Just the queen and I. Oh, and the Prince of Wales came in for a moment."

"Really?" She blinked rapidly and one could see the wheels of her brain turning, demanding to know why I should have a tête-à-tête with the queen and not she.

"I'm glad you're going to be staying with us for a long while, Aunt Georgie," Podge said.

"Unfortunately I won't be here as long as I had thought, Podge," I said. "But I will come to visit and maybe I can take you out to the park."

"You won't be staying here after all?" There was a note of hope in Fig's voice.

"Unfortunately no," I said. "The queen wants me to move into Kensington Palace and look after Princess Marina."

It gave me great satisfaction that those words had the effect I had hoped for.

Chapter 7

SATURDAY, NOVEMBER 3
KENSINGTON PALACE, LONDON

Dear Diary: Today I move into Kensington Palace. Moving
up in the world. Actually I'm partly excited and
partly terrified. Please don't let me break anything
or knock an elderly princess down the stairs!

Kensington Palace is not like its sister Buckingham. It sits
in the middle of a public park with a much-traveled walkway
going past it. There are no guards and only the southern side
has gates. And some of it is open to the public. In fact as I
approached, a group of schoolchildren were huddling
together and looking miserable in the rain as they waited to
be escorted around the state rooms. I had actually never
been inside before so I went to the reception desk and was
about to be handed a ticket when I let the woman know that
I was looking for the way to apartment 1.

"You can't get into the private apartments this way, miss,"
she said. "The private rooms are quite separate from the
public. You'll have to follow the path around and it's on the

other side, at the back of the building." She looked at me suspiciously. It was raining and I was wearing my mack again and probably didn't look much like a person who visited royal apartments. "Are you delivering something?" she asked. "I could have it sent around there for you."

"No, I'm coming to live there," I said and departed, giving her a bright smile and something to think about. I went back into the rain and then found the path that would take me to the back of the palace. The rain came down harder and the wind buffeted me as I finally came to what I hoped was the right door. I rang the bell. Nobody came immediately so I tried the knob and the door swung open. I stepped into a foyer and looked around with surprise. I had expected something like Buckingham Palace—walls lined with royal portraits, antiques and statues everywhere. But this was more like an ordinary home, slightly outmoded and with a lingering smell of furniture polish and damp. I gave a sigh of disappointment, mingled with a small sigh of relief. At least I wouldn't have to worry about knocking over priceless objects every time I turned around, the way I did at Buckingham Palace. It was also rather cold in that foyer, with a draft swirling about my legs. Not too welcoming a first impression for a newly arrived princess, I thought. But perhaps they were not planning to turn on any form of heat until she arrived.

I wasn't quite sure what to do next. I wondered if the queen would have supplied servants or if Princess Marina was bringing her own and they weren't here yet. I realized that I should have asked to be taken to Major Beauchamp-Chough, not have gone straight to the apartment. Protocol probably demanded that he escort me to my quarters. But it was a long, wet walk back to the front of the building. There was an archway at the end of the entry hall leading to a passageway beyond. As I looked toward it I saw a woman walk across it. She was moving swiftly, almost gliding and making no sound.

"Hello," I called. "Wait a minute, please."

When she didn't stop I ran after her, and found myself

standing in a long dark corridor that was completely empty. Where had she gone? There were no side hallways and she would not have had time to open and close a door. That was when I realized she was wearing a long white dress and her hair had been piled upon her head in little curls. I felt the hair on the back of my neck stand up. At that moment I heard the brisk tap of feet on the marble-tiled floor and a woman came across the foyer toward me. This one was all too solid. She was probably in her thirties, well fed, in a wool dress that was a little too tight for her, pale faced and with pale hair piled in an old-fashioned bun. She spotted me and bore down upon me, wagging a finger.

"Ah, there you are, you naughty girl," she said in strongly accented English. "Where have you been? I have been waiting for you."

"I didn't realize there was a specific time for my arrival," I said, taking aback by her ferocious approach.

"That is no way to address your betters," she said, giving me a haughty stare.

"My betters?" Indignation now overtook surprise. "I'm sorry. I don't know who you are, but I rather think we must be equals, unless you are Queen Victoria reincarnated."

I saw uncertainty cross her face. "Are you not the girl who was sent to bring me pickled herring from Harrods?"

I tried not to grin. "I am Lady Georgiana, cousin to His Majesty," I said. "May one ask your name?"

"Oh, thousand pardons," the woman stammered, thoroughly flustered now. "I did not expect . . . we were not informed that His Majesty's cousin would be visiting. And I did not expect a royal person to arrive alone in such a manner." And she looked at my sodden mack and the puddle accumulating around my feet.

"Yes, I'm sorry. I realize I don't look very royal," I said. "But it's raining cats and dogs out there and I don't have a motorcar."

She went and peered out of the window. "I do not see any cats and dogs," she said.

"Just an expression."

"Ah," she said solemnly. "An English idiom. I must learn these things. Cats and dogs." She nodded as if her brain had processed this information, then she gave me a little bowing jerk of the head. "I am the Countess Irmtraut von Dinkelfingen-Hackensack. I am the cousin of Princess Marina. Our mothers are related. My mother was a Pushova."

I didn't think I'd heard correctly. "I beg your pardon?"

"A Pushova. My mother was a Pushova. The daughter of Prince Vladimir Pushov, related to the czar."

"Oh, I see." Thank heavens I hadn't started to laugh!

"How do you do, Countess." I held out my hand and she shook it heartily.

"Has the king sent you perhaps to assure that the accommodations are suitable?"

"Actually it was the queen who asked me to come and stay here to look after Princess Marina until her marriage."

Countess Irmtraut frowned. "To stay here? Look after Her Highness? Why should this be necessary? She has me to look after her. And I know her wishes."

Oh dear. She looked seriously put out. "I'm sure you do," I said. "But the queen suggested that I acquaint Princess Marina with the way things are done in England and show her around London."

"I see." She did not look very happy.

"I don't know which rooms I am to have," I said. "I presume Major Beauchamp-Chough will show me to my quarters."

"This major is the very correct Englishman who lives here?" she asked.

I nodded. "I believe so."

"He is very military, I think," she said. "Not a sympathetic man. Prince George, is he a sympathetic man? I do not wish someone like this major for Marina."

"Prince George is very nice," I could say with complete truth. "Very kind. Good sense of humor."

"This is good. Not all princes are sympathetic. We have met some recently who are . . ." She broke off, weighing whether to proceed with this topic. "You are acquainted with Prince Siegfried perhaps?"

"Of Romania? Oh dear, yes. There was a push to make me marry him once."

"Somebody pushed you? This is dangerous. Did you fall?"

"No, I meant that my relatives were keen on such a match for me. But he was awful. Arrogant. Cold. We called him Fishface."

She looked troubled. "But he does not have the face of a fish, I think. He has the face of a human."

I was beginning to find this conversation really tiring and was relieved when a door nearby opened and a man came out, striding toward me with purpose.

"Lady Georgiana," he said, extending his hand to me. "I was just told that you were in the building. Forgive me for not welcoming you. Beauchamp-Chough. Major, Life Guards. I'm currently acting as His Royal Highness Prince George's equerry and have been put in charge of this upcoming bun fight."

"Bun fight?" Countess Irmtraut exclaimed. "There is to be a fight with pastries? This is an old English custom?"

The major and I both laughed.

"Actually it's a familiar term for any kind of celebration, hence, the wedding," the major said.

"I see. Another English joke." Her face did not crack a smile, but the major exchanged a brief glance with me and there was a flicker of amusement in his eyes.

He was younger than I expected, but certainly of military bearing, tall, erect, with a neat little blond mustache. Quite good-looking, I noted.

"How do you do, Major Beauchamp-Chough." I shook his hand while Countess Irmtraut stood and glowered.

"Most people call me B-C," he said. "Or Major B-C, if you wish." He grinned. "It refers to my initials, not my age."

"But it is impossible for you to have been born before Christ," Irmtraut said. "Surely you did not think we would believe you to be so old."

When neither of us replied she sighed. "I see. Another English joke. Your country has much humor, I think."

"Oh, absolutely. A laugh a minute," he said, and to my amusement she checked the watch that was pinned to the front of her dress.

"Major Beauchamp-Chough," she said, "I requested that someone be dispatched to find me some pickled herring. So far nobody has returned with any."

"Perhaps they are still fishing for it in the Round Pond," he suggested, his face expressionless.

"But no." Countess Irmtraut shook her head emphatically. "They will find no herring in a pond. It is a fish of the oceans."

The major caught my eye again and almost winked. I decided that I liked him.

"It was more English humor, Countess."

"I do not understand this English humor," she said grouchily. "I will await news of my herrings in my room." And she swept out.

"Not the easiest lady, I'm afraid," the major said. "Fortunately the princess is quite charming and easy to get along with."

"You've already met her?"

"I was lucky enough to visit her parents with His Royal Highness," he said. "Prince George and his parents will be going to meet her from the boat train tomorrow afternoon. They will be bringing her here and tomorrow evening there will be a dinner at Buckingham Palace for her to meet the family. You will be invited, of course, and will travel with Princess Marina in her motorcar."

"Thank you very much," I stammered. "Now if you would please have someone show me my room. I think I need to get out of these wet clothes before I make a bigger puddle on the floor."

"I'll be happy to escort you," he said. "This way."

He led me under the arch and up a spiral staircase. For a palace it was quite plain, with whitewashed walls and plain stone steps. "I hope you don't mind stairs," the major said. "This is one of the smaller apartments and I've given the first floor over to Princess Marina and her maid. You and the countess have rooms on the second floor and there are small bedrooms for your maid on the third. Your maid did not come with you?"

I swallowed hard. "She will be arriving later with my luggage." The thought of the major meeting Queenie made me feel positively sick.

The major went up the next flight at great speed, proving that he was as fit as he looked. "Here we are," he said, opening the first door we came to. The furniture was rather old-fashioned and the wallpaper a trifle dingy, but it was large and pleasant enough, with windows opening onto an inner courtyard, rather than the park.

"I'm afraid this apartment is in serious need of modernization," he said, "but it is the only one unoccupied that is big enough to house the royal party. As you probably know we have four elderly ladies occupying other apartments here."

"The Aunt Heap," I said with a grin.

"You've been talking to the Prince of Wales." He returned my smile. "Yes, two of Queen Victoria's daughters and two granddaughters are all in residence. Your great-aunts and your father's cousins, are they not?"

"I suppose they are. I always get confused with family relationships."

"Oh, and before I forget," he went on, opening a wardrobe door to check inside, "Princess Louise asked me to invite you to dine with her this evening in her apartment. It's 1A—the apartment that runs the length of the south side. Seven thirty, she said."

"Thank you. How kind of her."

"I'll leave you to settle in, then," he said. "I am in apartment 10 if you need me. The official entrance is around at the front of the building, through the public foyer, but luckily I have a bolt-hole back door into the courtyard so I don't have to negotiate hordes of schoolchildren. They always want to know which member of the royal family I am." He gave an exasperated smile, nodded to me and left. I heard his footsteps retreating down the stairs again.

IT WASN'T UNTIL I was alone in my new room that I
thought about the woman in the long sweeping white gown.
I should have asked the major whether Kensington Palace
was haunted. I had been brought up at Castle Rannoch where
the servants certainly had enough tales of ghosts, but I had
never encountered one personally. I found myself looking
around uneasily.

"Buck up," I said to myself. Surely no Rannoch should
be scared of ghosts, especially as they were likely to be my
own ancestors. I wondered how Queenie would react, however. Golly, I hoped none of the ghosts was headless. . . .

Then the reality of Queenie being in the same building
as Countess Irmtraut and Major Beauchamp-Chough hit me.
I couldn't risk her arriving and bumping into one of them.
So, much as I was loath to go back out into the rain, I decided
I had to be in that taxicab with her when she arrived with
my luggage from Rannoch House. I trudged home in the
rain, feeling thoroughly miserable and wondering why I had
agreed to this assignment, in a cold gloomy house where I
was clearly not wanted or needed. Then, of course, I knew
why. Because one does not say no to the queen.

When I arrived at Rannoch House I was pleasantly surprised to find Queenie waiting for me with my bags ready
packed. Maybe she was finally trying hard to be a proper
lady's maid. Hamilton secured us a taxicab and it pulled up
at the entrance to our apartment at Kensington Palace.

Queenie eyed it critically. "It ain't as nice as that place
we stayed with the duke in Eynsford, is it?" she asked.
"Rather dowdy, if you ask me."

"Nobody is asking you, Queenie," I said. "Whatever we
think, it's a royal palace and you must be on your very best
behavior. You must promise to stay in my room or your room
and not go wandering around. There will be royal persons
who would be horrified to meet you. To them servants are
supposed to be invisible and have perfect manners."

"There's quite a lot of me to be invisible," she said with a grin. "But I'll give it a try, miss."

All went well until we were inside and Queenie saw the stairs. "Bloody 'ell, miss. I ain't supposed to lug your bags up all them stairs, am I? What do they think I am, a ruddy porter or a donkey?"

"I'll see if I can find a footman to help you," I said and shooed her up the stairs to my quarters.

No footman was to be found, but in the end I did manage to collar a gardener and soon Queenie and bags were installed in my room.

"What about our dinner then?" Queenie's thoughts were never far from food.

"Remember I told you that we have luncheon in the middle of the day and dinner at night," I said.

"Your sort may do. We have our dinner at midday and our tea in the evening," she said. "And right now my stomach wants dinner."

"I'd like you to unpack my things first, then we'll go up another flight of stairs and locate your room," I said. I wasn't going to risk her wandering alone, not even once. "I'll go and find out about meals while you unpack."

Queenie sighed. I went downstairs again and looked for signs of life. I opened doors to a gloomy salon, a library, a smaller sitting room that would be charming once a fire was lit, and finally a dining room. A mahogany table stretched the length of it, big enough to seat thirty. But no signs of food. I pictured Countess Irmtraut sitting alone in her room eating her pickled herring and was wondering if I'd also have to send out for something to eat, when a maid appeared.

"Begging your pardon, Your Highness." She dropped a curtsy. "I didn't know anyone would be in here."

"That's all right. And I'm a lady, not a highness," I said. "Lady Georgiana. I was looking for luncheon."

"There's only the countess here at the moment, my lady," the girl said, "and she has a tray sent up to her room."

"Well, I'm now staying here too, and I'd also like to eat," I said.

"Should I set the table for you then, my lady?" She looked worried.

I thought of eating alone in that cold, dreary dining room. "I could also have a tray sent up, if it's easier," I said. "And maybe one for my maid."

"Very good, my lady. Is there anything special you'd like Cook to prepare for you?"

"I'm sure whatever she has prepared will be fine," I said, hopefully. "And can you please arrange for someone to come and light the fire in my bedroom, if I'm to eat up there. The whole place is rather cold and gloomy."

"I know." She made a face before she remembered to whom she was talking. "Sorry, my lady, but I've been sent over from Buckingham Palace where everything's ever so nice."

"It's only for a couple of weeks." I gave her an encouraging smile and she smiled shyly in return. She bobbed another curtsy and off she went. I retreated to my room and after a meal of hearty soup, grilled fish and a steamed pudding, I was feeling much better. Queenie also tucked in with relish. "Well, the grub's not bad," she said. "I'll take the trays downstairs to the kitchen, shall I?"

"No, I'll have somebody come up and fetch them. A lady's maid does not carry trays in a palace." This, of course, was not true, but I wasn't going to let Queenie out of my sight.

Chapter 8

Dinner with royal aunts I've never met. What could be more terrifying?

At seven thirty I presented myself, dressed in my burgundy velvet evening dress, at the door of apartment 1A. The annoying thing about Kensington Palace was that the apartments were all separate units and not connected by internal corridors. That meant another walk in the rain with an umbrella protecting my face but the hem of my skirt getting decidedly wet and muddy. The maid who opened the door did not let her expression betray that I looked windswept and bedraggled, but she did let me pause in front of a hall mirror while she took my coat and brolly.

This apartment had the feel of being inhabited for a long time. It was also old-fashioned but felt warm and cozy. It had that smell I associated with old ladies—lavender and furniture polish and pomades.

"Her Royal Highness is waiting to welcome you in the drawing room," the maid said and walked ahead of me.

"Lady Georgiana Rannoch," she announced and I stepped into a very Victorian room. Although large it felt cluttered and the décor was decidedly eclectic with Victoriana in the shape of stuffed birds under glass competing with interesting pieces of sculpture. A fire roared in the grate and seated beside it were not one but two elderly ladies who also looked as if they had stepped straight from the Victorian era. One had a beaded shawl around her shoulders. The other was dressed in a long, tight-waisted black dress with a high lace collar around the neck. Her face was remarkably unlined, however, and her eyes bright and intelligent. They lit up when she saw me.

"Georgiana, my dear, how lovely to meet you at last," she said.

I went over to her and curtsied. "How do you do, ma'am."

She laughed. "Oh goodness gracious, we don't go in for stuffy court formality here. I'm your great-aunt Louise and that's what you can call me." She studied me. "Yes, I see a remarkable resemblance to your father. What a charmer he was, even as a little boy. Such a pity he died so young."

I nodded. I had hardly known him since he spent most of his time on the Riviera, but he had always struck me as a warm sort of person. A fun sort of person who liked to laugh.

"And this is your other great-aunt, my sister Beatrice," she said. "She was also interested to see a great-niece she had never met."

I gave her a little curtsy. "How do you do, ma'am," I repeated. One can never be too careful with royals. This one did not contradict and tell me to call her "Great-Aunt."

I took the seat Princess Louise indicated and was offered a glass of sherry on a silver tray.

"You also live in the palace here, do you, ma'am?" I asked Princess Beatrice. "Is your apartment close by?"

"On the far side of the building," Princess Beatrice said. "Actually it is the very same apartment that our dear mama lived in as a child. I moved into it when she died in 1901, with my dear husband and children. My husband is no longer with us and my children are leading their own lives, but it gives me consolation to know that Mama was happy there as a young girl."

I nodded with understanding.

"The only drawback is the constant tramping of feet as visitors go around the state rooms above my head," she said. "You've discovered that certain rooms are open to the public, I take it?"

"I saw schoolchildren waiting to tour the palace today," I said.

She gave a tired little smile. "Of course, it is only during the day. On the whole I enjoy seeing them. It can be rather lonely at times and I like seeing young fresh faces. We are glad that you have moved in here, and we're most anxious to meet Marina, aren't we, Louise?"

"We are," Princess Louise said. "When she has settled in we'll have a luncheon or a sherry party to introduce her to the rest of the aunts in this Aunt Heap, as your wicked cousin calls this place."

Princess Beatrice leaned toward me. "Tell me," she said, "have you met David's mysterious lady friend?"

"I have and she's no lady."

"You mean his friend is really a man?"

I laughed. "No, ma'am. I meant that she is N.O.C.D. Not one of us. A brash American divorcée. Trying to divorce for a second time, so one gathers." (Perhaps I should explain that N.O.C.D. is shorthand for Not Our Class, Dear, but one could hardly say that to a royal aunt.)

"An adventuress!" The two aunts exchanged a look.

"Well, nothing can come of it in the end," Princess Louise said. "He certainly can never marry a divorced woman. Not as head of the Church of England."

"He was such a charming little boy," Princess Beatrice said wistfully. "Of course, his father rather favored him and gave him too much leeway, I always thought. And was too harsh on the second son. The poor little chap stuttered, you know, but his father couldn't see that his shouting and bullying only made the stammer worse." She paused and pulled her shawl more tightly around her. "But I rather think the second boy will end up showing more mettle than his brother. He's married a lovely girl. She brings the two little daughters to visit occasionally, doesn't she, Louise?"

Louise chuckled. "And that little Margaret Rose—she's a firecracker. My, she's going to be a handful when she grows up. She asked me if princesses could still have people's heads chopped off."

I laughed but I noticed that Princess Beatrice hardly smiled. "I'm going to have a word with that boy," she said. "The Prince of Wales, I mean. It's about time he learned that duty and family come before anything. He has been born to a great heritage. If Mama saw the way he was carrying on now, she'd turn in her grave. And Papa—he'd give the boy a horsewhipping and tell him to buck up or else, wouldn't he, Louise?"

"I expect he would. But times have changed, Bea. There has been a great war. Young people ask themselves if anything really matters, because life is so precarious, don't they, Georgiana?"

"Maybe those who remember the war. I was too young and things certainly matter to me."

"You're a good girl." She nodded. "A credit to the family. Our mother would have approved."

I had been looking around me. "This is an interesting room, Great-Aunt Louise," I said. "Are those sculptures modern or from classical times?"

She gave a delightful peal of laughter at this. "Not modern by your standards. I did them as a young woman."

"You are a sculptress? They are wonderful."

She nodded in appreciation. "I did have a certain talent. I had to give it up. It requires too much strength to chisel away at marble. Do you have artistic talents?"

"None at all; in fact I'm not sure I have any talents," I said.

"You should never sell yourself short," she said. "Young

women are brought up to prize modesty. I think one should shout one's abilities from the mountaintops."

She looked at my face and laughed. "My mother approved of my sculpting, but not of my views. I have always been a great champion of women. I championed the suffrage movement, you know, and I had a woman doctor for years before it became fashionable."

When I looked surprised Princess Beatrice added, "She had to keep it from dear Mama, of course. She would never have approved."

"You young people are so lucky," Princess Louise said wistfully. "In our day a girl was never allowed out unchaperoned, was she, Bea? A match was made for her. No career was possible for a girl of good family."

"It's not much easier these days to find a career," I said. "Too many unemployed men."

"Ah yes," she said. "I see men sleeping in the park when I go for my early morning walk. It distresses me. Such a sad time for so many. But let us not dwell on sad things. You are here to celebrate a wedding in the family."

A gust of wind moaned down the chimney, sending sparks and soot out into the room. I remembered what I had seen that afternoon.

"Tell me," I said, "is the palace haunted?"

The two great-aunts exchanged a look. "Oh yes, extremely haunted." Louise gave me a mischievous grin. "You'll bump into ghosts everywhere you go. Most of them royal, of course. Our ancestors, keeping an eye on us. I don't think any of them is malicious, so nothing to worry about."

"I saw a woman this afternoon," I said. "She wore a long white dress and her hair was piled on her head in pretty little curls."

"Ah, that would be Princess Sophia," Princess Louise said, glancing across at her sister for confirmation. "We've both seen her, haven't we, Bea? George the Third's daughter. Never allowed to marry, poor girl. Kept secluded here all her life. They say she had an incestuous affair with her brother the Duke of Cumberland, and also had an affair with her father's equerry. Either way, she produced an illegitimate child. The baby was whisked away and the whole thing was kept hushed up, but I think she walks the halls looking for that child, or maybe for the man who fathered it."

I thought of poor Princess Sophia, spending her life in this seclusion, and then having her child taken from her. No wonder she wandered the halls.

"Most of the other ghosts prefer the royal state rooms," Princess Beatrice said. "So we don't encounter them often. But the clock tower is supposed to be haunted."

"The clock tower?" I asked.

She nodded. "At the entrance to the courtyard behind us. Several times I've seen a strange light glowing there. But I've lived here long enough that ghosts no longer bother me. They do result in a large turnover in servants throughout the palace, I'm afraid. The lower classes are not used to meeting our ancestors on staircases." She chuckled again. She really was delightful.

We had a good dinner of mulligatawny soup, roast pheasant and apple dumplings, a pleasant evening, and as I said good-bye I wondered why I had never thought of visiting the aunts before. I supposed because I had spent my formative years far away in a Scottish castle and we'd never been introduced. And it's not quite as easy to drop in on a royal person as it would be if my aunts had been ordinary.

"Do you find it lonely or restricting living here on your own?" I asked.

"Oh no, dear," Princess Louise said. "Beatrice and I have each other and the nieces close by and if I want to get out, I just walk through the park to Harrods or a concert at the Albert Hall. And if I want to go farther afield I jump on a number nine bus. Nobody knows who I am. It's quite refreshing."

I thought that people might just notice an old woman in Victorian garb, but I nodded and smiled. A maid was sent to find my things.

"I can't think why we've never met you before, Georgiana," Princess Beatrice said and got a warning look from her sister.

"I'm afraid my mother left us and I was stuck alone in the nursery at Castle Rannoch," I said.

"But you must have been down in London when you were presented."

"Of course," I said.

"She wouldn't have wanted to waste her time visiting elderly relatives, Bea," Princess Louise said. "She would have been fully occupied with parties and balls and such."

"But you didn't find yourself a husband during your season?" Beatrice asked.

"I'm afraid not, ma'am."

She patted my hand. "Never mind. A nice healthy-looking girl like you will be snapped up soon enough. You'll see, the next wedding we celebrate in the family will be yours."

"I hope so." I gave her a smile.

The maid appeared with my coat and brolly.

"Take Lady Georgiana out through the back door, Phyllis," Princess Louise said. "She can go home by the courtyard and won't have to walk in that dreadful wind."

I kissed both great-aunts dutifully on the cheek without knocking either one of them over. Then I followed the maid down a narrow hall and was let out into a dark courtyard. Here it was quite still, apart from the drip, drip of rain. It was also quite dark. No lights shone out from windows, except for one on the second floor that must have been mine. But the heavy curtains were drawn and only a sliver of light showed. I put up my brolly and picked my way over the slippery cobblestones. As I approached the archway at the end of the courtyard I was relieved to see some sort of lamp was glowing, illuminating the dark shape of the building around it. As I drew closer a cold wind rushed at me and high above a clock began to chime ten.

The haunted clock tower, I thought. At that moment the light vanished and I was left in total darkness. I have to confess I plunged through the archway and ran all the way to the front door.

Chapter 9

Princess Marina arrives today. I hope she won't be as awful as her cousin!

The next day the apartment was full of hustle and bustle as we awaited the arrival of Princess Marina. Men appeared with large flower arrangements. Shelves were dusted. Fires were lit. Servants were in evidence and a good luncheon was served in the dining room. Civilization had come to apartment 1. I knew that the boat train was due in about four, so I made myself look as presentable as possible and went to the long salon to await the princess's arrival. Countess Irmtraut was already there.

"I did not see you at dinner last night," she said. "You were unwell?"

"No, I dined with my great-aunt, Princess Louise," I said. "She has the apartment next to this one."

"Ah yes, I am told that this house is full of old royal

ladies, but they do not invite me. I am not related to them, I suppose."

What was I supposed to say—that I was sorry she wasn't related to the English royal family? When I said nothing she went on, "So why are you not a princess yourself if these ladies are your aunts?"

"My grandmother was Queen Victoria's daughter. The offspring of a princess do not inherit her title. My grandfather was a duke, so my father was also a duke, and I'm merely a lady."

"Hmph," she said, obviously weighing whether a mere lady might rank below her. She looked out of the window. It was still as dreary and blustery as November can be in England.

"I hope Marina had a good journey. I do not think the Channel would have been smooth."

"Probably not. But it's only an hour, isn't it? One can endure most things for an hour."

"It will be longer if she comes from Hook of Holland," she said. "And rougher. I am always seasick, even on fine days. I have the delicate constitution of my ancestors."

I was extremely glad that Major Beauchamp-Chough joined us at that moment. "Won't be long now," he said. "The princess will be tired from her long journey, so I propose we let her rest until the motorcar comes for you at seven."

"The motorcar?" Countess Irmtraut asked.

"The princess has been invited to dine with her new family," the major said.

"We are to accompany her?" Irmtraut asked.

"Only Lady Georgiana, since she is a family member," he said curtly.

Irmtraut glared at me.

At that moment there was the crunch of tires on gravel and a Daimler drew up outside. Major B-C jumped up and strode briskly to the front door. We heard his big voice booming, "Welcome to Kensington Palace, Your Highness.

Inclement weather, I'm afraid. I hope the Channel wasn't too rough."

"Quite big swells. Rather exciting, actually," answered a woman's voice. And they came through into the room. From what I had been told—that the family had lived in exile with relatives and were rather poor—I had formed an image of a shy, rather dowdy young girl, a younger, fresher-faced version of Irmtraut. Instead into the room strode this tall and beautiful young woman. She was dressed in the height of fashion with a fox-fur-trimmed coat, beautifully cut, and a daring little hat perched on one side of her head. She gave a radiant smile when she saw Countess Irmtraut and held out her hands.

"Irmtraut. You're here. How good of you to come." They kissed on the cheeks.

Prince George came into the room behind her. "Hello, Georgie," he said, giving me what I interpreted as a slightly warning look. It was saying clearly, "You've seen me at a naughty party. Please forget about it."

"Hello, sir," I replied. "May I offer my heartiest congratulations on your upcoming wedding."

We exchanged the briefest of looks of understanding and he smiled.

"My dear," he said to Marina, "this is my cousin Georgiana I told you about. She has volunteered to stay with you here and show you around London."

"Georgiana, how delightful." She held out her hand to me. "How kind of you to give up your time to introduce me to London," she said. Her English was perfect and almost accent free. "I still have so much shopping to do for my trousseau. I've been away from Paris and the good shops for too long. Most European cities are too dreary and old-fashioned for words, especially Copenhagen, where I was staying. You can take me to the most fashionable shops in London. We'll have such fun."

Oh golly, I thought. I was the last person to escort someone around the most fashionable shops. I had never had the money to shop at any of them and my experience ended with

Harrods, Barkers, and maybe Fenwick. Certainly not the most fashionable boutiques London had to offer.

Major Beauchamp-Chough came in announcing to Princess Marina that her bags and her maid were now in her suite and he would escort her to it anytime she was ready. He suggested that she might want to rest after her long journey.

She gave a chuckle at this. "I've been sitting in a train carriage for most of the day. Hardly strenuous. What I'd really like is some tea. I have to say that English teatime is the best thing about moving to England."

"I'd rather hoped that I was the best thing," George said.

"Apart from you, my darling." She reached out a hand to touch his and I saw genuine affection there.

"I'll leave you to settle in, then," George said. "I'll see you tonight at dinner." He blew her a kiss as he left. Marina smiled fondly after him. I began to feel hopeful that this might be a true love match after all.

As soon as he was gone we enjoyed a good tea around the fire.

"I really missed having a proper tea when we lived in Paris," Marina said.

"Was it the custom to have tea in your family?" I asked.

"We had an English nanny," the princess said. "She expected tea to be served every day in the nursery."

"Ah, that explains your perfect English," I said.

She nodded. "Miss Kate Fox. Terribly strict and correct. You know, made us sleep with the windows open in a howling gale, and we had to mind our p's and q's. I expect you had one too?"

"My nanny was actually quite kind, which was good as neither of my parents was in evidence. But windows are always required to be open at Castle Rannoch, even in Scottish gales."

Marina smiled. "George has told me about the obligatory visits to Balmoral. I expect it will be much the same there."

"Definitely. And the piper waking everyone at dawn."

We laughed, at least Marina and I did. Irmtraut sat silent and staring past us, out of the window.

"Where are you to live, ma'am?" I asked. "Here at Kensington Palace?"

"Oh gosh, no. Too depressing for words, don't you think?" she said. "We'll be living in Belgrave Square. George is anxious to be moving out of his rooms at St. James's Palace. Do you know Belgrave Square?"

"Our family's London home is also there. What a coincidence."

"Then we shall be neighbors. How lovely." She reached out to me this time.

Irmtraut glared.

We chatted on as Marina worked her way through crumpets and scones and shortbread. It was all very pleasant and we probably lingered a little too long before finally realizing that we should go up and change for dinner at the palace. I found Queenie in my room, reading a magazine.

"Did you get your tea sent up to you?" I asked.

"No, I told them not to bother and I came down to have it in the kitchen. When it comes on a tray you only get one slice of cake."

The thought of Queenie coming down the stairs at just the time that Princess Marina was obviously arriving made me go cold all over. "I'd prefer it if you stayed put, Queenie."

"But it's lonely up here all by myself. And it's a bit creepy too. I kept hearing noises last night."

"I'm sure it was just the wind," I said brightly. No sense in telling her about the ghosts. "But now I have to get ready for dinner at the palace so please get out my blue evening dress."

"Your blue one?" she asked.

"Yes. The cornflower blue silk with the beading. The one my mother bought for me in America when my best clothes were lost in the fire. And those nice silk evening shoes too. I have to look my best."

There was a long pause. A feeling of doom began to creep over me. "Queenie, has something happened to my evening dress? You didn't try to iron it, and melt it, did you?"

"Oh no, miss. Nothing like that. It's just that . . . it ain't here."

"What do you mean?"

"I must have left it behind when we had to get out of your friend's place in a hurry. I remember that I couldn't fit all of your things into the wardrobe in the box room, so I shoved some into Miss Belinda's wardrobe. I suppose I must have forgotten them."

"You've forgotten my one good evening gown?" I tried not to shriek. "Queenie, I'm about to dine at the palace with the king and queen. All I have here are the burgundy and bottle green velvet and they are decidedly old and unfashionable and there is that place on the skirt where you ironed the velvet once. Queenie, you are hopeless. And it's too late to send you round to Belinda's in a taxi now."

"Sorry, miss," she said. "My old dad only said the other day that I'd forget my own head if it wasn't attached to my shoulders. That was when I forgot to turn off the gas and nearly blew up the house." And she gave an apologetic grin.

"Well, I have to make the best of it, I suppose," I said. "I'll wear the burgundy I wore last night."

"Oh, that one?" She was looking sheepish again.

"Please tell me something hasn't happened to the burgundy velvet dress."

"Not exactly," she said. "It's just that you wouldn't want to wear it tonight."

"And why is that?" Doom was enveloping me in a shroud.

"Well, you got a little spot on it at dinner last night and I was sponging it off and I turned around and me bum knocked the basin of water off the washstand. And it sort of went all over the skirt. So, I'm afraid it's a bit wet."

"Queenie, I should sack you on the spot," I exclaimed.

She hung her head. "Yeah, I know, miss. But accidents happen, don't they? Remember that time you bumped into someone with the tray of wine?"

I'm afraid she had me there, reminding me of my own clumsiness again. Maybe she wasn't quite as thick as she pretended.

"Go and find the bottle green dress and if you've damaged that one I'll throttle you personally."

The bottle green dress emerged from the wardrobe undamaged, but it had certainly seen better days and there was that patch of skirt where Queenie had ironed the velvet the wrong way. I now owned a silver fox stole, courtesy of my mother, so I planned to drape that over as much of me as possible. I was in low spirits when I went down to await Marina. And they sank even lower when she appeared in a stunning white dress dotted with pearls.

"Nobody will pay any attention to you anyway," I told myself.

The Daimler arrived and we set off.

"I'm very glad you are coming with me, Georgiana," Marina said in a whisper. "I am a little nervous about dining with my future family. The queen always seems so haughty and severe. Rather frightening after my own family, who are so easygoing."

"Yes, they can be rather alarming," I said. "I am invited to the palace quite frequently and every time I tremble at the knees. The king and queen are very hot on protocol. I always have to remember to curtsy and call her ma'am."

She took my hand. "Then you and I will support each other."

How charming she was, I thought, and I hoped fervently that Prince George could really learn to behave himself and to love her as she deserved. I tried to picture myself if I had agreed to marry Prince Siegfried, moving to a strange country with unfamiliar customs and a groom who would never love me. And I thought how lucky I was that I had found Darcy.

It was certainly less alarming to arrive at Buckingham Palace in a suitable Daimler motorcar and to drive past the guards, into the palace forecourt, through the arch and up to the main entrance. We were escorted up the stairs and into the Music Room, where the king and queen, together with the Duke and Duchess of York, were awaiting us. There was no sign of the Prince of Wales or the bridegroom. The queen came forward to meet us.

"Marina. Welcome, my dear. How very good to see you looking so well. And Georgiana too. Such a pleasure."

Marina was kissed on both cheeks. I curtsied. Marina

then kissed the king and was introduced to the duke and duchess.

"I must apologize for my sons," the queen said, looking around with obvious displeasure. "The king is extremely punctual and my sons appear to be more Continental in their approach to time. The Prince of Wales did tell me that he feared he would not be able to join us on this occasion, but your future husband was with us only a short time ago and went home to change into his dinner jacket. I can't think what could be delaying him."

"No sense of duty, this younger generation," the king growled.

"Oh, come now, Papa. We are here on time," the Duchess of York said with her sweet smile. I noticed the duke said nothing. He was always afraid of revealing his stammer in public and was very shy among strangers.

"You two are the salt of the earth," the queen replied.

"If only the boy would get over that blasted speech impediment," the king said. "It's only a matter of practice."

"I d-d-d-do try, Father," the duke said.

There was an awkward silence. Mercifully champagne was served. Nibbles were brought around and finally, when the king was clearly beginning to fume, Prince George came running up the staircase, out of breath and straightening his bow tie as he ran.

"Awfully sorry to be so late, Mama," he said. "The motorcar was involved in a minor prang. Nothing serious. Nobody hurt, but it delayed us."

"An accident on the way? Surely you only had to come a few yards from St. James's, didn't you? You could have walked," the king said testily.

"Actually I had to pop over to the new place to check on something the decorator wanted me to see, and as I said, no harm, no foul."

"You're here now, George. That's all that matters. And now that you are here, your father has something to tell you." The queen looked expectantly at the king, who cleared his throat.

"This is the time in your life when you take on responsibility, my boy," he said. "Until now you've had free rein to enjoy yourself when you were not out and about with the navy. From now on we expect you and your bride to be active members of the royal family, to take on royal duties, and to be a credit to our good name and to our ancestors. So I plan to make you Duke and Duchess of Kent."

"Gosh, thanks awfully, Father." He looked across at Marina. "Do you hear that, my dear? You're to be Duchess of Kent."

Marina was standing next to me. "Isn't that a step down from princess?" she whispered with the hint of a grin.

"These titles come with property and income, I believe," I whispered back. "Most royal sons are made dukes."

"Ah." She nodded.

The gong was sounded. Prince George took Marina's arm to escort her in to dinner. I followed behind, unescorted. I suppose the Prince of Wales would have made up even numbers, as he wouldn't have dared to bring Mrs. Simpson with him. Dinner passed smoothly but without the Prince of Wales putting in an appearance, which clearly vexed his mother. When we were driven back to Kensington Palace, Princess Marina seemed in good spirits and satisfied with her lot.

"The queen was kinder to me than I expected," she said. "And I could tell that the king liked me too."

"Who could not like you?" I asked.

She squeezed my hand. "You're so sweet, Georgiana. Will you have to marry someone the family finds for you, or will you be able to make your own choice?"

"Hopefully the latter," I said. "They tried to hitch me up with Prince Siegfried of Romania."

She gave a peal of laughter. "Me too. Isn't he awful? And do you know what I found out? He likes other men. Can you imagine how horrid that would be?"

Should I tell her? I wondered, then decided against it. After all, her future bridegroom George was also reputed to have had affairs with unsuitable women. He was an equal opportunity offender. And maybe he'd shape up and become a model husband. He certainly seemed fond of Marina, the way he looked at her.

It was not raining for once as the car drew up outside Kensington Palace, but a large puddle had formed outside the entrance to our apartment. "I'll stop a little farther down, Your Royal Highness," the chauffeur said, "so that you don't get your feet wet. There's a raised pavement beside the house where you can walk back."

"How kind. Thank you," Marina replied.

We were helped out of the backseat. Marina went ahead of me. I was about to follow when I glanced back and thought I saw that strange greenish glow coming from the archway below the clock tower. I had to see for myself where the light was coming from and began to walk toward it. Then I stared harder. Surely something was lying there. Something white. My heart was beating faster and I wanted to turn and hurry into the safety of our apartment but I couldn't help myself. I was drawn toward it. If it was the ghost of Princess Sophia I had to see it for myself. But why would a ghost be lying anywhere? Surely ghosts wafted about as they wished and didn't linger too long. As I approached the thing lying on the cobbles, I could make out the form of a dark-haired young woman in a white silk dress, lying slumped over, facedown. I kept moving closer, walking more slowly now. Surely the specter would vanish when I came too close, wouldn't it?

But it didn't. I stood there, taking in every detail—the rather flashy rings on the hand that lay outstretched a few inches from my foot, the very modern short haircut with its permanent waves, and then, as I moved around to get a better view I saw her eyes, open and staring at me blankly from a deathly white face, contrasting with the bright red lips.

Whoever she was she was no ghost. She had been recently alive and now she was very dead.

Chapter 10

I stood there in the darkness with my heart hammering, not knowing what to do. I had seen dead bodies before but one never gets over the shock. I put my hand to my mouth, feeling queasy. Marina had gone ahead of me into the house. I had no idea how long the girl had been lying there, if she had been murdered, or even if the murderer still lurked nearby.

"Your ladyship?" a voice called and the chauffeur was coming toward me. "I don't believe you can get into the apartment that way. May I escort you to the front door?"

"Thank you so much." I came hurriedly to meet him so that he wouldn't catch a glimpse of the dead girl. He delivered me safely to the front door and I heard the motorcar drive away as the door was closed behind me by a maid.

The police should be called immediately, I thought, and I was about to tell the maid to take me to a telephone. But I realized that Princess Marina should not be made upset. Then I remembered Major Beauchamp-Chough. There were rules of protocol to be followed in a royal palace and he was currently master of the house. So if anyone summoned the police it should be he.

"Do you know where one would find Major Beauchamp-Chough?" I asked the maid.

"I expect he would be in his own apartment at this time of night, my lady," she said, looking at me strangely.

"It was apartment 10, I believe. Do you know which one that is?"

"I'm not sure. I'd have to go and ask," she said.

"It's important that I see him right away," I said. "A situation has arisen that demands his immediate attention. Where can I find a writing desk?"

She took me through to a small sitting room and seated me at a Queen Anne desk by the window. I found an old-fashioned inkwell, pen and paper. I started to write as the maid went to find out how to locate the major's suite.

Dear Major Beauchamp-Chough,

I am sorry to disturb you at this time of night, but a difficult situation has arisen that demands your immediate attention. Please come to apartment 1 as soon as you receive this.

By the time I had finished, the maid had returned. "His apartment is all the way around at the front of the building," she said, her expression betraying that she didn't want to walk all that way in the dark.

I felt for her, but speed was of primary importance. "Then please take him this letter," I said.

"Now, my lady?" She looked scared and I wondered if she'd heard the stories about Kensington's ghosts.

"Yes, now. I'd go myself, but that would not be seemly. It's most urgent, you understand, or I would not be asking you to do this."

"Very well, my lady." She bobbed a curtsy and went. I sat at the desk, staring out into blackness, waiting. The image of that white face with staring eyes swam before me and I found I was shivering. It wasn't long before the major appeared, looking absolutely resplendent in full dress uniform with much braid and a row of medals that were most impressive.

"Lady Georgiana, what on earth is the matter? You look quite white. The maid said it was most urgent. Has the princess been taken ill?"

"Nothing like that, Major. I'm so sorry to disturb you, but it is indeed crucial," I said. "There is something that you must see. If you'd kindly come with me." I turned to the maid, who was still hovering in the doorway. "Thank you. You may go now."

As the maid departed with a look of relief, Major B-C looked at me questioningly. "You're lucky to find me at home. I only just returned a moment ago from my monthly regimental dinner. In fact the maid just caught me letting myself into my apartment. Now out with it. What is it that's troubling you?"

"Please follow me," I said and walked resolutely toward the front door. The major followed.

"Where on earth are we going?" he asked as I stepped out into darkness.

"I have to show you something."

Now that there was no Daimler with headlights shining, it was pitch-black outside.

"Is this some sort of prank?" he asked.

"No prank, I assure you, Major. This way, please."

I felt my way over the cobbles until I could just make out the archway beneath the clock tower. Strangely it had been light enough for me to spot the body instantly before but this time I almost stumbled upon it before I picked out a vague hint of whiteness.

"What on earth is that?" Major B-C demanded, his voice now taut.

"It's a body," I replied and my voice bounced back, alarmingly loud as it echoed from the cobbles and vaulted arch above. "A young woman. She's dead. I'm afraid she might have been murdered."

"Good God," he said, bending forward to peer more closely at the body. "Is it one of the maids?"

"No, she's dressed in a white silk evening gown. I've no idea who she is."

"Are we sure that she's dead? She might have been drinking too much at a party and lost her way in the dark and collapsed here." He bent down even farther to examine her.

"Oh, I'm sure she's dead. Look at her face." I shuddered.

He was kneeling on the damp cobbles beside her, felt for a pulse, then got hurriedly to his feet. "I'll go and find a torch," he said. "You come back into the house. You shouldn't be out here alone."

I followed him as he walked briskly back into the building. I waited in the foyer, hugging my fur stole around me, as I was suddenly extremely cold. He seemed to take forever. At last he returned carrying a large silvery flashlight.

"It wasn't easy explaining why I wanted this without raising curiosity," he said. "It required some quick thinking."

I followed him back to the archway. He shone the torch onto the dead girl.

"My God." I heard his sharp intake of breath. He looked around. "We should move her out of sight as soon as possible."

"You can't do that," I said. "This is a crime scene. We must stay with her until the police get here."

"My dear girl," he said, forgetting to use my correct title, "we can't just call the police. I don't think you realize the delicate nature of this situation." He moved closer to me, even though we were alone in a dark courtyard. "You say you didn't recognize her. I rather fear most people would. This is, or rather, was, Bobo Carrington. Surely you've heard of her? Her photographs are splashed all over the picture papers."

"I may have seen them," I said tentatively.

"She's a well-known socialite and partygoer and also at one stage her name was linked with Prince George."

"Oh crikey," I said, too shocked to worry about schoolgirl expressions and the need to sound sophisticated.

"So now you see," he said. "We can't just call the police. If any word gets out, any hint to the press, it would ruin everything. The scandal would be horrendous. The marriage could never take place."

I nodded. I did see, all too clearly.

"But we shouldn't move her," I said. "There are bound to be clues, pieces of evidence."

"I have a dark gray blanket on my bed," he said. "We could cover her with that until morning. But something will have to be done before the first grounds staff pass this way." He looked up at the building, frowning. "Luckily there aren't many windows that look onto this courtyard. One up in Princess Louise's apartment, but she usually goes to bed early and I believe it's a bedroom that is not used. And the one on the second floor of your apartment with the light still on is surely your own room."

"Yes, it must be," I said.

"Might your maid have looked out of the window?"

"It's possible. But she's quite susceptible and already finds the place rather spooky. If she mentions anything I'll tell her about Princess Sophia's ghost."

"Good girl." He smiled at me.

"So I'll go and get the blanket to cover her and I suggest you go inside and have someone bring you a brandy. You'll need it for shock and it's devilish cold out here. You don't want to come down with a chill."

I was going to tell him that I'd been involved in murder cases before and I was strong enough to help him, but I realized I did feel quite shivery.

"If you're sure there is nothing more I can do?"

"You've been very brave, Lady Georgiana. But I suggest you go to bed," he said. "There's nothing else you can do now."

A great gust of wind swirled up, stirring the dead girl's clothing. The sequins on her dress sparkled suddenly in the beam from the flashlight. I wanted nothing more than to get away from that spot.

"Very well," I said. "But we must do something. A girl

has been murdered. We can't let it be hushed up just so that a wedding can go forward."

"Of course," he said. "But this is a royal palace and it will need to go through the correct channels. I will pass this information on to His Majesty's private secretary and see how I am instructed to proceed. And in the meantime please behave as if nothing is amiss. The word will have gone around that you summoned me late at night. You might want to think up a plausible explanation for that."

"All right, I'll try," I said. "Although my brain isn't working very well at the moment."

"I'll escort you back to your front door." He took my arm and steered me along the narrow pavement while I wracked my brains thinking of something plausible to say.

"Oh, there you are, your ladyship." The same maid came to meet me in the foyer. "Is everything all right? Major Beauchamp-Chough looked quite upset and he wanted a flashlight."

"Yes, my fault, I suppose," I said. "I was wearing a very valuable diamond brooch lent to me by Her Majesty for the occasion and the pin must have come loose. I realized it must have fallen off when I got out of the car and I knew how upset Her Majesty would be if something happened to it, so I'm ashamed to say I panicked."

"You could have asked us to help you find it, my lady," she said. "There's enough servants still awake."

"Actually I didn't want word to get back to Her Majesty," I said. "So please don't mention it, all right?"

"But did the major find it for you?"

"Yes, he did, thank goodness." I gave her what I hoped was a convincing smile. "And he's taken it away for safe-keeping, ready to be returned to Buckingham Palace in the morning. Now that I know the clasp is loose I won't risk wearing it again."

"Well, that's good then, isn't it, my lady?" She gave me an encouraging smile. "Everything's all right and we can all go to bed."

"Yes. Everything's all right. But I would appreciate a glass of brandy to warm me up. I'm really cold now."

"Of course, my lady. Would you like the brandy in hot milk?"

"That's a lovely idea." I smiled at her again.

"I'll bring it up to your room," she said.

"Oh, that's not necessary."

"No trouble, my lady. You go up and I'll bring the hot milk."

Why couldn't Queenie be more like that, I thought as I trudged up the two flights of stairs. Cheerful, willing, thinking of my needs. I sighed. Queenie would probably be snoring on my bed when I got to my room.

I opened my door and jumped as Queenie stepped forward to greet me. "Oh, there you are, miss. I've been that worried about you. I heard the princess come upstairs a while ago and then you didn't show up and something funny was going on down in the courtyard below."

"Nothing to worry about, Queenie," I said. "We were just looking for a piece of jewelry that must have fallen off when the princess got out of the car."

"Oh, that was you down there, was it? Thank God for that. I thought it was one of them ruddy ghosts. They say this palace is bloody well haunted. Down in the kitchen they said there's ever so many ghosts drifting around. In fact I think I saw one, earlier this evening. Something in white, wafting across the courtyard. Horrible it was."

"Yes, I'm afraid that must have been one of the ghosts," I said rapidly. "Princess Sophia, the daughter of George the Third, but don't worry. She's quite harmless. She drifts around looking for her lost child."

"She might be harmless but I don't want to bump into her. Gives me the willies just thinking about it. I sat here all evening wondering if ghosts could come up the stairs and through walls."

"I think you're quite safe, Queenie," I said. "And anyway, I'm back now. As soon as I'm undressed you can go to bed and you know very well that no princess would haunt the servants' quarters."

"Yes, that's right, ain't it?" She perked up then. "Come on then. Turn round and I'll take your necklace off."

Queenie finished undressing me and I climbed into bed. The fire had burned down to embers and it was cold in the room. I couldn't resist going over to the window and pulling back the curtain to take a peek at the courtyard below. Someone was moving around down there. I could see a torch dancing but the person holding it was invisible beneath the archway. Fortunately so was the body. And I realized that the holder of the torch must be the major, covering the body with his blanket. There was nothing else to do but to get back in bed. My hot milk was delivered. I drank it but it didn't seem to warm me. I curled up into a ball and tried to sleep, but sleep wouldn't come.

Bobo Carrington. Now that I thought about it I had heard the name before. One of the glamorous young women who was always photographed at nightclubs or at the races. But what on earth was she doing here, trying to get into Kensington Palace?

Chapter 11

I was in a deep sleep when I began to be shaken violently.
I started and sat up with a gasp to see a strange young
woman, dressed in servant's garb, standing over me. It was
still dark outside.

"What's wrong?" I asked. "What time is it?"

"Five thirty, my lady, and I didn't mean to startle you,"
she whispered, "and sorry to wake you so early, but the
major is downstairs and he wants to talk to you right away.
I've no idea what it's about but he said it was urgent and I
should go and wake you."

I swung my legs over the side of the bed and my feet
sought my slippers. It was horribly cold. The maid took
down my dressing gown from the back of the door. "Should
I go and wake your maid, my lady?"

"No. Let her sleep," I said, thinking that by the time
Queenie could be roused and ready it would be broad day-
light. "I'll go down to the major in my robe and slippers."

I tied the dressing gown firmly at my waist and then made

my way down the stairs. The major was waiting in the foyer, already dressed and looking military and ready for action.

"Lady Georgiana," he said. "I'm so sorry to get you up at this ungodly hour, but I wonder if you'd be good enough to come with me."

"Uh—yes. Of course," I said, conscious of the maid still standing behind me.

He looked at my attire. "I think you might need proper shoes and an overcoat. I'm afraid we need to go outside for a moment."

"Oh, right. Very well."

The major turned to the maid. "Perhaps you would make sure there is hot tea for Lady Georgiana when she returns in a few minutes."

"Very good, sir." The maid bobbed a little curtsy and fled. I went back upstairs and put on shoes and an overcoat. The major was waiting by the front door and I followed him. When we reached the archway under the clock tower I saw that the body had already been taken away and there was no sign she had ever been there.

"Did you get permission to move the body?" I whispered even though we were alone and my whisper hissed back at me from the vaulted roof of the arch above our heads.

"Yes. The Home Office had some chappies here within the hour last night. They took photographs and examined the area well before the poor young woman was carted off to the mortuary. There wasn't actually anything to see. In fact one of the chaps suggested that the girl had been killed somewhere else and the body dumped here."

"Why would anyone do that?" I asked. "If you wanted to dispose of a body surely you'd drive out to a wooded park or throw it into the Thames."

"Unless you wanted it to be found," he said, turning back to look at me. He opened a door at the far end of the courtyard and we stepped into an austere, white-painted hallway. There was no form of adornment on the walls, but the carpet underfoot was rich and thick and the place was delightfully warm.

"Through this way, if you don't mind." Major B-C opened a door and stood aside for me to enter first. I stepped into a small sitting room, definitely a man's room with leather armchairs and the lingering smell of pipe tobacco. Two men had been sitting in the chairs facing the fire. Both rose to their feet as I came in. I hadn't been expecting to face strangers and was horribly conscious that I was in my nightclothes under the overcoat, with my hair still tousled. This put me at an awful disadvantage.

"Lady Georgiana, I'm so sorry to have to disturb you at this hour," one of the men said. He was dressed impeccably in a dark gray pin-striped suit and had silver gray hair smoothed back to perfection. What's more, I recognized him at the same moment that he said, "We have met before. Jeremy Danville of the Home Office. We are forever grateful for the way you helped us with a difficult situation in Scotland a couple of years ago."

"Sir Jeremy, of course." I shook his hand. When I had last encountered him it had been on a case involving royal security and I suspected that his job was not that of the usual civil servant.

"I'm sorry we meet again under such difficult circumstances," Sir Jeremy said. "A tricky situation indeed."

I nodded as my gaze went to the other man. At first glance he seemed more nondescript and unassuming but he was examining me with a keen gaze and my brain said *policeman* at the same time that Sir Jeremy said, "And this is Detective Chief Inspector Pelham from the Special Branch, Scotland Yard. He has plenty of experience handling difficult situations like this." I caught a flicker of annoyance and realized of course that if Sir Jeremy was really in some kind of secret service the last person he'd want to work with would be someone from Special Branch. It was rumored that both departments thought the other was superfluous.

"How do you do, Lady Georgiana." Chief Inspector Pelham nodded to me but didn't shake hands. His voice betrayed a trace of a northern accent and I noticed he didn't smile.

Special Branch, I thought. Usually handles matters of national security. The royal family was certainly taking every precaution to make sure this news did not leak out.

"Please do take a seat, Lady Georgiana." Sir Jeremy indicated the armchair by the fire where he had been sitting, then drew up a wooden chair from the desk in the corner for himself. "So you were the one who actually found the body, I understand?"

"That's right," I said.

"What time was this?" the chief inspector asked.

"I would say about ten thirty last night. We left Buckingham Palace a little after ten, that much I know."

"And how did you happen to come upon this body, Lady Georgiana?" the chief inspector continued. "Since the place where she was lying was nowhere near the door to the apartment where you are staying?"

"Well, there was a puddle outside the front door," I said, "so the chauffeur had to stop the car quite a way farther along, so we didn't get our feet wet. Princess Marina got out of the motor first and walked straight to the door. I was about to follow but as I got out of the car I thought I saw something under the archway and went to look closer." I had been going to say that I saw a strange sort of glow and I wanted to see if it was the ghostly light, but that would have sounded silly.

"But surely the body wasn't visible from where the car stopped?" the inspector asked sharply. "And I don't know how you could spot a body in that kind of darkness."

"I'm not quite sure what made me go and look," I said. "I thought I saw some kind of light first and it was only when I came close to the archway that I saw something lying there."

"Some kind of light? Like a torch shining, you mean?"

"No." I shook my head. "More like a gentle glow."

"I suppose a light could have been shining out from a window," the major said. He was still standing beside my chair, ramrod straight, a military man to the core. "There are a couple of windows that look onto that courtyard. Lady Georgiana's room, for example. And my own bathroom."

"And you didn't hear or see anything, Major?" Detective Chief Inspector Pelham asked.

"I'm afraid I'd been out all evening—our usual monthly regimental dinner in mess. Can't miss that, you know, even for a visiting princess." He gave an apologetic smile. "I had literally just come in when I was given a note from Lady Georgiana. And frankly even if I'd been here, one hears plenty of strange noises in an old building like this."

"If there were windows without the curtains drawn then someone might have seen something," Sir Jeremy suggested, looking up at the major.

"Hardly likely. The suite next to mine is unoccupied. I believe the rooms at the back of Princess Louise's suite are not in normal use, and the only room with a window facing the courtyard that is currently occupied is Lady Georgiana's own."

"Did you ask your maid if she saw anything?" the major asked me.

"She did," I replied. There was an intake of breath. "She said she saw something going on under the archway, but I think it must have been Major Beauchamp-Chough with his torch when I brought him to see the body." I looked up at them. "I can ask her again exactly what she saw, if you like, but she is rather an impressionable girl and has heard the stories about ghosts in the palace."

"Ghosts?" Chief Inspector Pelham looked amused.

"Yes, apparently the palace has more than its fair share of ghosts," I replied. I didn't add that I had seen one of them.

"That may be useful." The men exchanged a glance.

Sir Jeremy leaned toward me. "Lady Georgiana, I do hope that Major Beauchamp-Chough has impressed upon you the sticky situation in which we find ourselves. We are weeks away from a royal wedding. The eyes of the world are already on London. Photographers are crawling out of the woodwork. And now this young woman—rumored to have been a . . . well, rumored to be a close friend of the groom—is found dead a few yards from his future wife."

Detective Chief Inspector Pelham cleared his throat.

"You can thank your lucky stars that you and the princess were out all evening at the palace," he said, "otherwise suspicion could have fallen upon the bride. Jealously is a powerful motive."

"That is absurd," I said angrily. "Have you met Princess Marina? She is not the type at all."

"Oh, I think most women have a streak of jealousy running through them." The DCI gave the hint of a smirk. "More deadly than the male, isn't that what they say?"

"Then, as you say, it was lucky we both have a perfect alibi all evening," I said calmly. "Has the time of death been established?"

"An autopsy is being performed at this moment," Sir Jeremy said. "Presumably we'll be able to know whether it was murder or suicide."

"Suicide?" I said. "Why would anyone come to Kensington Palace to commit suicide?"

"Suicide or even accidental death," Sir Jeremy went on, looking across me at the other men. "I understand you were not acquainted with the young woman. So let me tell you she was known in fashionable circles as 'the girl with the silver syringe.' She was a drug addict: cocaine and morphine. So it's possible she took her own life."

"And she came here to do it to punish Prince George for getting married," Chief Inspector Pelham said, nodding agreement. "Killed herself while of unsound mind in a moment of despair."

I realized, as I looked from one to the other, that they were writing a plausible scenario, just in case word ever got out. Unstable Young Woman, Known Drug Addict, Kills Self at Royal Palace. They were determined to make this a suicide.

"So you are not going to investigate this further?" I asked. "You're already writing it off as a suicide?"

"Of course not," Chief Inspector Pelham said. "If it is proven to be murder then naturally we will investigate to the fullest. But let's just hope she died of a mixture of drugs and booze, shall we?"

And the three men nodded.

"So nothing was found at the scene to indicate that someone else had been there with her?" I asked.

"My men examined the scene thoroughly," Chief Inspector Pelham said. "There was no sign of a struggle or of foul play. No obvious wounds on the body. The sequins on her dress were intact, so were the long strings of beads around her neck. They probably wouldn't have lasted through any kind of assault. And surely someone in one of the apartments would have heard her scream if she had been attacked."

"I believe it was suggested that maybe she was killed elsewhere and her body was dumped here," I said.

"If she was murdered," Chief Inspector Pelham said. "But then the sound of a motorcar in this private area behind the palace would have made somebody look out of a window."

"All this speculation is worthless at the moment. Let's just wait for the autopsy results, shall we?" Sir Jeremy said. "Because if the results indicate murder we have the most difficult of tasks ahead of us, keeping the investigation entirely out of the public eye." He turned to me. "The newspapers have been remarkably cooperative about turning a blind eye to royal scandals, but I don't think they could be persuaded to stay mum about a murder. This is where you can be of help to us, Lady Georgiana. You are one of their inner circle. You can ask seemingly innocent questions."

"Their inner circle?" I asked in surprise. "Surely you don't think that anyone connected with the royal family is involved?"

"Of course not, but given the young woman's tenuous connection . . ." He left the rest of the sentence hanging. "And there are the servants. I don't want to raise any alarms by questioning any of them officially yet. You could find out if anyone here saw anything strange last night." He got to his feet. "I know we can count on you. You did a stellar job for us last time. Absolutely stellar."

Detective Chief Inspector Pelham raised an eyebrow as

if he found this hard to believe. "And we don't need to impress upon you the complete need for discretion," he said. "Not a word of this conversation is to go beyond these four walls. You do understand that, don't you?"

"Of course," I said. "Don't worry. I'll do anything I can to help you."

Sir Jeremy smiled. "We're most grateful, Lady Georgiana. I told them we could count on you."

"How do I contact you?" I asked. "Or will you contact me when you need to?"

I realized that he worked in one of those nebulous departments that the Home Office would probably deny even existed.

"I've no doubt you can contact Sir Jeremy through me," the major said.

Sir Jeremy reached into his breast pocket and produced a card. "This is my private telephone number," he said. "It doesn't go via the usual sort of exchange."

I took it from him.

"Actually I will be officially handling the investigation." DCI Pelham cleared his throat.

"Quite." Sir Jeremy gave the major the briefest of glances that said clearly the policeman was not of our class, not one of us, but had to be tolerated at this stage.

"We'll be in touch, then," Sir Jeremy said. "As soon as we know the autopsy results."

I was shown out of the room and crossed the courtyard in a bit of a daze.

$\mathcal{C}hapter$ 12

STILL NOVEMBER 5
KENSINGTON PALACE

It wasn't until I was back in my own bedroom, sipping tea as I watched the maid lighting the fire, that the full implication of what I had agreed to do hit me. They had not ruled out the royal family and they wanted me to question them. If it was murder, clearly the whole family had a motive. An unstable girl, addicted to cocaine, who had once been Prince George's mistress, could do incredible damage if she decided to sell her story to the newspapers. She would have to be silenced at all costs. But then I realized that the royal family would not do their own killing and anyone they detailed to do the dirty deed would have made sure that the body was found far, far away, if it was found at all. Preferably it would have been taken out to sea, or buried conveniently in a royal wood. Leaving it for all to see at Kensington Palace would be an act of profound stupidity.

So it was therefore more likely that someone else had a reason to want Bobo Carrington dead and wanted to pin the murder on the royals. Like the three men in that room, I just hoped it would turn out to be suicide.

I got up, ran myself a long bath in a tub big enough to float the royal yacht in and was already out and dressed by the time Queenie appeared, bleary-eyed and still trying to button her dress.

"Blimey, you're up early," she said. "What's happening today, then? You didn't tell me you wanted me earlier than normal this morning."

"Don't worry, Queenie, for once you're not in the wrong," I said. "I merely woke early and it seemed silly to stay in bed."

"Right, then. Do you want your breakfast brought up on a tray? I'll go and fetch it for you."

"No, thank you. Remember I said that I didn't want you wandering around the palace? I'll have mine downstairs. You stay here and I'll have someone bring up your breakfast to you."

"It's like being a bloody prisoner in a cell," she said.

"I think it's very nice to be waited on. You can pretend to be me for once."

"Well, make sure they put more than one slice of toast on the plate," she said. "That supper last night wasn't enough to feed a ruddy sparrow."

"You can hardly do up those buttons as it is," I said, chuckling. "A few weeks of dieting won't do you any harm."

"How am I supposed to keep up me strength then?" she asked. "It takes a lot of energy lugging your ruddy trunks up and down stairs all the time."

"You'll survive," I said. "Oh, and Queenie, about last night . . ."

"Yes, miss?"

I walked over to the window and looked down. Below me the cobblestones glistened in watery sunshine. I tried to picture where the body had lain. Could I have seen it from this window? If a motorcar had drawn up outside the building and dumped the body it wouldn't have been seen from here. I looked at the wall opposite. There were not many windows looking onto this courtyard. The one at the far end must be the major's bathroom. Apart from that there were only the ones at the back of Princess Louise's suite.

"You said you saw something last night. What exactly did you see?"

"Do you mean them lights flashing around?"

"No, you said you saw something white earlier in the evening. Was it a lady in white?"

"I couldn't tell, miss. It was right dark down there. I just saw this white thing, moving slowly across the courtyard. I couldn't even tell if it was a person. It just sort of oozed across the cobblestones toward the arch."

"Oozed?"

"Yeah. Or wafted. I couldn't exactly tell. Not going in a straight line anyway. Not someone walking. All I can say is it moved slowly in a funny way—this blob of white. I can tell you I closed them curtains pretty quick."

"What time was this, Queenie?"

"I couldn't tell you, miss. I was sitting here, feeling bored, and I thought I heard a motorcar, so I pulled back the curtain and that's when I saw it. I'm sure it was one of them ruddy ghosts. You should hear what the servants say about this place being haunted. There's the man with no face, and the boy who jumps out at you and laughs. So now I come to think of it, I'm quite happy to stay up here. If I ran into one of them on the stairs I think I'd die of a heart attack."

"I don't think ghosts can hurt us, Queenie. They are not solid flesh and blood."

"That's as may be," she said. "I ain't going to give them a try."

I thought of Bobo's sparkly white dress. It did appear that Queenie may or may not have seen her crossing the court-yard. If she had been tipsy or on drugs might she have staggered around, giving the impression of wafting, as Queenie put it. That was interesting. If true, then a motorcar had not pulled up and dumped her body, but she had been alive down below my window.

I went down to see if breakfast might have been put out

for us and found Countess Irmtraut already seated at the table, tucking into a plate piled high with food.

"This I like. The English breakfast. It is most nourishing," she said.

"Yes, there's nothing to beat a good English breakfast," I replied, starting to help myself to kidneys and bacon. "Did you sleep well last night? I hope we didn't wake you when we came home."

"I was still awake," she said. "You do not think that I would fall asleep before the princess returned? She might have needed me. And the maid said that someone lost a piece of jewelry when you came out of the motorcar? Was it you or Princess Marina?"

"It was me. But easily found again. The major had a flashlight and helped me find it."

"This is good." She nodded.

"Your room faces the outside of the palace," I said. "You didn't hear any vehicles drive up before we arrived home, did you?"

"What kind of vehicles?" She was looking at me suspiciously, a kidney poised on her fork.

"My maid said she heard a motorcar outside the front door and I wondered who it could have been."

"I heard nothing," she said. "I ate my dinner alone in the dining room. And a terrible dinner it was too. They served me something called toad in the hole. Do you know this? Is not a toad some kind of frog? Me, I do not eat frogs. I am not French."

I tried not to laugh. "That's just its name. Actually it's only English sausages in a batter. You know—English bangers?"

"Bangers?" Her eyebrows shot up. "They explode?"

"Not usually." I smiled. "I'm sorry you didn't like the meal. It's a favorite of mine but not served often in fashionable circles. More like nursery food."

"They think I am only worth serving nursery food." Irmtraut sniffed. "I had this frog for dinner and then I sat alone and read until Marina returned. A very boring evening. I trust your dinner at the palace was more lively."

"Very pleasant, thank you. And the family has clearly taken to Princess Marina."

"This is good," she said. "I hope she will be happy with the English prince. He has not the good reputation, so I have heard."

"He might have been a bit of a playboy," I said cautiously. "But I'm sure he will settle down now and take his responsibilities seriously."

"A playboy? At what does he play?" she asked. "Does this mean like an actor in a play?"

I smiled. "No, it means he likes to have a good time."

"Ah. This is what we heard," she said. "I do not wish Marina to be disappointed in her choice."

"The king has just made Prince George the Duke of Kent," I said. "That means that Marina will become Duchess of Kent upon her marriage."

"A duchess is of higher rank than a princess?" She echoed Marina's question.

"A royal duchess, yes. The title comes with property and income. Kings' sons, other than the heir, are often made royal dukes in England."

"Ah, so this is good. I am pleased." I think it was the first time I had seen her smile.

I waited for Marina to appear and ask to be taken to fashionable shops, plays and even nightclubs. All outside of my sphere of experience. I sighed. If only Darcy were here, he'd know about such things. He had certainly lived enough of the playboy lifestyle. I wondered where he was and why he could never even drop me a postcard. Was this what married life would be like, with my husband away in unknown parts of the world and my never knowing when he would return home? And whatever he was doing, of course he couldn't tell me. Annoying man!

Then suddenly I had a brain wave. I did know someone who moved in fashionable circles and knew about boutiques and nightclubs. What's more, she had my blue evening gown hanging in her wardrobe, thanks to Queenie. I'd go to collect the dress this minute and see if I could persuade Belinda to help me escort Marina around fashionable London.

Now I felt much better. I told Irmtraut to tell the princess that I had to pay a call but would return soon to take her wherever she wanted to go. Then I put on my coat and hat and stepped out into a fine, brisk morning. There was no sign of any kind of police vehicle and the archway was deserted, with no indication that anything had ever happened there. I searched around, looking for any kind of clue that might have been missed, but rain-washed cobbles do not favor telltale footprints, or even the tread of motor tires.

Then I set off across the park for Belinda's Knightsbridge mews cottage. It was a grand day to be out and walking and I felt my spirits rise as they always did when I was in the open air. Nannies pushed prams along the gravel paths while their older charges ran ahead or pushed their own dolls' prams. It was a peaceful and friendly scene and it was hard to believe that a young woman had lain dead in an archway just on the other side of the palace. The men in the major's study clearly wanted her death to be a suicide. I just hoped they were right and the autopsy would prove that she died from a drug overdose. But it still wouldn't explain what she was doing under an archway at Kensington Palace.

I hadn't gone far before two young boys came barreling toward me, pushing a pram with a hideous stuffed figure in it. I leaped back, startled, before they yelled, "Penny for the Guy, miss!" And I realized the date. Guy Fawkes. Bonfire night. All over Britain bonfires would be lit in back gardens and fireworks would be set off. I fished in my purse and found a penny, then was accosted by two more lots of boys and Guys before I reached the entrance to the park.

I rapped on Belinda's front door. I had to wait quite a while and had almost given up when the door opened and a bleary-eyed Belinda peeked out.

"Oh, Georgie, it's you. What are you doing here at this ungodly hour?" she asked.

"It's nine thirty, Belinda. Most of the world is up and busy. Were you out gambling again late last night?"

"No, but I haven't quite got used to the difference in times between California and here. My body still thinks it's on California time."

"I know. I had the same trouble when I first arrived home," I said. "Aren't you going to let me in?" Then a thought struck me. "Or are you perhaps entertaining some gentleman I should not meet?"

"No, it's just me. All alone," she said. "Come on in. I'm afraid I haven't made tea or coffee yet."

I stepped into a rather untidy sitting room. "Where is your maid, Belinda?" I asked. "Has she not come back into your service yet?"

"Gone," Belinda said. "Deserted me. Abandoned me in my hour of need, the rotter."

"Oh no."

She nodded. "Oh yes. I paid her wages for a month when I left England. And of course I was gone longer than a month so she ups and finds herself a new job. And listen to this—not as a maid, either. She took a course in typewriting and now she works in a typing pool where she has regular hours and weekends free, and she earns more money than I paid her." She shook her head. "What are the lower classes coming to, Georgie?"

"The world is changing, I suppose," I said. "Although it's rather galling to think that she can get a job just like that when you and I are unemployable."

"You wouldn't like to make me some tea, would you?" Belinda said. "You're so good at domestic things."

"All right." I smiled as I went through to the kitchen. I'd had to learn the hard way how to survive on my own. If Belinda didn't find a new maid soon, she'd also have to learn how to look after herself. I lit the gas and spooned tea into the pot. Belinda came to stand in the kitchen doorway. "I don't suppose you'd like to move back into my box room, would you? I am hopelessly undomestic."

"Sorry, but I've got better digs at the moment," I said. "I'm living at Kensington Palace."

"What on earth for? Have you been given a grace and favor apartment because of your royal connections?"

"No. I've been asked to look after Princess Marina until her marriage and she's staying there."

"To Prince George? Poor girl. Does she know what she's in for?"

"Not exactly. I did say he had been a bit of a playboy."

"That is a classic understatement," she said.

"Maybe he'll reform. He seems to be fond enough of her."

Belinda took the cup of tea I had just poured for her. "I doubt he'll change. Maybe long enough to produce the heir and the spare. But then in most royal marriages it's back to the little wife turning a blind eye to the husband's wandering, isn't it?"

"It does seem to be. Although the Duke and Duchess of York seem happy with each other."

"Well, he's never been exactly the playboy type, has he?" Belinda took a tentative sip of tea. "I needed that," she said. "Georgie, you're a godsend. But what exactly are you doing here this early?"

"Two things," I said. "I discovered to my chagrin last night that Queenie had left my blue evening gown hanging in your wardrobe. I had to wear the bottle green velvet to dinner at Buckingham Palace."

"Not the one that Queenie ironed the wrong way?" Belinda looked horrified. "Darling, how utterly awful. Didn't you die of embarrassment?"

"I think I managed to drape my mother's fox fur stole effectively. At least I hope I did."

"Darling, has it ever occurred to you that you'd be better off without a maid?"

"Many times. But unfortunately if I go and stay at Kensington Palace it is expected that I bring my maid with me."

Belinda looked up from her tea with horror. "You are letting Queenie loose in a palace? With royal persons?"

"Not exactly," I said. "I've told her she is not to leave my quarters and I'm having meals sent up to her on a tray."

Belinda shook her head. "You're living with a ticking time bomb. Do go up to my room and retrieve your gown.

I saw it hanging there last night and wondered when I had ever bought that shade of blue. It's just not me."

I went up and retrieved it. When I came down Belinda was examining herself in the mirror.

"God, I look a sight, don't I?"

"Are you well, Belinda?" I asked. She did look a little hollow-eyed and I wondered if too many late nights were finally catching up with her.

"Me? Of course. Yes, I'm fine. I probably picked up a little chill on the ship. You wouldn't like to be an angel and make me some toast, would you?"

I laughed. "Belinda, surely you know how to make toast! You'd better find yourself a new maid before you starve."

"The problem is that I don't know whether I can afford to pay one. A proper maid, I mean. Not another Queenie, although God forbid that there are two of her in the world."

I went back into the kitchen and sliced bread to put under the grill. "The other reason I came to see you was that I need a favor," I called through to her. "I've been asked to take Princess Marina around London. She's frightfully chic and I realized I don't know any of the smart shops or evening spots. So can you give me some pointers? My experience of clothes shopping stops with Harrods and Barkers."

She looked up in horror. "Darling, you can't take a visiting princess to Barkers, especially not a chic one. Barkers is for elderly matrons of the county set. All right for tweeds to wear between hunts. But one doesn't take a visiting princess to a shop."

"One doesn't?"

"No. Of course not. You take her to a designer and let her view their collection. Much more civilized—gilt and brocade sofas, chandeliers, champagne and privacy. It's what I'd do all the time if I could afford it. And London has some wonderful designers' salons now. Schiaparelli has a salon here now, you know. And darling Molyneux." (She pronounced it Molynucks, as one does.) "And Norman Hartnell is an up-and-coming who is worth visiting. I know some of the other royals like him. A little too stuffy for me, but then, I design my own clothes."

"But what if Princess Marina wants to shop for undergarments?"

"Then you go to a designer who makes those things. Lucile still is the one, I suppose. Really, Georgie, you haven't a clue, have you?"

"I've never had the money to have a clue," I said. "When I came out we had our dressmaker copy from pictures of fashionable gowns. The result wasn't always successful. Golly, I should find out if Marina has the money to afford designers. I was told that her family was not at all well off, but she looks stunningly chic to me."

"Anyone who has lived in Paris knows how to look chic by nature. They take a little black dress, throw on a scarf and voila," Belinda said. "If ever I can open my own salon I'll show British matrons that they don't have to be dowdy."

"You just have to marry a rich husband, Belinda," I said.

"Just like that," she said, turning away. "One doesn't always get what one wants in life, does one?"

"No, I suppose not," I said, upset by the note of bitterness in her voice. "But why don't you come with us when I take the princess around London. You know all the chic places and where to buy cosmetics and get one's hair done. And then there are nightclubs. What if she wants to go out on the town at night? I've never even been to a nightclub. Where does one start?"

"Don't take her to the Embassy," Belinda said quickly. "She's likely to meet her future husband there, and God knows who he might be with."

"Not the Embassy," I repeated.

"Ciro's is safe, I suppose. Usually has a good cabaret. And then there's the Kit-Cat and El Morocco. Also safe. But it's not really done to go to a club without an escort. Only ladies of the night do that."

"I suppose her future husband might want to come with us," I said.

"I doubt it. He'd be bound to run into one of his past conquests who might say the wrong thing. He has been far too friendly with far too many people."

"Bobo Carrington, for example," I said, realizing I might have a mine of information in my friend. "You move in smart circles. What do you know about her?"

"Who doesn't know everything about Bobo?" Belinda laughed. "She's one of the most visible people in London. So now that I think about it, you might not want to take Princess Marina to any nightclub. The risk of running into Bobo is just too high and Bobo is not always discreet in what she says, especially after she has had a few cocktails and has injected herself with something stronger. She's quite likely to breeze up to Marina, introduce herself as George's mistress and offer her some cocaine."

"Do you think she was"—I corrected myself, not wanting to reveal the truth to Belinda just yet—"is still his mistress or has the relationship ended?"

"I don't know. I don't follow the ups and downs of Prince George's sex life." And she laughed.

"Have you seen Bobo with him recently?" I asked. "Is there anyone else she's involved with?"

Belinda looked up, amused. "Why this interest in Bobo?"

"Oh, simply because someone at Kensington hinted that she'd been involved with Prince George and suggested that we try to shield Princess Marina from gossip," I said hastily.

"Darling, Bobo has always been just one of many. There was Poppy Baring, the banking heiress. And let me see, who else? He's worked his way through the top layers of London society, both male and female."

"Bobo is in the top layer then, is she?"

"She likes to pretend she is. Between ourselves I think she started life more humbly and has learned to reinvent herself. She's a great opportunist, our dear Bobo, I'll tell you that much. Has a nose to sniff out anyone with money and then makes a beeline for them, turning on the full force of her charm." She paused, thinking, then added, "One hasn't seen her around as much as one used to. But then she's not as young as she used to be. And drug use does take its toll."

"So you haven't seen her with anyone else recently, then?" I asked.

"Of course I've been away, but I hadn't seen her for some time, until I bumped into her at Crockford's the other night. She was being frightfully gay and witty as usual. Almost as if she was trying too hard. But then she went into another room and I saw her talking to some American. I don't know who he was. I hadn't seen him before, but Bobo suddenly started acting differently around him. Awkward. Uneasy. Maybe she had him in her sights and was playing the 'innocent little miss and it's my first time at a gambling club and I need a big strong man to show me what to do' routine."

"As you often do," I reminded her.

She grinned. "It usually works wonders."

"Did she go off with the American?"

"I can't tell you. I think he left soon after. He didn't look as if he was enjoying himself. Not the usual Crockford's type. Didn't look comfortable in evening dress, if you know what I mean."

A strange look came over her face. "In fact the odd thing is I thought I saw her leaving with—" She broke off suddenly, then shook her head. "No, it couldn't have been."

"Who?"

"Nothing. It doesn't matter." She waved a hand expansively. "Take Princess Marina to the Café de Paris. That's grand enough and staid enough that none of George's or Bobo's cronies will be there."

"I'd better be getting back to the palace. I'm supposed to be at the princess's beck and call," I said. "Will you come with me when I have to take her around? It could be fun, shopping for a trousseau at all the salons."

"Maybe," she said. "I'm not sure if I'll have time."

"What do you mean? You've just come home. Of course you have time."

As I stood up to walk to the front door I turned back

suddenly. "And I have a brilliant idea—you could design her an outfit. If she wears it, it would really put you on the map."

I didn't get the response I expected. "I suppose I could," she said hesitantly.

I'd expected her to jump up, hugging me and yelling, "Darling, you're a genius."

"Come on, Belinda," I said. "This could be your big chance. If Princess Marina wears your clothing, everyone will want it."

She nodded. "You're right. I wonder if I have time to pull it off."

"Time to pull it off? What else are you doing right now? Buck up and get on with it!"

"Right." She gave me a resolute smile. "I will. She's tall, isn't she? About my height?"

"Wait until you meet her and then you'll get an idea of what she likes to wear. I'll keep you posted on what she wants to do," I said. A sudden dreadful thought struck me. "Crikey, Belinda. What if she says she wants to mingle with London society and I can't take her to nightclubs?"

"Lunch at the Savoy Grill, darling. That's a good start. You'll see everyone you know if you sit there for half an hour. And bring her to the new Noel Coward play—oh, I know, all those rumors about Noel and the prince, but who could resist Noel's charm, and you know him quite well, don't you? Feather in your cap."

"He did stay with my mother last Christmas, so I know him a little," I said.

"There you are. You introduce her to the great man. She's impressed. Noel will invite you both for cocktails and you'll meet everyone who matters. Situation solved."

"Belinda, you're brilliant," I said. "Now let's hope the palace has allotted sufficient funds for all this. Designers and the Savoy aren't exactly cheap."

"They surely don't expect you to pay to host her?"

"They did when that princess came from Bavaria, remember?" I said. "The queen has no clue about money, or that some of us don't have any. But this time Major Beauchamp-Chough is in charge at Kensington and I suspect he's the keeper of the purse."

"Major Beauchamp-Chough," she said. "That name rings a bell."

"Life Guards. Recently Prince George's private secretary. Frightfully stiff upper lip. But quite good-looking."

"Married?" she asked.

"I've no idea. There is no Mrs. Major at Kensington and he hasn't mentioned one, but that doesn't mean she's not happily at home in Shropshire with the children."

"I don't think a military man is my type," Belinda said. "Even if he is good-looking. Too bossy and correct. And I couldn't exist on a major's pay."

"I'll let you know when shopping sprees are planned," I said. "This could be a lot of fun."

"You're right," she said. "A lot of fun."

Chapter 13

When I arrived back at Kensington Palace, my cheeks burning from the strong north wind that swept across Kensington Gardens, I found that Princess Marina had finished breakfast and was sitting in the morning room, reading the newspapers. Countess Irmtraut sat at the desk in the window, writing a letter.

"So many pictures of me," Marina said, holding up a paper with a look of incredulous delight on her face. "Even in the *Daily Mirror*, which I gather is rather socialist in leanings. I had no idea my arrival would be such big news."

"The world has been rather short of good news for some time," I said. "A royal wedding is something everyone can look forward to." I poured myself a cup of coffee from the carafe on the tray and sat down beside her.

"It's rather nice being the bringer of good news to people, isn't it? Makes one feel useful. I'm looking forward to taking on royal duties with George as soon as we marry. The queen said how glad she was that we could relieve them of some of the burden. The poor king looks so fragile now, doesn't he, and Queen Mary doesn't like to leave him."

I sighed, because I too had noticed how old and drawn he looked. "He never really recovered from that bout of pneumonia he had," I said. "And I think worry about his oldest son is also contributing."

"But I've met David," she said. "He seems delightful. Why should his father worry?"

"Because he refuses to marry someone suitable, like you. And an awful American woman has him in her clutches."

"I did hear a rumor to that effect," Marina said, glancing across at Irmtraut, who had looked up. "Isn't she still married to someone else?"

"I believe so, but she wants to divorce him. And she's been divorced before too."

"Quite unsuitable," Irmtraut sniffed. "Why was this man not brought up to put duty first? We all were."

"So was I," I said. "And so was the Prince of Wales, I'm quite sure. He just prefers to put himself first."

"You've been out for a walk," Marina said.

"Yes. I went to visit a friend of mine who knows all about fashion," I said. "I asked her which designers she would recommend for you to visit. She suggested Norman Hartnell and Molyneux. Schiaparelli has a salon here now too."

"Molyneux is designing my wedding gown," she said, her face lighting up.

I must have shown surprise, having been told how poor her family was since they were ousted from Greece.

"I met him when he was in Paris. He said he'd be honored to design the gown for a royal wedding," she said. "He's sent me sketches, but I haven't tried anything on yet. But he's wonderful, isn't he?"

I didn't answer, having no idea what his designs looked like. So she went on. "I have to arrange for my fittings with him. But what I really wanted to do was to go to ordinary shops. I've heard about Harrods and Selfridges. I think shopping there would be such fun. I have most of the important items for my trousseau. It's just the little things I still need.

Cosmetics and undergarments and a sinful negligee, maybe?"

There was an intake of breath from Countess Irmtraut. Marina turned to her. "Traudi, don't be so stuffy. I will be a married woman, after all."

"I can certainly take you to look for those sorts of things," I said.

"And a theater, maybe? I want to make the most of being an invisible person."

"After all those pictures in the newspapers, I rather suspect you'll be recognized," I said. "But I'm happy to take you to Harrods. And even Selfridges, although my friend would say it's a shop for housewives up from the country and typists."

"Then I'll pretend to be a housewife up from the country," she said. "Mrs. Smith."

We laughed.

"My friend suggests we start by lunching at the Savoy Grill," I said. "It's the sort of place one goes to see and be seen."

"All right. I'll go up and change into something a little smarter then," she said. She put down the newspaper and left the room. I was about to follow when I remembered Irmtraut. Oh crikey. She'd have to come too, wouldn't she?

"Of course you are invited as well, Countess. A good luncheon to make up for the toad in the hole?"

"Thank you," she said. "There is no point in my changing clothes. I do not own items of fashion."

I left her sitting at the writing desk scribbling away furiously. I suspect she was telling her mother or sister how badly she was being treated in England. Before I went up to change I went to look for the major. I found him coming around the side of the building, striding out in true military fashion.

"Oh, Major," I said, "I was coming to see you."

"How are you bearing up?" he asked. "You've had a nasty shock, Lady Georgiana. Are you sure you shouldn't stay in bed today to recover? Most girls would have swooned at the sight of a dead body."

"I'm made of sterner stuff, Major," I said. "I come from a long line of Rannoch chieftains who went on fighting as their limbs were hacked off."

He laughed. "Good sense of humor too. I think the queen chose well. So what can I do for you now?"

I chewed on my lip. "It's the delicate question of money. I'm supposed to take Princess Marina out and around and nobody mentioned how the financial side would be handled. I mean, am I supposed to—"

"Oh good Lord no. Simple enough," he cut in. "You tell me where you'd like to go. I'll telephone ahead and let them know who is coming and ask that the bill be sent to Kensington Palace. Just in case there is any difficulty I'll give you a letter to show them. But I don't anticipate any problems."

"Oh, that sounds splendid." I sighed. "So it would be all right to take the princess to lunch at the Savoy Grill, wouldn't it? A friend suggested that would be a suitable place to see and be seen."

"Admirable choice. Of course." He nodded approval. "Now off you go and show the princess the best of what London has to offer."

I returned to the apartment with a grin on my face. Carte blanche to go out and have a good time when someone else was footing the bill. What could be nicer? For a moment the dead girl in the courtyard and my commission to question people at the palace had faded into the background. I went up and changed into the cashmere cardigan and soft jersey skirt that had become my acceptable winter outfit. I had been given both by my mother last Christmas. It was too bad that she was a petite five foot three while I was a healthy five six, as she had oodles of lovely clothes I could have inherited when she discarded them. But I looked presentable enough as I examined myself in the mirror.

"I'm going to take the princess out for lunch," I said to Queenie. "Don't forget to stay put. Remember the ghosts."

"Yes, miss," she said. "Don't worry. I ain't leaving this room. Not for love nor money. Ruddy ghosts!"

A taxicab was summoned to take Marina, Irmtraut and

me to the Savoy. The outing was a huge success. We happened to pass the horse guards out training in the Mall, the plumes on their helmets and their horses' manes floating out behind them in the breeze. This produced an "ah" even from Irmtraut.

They thought Trafalgar Square was charming and expressed an interest in going to the National Gallery and then we pulled out under the brightly lit canopy of the Savoy. Major Beauchamp-Chough had clearly done what he promised and telephoned ahead because we were welcomed with great reverence and whisked to the best table. I hadn't had enough luncheons at smart establishments to know what to recommend but Marina confidently ordered lobster bisque, pâté de foie gras and veal dijonnaise. Irmtraut and I followed suit. Marina also chose a light French wine to accompany the food.

"I don't think I want a cocktail to start with," she said. "Too much alcohol at midday and I'm useless for the afternoon. And I think we should visit Molyneux just to set up times for my fittings and see how he's getting along with the dress."

The wine was brought and approved. I noticed many heads turned in our direction. It's funny the rush of pleasure that this brought. Marina didn't seem to notice, but I think she was just more poised than I. The first course arrived. Deliciously light and creamy. The foie gras was superb. We were in the middle of the veal when a voice said, "What-ho, Georgie, old bean. Long time no see."

And there in front of me was the chubby form of Gussie Gormsley, son of a newspaper magnate. He was the closest thing to a playboy with whom I had ever been involved and I remembered that I had encountered Prince George at one of his naughty parties with a Negro jazz band playing and cocaine being snorted in the kitchen. As he approached I also remembered he had tried to seduce me once. Obviously he had forgotten the circumstances in which we parted because he was beaming. "Hello, Gussie," I said. "Let me introduce my table companions. Your Royal Highness, may I present Augustus Gormsley."

Gussie obviously recognized her and went rather pale. "Frightfully sorry to barge in on you, Your Royal Highness," he said. "Damned bad form."

"Not at all. I'm pleased to meet Georgiana's friends and the London smart set."

Before Gussie could inform Marina that I was certainly not part of any London smart set, I said, "Augustus's father owns newspapers and magazines and Gussie is very much a young man about town."

"Not for much longer, old thing." Gussie made a face. "Haven't you heard? I'm getting married. Finally getting hitched. What a blow to the womanhood of the nation, eh?"

"Congratulations, Gussie," I said. "Who are you marrying?"

"You know her. Primrose Asquey d'Asquey. She was at school with you."

"But I went to her wedding a couple of years ago," I said. "Didn't she marry Roland Aston-Poley?"

"Only lasted a few months," he said. "Marriage was doomed from the start, wasn't it? I mean, Asquey d'Asquey becoming Roley Poley? Hopeless. And of course he had a severe gambling problem, didn't he? And drank like a fish and got very maudlin when in his cups."

"Please give my very best to Primrose," I said. "I hope you'll both be very happy."

"And may I extend my best wishes for your happiness, Your Highness," Gussie said. "I'm a pal of your future husband. Jolly nice chap, old George. Ripping fun."

Marina smiled politely.

"What does the prince like to rip?" Irmtraut asked. "He has fun ripping paper or fabric?"

Gussie stared as if he had just noticed her.

"No, it's just a word. Just like 'smashing' doesn't mean actually smashing anything."

"This English language is very peculiar," Irmtraut said.

"Oh, you'll get the hang of it," Gussie said.

"Hang?"

Oh golly. This could go on for hours. I realized I hadn't

introduced them either. Irmtraut would not like that. "Gussie, this is Countess Irmtraut von Dinkelfingen-Hackensack," I said. "A cousin of the princess."

"How do you do?" Irmtraut nodded in regal fashion.

"Absolutely tickety-boo, thanks," Gussie said.

"Gussie, our meal is getting cold," I said, before I had to explain to Irmtraut what "tickety-boo" might mean.

"Right-o, old bean. Where are you staying? I'm having a little party and I'd love you to bring Her Highness. Show her what London has to offer, what?"

"How kind," Marina said, before I could answer. I wasn't at all sure that one of Gussie's parties would be the sort of place one should take a princess, especially since her future husband would have had flings with most of the other participants.

"Tomorrow night. My place. You know where it is, don't you, Georgie?"

"The flat on Green Park. Yes, of course." I gave him what I hoped was a warning look, meaning no drugs, no hints about Prince George's past life.

"Jolly good show. About nine-ish, then?"

And off he went.

"You have charming friends, Georgiana," Marina said. "I am so happy to attend a London party. My life has been quite boring recently. This can be my final fling, yes?"

"Fling? What do you wish to throw?" Irmtraut asked.

Chapter 14

After luncheon we visited the House of Molyneux, met Edward Molyneux himself, who was utterly charming, and saw the princess's absolutely lovely gown. I found myself daydreaming wistfully about having such a gown made for me one day. About getting married someday to a certain tall, dark and handsome man. Fittings were arranged for the princess and we came home with her looking forward to her English tea. As I came through the door one of the maids took me aside. "Don't take off your coat and hat yet, Lady Georgiana. There is a motorcar waiting for you outside."

"A car? Whose car?"

"I'm not sure, my lady, but the man just said that your presence was wanted urgently."

"I see." I looked around but Marina had already gone upstairs. "Please inform the princess that I have been called away unexpectedly and will join her as soon as I can."

Then I went out again. Sure enough a dark sedan was parked under the trees. As I approached, a man jumped out of the front seat and opened the back door for me.

"Lady Georgiana?"

"Yes, what is this?"

"I believe that my superior would like a word with you, but somewhere private, away from this place. If you'd be good enough to get in, please."

The thought crossed my mind that I'd look silly if I were actually being kidnapped by some kind of criminal organization or foreign power. Then I decided I wasn't important enough for anyone to want to kidnap me.

"Where are we going?" I asked.

This time he pulled out a warrant card. "I'm DC Coombs. You're wanted at Scotland Yard."

We set off, then turned from Victoria Street into Whitehall and the familiar red and white brick of Scotland Yard appeared in front of us. I think I gave a little sigh of relief that it really was our destination. We passed under the archway and into the courtyard. My driver got out, opened the door for me. "Follow me, please," he said.

I was taken up in a lift, whisked along corridors and finally halted outside a door. My guide tapped and was answered with a deep "Come in."

I stepped into a bright office with a view toward the Thames. I had rather hoped I was going to meet Sir Jeremy, but it was DCI Pelham who sat at a large dark oak desk.

"Good of you to come, Lady Georgiana," he said.

"Did I have a choice?" I smiled. He didn't. Instead he said, "Please take a seat."

I did so. He was seated in a leather armchair; I was offered a wooden upright. He leaned forward toward me, resting his elbows on the desk so he was staring straight at me. "We've been waiting to give you the results of the autopsy, but before I do, I must impress upon you again that what I tell you must go no farther than these four walls. I have your word on that?"

"Oh absolutely," I said.

"Right. The doctor has finished the preliminary tests on Miss Carrington, and I'm afraid you were right. It was murder."

"So not a drug overdose?"

"No trace of cocaine or heroin in her body."

"I see. So how was she killed?"

"Suffocated," he said. "The doctor found both alcohol and Veronal, which you probably know is a strong sedative, a barbiturate, in her system. A significant amount of both, but he reckons not enough to kill her."

"But enough to put her to sleep? To knock her out? And then someone finished her off?"

"It looks that way, yes."

"Could she not have vomited and aspirated into her lungs, thus suffocating herself?" I asked.

He looked surprised. "Now how does a young lady like you know about such things?"

"I've had a couple of brushes with murder before," I said. "I can assure you I'm not squeamish."

"Obviously not. And in answer to your question, no. She was suffocated manually. There were signs of bruising around her nose and mouth where someone clearly clamped a hand to stop her from breathing."

"How horrid," I said. "And your men turned up no clues in the courtyard to indicate who that person might have been?"

He shook his head.

"I wonder what she was doing at Kensington Palace," I said. "She must have known she wouldn't find Prince George there."

"But expected to find Princess Marina?" He raised an eyebrow. "I suspect it's more likely that she was killed elsewhere, maybe in a motorcar, and her body was left at Kensington Palace to try to place the blame on the Duke of Kent."

"Who would do such a disgusting thing?"

He smiled. "You've led a sheltered life, my lady. If a man can kill, then besmirching a good name means nothing to him. Especially if he is desperate. It might even be the work of communists or fascists using this as a means to bring down the British monarchy."

"You said 'he.' We are assuming the killer was a man, are we?" I said and noticed his eyebrows rise. He had big bushy brows and the effect was startling. "If Miss Carrington had been knocked out then it wouldn't have taken much strength to suffocate her."

"Yes, I suppose we have to consider that a woman could have been capable of killing her, but it would take a strong woman to haul her out of a motorcar and deposit her under the arch."

There was a silence punctuated only by the ticking of the clock on the wall and the cooing of a pigeon outside the window. Then he cleared his throat. "There is something else that you should know. The doctor states that the young woman had recently been pregnant."

I stared at him, trying to digest this. "She'd had a baby? When?"

"Within the last three months, the doctor thinks."

I remembered Belinda saying that she hadn't seen Bobo at the nightclubs. That would explain it. I swallowed back the desire to say "Golly."

"Do you know what happened to the child?" I asked. "Was it a live birth, or did she perhaps have an abortion?" It was hard to bring myself to say the word to a strange man.

"The doctor says it was a full-term baby. And no, we have no idea where the child is now."

"Not at Miss Carrington's flat in any case?" I said. "I take it you have searched her flat?"

"We've made a preliminary search, but no sign of a child there." He paused, then took a deep breath. "You can see our dilemma, can't you, Lady Georgiana?" CDI Pelham said.

I nodded. "It would depend on whether the Duke of Kent was the father of the child."

"Precisely. We need to know whether he was involved with the young woman within the last year, and whether she had told him about the child."

He leaned even closer to me. "Normally in a case like this I'd have a team of men already questioning everyone in Kensington Palace, in Miss Carrington's block of flats, everyone in her address book. But I've been given orders from the top brass to lay off. Frankly I think their feeling is that they don't care why this girl was murdered or who did it as long as nothing appears in the press. I didn't become a policeman to sweep dirty crimes under the rug, Lady Georgiana. Whoever this woman was, whatever her lifestyle, she deserves justice. But any move I make has to be sanctioned by Sir Jeremy. I am not allowed to question the prince, nor anyone at Kensington Palace. Sir Jeremy is adamant that Princess Marina hears nothing about this."

"I can understand that," I said. "She might call off the wedding and cause great embarrassment to the royal family."

"Precisely. That's where I hope you might come in." He sat up straight again and toyed with the fountain pen in his right hand. "You're one of them, Lady Georgiana, and Sir Jeremy thinks highly of your abilities. You could ask questions. Not directly interrogate, of course, but in a subtle way. You could find out if anyone at the palace saw or heard anything."

"I already started to do that this morning," I said. "And I could certainly question the servants."

"And the elderly princesses?" he said. "They are your aunts, aren't they?"

"Great-aunts. Yes, I could ask them too, but it wouldn't be easy if I was not to mention that somebody died outside their door. They'd certainly be curious why I wanted to know whether anyone had heard or seen anything strange outside their windows."

"Maybe we could invent some sort of crime or incident that did not involve them in any way." He frowned. "Something that didn't make anybody put two and two together and come up with four."

"What sort of crime would not involve any of us and not raise suspicions?" I asked.

"A robbery, maybe? We found a thief trying to hide out in the courtyard?"

"Possible," I said. "What if one of the servants actually spotted the body but has said nothing so far?"

"Or vagrants," he said. "There are quite a few homeless men sleeping rough in the London parks these days, aren't there? A falling-out among vagrants? A vagrant taking shelter at the palace on a stormy night, who died of natural causes?"

"I don't think anyone would mistake the body of a silk-clad young woman for a vagrant," I said.

"That's presupposing anyone saw her body. Ghosts," he said, suddenly animated and wagging a finger at me. "You said the whole place is haunted. How about asking everyone if they saw the ghost of a white lady going through the courtyard?"

"That's a better sort of idea," I said. "Servants are very susceptible to the palace ghosts, particularly those who don't normally work there. If one of them saw her at least we'll know what sort of time she came there and whether she actually went into the courtyard and for what reason."

"Good," he said. "So I'll leave that to you then."

"Very well." I nodded, my brain still racing as I tried to process everything he'd told me. "But surely one of the first things to do is to find out where she gave birth and if she named the father on the birth certificate," I said.

"Yes, we'll certainly try to do that. It wouldn't have been a public hospital, obviously. She couldn't risk being recognized even if she checked in under a phony name. One of those fancy private clinics where ladies go for vague and undetermined female illnesses, nervous cures and no questions asked."

"It could have been abroad," I said. "I hear some women go to France or Switzerland for such things."

"It's not going to be easy, that's for sure," he said.

"What about her maid?" I asked as the thought occurred to me. "What does she have to say? She must know where her mistress went. She may have been sworn to secrecy but she can be frightened into telling the police."

He gave a long and heavy sigh, stroking at his fawn-colored mustache. "The young lady was apparently one of the modern set who has no maid. There is a woman who comes in to clean but I'm sure she'll know nothing."

"And her family? Do we know anything about them? Did she go home to give birth, maybe?"

"There doesn't seem to be a family. Of course, Carrington might not be her real name." He looked glum. "But she had friends. She was always photographed in the middle of a group of people. She attended parties and nightclubs with her chums. She would have told at least one of them the truth. Women always find someone to confide in, in my experience. She might well have told the father." He paused, sucking air in through his teeth. "Again, it's going to be tricky questioning people who knew her and finding out what they knew without giving away that she's dead."

I nodded agreement.

"We certainly have a good motive for murder," he went on. "Whoever the father was might have a lot to lose if the news was made public."

"Gosh, you're not suggesting that Prince George might have been involved in her murder?" I stammered out the words, because it was impossible to think of my likeable cousin as a murderer.

"He's a royal, isn't he? They get someone else to do their dirty work."

My thoughts went instantly to Major Beauchamp-Chough. The prince's private secretary. A military man. A trained killer. Would he have been willing to do what it took to make sure the prince was not involved in scandal and the wedding took place? And yet he had been away all evening, at a regimental dinner, arriving home around the same time as us. And surely plenty of fellow officers could verify his attendance. And he had seemed genuinely shocked to discover the body, and recognize who it was.

"Someone will have to tell Prince George," I said. "But please don't look at me. That's something I absolutely shouldn't undertake. And couldn't."

"I agree. If Sir Jeremy wants to play puppet master and pull the strings, I'll suggest he is the one to face the prince."

"Of course, he could have a word with Major Beauchamp-Chough first," I said. "He's the prince's private secretary, after all. He'd probably know many of the prince's dark secrets. He'd certainly have known if Bobo Carrington had told the prince she was expecting his child."

"The major was with us this morning. Why did he not mention any of this if he was privy to the prince's secrets? He seems like an upright sort of bloke. Straight as a die. He wouldn't have approved of such goings-on."

"Perhaps he was hoping it would never come out. Perhaps he thought Miss Carrington's death was a suicide, an overdose of drugs." I looked up. "That is our biggest weapon in guarding the palace, you know. That she was a drug addict. People who take drugs have to obtain them from somewhere. This murder could have nothing at all to do with her liaison with the prince, or with her illegitimate child. She might have fallen foul of a drug kingpin and they are known to mete out their brand of justice swiftly and ruthlessly, aren't they?"

"That's definitely another angle we'll follow up on," he said. "I have my contacts in the underworld. But I'd still like to start off with her closest friends. They would know if she was scared, worried, and also what she did with the baby."

Another horrid thought crossed my mind. "I suppose you should also check whether any newborn babies have been found abandoned or dead in the last three months," I said. "She may have gone away to have it and then not been able to face the future and killed it. Dumped it in a river. In which case one might even have thought that she took her own life in remorse. You're sure about the bruises on her face? They couldn't have been formed by falling onto the cobbles?"

"Interesting thought, Lady Georgiana. But the medico was pretty sure. He said you could see where a thumb had pinched her nose shut. And her eyes showed indications of hemorrhage brought on by suffocation."

"I see." I shuddered, wondering if she was already unconscious at the time or whether she had struggled, fought to live.

"You're one of the bright young things, aren't you?" he said suddenly. "So maybe you'd know how we get in touch with her chums. There's a young man in particular we know visits her flat from time to time. Don't know if he's a romantic interest or not, but he should certainly be able to tell us where she went to have the baby. He may even know who the dad might have been. Come to think of it, he may well have been the dad himself."

"Oh, I'm afraid I don't move in Bobo's circles," I said. "I'm not often in London."

"He was a fellow aristocrat," the DCI said. "I'm sure your type bump into each other at hunt balls and things. The name is Darcy O'Mara. The Honorable Darcy O'Mara."

Chapter 15

The world stood still. I felt as if I had been punched in the gut. I couldn't breathe. Inside my head words were screaming, "No, you've got it wrong. Darcy would never have been involved with a woman like that. Darcy would never . . ." But I had been raised to be part of a family that takes everything in its stride. A lady never displays emotion. If a native suddenly hurls a spear at a royal person and it misses, a slight nod of the head and royal smile are all that are permitted. That training kicked in now.

"I'm afraid I have no idea where you might find the Honorable Darcy O'Mara," I said. "He is often out of the country. In fact you might ask Sir Jeremy. I believe Mr. O'Mara works for him, or in conjunction with him from time to time."

"But you do know the young man?" he asked.

I wondered if it was a trap, that maybe he had known all along that I was close to Darcy. Maybe he already had him in custody.

"Yes, I know him." I tried to sound frightfully breezy and offhand.

"Quite chummy with him, are you?"

This use of the words "chum" and "chummy" would have been irritating to me even if my nerves hadn't been torn to shreds. "I haven't seen him for several months, Detective Chief Inspector," I said. "I hope that answers your question."

"Not even a postcard from him?" He made a face that I wanted to slap. "Sir Jeremy seemed to think you were quite good pals."

"Which we are. I have lots of good pals, but our class of person tends to travel a lot. Especially Mr. O'Mara."

"So where did you see him last?"

"When I last saw him he was heading for the train station in Los Angeles. That was in August. Now, is there anything else I might be able to help you with?"

I was feeling really proud of myself. I went on, "So what makes you think that he has been staying at Miss Carrington's flat recently?"

A smirk crossed his broad face. "I think a dressing gown behind the bedroom door with his initials on the pocket and his name on the laundry tag might do it. Oh, and it was behind *her* bedroom door. Not the spare room."

He was enjoying this, I could see. Perhaps Sir Jeremy had told him that I had been sweet on Darcy. Perhaps he had a chip on his shoulder against aristocrats. Perhaps he just liked the feel of ruining other people's lives. But I was not going to let him see my distress. I fought with every ounce of my being to keep my face a mask with a half-interested smile on my lips. I took a very deep breath before I spoke again. "Do you consider this gentleman a possible suspect in the case?"

"Only if he's still in London and not in some far-flung part of the world. I would still need to rule him out as the father of the child. And as a potential suspect, for that matter."

I couldn't wait to escape. "Are there any other friends of mine you might want to check on?" I said. "As I told you before, I don't spend much time in London and don't have a large acquaintanceship here. If there's nothing more, I should get back to Princess Marina. I'm charged with taking care of her, you know." I stood up.

"We'll be in touch, then," he said. "And should Mr. O'Mara decide to contact you, please make sure he comes to have a little chat with me."

I nodded, graciously, as my relative the queen would have done. And I tried to walk to the door without falling or staggering or knocking something over. As I reached for the doorknob I remembered something. "There is one thing." I turned back and saw his eyes register instant interest. "Another friend of mine was at Crockford's recently and she saw Bobo talking to a strange American. She said that Bobo appeared nervous and uneasy. She didn't know who the man was, but you can check the Crockford's registry to see which men were there on the same evening as Bobo Carrington."

I felt I had scored a small point as I made my exit, but I was only halfway to the lift when the enormity of the truth hit me. Belinda had said that someone else had been at Crockford's with Bobo and she had left with him. She had been going to tell me and then rapidly changed the subject. She had been going to say that she had seen Darcy leaving Crockford's with Bobo that night.

His dressing gown was hanging behind her bedroom door. It was almost a physical pain to think the words. What more proof did I want? I knew that Darcy had been no saint when I met him. I knew that young men of my social class were often wildly promiscuous, but he had said that he loved me. He wanted to marry me. My hand went to the silver Devonshire pixie I wore around my neck. Darcy had given it to me last Christmas, when he had proposed to me. Was I stupidly naïve to think that he'd be living a chaste life now? Men were different, weren't they? They had needs, apparently. But Bobo Carrington? The girl with the silver syringe? And not just a one-night stand either, but leaving his dressing gown behind her bedroom door.

I squeezed my eyes tightly shut so that tears would not come.

As the car drove me back to the palace I tried to push

Darcy from my mind and focus instead on who might have killed Bobo Carrington. This was not easy as I knew nothing of her friends or her wicked lifestyle. It did occur to me that going to Gussie Gormsley's party tomorrow night might be a worthwhile thing to do as he did move among the bright young things. I'd seen people snorting cocaine at one of his parties, and Noel Coward had been there, and . . . Oh. I paused, reconsidering. And Prince George also. So maybe it was a dangerous place to take Princess Marina. But if George himself showed up, he'd have to behave with his future wife there, and someone in that set might well have been friendly with Bobo Carrington.

I toyed with Prince George as a suspect. He had always come across as an easygoing sort of chap. Everyone liked him. He had an infectious smile. But if his former mistress had come to him right before the wedding and told him she would go to the newspapers and tell them about their affair and the baby, might he have been driven to silence her at all costs? That was clearly what Sir Jeremy and Major Beauchamp-Chough were fearing. But Prince George had a perfect alibi. He had been at dinner with his family last night. He had still been there when Marina and I left to go back to Kensington. In fact he had offered to drive us until we told him we had a car waiting.

Cars. Something to do with cars. Then I remembered. George had arrived late, breathless and straightening his bow tie. And had apologized to his parents that he was late because his car had had a crash. Golly, I thought. Could he have arranged to meet Bobo at Kensington Palace, drugged her and then killed her earlier in the evening? And then thought he was perfectly safe because he was having dinner with the family at Buckingham Palace—surely a cast-iron alibi?

I felt quite sick. I'd had enough shocks for one day. I didn't want to believe that Prince George could kill anyone, but then I hadn't wanted to believe that Darcy, my Darcy, had been intimate with Bobo Carrington. An image flashed through my mind of them together, in each other's arms in that bedroom, while I was in Belinda's flat, not far away, and he hadn't even bothered to come looking for me.

They are all so right, I thought. Belinda said I'm hopelessly naïve and I am. I'd convinced myself that Darcy was different from the rest. I gave a long sigh. At least I'd found out before I married him. But I didn't find that thought comforting.

I ARRIVED BACK at the palace to find the princess and countess enjoying afternoon tea.

"Lovely crumpets, Georgiana," the princess called as she spotted me. "Take off your coat and come and join us."

"This English crumpet I like," Countess Irmtraut said. She was in the process of eating one with about an inch of strawberry jam piled on top while butter dripped onto the plate. "I tell the servant I want some crumpet. Lots of crumpet. Yes, I am looking for crumpet. And she start to laugh. Why is this? Anther strange English joke?"

"Perhaps she was nervous, trying to understand your English, Irmtraut," the princess said sweetly. I wondered if she understood the double meaning. We English used the term to refer to a person of sexual interest. Perhaps not. I studied Irmtraut as she ate. She wasn't really that much older than Marina and I, I realized. And yet she might well have had the word "spinster" tattooed across her brow. And a sudden wave of fear shot through me. Was this destined to be my future? Would I be better off agreeing to marry some minor half-lunatic European princeling that the family found for me? I shut my eyes, not wanting to think about the future.

Duty. My duty was now to look after Princess Marina.

"Would you like to go out this evening, Your Royal Highness?" I asked. "I could have Major B-C see if he can get us tickets for a play."

"That would be lovely. But please, do call me Marina. We are, after all, to be related." She turned on the full force of that radiant smile and I found myself thinking about her future as Duchess of Kent. Would she have to learn to turn a blind eye to her husband's infidelities? Would he break her heart the way Darcy had broken mine?

"I'll go and ask the major right away," I said and left them to their tea. I wasn't in the mood to eat anyway.

I went around to the front of the building, negotiated the crowd of tourists and found the major's front door open and the major inside, brandishing a feather duster. "Doing a spot of housekeeping," he said, looking embarrassed. "I'm afraid the servants they employ here are not up to my army standards. I really miss my regimental batman. I like to see everything sparkling—not a spot of dust."

Sparkling. The word flashed through my brain. Something significant. Something I had seen.

"So how did the lunch at the Savoy go?" he went on and the thought vanished like a bubble on a sunny day.

"Very well, thank you," I said. "We met a friend of mine there and are invited to a party he's hosting tomorrow night."

"A party suitable for a princess?" He gave me a questioning look.

"I hope so. Gussie Gormsley. Do you know him? Oodles of money."

"I know the name. I don't move in those circles personally. Not my cup of tea. But the prince does, as you know."

"Gussie knows the prince," I said. "And he has some questionable friends, but I'm sure they'll behave if they know Princess Marina is to be a guest," I said. "And Gussie himself is also getting married soon. Settling down, you know."

"It happens to most people in the end," the major said.

"Tell me," I couldn't resist saying, "you are Prince George's private secretary. Do you think . . ." I couldn't go on. I had wanted to know whether he thought the prince might be capable of killing a former mistress, whether the prince might have told him Bobo was pregnant. But I couldn't. Perhaps Sir Jeremy would have asked him those things, but for me they constituted a betrayal of family. Instead I said, "Do you think he will settle down?"

"I rather think he will," Major B-C said. "He's a good chap

at heart, you know. And he's certainly sown his share of wild oats before the marriage." He flashed me a wicked grin.

I came away somewhat reassured. Either Prince George kept secrets from his equerry or the major really didn't think the prince was involved in Bobo's killing. But the question was still there: what was she doing at Kensington Palace?

I could think of several possible answers: The first was that she had been killed elsewhere by an unknown person. Probably not Prince George in that case. Surely he wouldn't have been stupid enough to leave a body where all evidence pointed to him. But perhaps he was not the child's father, and the man who was feared exposure. Or it could have been a drug lord to whom she owed too much money. Or even a thwarted suitor. I pushed that last thought quickly out of my mind. In any of these cases her killer had dumped her at the palace, hoping to pin the crime on the royal family. Knowing, maybe, that the family would do anything in their power to avoid a scandal at this moment and thus probably not have the crime investigated too fully.

Or secondly Bobo had come to see Princess Marina, either to demand money, to threaten or to warn. But Marina hadn't been there. How had Bobo discovered that? Had she knocked on the front door? Asked for the princess? Found that nobody was home . . . and then what? Someone had been following her? Or . . . Suddenly I realized something important. Somebody had been home. Countess Irmtraut, who would do anything in the world to protect the princess she loved.

Chapter 16

**I have had the very worst news in the world. I can't bear
to think about him. I won't think about him. I'll
push him right out of my mind and get on with the
task I've been charged with. I'm a Rannoch, damn
it. Duty comes first!**

Countess Irmtraut. I added her to my list of suspects. And
now that I thought about it, she seemed the most likely.
Perhaps she had opened the front door to find Bobo there.
Bobo had been drinking. We knew there was a goodly
amount of alcohol in her system. She told the countess things
she didn't want to hear, threatened to expose the prince, to
harm Marina. So Irmtraut had given her a drink laced with
Veronal. And when the drink didn't kill her, Irmtraut had
smothered her and dumped her body outside.

It seemed a little far-fetched but possible. Irmtraut was a
big, beefy woman. Certainly strong enough to overpower a
delicate, fine-boned specimen like Bobo, already rather

tipsy. The one problem was that there were servants at the palace. Even if Countess Irmtraut had opened the front door herself, a servant would have surely seen, surely heard Irmtraut talking to someone. Then I remembered what had happened when I arrived at Kensington. Nobody had answered the front door. Nobody had seen me cross the foyer. In fact the person who had first encountered me was none other than Irmtraut.

And she did have the temperament, I decided. She was emotional, jealous, high-strung. And she adored Marina. Now I'd have to find a way into tricking her to reveal a morsel of the truth. As I came back to apartment 1 I let myself in through the front door. No servant appeared and I was able to cross the full length of the foyer unseen. So it might have been possible that Bobo let herself in, or was admitted by the countess. But if she had been killed here, someone would have had to drag or carry her out to the archway beneath the clock tower. That would take strength, and such an undertaking would have had to leave a trace. I remembered Bobo's sparkly gown, the beads around her neck. Wouldn't sequins have come off, beads have snapped if she had been dragged along the cobbles?

I went back outside and retraced my steps along the side of the building and around to the archway. I didn't notice a single bead or sequin lying along the path. There was another difficulty with my theory: Bobo's white dress would have been covered in mud. And it wasn't. Which brought up another problem—what happened to her overcoat? It had been a beastly night earlier on. She wouldn't have walked across the park to Kensington Palace with no coat on. So where was it? Hanging in someone's wardrobe at the palace right now? Or in the boot of somebody's car, or already dumped into the Thames? I went back inside. I could hear Irmtraut and the princess still conversing in the sitting room.

Without hesitating I tiptoed up the stairs. Irmtraut's room was on the same floor as mine, but overlooking the front door, where our car had picked us up last night. Outside her door I hesitated. I didn't know whether she had brought a maid with her from whatever country she lived in. I hadn't seen one, but good servants are trained to be invisible, as I had told Queenie. And I suspected Irmtraut would insist on well-trained servants. I gave a tentative knock. No answer. I glanced down the hallway, then turned the handle. The room was unoccupied and I breathed a sigh of relief as I stepped inside and closed the door behind me.

I looked around. A meticulously neat room, as one might have suspected. A prayer book on the table beside the bed. A silver-backed hairbrush, small box of hairpins and powder compact on the dressing table. But no clothing draped over the backs of chairs. No shoes left beside the bed. On the table by the window was a pad and envelopes, a half-written letter and what looked like a scrapbook. I glanced at the letter. It was in what was probably Russian and I couldn't read that language, although I could make out the word "Mama." A letter to her mother, then. And the scrapbook contained newspaper cuttings pertaining to her cousin's wedding, some cut from that morning's papers.

On one wall was a huge carved oak wardrobe. I opened it, and my nose wrinkled at the smell of mothballs and stale scent. She had almost as few items of clothing as I did. Either she had not brought many garments with her or she was the proverbial poor relative, as I was. One couldn't help feeling sorry for her and I suspected that coming to England to be part of her cousin's wedding was a very important happening in a dull life.

I examined the items of clothing. All good quality but not of the latest fashion and showing signs of wear. At the back was a good-looking fur coat that caught my eye. I stroked the softness of the fur. Not mink. Not sable. Something more rugged. Beaver, maybe? Could it possibly be Bobo's missing overcoat? I felt for pockets and thrust my hand into one, finding nothing more than a handkerchief. The other contained a bus ticket in a foreign language and a couple of hairpins. I removed the coat from its hanger to see if there was a name inside. There was a manufacturer's label. It said *Silbermann, Berlin.*

A lot of effort for nothing. I didn't think Bobo would go to Berlin for her clothes. I was just hanging it up when to my horror I heard a noise. Footsteps coming down the hall. The door handle started to turn. For a second I froze, not knowing what to do. Then I plunged into the wardrobe and pulled the door to behind me, still clutching the heavy fur coat. I heard Irmtraut's heavy tread come into the room. I eased the wardrobe door open a fraction more so that I could see out. I just prayed she hadn't come upstairs to take a nap or to change for dinner. I watched her go over to the table and pick up the letter and envelope. She was heading back for the door again when she looked in my direction.

"Ach!" she said in an annoyed voice, strode over to the wardrobe and shut the door firmly. I heard a lock click into place as I was plunged into complete darkness.

"Now look what you've done, you idiot," I said to myself. The fur tickled my nose. The unpleasant smells added to my discomfort and I was terrified I'd do what I had done before and give away my presence by sneezing. I pressed my nostrils firmly shut and kept them clamped until I had to breathe. There was no sound in the room and I suspected Irmtraut had gone downstairs with her letter. But that was of little comfort. I was trapped in a wardrobe until Irmtraut came up to change for the theater. And then she'd find me and I'd have to come up with some kind of plausible excuse for hiding in her wardrobe. Another English joke, maybe? In England we always hide in wardrobes on a special saint's day and leap out to scare the occupants when they are changing for dinner. It might just work. She might just be gullible enough to believe it. But I didn't think I could bear to be trapped with the smell of mothballs and lily of the valley scent for that long. I felt along the surface of the door. There was a plate but no handle inside. I was indeed in a pickle. Then I remembered the hairpins in the coat pocket. I retrieved them and poked hopefully into the hole on the plate. I'd read about opening locks with hairpins but unfortunately I hadn't actually been given the specifics of how to do this. Had there been a key in the lock? Had she turned the key? Perhaps the door automatically locked itself, in which case I was definitely doomed. I started to go through other pockets, mostly empty. Really, what was this woman thinking? How could she exist with no makeup or coins or anything else useful? Then finally I found something—at first I thought it was a nail file, until I recoiled in pain and examined it more carefully. It was a little knife, rather sharp. What on earth was that doing in a jacket pocket?

I inserted the knife into the crack and kept jiggling until the latch gave and the door swung open. I took big gulps of air as I stepped out into the room, then I stood examining the knife in my hand. It was designed like a miniature sword, with an ornate handle. Very pretty, but also quite deadly. Did Irmtraut feel she needed such a hidden weapon for protection? Or something more sinister? But then Bobo had been drugged, then suffocated. The autopsy had not mentioned her having been stabbed with a stiletto-like blade. I went to return the knife to the pocket and realized I had no idea which pocket it had come from. An overcoat and two boiled wool jackets had pockets. I tried to remember the feel of the fabric as I searched pockets. Not rough. Probably boiled wool. But which of them? Irmtraut would know. If I put it back in the wrong one, she'd realize that someone had been through her things.

I strained my ears for the sound of approaching feet, afraid she'd come back and catch me with the knife in my hand. At least I'd have the weapon, I thought, and giggled nervously. I have been known to giggle in moments of extreme stress. I examined the two jackets and noticed something—the slight odor of wet sheep coming from one of them. The dark blue one. I picked it up and sniffed. This jacket had been out in the rain in the not too distant past. I put the knife back into what I hoped was the correct pocket and made my way hastily out of the room.

A stupid exercise for nothing, I told myself as I made my way along the corridor. Or was it? I knew that the blue jacket had been out in the rain. And Irmtraut had a knife in her pocket. Perhaps she had taken it with her, just in case, but had not needed to use it. I still wasn't ready to cross Countess Irmtraut from my suspect list.

I went back downstairs and found Irmtraut alone with the remains of the tea.

"Marina went up to change for the theater," she said. "It will be a dramatic play tonight? Your Mr. Shakespeare, perhaps?"

"Oh dear no," I said. "Quite the opposite. A musical comedy by Mr. Noel Coward."

"With many English jokes?"

"I'm afraid so." I smiled at her face. "At least it will be more cheerful for you than last night, eating your toad in the hole all alone," I said. "And with the major also gone, I presume you had no visitors all evening?"

"Nobody." She sniffed. "But I am used to being alone."

"So nobody even came to the front door?" I asked. "You didn't hear a knock, perhaps? Or see someone moving around outside?"

"Why should I hear this? It is not my place to answer doors. Did someone inform you that a visitor came to the front door?"

I nodded. "I was told that someone came to deliver a message to me," I said, saying the first thing that came to mind. "A friend who thought she would find me here. But she could make nobody hear and thought nobody was home."

Irmtraut sniffed. "I heard nothing. You should ask the servants. But they do not pay proper attention, I think. They remain shut away in their own quarters, enjoying themselves. They are very lazy, these English servants. I never got the pickled herring I sent for. This is always the way without a butler or proper housekeeper to watch over them."

"Your room is above the front door," I went on, trying desperately to think of what to ask her that might be revealing. "You didn't hear a car pull up all evening?"

"Only when you and the princess returned home. Until then nothing. It is very boring."

"I'm sorry. It must have been. But tonight will be better."

"With English jokes I do not understand," she said. "You will please tell me when I should laugh."

I left her then and went up to my own room. She had not seemed at all rattled by my questions and one would have expected such a person to become easily flustered. But perhaps Countess Irmtraut was made of sterner stuff.

Queenie was sitting on my bed, tentatively brushing the hem of my burgundy velvet dress.

"You got this in a right mess, didn't you?" she demanded, looking up as I came in. "Caked with bloody mud."

"Sorry. I had to walk in the rain when I went to have dinner with Princess Louise," I said, then wondered why I was apologizing to a maid. I'm sure none of my royal relatives would have done so.

"Well, it's ruddy hard work trying to brush off the mud without brushing off the nap and getting a right earful from you," she said. "And nobody even bothered to bring up me tea."

"Oh dear. Hold on a minute. I'll go down and find you some. The tea things are still out in our sitting room." I knew I was being too soft, but I couldn't help it.

As I came back into the sitting room Irmtraut was standing at the window, looking out. When she heard footsteps she let the curtain fall and spun to face me. Was I mistaken or was that a guilty look on her face?

I couldn't say that I'd come to fetch my maid some cake. She'd be horrified.

"I decided I did want a little sustenance after all," I said, putting a scone and a couple of pieces of shortbread on a plate. "Almost time to get dressed for the theater." And I breezed out again.

Queenie was duly grateful and wolfed down the food while I laid out what I wanted to wear with the burgundy dress to the theater. But my thoughts were racing. What to do next? Obviously someone should have a little heart-to-heart with Prince George to find out why he came in late to dinner last night. I didn't want to do that, but I could take a look at his car to see if it had really been in an accident. And maybe ask his servants what time he left St. James's.

Then I should interview the servants here. The lie I had made up on the spot for Irmtraut was a good one, I decided. Nothing to do with any sort of crime. A friend had heard I was staying at the palace and came to say hello. But she couldn't make anyone hear when she knocked on the front door. She wandered around a bit, looking for a way in, then gave up and went home. I'd ask indignantly if nobody heard or saw her.

My thoughts went back to Irmtraut and the damp jacket with the knife in the pocket. But the method of the murder was so different from a quick stab in the dark. If someone had fed Bobo a cocktail or two, and one of them was laced with Veronal, then it had to be someone she knew. A complete stranger couldn't force alcohol down her throat. So that probably ruled out the drug lord. Such subtle killing was not their way of operation. The quick knife or bullet in the dark or kidnapping and dumping someone in the Thames would be what I'd expect from them. And if Bobo was a habitual drug user, it would make no sense to kill the goose that laid the golden egg, would it?

"Do you want me to run your bath?" Queenie asked, interrupting my reverie.

I REALIZED THAT the next thing I should do would be to question the servants, but there wasn't time before the car arrived to take us to the theater. We set off and had not gone far before there was an enormous flash of light, followed by an explosion to our right.

We all jumped but Irmtraut screamed, "Assassins! We will all be killed by Bolsheviks!"

It had taken me a minute but when the second flash and bang went off I realized. "Don't worry. It's only Guy Fawkes Night."

"Guy Fawkes?" Irmtraut asked. "What is this?"

"Who is this," I corrected. "He was a person who tried to

blow up the Houses of Parliament many years ago. We still celebrate his beheading by burning his effigy on bonfires and setting off fireworks every November fifth."

"You burn people? This is most barbaric," she exclaimed.

"No, not real people. Just an effigy—Guys made of old clothes, stuffed with straw. And we set off pretty fireworks. Children love it."

A rocket shot into the sky, sending down a trail of colored stars. Marina and Irmtraut gazed out of the window, entranced. It had occurred to me that tonight would have been a good time to kill somebody, with all the flashes and bangs going off. Which seemed to indicate that the earlier killing of Bobo Carrington was not premeditated. Or the killer knew he or she could carry out the planned killing without risk of being disturbed.

The play was a big success—a witty period piece with some good musical numbers, Noel as the duke and a lovely French actress as the female lead. Even Irmtraut laughed, although I suspected she didn't understand the jokes. I went to the stage door during the interval and sent a note to Mr. Coward, telling him that we were in the audience, and was rewarded by being invited backstage at the end of the show. Noel, sitting in his brocade dressing gown, an ebony cigarette holder held nonchalantly between his fingers, was his utterly charming self and promised to set up a little soiree for Princess Marina to meet the stars of the London arts world. She was, like most people, quite dazzled by him. She didn't even blink when he said, "Your future spouse is a good pal of mine. Charming boy. Utterly charming. You'll have fun with him."

I was terrified he was going to add, "I know I did."

"Georgiana, your friends are wonderful," Marina said during the car ride home. "What a kind man. And so clever too. Is he married? Will we meet his wife?"

"No. He's not married, at the moment," I answered vaguely.

I was suddenly overcome with fatigue. I had been awoken before dawn and had had to undergo too many shocks to the system for one day. It was all I could do not to fall asleep in the car. We arrived back at the palace to find a late supper

awaiting us. A thick brown Windsor soup, cold meats, veal
and ham pie, baked potatoes and pickles. Simple but satisfying. Only I could hardly eat a thing. Now that I wasn't
absorbed in watching a play my stomach had clenched itself
in knots again. My thoughts jumped from the body under
the arch to Countess Irmtraut's damp jacket with the knife
in the pocket to the unpleasant session with DCI Pelham
and Darcy's dressing gown behind that bedroom door. And
they wanted me to help get to the bottom of this before the
news leaked out and became a national scandal. And if the
press did get wind of it, then it was quite possible that Darcy's name would be in the papers, or even that he'd be seen
as a suspect. I found myself praying fervently that he was
currently in some far-flung part of the world, even if I knew
I should hope he got all that he deserved.

Chapter 17

**I don't want to think anymore. Everything is just too
horrible. I just wish I could get away from here, go
to Granddad, curl up in a nice warm bed and never
get up again.**

Needless to say, I did not sleep well. There were still odd
shouts and explosions from Guy Fawkes Night revelers. I
awoke several times from vague nightmares with my heart
pounding. When I got up and pulled back the curtains to
look down onto the courtyard and the archway I was peering
into blackness. Only in the major's bathroom window at the
far end did a light still glow. Maybe he too was worried
about what had happened and could not sleep. He probably
realized more than any of us what was at stake if the press
got hold of the story and dragged Prince George's name
through the mud. Did he secretly suspect the prince? I wondered. Did he actually know whether the prince had fathered
Bobo's child and where it was now? Was I really being kept

in the dark while I was expected to help the police to solve the case?

In the morning I was up early again. The early November rain had turned to the more classic November fog and I looked out onto a sea of swirling whiteness. This would have been better weather in which to dump a body, I thought. It could have lain there for ages before it was discovered. Which made me wonder about the time of death. I hadn't asked that question, had I? The only doors leading from that courtyard were the back doors to Princess Louise's suite and to that of the major. I was sure that both exits were hardly ever used and it was possible that a body could have lain unnoticed for a good while under that archway. I'd have to ask the servants if any of them had had to pass the entrance to the courtyard at any time during that day.

Naturally there was no sign of Queenie. I had bathed the evening before so I dressed and went downstairs. The house was in the normal bustle one finds before its upper-class occupants have arisen. Fires were being laid, floors were being swept, maids were staggering under scuttles full of coal. They looked up in horror when they saw me, murmuring, "I'm sorry, my lady," as if it were their fault that I had interrupted them at work.

"Please don't mind me," I said when a skinny young girl looked as if she might pass out on encountering me while she carried in the coal. "I couldn't sleep and my maid isn't awake yet."

"Should I ask one of the parlor maids to bring you tea?" the girl asked. "In your bedroom or the morning room, perhaps? The fire is already going in there."

"There's really no hurry," I said, "and I don't want to disturb your work. But you can tell me one thing: whose job is it to answer the front door?"

She frowned. "We don't have a proper butler, so it would be Jimmy, the first footman. But Elsie, the parlor maid, she'd also do it if she heard a knock."

"And if you heard a knock, while you were cleaning, maybe?"

"I'd go and find one of them, my lady. It's not my place to answer doors, especially not if I'm wearing a coarse apron like now."

"What's your name?" I asked.

"Ivy, your ladyship." She studied her toes as she muttered the words, probably scared she'd now be in trouble.

"Well, Ivy, I wonder if you can think back to Princess Marina's first evening here. We went to dine at Buckingham Palace, and the countess had dinner alone here."

She looked up, a relieved smile on her lips. "Oh yes, my lady. Of course I remember."

"Do you know if anyone came to the door that evening? Or was anyone seen outside at all?"

"I wouldn't know, my lady. I was put to polishing silver and didn't leave the kitchen. And I go to bed early on account of having to be up at five."

"Thank you, Ivy. You can get on with your work. But tell me, what time do the servants have their breakfast?"

"At seven thirty, my lady."

"Would you please pass along the message that I'd like a word with them at that time?"

She looked terrified and I decided I should go back to my room for a while, rather than alarming more of the maids. I sat there, waiting impatiently, staring down at the fog swirling through the courtyard. This morning I would try to pay a visit to Prince George's garage at St. James's and see if his chauffeur would let me take a look at the motorcar. I wondered if he had driven himself that night or if the chauffeur could verify the crash. And if I could get away from my duties to the princess, I'd really like to take a look at Bobo Carrington's flat for myself. I was sure DCI Pelham would have gone over it, and probably removed anything incriminating or interesting, but you never know what might still be lying around. Wouldn't there be correspondence with the father of the child? A photograph of the baby? A rattle or a bootie lying somewhere? The problem was, I wasn't sure what I was looking for. All I knew was that somebody must have planned to kill Bobo Carrington.

One does not carry Veronal in a pocket unless one means to use it. I made a mental note to ask Countess Irmtraut whether she had trouble sleeping and if she had a sleeping aid she could perhaps let me use.

At seven thirty, with still no sign of Queenie, I went downstairs again and found my way through the back door of the dining room then down a dark passage until I heard the sound of voices and the clatter of pots and pans. I pushed open a door and found myself in the sort of old-fashioned kitchen we have at Castle Rannoch (although not quite as cavernous). Seven people were seated at a long scrubbed pine table while a scullery maid went around serving them porridge and a cook hovered watching critically in the background. They all rose to their feet as I came in.

"Please sit down and get on with your meal," I said. "I must apologize for interrupting but I just wanted to ask you a question."

"Yes, my lady?" The cook still glared, perhaps thinking that her cooking was about to be criticized.

"On the evening after Princess Marina arrived, she and I went to dine at Buckingham Palace," I said. "Countess Irmtraut was left here alone. Now, a friend of mine heard I was staying here and decided to pay me a surprise visit. She tells me that she knocked on the door but nobody answered so she assumed I must not be in residence."

Guarded faces stared at me, still waiting to find out whether they were in trouble.

I smiled at them. "I can see now that, the way this apartment is built, it would be hard to hear a knock at the front door from this room if you were all having your supper."

"There is supposed to be a bell, my lady," the footman said. "But it doesn't seem to be working. We've got an electrician coming to take a look at it."

"So none of you heard a knock that evening?"

Heads were shaken. "No, my lady," was murmured.

"And nobody saw anybody walking around outside, or heard the sound of a motorcar?"

"Your maid said she saw someone in the courtyard," one

of the girls said. "But that was right after we told her about the ghosts. Ever so upset, she was."

I smiled again. "Yes, my maid tends to be rather impressionable. So nobody else saw the white figure in the courtyard?"

"We don't have any windows that look out on the courtyard, my lady," the same girl replied. "And I don't think we'd have heard a motorcar outside either. I'm sorry we didn't answer the door to your friend. Please tell her about the bell not working."

"Of course. It's certainly not your fault and my friend only paid a surprise visit on the off chance she'd see me. No harm done. But one more thing, before I let you get back to your porridge. Did any of you go out that evening?"

"No, my lady," the footman said. "It was raining, if you remember, and we wouldn't have been allowed an evening off when royalty was in the house."

"What about Countess Irmtraut? What did she do all evening?"

"We served her dinner and then she had coffee in the salon," one of them said. "She wasn't very happy. Didn't like the food."

"I take it she didn't go out in the rain either?" I asked.

Heads were shaken but one girl said, "She must have popped out for a minute. I don't know why. But when I came to clear away the coffee she was standing by the door. I could see raindrops on her hairnet and she was wearing a jacket."

"What time was this?"

"Must have been about nine, my lady."

I smiled at them all then. "Thank you. I'm sorry to have interrupted your breakfast." And I left them glancing at each other uneasily.

WHAT REASON COULD Countess Irmtraut have had for going out into the rain? And why had she denied it? I realized I should pass this information along to DCI Pelham, but I was loath to cast suspicion until I was absolutely sure. I think it must have had something to do with sticking up for my own kind and an instinctive dislike of the DCI. Should I confront Irmtraut and tell her I knew she had been out? I'd have to wait for the right moment, but it was looking more and more as if I might just have a plausible suspect. But as to the opportunity to slip Bobo a drink with Veronal in it—when could that have happened? The servants did indicate that they could hear nothing from the kitchen if they were eating their meal. And if Irmtraut answered the front door, could she have invited Bobo in, fed her a drink, killed her and dumped her body outside all without being seen or over-heard? I supposed it might be possible. The servants clearly weren't enamored with Irmtraut and probably stayed as far away as possible without being obviously rude. However, Irmtraut wasn't to know that. If she'd invited Bobo in and then killed her, she was taking an enormous risk.

I HAD A cup of tea brought to me in the morning room, read the newspapers, which included pictures of myself with Princess Marina at the play the previous night, and waited for the others to show up. Eventually they both did. Irmtraut looked rather bleary-eyed.

"I did not sleep well last night," she said. "This place does not feel agreeable to me. I hear it is haunted. I myself spotted a ghost, I think."

"You did? Was it a white lady?" I asked.

"No. A fat man," she said shortly. "He walked through a wall."

"I think that would have been King George the First," I said.

"I don't care which king he was, I do not want him walk-ing through my walls."

"I also found it hard to sleep last night," I said. "So how did you get to sleep in the end? Do you have any sleeping drafts with you?"

"The draft in my room does not help me sleep," she said angrily. "It blows in under the door and hits me in the face. It is most disagreeable."

Marina smiled. "She means medicine to help you sleep, Traudi. I have some Veronal if you need some. I always carry it when I travel because it's hard to sleep in strange houses, isn't it?"

"Thank you, but like Irmtraut I try not to take those things," I replied. "It makes me rather groggy in the mornings." I was watching Irmtraut's face. Was she looking away on purpose?

"So what would you like to do today, Marina?" I asked.

"You promised to take me shopping," she said. "Let's start with Harrods, shall we?"

"Absolutely. If the car can find its way there in this fog."

She looked out of the window. "Goodness, it is quite dense, isn't it?" she said, then added, "There's a car pulling up outside now. Is it for us, do you think?"

I went over to look, worried it might be more policemen, which would certainly alarm the others or at least make them suspicious. But instead Marina said happily, "Oh, it's George. How lovely."

And Prince George himself headed for the front door. The knock was answered promptly, I noticed, and a rather flustered maid came in to announce, "His Royal Highness, the Duke of Kent."

George came striding into the room looking remarkably jaunty and debonair. "Well, that's what I call a sight for sore eyes," he said. "The Three Graces."

"You should have warned us you were coming, George," Marina said. "We are not yet dressed to receive visitors."

"Ah, but I'm not really a visitor. I'm a husband-to-be and will soon be gazing upon you in your night attire. Besides, you look absolutely charming." He went over and kissed her cheek. "I've come to whisk you away, my dear. I'm meeting the decorator at the house and I thought you'd want to see his suggestions for wallpaper before he puts it on the walls."

"Oh yes, of course." Marina looked pleased. "But we can't take too long. Georgiana and I have a shopping spree planned for my trousseau."

"Ah well, we can't get in the way of your buying dainty

little things, can we. Just make sure they can be taken off easily." He gave her a wicked grin.

There was an intake of breath from Irmtraut, and Marina said, "George, we're at the breakfast table, with young ladies present."

"Sorry, old thing." He didn't look particularly sorry. "Didn't mean to offend. I promise not to keep you from your shopping too long."

"You must let me finish my breakfast first and then go and change. I'm not appearing in public unless I'm looking my best. Too many cameras around."

"Yes, you have become the darling of the press, haven't you?" George said. "I'm pleased they've taken to you so well. The public is glad that at least one prince is doing the right thing. And my brother is glad because it's taking the spotlight off him. So come on. Eat up and off we go."

"And I'll go and round up my friend," I said, rising from my seat. "The one who knows all the best places to shop in London."

"Splendid." Marina smiled at me. "We'll meet back here at eleven, shall we?"

"And I? What am I to do?" Irmtraut asked.

"Oh, you can come shopping with us, of course," Marina said as if she'd only just remembered that Irmtraut was in the room with us.

"Shopping is of no interest to me. I do not have money for clothes," Irmtraut said.

"Then you could go and feed the swans in the Serpentine," George said. "Or take out a rowing boat."

Irmtraut looked at him as if he was an imbecile. "In case you have not noticed, there is thick fog. I do not wish to walk through the park in thick fog. I might lose my way or bump into undesirable persons."

"I always find it quite fun bumping into undesirable persons," George said, with the hint of a wink to me.

Marina looked out of the window. "The fog is lifting a little. Is that your motorcar outside or do we need to summon a car?"

"No, that's my old banger," George said.

"A banger—is that not an exploding sausage?" Irmtraut asked and I'm afraid we all laughed.

I HURRIED UPSTAIRS to put on my coat and hat, because I realized what a great opportunity I had. Prince George's car was actually outside the front door, and it was foggy so I wasn't likely to be seen. I slipped out into the cold, damp air. The black shape of the Bentley loomed in front of me. I started to inspect it, walking around it carefully. I was bending to examine the front mud guard when a voice asked, "Can I help you, miss?"

I jumped up guiltily to see a chauffeur standing over me. Oh golly, I hadn't thought Prince George would have his chauffeur with him.

"I'm Lady Georgiana, the prince's cousin," I said, just to establish that I wasn't a deranged stranger. "And I was at dinner at the palace with him the other night when he told us his motorcar had been in an accident. I was on my way out and was curious as to what sort of damage the motorcar might have sustained."

"An accident, my lady?" He looked perplexed. "The prince was driving himself that night and he certainly didn't mention any accident to me. And I've polished the motor since. There's no damage that I can see. But then these Bentleys are good solid motors, aren't they? It was probably the other vehicle that came away with a dent or a scrape."

"Yes, I expect so." I smiled at him then. "I'm glad his lovely motorcar wasn't scratched. Now I must be off to visit a friend."

And away I went. So there wasn't a mark of any kind on the prince's motorcar. Surely if it had been involved in an accident there would have been some trace—a chip of paint gone, a small scratch at the very least. But the chauffeur would have noticed when he polished the motorcar. So either he was not revealing any damage out of loyalty to his master or Prince George had not been in an accident that night.

Which of course made one wonder what else might have made him arrive late at dinner.

I REALIZED IT didn't look good for my cousin the prince. Means and motive, wasn't that what they said in the police force? He clearly had both. I realized I should inform DCI Pelham of my suspicions—both about Prince George and about Countess Irmtraut. But I worried that the DCI's approach might be heavy-handed, and I could see the press would have a field day if Prince George was dragged into a police motorcar. That would make newspaper reporters start digging deeper and who knew how much they might find out. At the very least it could upset the wedding plans.

And if he did it? I asked myself. If he really did kill Bobo? Wasn't it my job to help bring a murderer to justice? I sighed. Then I remembered Sir Jeremy. He had given me his card with a personal telephone number on it. He would be the one to tell. And it would be up to him if and when he informed Scotland Yard. I came out of the southern gates of the park and saw a red telephone box glowing through the fog. I went inside and dialed the number. A strange voice answered but when I asked for Sir Jeremy I was put straight through.

"Lady Georgiana—you have something for me?"

"I'm not sure," I said. "There are two things you should know about."

"Don't tell me now," he said. "Can we meet somewhere later today?"

"I'm taking the princess shopping this morning and we are attending a party this evening," I said.

"Then let's meet for tea. There's a little tea shop on Knightsbridge called the Copper Kettle. I know the owner— we can talk safely there. Shall we say three thirty?"

I put down the receiver and came out into the fog. Indistinct shapes of people bundled up in scarves passed me as I headed for Belinda's mews cottage. I knocked on the door and waited. It was distinctly chilly and unpleasant standing in the mews. I knocked again, more loudly this time. She was known to be a sound sleeper and a late riser, but my hammering on her front door should have awakened the dead. I squatted down.

"Belinda," I called through the letter box, "come and open the door. It's me, Georgie."

There was no answer. Surely she couldn't have gone out so early on a day like this. I stood there in the mews, the cold gnawing me, feeling indignant and uneasy at the same time. Belinda sometimes spent the night in a bed other than her own, that I knew. But we had talked about going shopping together only yesterday. All right, so Belinda was not the most considerate of people either. She definitely took care of her own needs first and if those needs included going off somewhere with a dashing man she met at Crockford's, then it probably would slip her mind that she was supposed to be going shopping with her friend and a visiting princess.

I gave one last rap on the front door, then stomped off down the mews. Really, she could be most infuriating. Of course, we were only planning on a trip to Harrods and I didn't really need her today, but all the same . . . As I walked away I couldn't shake off the lurking feeling of uneasiness. Belinda lived the same kind of life as Bobo Carrington. She went to gambling clubs and was not too choosy about her bedmates. And Bobo Carrington was now dead.

Chapter 18

I was going to return to Kensington Palace when it struck me that I wasn't too far from Bobo's Mayfair flat. I was sure the police would have been through it, but I wanted to get a look for myself. You can learn a lot about a person from seeing the kind of place they live in. Even though I knew I would be putting myself through more torture if I saw Darcy's dressing gown, or any other item I recognized as his, it had to be done. Until now all I knew about Bobo was what I had been told. She was a society beauty, she moved with the smart set, one of the bright young things. She had had an affair with Prince George, among others, and she had given birth to a child recently. Also she was a drug fiend. And apparently she had no family and no maid. But I knew nothing at all about what kind of person she was. Did she have many friends? How did she manage to live in Mayfair? And why did she have no maid? And the most important question of all—who had wanted her dead?

I turned onto Knightsbridge and made my way to Hyde

Park Corner, then up Park Lane until I came to Mount Street. The world was eerily silent with the odd bus and taxi passing at a snail's pace and almost nobody on the pavement. My own footsteps seemed to echo unnaturally loud and I found myself glancing over my shoulder, even though I knew I should have nothing to worry about.

The building on Mount Street was brand new—an impressive art deco affair of white marble and glass. A uniformed doorman stood in the foyer and sprang out to open the glass door to admit me.

"Miserable old day, isn't it, madam," he said. "How can I help you?"

I realized as I went to open my mouth that I hadn't thought through a credible plan of campaign as I walked and also that DCI Pelham would probably not approve, so I blurted out, "Actually I've come to visit Miss Carrington. I take it she is home."

His expression became troubled and I wondered how much he knew. Presumably he must suspect something was wrong if he'd had to admit the police.

"I'm sorry, madam, but I'm afraid she is not at home at the moment."

I wasn't going to let him know that I knew. I put on my bright and innocent face. "Oh, how annoying. Who would want to step out on a day like this, and when she knew I was coming too." I gave him what I hoped was a winning smile. "Do you have a key? Could you let me into her apartment to wait for her?"

"Let you in? Wait for her?"

"Yes. She knows I'm coming. We're old friends. I wrote to tell her I was coming up for Gussie Gormsley's party tonight and she said she was going too and why didn't I come over to her place and we'd go together?"

He was looking most uncomfortable now. "I'm afraid there has been some mistake. Miss Carrington is not at home. I really can't tell you when she'll be returning, but certainly not today."

"Not today? Oh, that's too bad of her," I said. "Now where

am I going to get ready for the party? And where am I going to stay tonight? That's not at all like Bobo. She's usually such a sweet girl, isn't she?"

"I wouldn't know, miss," he said. "I'm just the doorman." His expression, however, betrayed that he hadn't found Miss Carrington to have displayed much sweetness.

"I say," I said. "Is something wrong? She hasn't had an accident or something, has she? She's not in hospital?"

"I really don't know, miss," he said. "I'm sorry."

I was desperately trying to think of some way to get into that flat. "Look," I said, "would it be possible for you to take me up to her flat, if you don't want to give me the key? You see, I lent Bobo some earrings last time I saw her and I was going to collect them today. I wanted to wear them tonight. I told her and I thought she'd have them out and ready for me. So perhaps they are lying on her dressing table waiting for me."

"And your name is, miss?" he asked.

Goodness, that was a tough one. If I gave him my real name he'd know that I was reputable beyond doubt. However, he might then report my visit to DCI Pelham and that would probably not go down well. "It's Miss Warburton-Stoke," I said. "Belinda Warburton-Stoke. Bobo and I were at school together."

If Belinda hadn't bothered to be available for our jaunt to Harrods today, at least I'd use her name.

"Well, Miss Warburton-Stoke," the doorman said, still frowning, "I suppose it couldn't do any harm to take you up to the flat for a minute—just to recover a pair of earrings."

"You're most kind." I beamed at him. "What's your name?"

"It's Frederick, miss."

"Frederick. How nice." I gave him my most charming smile.

I think he went a little pink. He went into a cubby and took a key from the wall. I made a mental note of which hook it came from. I followed him across the foyer and into the lift. Up we went to the third floor. We crossed a landing with a big mirror and modern bentwood bench, then he turned the key in the lock and stood back for me to step into

Bobo's flat. It smelled of stale smoke and stale drink and rotting fruit—rather unpleasant, in fact. It was modern in the extreme—large plate-glass windows looked out onto Park Lane with glimpses of Hyde Park beyond. On the floor was a white rug and the furniture was sleek and low and chrome. There were modern paintings on the walls with great splashes of color. It was also rather untidy. A plate with an orange peel lay on a low table, along with a newspaper and an empty cocktail glass. An ashtray was piled high with cigarette ends. A silver fox wrap was draped over the back of a bentwood chair. Through in the kitchen I could see dishes piled in the sink.

"Dear me," I said. "Does Miss Carrington's cleaning lady no longer come?"

"Not for the last few days, miss," he said. "She was told not to."

"It's still Mrs. Parsons, is it?" I asked.

"Not Mrs. Parsons. You mean Mrs. Preston."

"Oh yes, of course. Mrs. Preston. Silly of me. Doesn't she have a key to come when Miss Carrington is away? I'm sure Miss Carrington won't want to return to this mess."

"Yes, miss. She does have the key to the flat, but she has been told not to come until further notice, so I understand."

"Who told her? Not Bobo, surely?" I looked at him. "I say, she's not in any trouble, is she? I know that at times . . . well, you know."

"There is some kind of complication, miss," he said, looking relieved to be telling me. "I won't deny that the police were here, looking for something. But they wouldn't tell me what, so I'm no wiser than you."

"I see," I said. "Well, I promise not to tell anyone you let me in." I gave him a conspiratorial stare.

Luckily the bedroom door was half open so I didn't have to reveal that I had never been here before. I walked purposefully across the room and pushed the bedroom door fully open. I didn't want to have to see what might be hanging behind that door. The bed was unmade. A pair of silk

stockings lay across it. A pair of frilly knickers lay on the floor. A dress was draped over the dressing table stool. Two things were clear: Bobo was sorely in need of a maid and she had certainly been living in this flat very recently.

I went over to the dressing table. Odd pieces of jewelry were lying scattered across it, but no earrings. And nothing else that might be of interest, like a note saying, "Meet me tonight in the park." In fact one thing that struck me about the whole flat was the absence of anything personal. No photographs of family members or of Bobo with friends. No half-written letters, or letters from others. Just cigarette stubs in an ashtray and a bright red lipstick. I remembered the red gash of her mouth against a white face as she had lain on the cobbles. And I felt a wave of pity. This had been someone who lived for the moment but had no real ties. A bright but lonely life.

This thought, of course, led to Darcy. I forced my face to stay serene as I asked, "So tell me, do you know Mr. O'Mara? Isn't he still one of Bobo's friends?"

He smiled. "Oh yes, Mr. O'Mara. He's a good sort."

"Have you seen him recently?"

"I can't say I have, miss, but then I go off duty at two and William comes on until ten. So if he came to visit Miss Carrington in the evening I wouldn't know about it."

And if he'd stayed the night, wouldn't Frederick have had to let him out in the morning, I wanted to ask, but couldn't. Instead I sighed and headed back into the sitting room. "The earrings don't appear to be here," I said, "and I don't want to go rummaging through her drawers for them. So thank you again. And if Miss Carrington does come back, please tell her I was here and had to go to the party without her."

"Right you are, miss," he said and shut the door firmly behind us. We rode down in the lift in silence. As we stepped out into the bright foyer an idea struck me. "I've just thought of something," I said. "If Mrs. Preston isn't working here at the moment, she'd have free time, wouldn't she? And I'm moving into a little mews cottage just off Knightsbridge.

I'm desperate for someone to come and clean the place for me and she'd be perfect, wouldn't she?"

"I expect she would, miss," he said.

"So do you happen to have her address?" I asked. "I'll go and see her right away."

"It's here somewhere." He went into his cubby and rummaged around, producing a stack of calling cards and papers. "Hold on. Just a minute. Here we are." He produced a grubby index card. "It's 28 Cambridge Mansions, Cambridge Street."

"Oh dear, where would that be, do you know?"

"Just behind Victoria Station, I believe. Not too far from here because she had to walk the last time we had a pea-souper fog and the buses weren't running."

I took out the small notebook from my purse and copied down the address. "Thank you, Frederick. You have been most helpful. But I'm so worried about dear Bobo. I wonder if any of her other friends would know more about what happened to her? Whom do you think I could ask? I've been living at home in the country so I'm completely out of touch with her friends these days."

"I couldn't say, miss." His face was expressionless. "Not many friends come to visit here. At least not when I'm on duty."

Was he hinting that most of Bobo's friends came after dark?

"Perhaps someone at Gussie Gormsley's tonight will know more," I said. "Thank you again."

And out I went into the fog. In a way it had been a frustrating visit. I hadn't learned any more about Bobo—or had I? One thing was obvious: she lived in a very expensive flat in the most expensive part of London. But her jewelry was flashy and paste, not real. She had no job and apparently no family. So how could she afford to live there? I'd have to find out from Sir Jeremy this afternoon who was paying the rent on that flat, and whether the person (presumably male) who paid the rent was also paying the doorman to keep silent.

I WOULD HAVE loved to pay a call on Mrs. Preston, to wheedle information out of her, and maybe even find a way to persuade her to lend me the key to Bobo's flat, but I knew that I should return to Kensington Palace in case Marina was ready to attack Harrods. I hopped on a bus that crept at a snail's pace along Knightsbridge, then into Kensington and finally stopped at the entrance to Kensington Gardens. I almost sprinted up the Broad Walk and into the palace, where I found Irmtraut staring out of the window with a petulant expression on her face.

"No, Her Highness has not returned," she said. "Prince George is not wise to keep her out in this fog. It will be bad for her lungs and is most disagreeable."

"Yes, I'm afraid it's a classic pea-souper," I said.

She frowned. "But no. Pea soup is green. This fog is dirty brown."

"I think it just implies that it's very thick," I said.

"Ah. Another English joke maybe?"

"Not much of a joke. It's horrible out there."

"You went for a walk in such weather?" she asked. "You English have great fortitude."

"No, actually I went to visit a friend I thought was coming to the party with us tonight. But she was not at home."

Irmtraut sniffed. "This party. There will be drinking and loud noise?"

"Oh yes. A lot of both, I'm afraid."

"Then I shall stay here. I do not like such things. But I trust you will watch over Princess Marina."

"Oh yes, don't worry. I'll keep an eye on her all evening," I said.

"No, you must keep more than one eye. You must keep both eyes," she said.

Luckily at that moment I heard voices and Princess Marina returned, accompanied by the major. They were both laughing, in animated conversation, and I thought how attractive they both looked, in contrast to the glum, surly Irmtraut.

"At last you return," Irmtraut said. "This fog, it is not good for the chest."

"Oh, nonsense, Traudi," Marina said. "I was in a car or in the house most of the time and the major arrived to give me a lift back here. You should see my house. It will be absolutely splendid. George has quite good taste and we even agree on wallpaper!"

"You've also been out in this foul weather, Lady Georgiana?" the major asked.

"Yes, I went to visit a friend and annoyingly she wasn't there. So a trip for nothing."

"I see." His eyes held mine for a second and I wondered if he thought I'd been out investigating. Then he turned and gave a polite nod to Marina. "I must get back to my duties, Your Royal Highness. If you will excuse me."

"Of course. Thank you for the ride."

"Major, I'd like to take Princess Marina to Harrods this morning, if a car will be available for us."

"Good idea. Of course. I'll have the motor waiting whenever you're ready."

As the major left she exclaimed, "He is really quite charming, is he not? But he is clearly unhappy with his present role of housekeeper. He'd rather be back with his regiment, he says. They are due to sail to the Far East soon and he wants to be with them."

"Yes, it must be hard to adapt to this kind of civilian life after a military career," I replied.

We had some coffee and then we went to Harrods. Marina enjoyed herself thoroughly, especially, I think, because Irmtraut was so shocked at her choice of underwear.

"You will live in a cold English house," she said. "Those knickers will not keep you warm."

We returned late for luncheon and the princess decided to take a rest before the party. I took my cue to go to meet Sir Jeremy at the Copper Kettle. It was a nondescript tearoom of the type favored by ladies up to town for a day's shopping. With neat little tables between large potted palms.

Sir Jeremy had chosen a table in a far corner and rose to meet me as I entered.

"Good of you to come in this beastly weather, Lady Georgiana," he said. "I've ordered tea and scones. I trust that will fit the bill."

"Super, thank you."

The tea arrived and I poured.

"You have something to tell me, I gather," he said as the waitress moved off.

"Two things that might be important." And I related the curious incident of Prince George's motorcar, that he had claimed to be in an accident when there was no sign of damage to his motor, and then later said he was held up with his decorator. Then I added the fact that Countess Irmtraut had been out when she claimed she hadn't. And with a knife in her pocket.

He looked grave. "Now that could be interesting," he said. "If Bobo Carrington had come to confront Princess Marina, you say this woman would do anything to protect the princess."

"Absolutely."

"I'm afraid we'll have to question her, although God knows how we'll do that without spilling the beans about the murder."

"I questioned the palace staff by telling them that a friend had come to the door after I had gone out and couldn't make anyone hear her knocking. I asked if anyone had seen her or heard a motorcar."

"That was clever of you. And had they?"

"No, but that was when one of the maids told me that Countess Irmtraut had been outside."

He nodded. "And Prince George's motorcar. That's interesting, but as it happens I've already had a little talk with him. He was visibly upset when he heard of Bobo's death. His first words were 'So it finally got her, did it?' And when I asked what he meant he said, 'The cocaine, of course. I knew it would only be a matter of time.'"

"Did he know about the baby?" I asked.

"I gather he did, but he claimed he had only had a casual friendship with her and ended it ages ago because of her drug use."

"So not his child," I said. I must have spoken a little too loudly, as two matrons looked across at us with raised eyebrows. I stifled an urge to giggle.

"Apparently not."

"Then finding the true father of the child seems the most important step to take, doesn't it?" I kept my voice low this time and noticed that one of the matrons was leaning toward us in an attempt to overhear. "If he's a prominent man he would be the one with most to lose if the news went public."

Sir Jeremy nodded. "I don't think it's going to be easy, especially given the cloak of secrecy under which we must operate. We've been looking into her life and her friends and it's devilishly hard to find out anything about her. It is as if she dropped from another planet. No past history. No birth certificate. Nothing."

"And what about the baby?" I asked. "Did you find out where she gave birth?"

"Apparently not in or around London," he said. "Of course she would have entered any nursing home under an assumed name, but none of the private clinics admits to her being a patient. So she went somewhere. And if we only knew where she came from, we might find that out."

"Perhaps Prince George knows something of her background," I said. "One inadvertently lets quite a lot of details slip when one is in a close relationship."

"Ah yes," he said. And from the way he looked at me I knew he was thinking about Darcy. "I can certainly talk with him again, but I found him testy about it before—obviously scared the news will leak to Marina and his parents. He wants nothing more than to distance himself from anything to do with Bobo."

"I went to her flat today," I said, deciding it was better to come clean with him. "I just wanted to get a feel of her surroundings for myself."

"And someone let you in?" He looked at me in surprise. "That really is most irregular."

"Only for a second. I pretended I had left some valuable earrings with Bobo and wanted to retrieve them. The doorman hovered over me every second."

"And did you find anything?"

"Not really. Only that she is in need of a maid. Her place was most untidy. But expensive. Have you found out who was paying her rent? That might be a start."

"Nobody paid her rent," he said. "She bought the place herself, two years ago. Paid cash."

"Paid cash," I said. "I wonder where she got that much money. She's not an heiress, is she? She was never a famous actress, never married to a millionaire. What did she do?"

He sighed. "As I said, her life is an enigma. True, her name was linked to various prominent men, but such relationships wouldn't have provided the money for a flat in Mayfair, unless she was the mistress of a particular millionaire . . . and then we'd all have known about it."

"So what do you want me to do now?" I asked. "Would you be prepared to turn a blind eye if I went back to her flat?"

"Pelham's men have been over it once and removed any letters or bills they thought might be of interest, so I'm not quite sure what you think you'd find. And of course you know he wouldn't thank you for interfering, but if you think there is something to be learned, then by all means . . . Only you and I never had this conversation." He shared the hint of a smile with me. "My department and Scotland Yard are not always on the friendliest terms, you know. Treading on their toes, going behind their backs . . . that's what they think of us."

"I'm going to a party tonight," I said. "Gussie Gormsley is giving it. I thought there could perhaps be some of Bobo's crowd there. I might ask a few questions."

He nodded. "And this countess. You think she is the type who might kill out of misplaced loyalty?"

"I do," I said. "I think she's absolutely the type."

As I left the café and made my way back to Kensington

Palace I couldn't help reflecting that Sir Jeremy had already had a chat with Prince George. Who knew what information had passed between them and what they were determined to keep from the rest of us? Sir Jeremy had been involved in protecting the royal family before. He was one of us, and I knew whose side he would take. He might not care about justice if it meant scandal and disgrace for a royal. And he might even have asked me to help in the knowledge that I'd just get in the way, tangle things up for DCI Pelham and not come anywhere near the truth.

Chapter 19

Jazz music spilled out of St. James's Mansions as our motor-car pulled up outside the modern block of flats overlooking Green Park. We joined the line of taxicabs outside, disgorging passengers in evening gowns, fur coats, tails or tuxedos. As we waited for our turn in the lift I was suddenly struck by a sense of déjà vu. It had been at one of Gussie's parties that I had witnessed a terrible tragedy, and I had put it from my mind until now. It had been the same kind of party, the same kind of music, the same crowd that night, and I had been there accompanying another princess. I found myself shivering in the icy blast that swept in across the foyer from the open front door. Around me voices chattered excitedly, the sound echoing back from the high ceiling, and I glanced back at the door, wondering if I could perhaps come up with a good excuse for abandoning the party and returning to Kensington Palace. But before I could make my mind work we were propelled forward into a packed lift and whisked up to the sixth floor.

As we emerged from the lift the music became so loud that I could feel the thump of the beat resonating through the floorboards. I wondered what the neighbors might be thinking. I hoped there weren't any stuffy old colonels in the building or we'd be having a visit from the police. The door to Gussie's flat was open. As I ushered Marina into the foyer I caught a glimpse of a Negro jazz band playing in the drawing room. The carpet had been rolled back and it was dark in there, but full of gyrating shadows. Marina turned to me with an excited little smile. I tried to return the smile but my insides were clenched. Golly, I was charged with looking after her, keeping her safe, and I was taking her to a place where a murder had once occurred. But the culprits had been caught and Gussie was a harmless enough chap, wasn't he? Besides, he was getting married too, and he knew that he'd invited a princess to his party. Coats and wraps were taken and we were just heading toward the barman dispensing cocktails when Gussie himself came out of the drawing room, mopping his face with a white silk handkerchief. He was a rather large lad—Clydesdale rather than Thoroughbred—but he looked distinguished in tails, and his face broke into a broad smile when he saw us.

"You came, old thing," he said, holding out his hands to me, "and you brought Her Highness with you too. Jolly good show. I made sure I vetted the guest list when I knew you were coming, Your Highness. None of my disreputable bachelor friends, don't you know."

"Oh dear," Marina said. "I hope it won't be too boring now."

Gussie looked worried for a moment, then he burst out laughing. "Good sense of humor. I like that. Let me get you a cocktail, Your Highness. What are you drinking?"

"I'm afraid I'm not too well up on cocktails," Marina said. "How about you, Georgiana? Do you have a favorite?"

"I had a sidecar last time I was here and your bartender made it very well," I said, not wanting it to be known that my experience with cocktails was limited in the extreme—

although it had broadened a little on my first transatlantic crossing.

"Splendid," Gussie said. "Two sidecars please, Albert." He turned back to us. "I've trained my man to be a splendid bartender, don't you think? He keeps threatening to leave me and get a job in the bar at the Savoy. Only they wouldn't pay him as well, isn't that right, Albert?"

Albert gave a wan smile so that we couldn't tell whether he agreed with this or not, and went on shaking the cocktail.

"So where is your intended, Gussie?" I asked.

He made a face. "At home with her mother, I'm afraid. Mother's just had an operation so my bride has deserted me to minister at her bedside."

"Oh, that's too bad," I said.

He gave me a knowing grin. "She doesn't actually like this kind of shindig anyway. I think it's a good excuse, personally. But never mind. We'll enjoy ourselves, won't we?"

Gussie put a hand on my shoulder, making me remember a not-so-pleasant experience with him once. But then he had been very drunk. "And I gather it's to be a right royal evening tonight. I've told everyone to be on their best behavior and practice their 'sir's and 'ma'am's."

"Really?" I asked, giving him a worried look in case he was referring to Prince George, who had been known to come to Gussie's parties.

Gussie's face lit up as the front door opened. "And here they are now. Jolly good." He abandoned us and pushed his way across the crowded foyer as the Prince of Wales came into view. He was dressed impeccably in evening attire as usual and I was not in the least surprised to see he was accompanied by Mrs. Simpson, wearing the black beaded evening gown she had worn on the ship crossing the Atlantic. I was, however, surprised to see Mr. Simpson in tow, looking broody and uncomfortable. Well, who wouldn't?

"Good of you to come, sir." Gussie pumped the prince's hand with enthusiasm.

"Wouldn't miss one of your parties for anything, Gussie,"

the prince said in his light drawl. "And I believe you've met my friends Mr. and Mrs. Simpson."

"Of course. So glad you could make it." Gussie was the soul of discretion. "What can I get you to drink?"

"A whiskey," Mr. Simpson growled. "And better make it a double while you're at it."

I wondered why he still bothered to accompany her when everyone in London society knew about his wife and the prince. Surely it must have felt most embarrassing. For that matter, why hadn't he divorced her yet? Perhaps chivalry was not dead and he was waiting for her to divorce him. Or perhaps she still needed his money to fund her expensive clothing habit.

Albert handed us our drinks and Gussie steered the prince in our direction. "I expect you've met your new sister-in-law, sir," he said. "And of course you know Georgiana."

"Hello, sir," I said.

"What-ho, Georgie. Looking stylish tonight." The prince nodded to me then took Marina's hand. "Actually we haven't met yet. How do you do, Marina? So glad to meet you at last. You're far too good for my brother, of course. Make sure you make him toe the line, what?"

"So pleased to meet you at last, David," she said. "However, I'm not sure it's always an easy task to make royal princes toe the line, as you put it." She was wonderful, wasn't she?

The prince grinned appreciatively and introduced Mrs. Simpson. Her husband had already melted into the crowd, nursing his double whiskey.

"Why, you're not at all what we expected, is she, David?" Mrs. Simpson said, holding on to Marina's hand. "So elegant. So composed. And that gown—it had to come from Paris!"

"From Worth," Marina said.

"See, David. What did I tell you? You can't find anything fashionable in London. One really has to have a flat in Paris to pop across and buy clothes."

"Oh, I disagree," Marina said. "Molyneux is making my wedding dress and it's absolutely lovely. And Georgiana and I had great fun at Harrods this morning buying things for my trousseau."

Mrs. Simpson turned that formidable gaze onto me.

"You're also looking quite elegant these days, Georgiana, honey," she said. "I take it Mummy helped you choose that gown. Is she still around or did she stay on to become a star in Hollywood?"

"She decided that America wasn't for her," I replied. "It was all too fake and insincere. I think she prefers a place where class can't be bought with mere money."

I saw the glint of venom in those dark eyes. "My, my, we are sharpening our claws these days, are we not? But don't get too catty, honey. Men don't want a woman who is too sharp for a wife. Especially the sort of man you'll wind up marrying." She took a long sip of her drink and gave David a smoldering glance over her cocktail glass. "They like to be babied, cosseted, made a fuss of, don't they, David?"

I heard an intake of breath in the crowd around us as Mrs. Simpson addressed him by the first name the family used and didn't call him "sir" as was required in public, even by close relatives like me.

"So is Mummy here?" Mrs. Simpson looked around hopefully. I think she enjoyed the verbal battles that always ensued with my mother, who certainly gave as good as she got.

"No, she went back to Germany."

"Sensible woman. That's the place where things are looking up these days," Mrs. Simpson said. "That Mr. Hitler. He seems to have the right ideas."

"Do you think so?" I asked, shocked. "He seems to be like a funny little chap who just shouts a lot."

"Oh no, honey. He's got what it takes. You'll see. He'll have Europe eating out of his hand," she said. "David's impressed too, aren't you?"

"He's doing a lot of good things for Germany, I must say," the Prince of Wales said. "Getting people back to work. Building roads. Giving Germans pride again. It's all good."

"Let's hope so," I said.

"So do you care to dance, Marina?" the prince asked. "I should probably trip the light fantastic first with my new relative, if you ladies will excuse us?"

He took Marina's hand and steered her into the fray. Mrs. Simpson looked at me. "That poor girl is in for a rough time," she said. "Does she have any idea what she's letting herself in for?"

"I think they may be all right," I said. "George seems quite smitten with her. He may shape up and do the right thing after all. You'd be surprised at the number of English princes who actually do, when the time comes."

I gave her a little smile as we were swallowed up into the crowd. I felt terrific and it wasn't the cocktails. Finally I was learning from my mother to hold my own in this cat-eat-cat society. I might even become the sort of clever, brittle woman who never lets herself be hurt. If only I could get that image of Darcy's dressing gown out of my mind.

I heard the band change tunes and the crooner started singing a song that had been popular a while ago. It went, "I've danced with a man who's danced with a girl who's danced with the Prince of Wales. It was simply grand, he said, 'Topping band,' and she said, 'Delightful, sir.'"

The dancers suddenly spotted the prince and there was laughter and applause. More people crammed in to watch David dancing with Marina. I'm slightly claustrophobic and hate the feeling of being trapped in a crowded, sweaty and noisy room, so I wandered instead into the dining room next door. This room was only populated with odd knots of people, it being too early for supper. A lovely spread had been laid out on the table against one wall—a whole cold salmon in the middle, oysters, prawns, cold chicken and pheasant, caviar and all the nice little things that go with it. When I had been one step away from starvation and living on baked beans I would have fallen upon it. Now I was content to scoop a little caviar onto a cracker and was just biting into it, careful not to spill it down my décolleté front, when I heard something that made me prick my ears up.

"No, I haven't seen her for ages, darling."

I turned around and saw two rather glamorous women, older than me and of that brittle, witty kind I had just been considering, standing together by the window, each with a cocktail glass in one hand, a cigarette holder in the other.

"She was away all summer, wasn't she? Let it be known that she was going to the Med, but that wasn't the case. I was there myself in August and she certainly wasn't at any of the parties." The voice was lowered. I could just make out the words. "Tell me, did you hear the rumor going around?"

"That she was preggers, darling? Oh yes, I did hear that. One finds it hard to believe. I mean, who knows how to take care of herself better than Bobo?"

The first voice grew even lower. I moved around the table, pretending to pick a grape from the bunch but actually positioning myself closer to the women. With the thump and wail of the music next door it was hard to overhear. "And if she was . . . you know . . . why didn't she just pop to Harley Street and have it taken care of like any civilized person?"

"Catholic, darling. Doesn't believe in that sort of thing." This latter phrase was whispered but I managed to lip-read. Our class of person does have such good diction.

"So you think she actually went away to have the baby?"

The first woman nodded. "Must have. She wouldn't have risked being recognized in London."

"Switzerland, do you think?"

"Possibly. But there are places closer by, aren't there? That one on the south coast . . ."

I took a deep breath and decided to take my chances. I went over to them. "Excuse me, but are you talking about Bobo Carrington, by any chance?" I asked. "Sorry to interrupt, but I was hoping she'd be here tonight. I've been wondering about her too. I caught a glimpse of her at Crockford's the other night, but that's the only time recently."

They were looking at me suspiciously, not quite sure who I was.

"I'm sorry. It was rude of me to barge in, but I've been trying to find out where Bobo disappeared to. I'm Georgiana

Rannoch, by the way," I said. "I brought Princess Marina tonight."

The frowns eased into smiles. "Oh. You're Binky's sister. I didn't realize you knew Bobo."

"Oh yes. Doesn't everyone?" I gave them a bright smile.

"Everyone in trousers, darling," one said.

"Yes, I was thinking about that the other day," I said. "She doesn't really have any close female friends, does she? If she does, I've never met them. One sees her at a party. One exchanges pleasantries, and that's about it."

"As you say, that's about it," one of the women said. "I never really took to her myself. Cold and calculating little minx." She looked at her friend, who nodded agreement. "And I don't condone that whole drug business. I know plenty of people at this party would disagree with me, and if the new little princess was not here tonight I can tell you there would be sniffing in the kitchen at this moment. But we're all on our best behavior. And most of them aren't stupid enough to inject themselves the way Bobo does. She's heading for an early grave, I'm afraid."

"So tell me." I moved closer. "If she really was preggers, does anyone actually know who the father of the child is?"

"Bobo does, presumably. But she's keeping a low profile," the first woman said.

Her friend looked around before saying, "Of course it's quite possible it was one of your royal relatives. But he says not. And he may not always be the best behaved, but he's as honest as any Boy Scout. So any one of the other candidates. Bobo isn't always too choosy after a night of booze and the other stuff."

"The other candidates? Any ideas who they might be?"

"Darling, she has worked her way through every male under sixty-five in London society. I suppose we'll just have to see who the poor little thing looks like."

"So she's never had one particular sugar daddy—someone who takes care of her?"

The two women laughed. "If anyone can take care of herself, it's Bobo. I hope I'm not putting my foot in it, running her down. She's a friend of yours, is she?"

"Not really a friend. Someone I've bumped into from time to time and we had a good laugh at a house party last year," I said, trying to keep my acquaintance with Bobo suitably vague. "I can't say I know her well or that she's ever shared confidences."

"She doesn't," one of the women said. "She's good at that. She gets other people to talk about themselves but shares no secrets."

"It's funny, isn't it?" I said. "Does anyone know who she really is? I mean, family background and all that? I've never met anyone who was presented with her."

"Rumor has it that she comes from Argentina," the first woman said. "That would explain the Catholic leanings. And there are plenty of ne'er-do-well sons of English aristocracy over there, presumably having their way copulating with local girls. But if you want my personal opinion"—she leaned closer—"I think she's a little upstart, pretending to be what she's not."

"Why do you think that?" I asked.

"One just gets the feeling that she's not really one of us. Of course she's very good at hiding it, and she's very lovely, and funny, and generous, and I'm sure she's divine in the sack, so nobody probes too deeply. But one day it will all come out, mark my words."

She broke off as a noisy group came into the room, laughing uproariously at something one of them had just said. I helped myself to more caviar, this time unfortunately letting a couple of beads drop down my cleavage, then moved away from my gossipy new friends. It seemed that nobody knew any more about her than the police had already found out. If I were to do my job well, I should dance with the various chaps here and see what reaction the mention of Bobo's name produced from them.

There was no sign of Marina as I came out into the foyer. Presumably still dancing with the Prince of Wales. It didn't seem I knew anybody else here from the crowd that milled around me, trying to get to the bar. And then Belinda popped into my mind. One might have expected her to be here. This was her kind of party, as it would have been Bobo's. Half the rich young men of London were attending. So why wasn't she here? Again a shiver of apprehension went through me. Bobo had gone to Crockford's and was seen to be agitated and talking to a strange American. And Belinda frequented Crockford's and wasn't at home this morning. I was determined to visit her mews place first thing tomorrow. What's more, I still had a key. I could let myself in.

I found myself in the line for the bar, even though I wasn't too keen on having another cocktail. But it was something to do, rather than standing around, feeling like a wallflower.

"Another sidecar for you, my lady?" Albert asked.

"Georgie?" said a surprised voice behind me. I spun around to see Darcy standing there.

Chapter 20

LATE NOVEMBER 6

Darcy was looking ridiculously handsome, dressed in a white tuxedo, his unruly dark curls tamed for once, and his face lit up. "There you are. I've been hunting all over for you. Someone said you'd gone to Germany with your mother."

He took my hand and attempted to drag me out of the line.

"I'm waiting for my cocktail, thank you," I said, stone-faced. I was too conscious that Princess Marina and the Prince of Wales were in the next room and I couldn't afford to have a scene. My hand was shaking as Albert handed me the glass. I started to walk away.

"Well, that's not what I'd call a warm greeting," Darcy said. "How about, 'Darcy, my love, I've been pining for you'?"

I moved with him out of the flow of traffic.

"Maybe I'd say that if I were your only love," I said.

"What do you mean?"

"Tell me one thing, Darcy." I turned to face him. "Have you slept with Bobo Carrington?"

"Bobo? Well, yes, but . . ."

"No buts," I said. "That confirms everything I've been

told, I'm afraid. I wish I were wearing the silver pixie instead of these stupid sapphires, then I could have thrown it in your face."

I was horribly close to tears. I pushed past him through the crowd until I found Marina, now dancing with our host.

"Gussie, I'm not feeling at all well," I said. "One of my headaches, I'm afraid. I'll take a cab back, if you could make sure Princess Marina is escorted to her motorcar. Please forgive me, Marina, but I have to go home now."

"Georgiana, I can come with you—" She reached out to touch my arm. That simple act of kindness was too much. I felt a fat tear squeeze itself out of my eye and run down my cheek.

"No, you stay. Have fun, but I simply must go."

Then I fled.

"Georgie, wait." Darcy tried to force his way through the crowd to me. Luckily a lift had just arrived. I leaped in and pressed the button. The doors closed and I descended to the street. A taxi was just disgorging more passengers.

"Kensington Palace, please," I said to the driver as I climbed in. "As quickly as possible."

It wasn't until I was back in my own room that I allowed myself to cry.

I didn't even care when Queenie arrived. I let her undress me and bring me a basin and face flannel.

"Can I get you a nice cup of hot milk, my lady?" she asked, proving that she knew perfectly well how to address me if she tried.

"Yes, that would be very . . ." I couldn't even finish the sentence.

I crawled into bed and soon Queenie reappeared with a tray with hot milk and digestive biscuits on it.

"Get that down yer. That will perk you up no end," she said. "I had the cook add some brandy to it. 'She ain't half upset,' I told the cook. 'I don't know who done it to her, but I won't half give him a piece of my mind if I ever catch him.'"

The thought of Queenie giving this Cockney address to a royal cook would normally have appalled me. You can tell

how deep in my own misery I was that I didn't even care.
Queenie went over and adjusted the curtains. Then she
stopped, peering out of the window.

"'Ere," she said. "There's that ruddy ghost again. Just
like before. Something white moving around the courtyard."

Curiosity got the better of despair. I climbed out of bed
and went to join her at the window. It was pitch-black in the
courtyard, apart from the thin sliver of light shining down
from my window. The archway itself was in absolute blackness but I could just vaguely see something white drifting
about.

"Give me my overcoat, Queenie," I said. "I'm going down
to see."

"Oh, miss, you don't want to go down there. I don't trust
them ghosts," she said.

"You can come with me to keep an eye on me. Come on."

"Me, miss?" she asked as I was already heading for the
stairs. "I ain't going out there for love nor money. And you
shouldn't either. What if you get haunted or possessed?"

"You can stand in the doorway and call for help if I yell."

She followed me unwillingly down the stairs. And
grabbed my arm as I was about to go out into the darkness.
"I don't think you should go out there. If it's one of them
ghosts, just leave it to mind its own business."

"I have to see for myself, Queenie," I said. I didn't add
that I was wondering if the ghost was Countess Irmtraut
prowling around or snooping. Nobody had any good reason
to be in a courtyard that went nowhere at this time of night.

It wasn't until I approached the arch and was swallowed
into complete darkness that I began to have second thoughts.
It's all very well to be brave when looking from a lighted
window. Going under a dark archway where someone was
recently murdered is another matter. I told myself that
Bobo's murder had nothing to do with the palace, but all the
same my nerve almost gave out as I peered into the gloom.
The gap between the curtains in my own window painted
only a small stripe of light across the far side of the courtyard. Not enough to cut through the total blackness ahead

of me. I stopped in front of the archway. No, I wasn't going to venture in there. If a ghost or a person was moving around, it was none of my business.

"It was probably only a maid returning from an evening off," I thought. "Going into the back door of the princess's apartment." And I laughed at my own terror.

Then without warning I was grabbed from behind, spun around and pushed up against the cold, damp wall of the archway. Before I had time to cry out, cold lips were kissing mine. It only took a second of terror in which my heart stopped beating before I recognized those lips.

I struggled, broke free and tried to push him away. "Don't you dare try to win me over in such an underhanded fashion, Darcy O'Mara." I could make out his eyes now, glinting at me like a cat's. "And what do you mean by following me here and then skulking around?"

"I followed you because I had to set things straight," he said. His eyes were flashing dangerously now. "And I was skulking, as you put it, to see if there was a way in without alerting the entire household. I never have got the hang of this place. It's like a warren. I didn't want to burst in on one of your aunts by mistake."

"You can't set things straight," I said. "It's over, Darcy. I know our kind of people like to go in for bed-hopping, but not me. I don't ever want to play that sort of game. I'm not prepared to share you. I'd rather marry Prince Siegfried. At least I know where I'd stand there."

He was still holding me fiercely, his fingers digging into my arms. "Look, Georgie, you knew when you met me that I wasn't a saint. I'm a healthy, red-blooded male, and as you said, our sort are not prudish. Bed-hopping is a recognized sport. But I don't know why this is upsetting you so much now."

"You don't know? You and Bobo Carrington, and I shouldn't be upset?"

"Of course not. It's all old hat. She meant nothing to me."

"Oh no? You leave your dressing gown behind her door? And that means nothing? That to me indicates more than a spur-of-the-moment fling. What's more, it indicates an affair that is still going on when you are supposedly engaged to me."

He gave a nervous little laugh. "Oh, so that's what's worrying you. You are silly. That was only there because . . ."

The sentence was never finished. We hadn't heard the approach of a motorcar, or we had been so intent on ourselves that we hadn't paid attention to it, but we were suddenly blinded by headlights shining directly on us.

Darcy shielded his eyes. "What the devil?" he asked. He released me and spun around.

Men were coming toward us. Policemen.

And leading the charge was DCI Pelham. "Well, well. Mr. O'Mara, isn't it?" He looked pleased with himself. "We've finally caught up with you. And you said you had no idea where he was, little lady."

"I'm not a little lady. I am addressed as 'my lady' and I tell the truth," I said. "I didn't know until tonight."

"What the deuce is this about?" Darcy demanded. "What do you think you're doing, man?" This to a copper who had now grabbed Darcy's arm.

"It means we're taking you in for questioning concerning a very serious matter, sir."

"What serious matter?"

"Let's wait until we get to Scotland Yard, sir. Now come quietly. We wouldn't want to make a fuss outside a royal residence and disturb the occupants, would we?"

"Georgie, listen," Darcy called out to me as he was led away. "I didn't do anything."

He was bundled into the motorcar, the door slammed. The motor reversed, then the car screeched away, spraying gravel. I stood watching, feeling sick and scared. However angry I was with Darcy, I knew he wouldn't have killed Bobo. What if the police thought he did? What if DCI Pelham was determined to pin this crime on somebody, thus removing any possibility of scandal for the royals?

There was nothing more I could do but go back to the front door.

"Someone trying to break in, was it?" Queenie asked. "Lucky the police arrived then."

I couldn't find any words to answer her. I trudged up the stairs, drank my milk and went to bed. Needless to say I didn't sleep very well. I tossed and turned. I got up and stared out of the window, looking down at that archway I could just make out in the darkness. And when I did doze off it was to frightening dreams of Darcy, wearing a dressing gown, with a noose around his neck saying, "You have to save me, Georgie."

In the morning there was a buzz going around the apartment that the police had caught an intruder trying to break in.

"Shocking business," the major said, as he came to check on us at breakfast. "A burglar, I suppose. It's too bad my regiment doesn't guard this palace the way they do the king's residence. We'd have dealt with any nasty little crook in a way he'd never forget." He gave me a meaningful look and I could tell he was wondering whether the intruder could have anything to do with Bobo's murder.

"I'm afraid I have a fitting for my wedding dress today, Georgiana," Marina said. "Don't feel you have to come. I'm sorry you weren't feeling well last night. Those cocktails were awfully strong, weren't they?"

"It wasn't that," I said. "I bumped into an obnoxious young man and had to get away from him."

"Oh dear. A rejected suitor?"

"Something like that." I tried to smile. "But I do have some important errands to run, if you're sure you don't need me."

"Of course." She smiled. "And you don't need to come either, Traudi. Why don't you go to a museum or something? There is so much to see in London."

"Perhaps I will." The countess nodded. "I should like to see the exhibit with the large dinosaur bones. Most educational."

"That's the natural history museum," I said. "It's not too far from here. Perhaps Princess Marina's motorcar can drop you on the way to her fitting."

Irmtraut looked horrified. "Drop me? Onto the pavement?"

"I meant give you a lift."

"A lift? I do not wish to be raised up either."

Oh dear. This was so tiresome when my nerves were already in shreds.

"English expressions again," I said. "I meant her motor-car can take you to the museum and then continue on to the dress fitting. All right?"

"Ah," she said, nodding.

"Maybe we can go to a nightclub tonight, do you think?" Marina looked first at me and then at the major, who was hovering in the doorway, having not yet been dismissed from a royal presence. "Or a gambling club? I hear there are good ones in London and it is something I have done so seldom."

"Gambling is a sin," Irmtraut said.

"Nonsense. A little flutter never hurt anyone."

The major gave an embarrassed cough. "I'm afraid those places are outside my territory, Your Royal Highness. I don't frequent nightclubs. Not on an army officer's pay. And also the regiment is strict on our behavior code. Doesn't do to be seen drinking or gambling. So I can't say which establishment I'd advise."

"I know fashionable people go to Crockford's to gamble," I said. "But I think you have to be a member to get in. And my friend who knows about these places suggested Ciro's or El Morocco as a nightclub. Both have good floor shows."

"Let's do both!" Marina clapped her hands like a small child. "Or rather all three."

"But again my friend says that ladies don't usually go to nightclubs without an escort."

"The major can be our escort." Marina's eyes sparkled. "What do you say, Major? Your chance to live the glamorous life too, for one evening, and to keep us out of trouble."

"If that's what you'd like, Your Royal Highness," he said. "However, it should not be somewhere that could create a negative impression in the newspapers. Somewhere beyond reproach. I'll do a bit of fishing today."

"Ah. You go back to the pond to do fishing, Major." Irmtraut nodded with satisfaction. "I hope you get a good catch."

As I left the room I realized I had been laughing. It had been good to break the horrid tension, if only for a moment. And I had a busy day ahead of me with little time to think. That was good too.

"He can take care of himself," I told myself firmly as I laced up my walking shoes. "He will only have to get in touch with Sir Jeremy and someone will set DCI Pelham straight." But I still worried. You can't stop loving a person overnight.

Chapter 21

Darcy has been arrested. Serves him right. No, doesn't
serve him right. I don't want anything bad to
happen to him. I know he didn't have anything
to do with Bobo's death . . . don't I?

My first task for the morning was to visit Belinda. We needed
her tonight if we were to visit Crockford's. And I also wanted
to reassure myself that she was all right. I went straight to
her mews and hammered on the door, loudly enough to wake
the dead. A window opened opposite and an indignant
woman looked out, but there was no sign of life from Belinda's place. The feeling of dread rose inside me again. I fished
in my pocket and produced her key.

"Belinda?" I called as I shut the door behind me. The
house had a cold, abandoned feeling to it. "Belinda, it's me,
Georgie."

I went cautiously up the stairs, not knowing what I might
find. On other occasions I would have been scared of finding

a strange man asleep in her bed. Today I would have welcomed it. Her bedroom door was closed. I pushed it open, inch by inch. Her bed was made. Nobody in the room. Belinda was not at home. But her wardrobe was open and several hangers had nothing on them. Her slippers were not beside the bed. Also the robe with the feather trim was not hanging behind the door. What's more, her A to Z railway timetable was on the bedside table.

I stared, frowning. It appeared that she had taken a trip. But if she had known she was going away, why hadn't she told me? Why did she agree to come with me to show Marina around London? An impromptu trip then. Maybe summoned home by a family illness? I knew she was fond of her father, but loathed her stepmother. Maybe it was simpler than that. Maybe she had met a man at Crockford's who suggested a rendezvous in the New Forest or a few days in Paris. That sort of thing happened to Belinda. I gave a sigh of relief. I was worrying for nothing. She had gone away. She was quite all right. And wherever she had gone it was none of my business.

I came downstairs, let myself out and locked the door again. Then I set out for Mrs. Preston's flat. I headed behind Victoria Station, down Sloane Street and across the Pimlico Road, and eventually found Cambridge Street coming off Hugh. It was a narrow little road, not nearly as grand as it sounded, and 28 Cambridge Mansions was really just a flat in a dingy building with a stone staircase that smelled of dog. I was rather out of practice for long brisk walks and had to stand on the landing catching my breath before I tapped on her door. It was opened a few inches by a woman with curlers in her hair. A small hairy dog yapped at her feet. Not a person I would immediately have chosen to clean my house if I ever owned one.

"Mrs. Preston?" I asked.

"Who wants to know?" she demanded.

"I'm a friend of Miss Carrington." I gave her a warm smile. "Can I come in for a minute? It's awfully cold out here."

"If you must." She opened the door and led me into a

threadbare sitting room, which was almost as cold as the landing had been. She nodded to a chair by an unlit fire. "I always sit in the kitchen myself," she said. "And I'm out during the day usually so there ain't no point in wasting coke."

She was a skinny, birdlike woman with sharp features and quick movements and she was still standing with hands on hips, watching me with suspicious dark eyes.

"I'm sorry to be barging in on you like this," I said. "And I feel rather awkward about doing it, but I've been sent to collect the key to Miss Carrington's flat. They said you still had one."

"They don't trust me no more?" she demanded. "Me, what's been doing for her for years now?"

"I'm sure Miss Carrington trusts you completely," I said hastily. "But you know what building managers are like. Always think the worst, don't they?"

"I suppose they do, ruddy lot," she muttered. "So she don't want me to clean no more, is that it?"

"I'm afraid Miss Carrington isn't going to be living there any longer," I said. "I don't know the details. It's all rather rushed and confused, but I suspect she may be moving abroad."

"I'm not surprised," she said. "She sails too close to the wind, if you ask me."

"Does she?" I sounded surprised. "In what way?"

"I thought you was a friend of hers." The suspicious look had returned.

"I live in the country," I said. "I usually only meet her at house parties and the like. She's a lot of fun, but I can't say I really know her terribly well. But then who does?"

"A lot of gentlemen, if you ask me." She sniffed. "Too many gentlemen. She's not choosy enough. I told her she'd get in trouble one day, and it's my belief that she did. Of course, she never told me nothing, but I've had seven children and I know what the signs are when someone is in the family way. She said she was going to the Continent, but I says to myself, 'Rubbish. She's going to have that baby somewhere private.'"

"That's what I suspected too," I said. "I didn't like to mention it, but now that you have . . . did she ever tell you who the father was?"

Mrs. Preston's gaze became really guarded now. "What are you, one of them newspaper reporters, trying to be all matey-like and worming information out of me?"

"Of course not!" I gave her an indignant stare. "I'm a concerned friend, that's all. I promise you I would never divulge any of this to the newspapers."

"Well, there's no point in asking, 'cos I don't know. She paid me well to keep me mouth shut," she said. "When I let meself in in the morning and there was a strange man's head on the pillow I went about me work and didn't see nothing. And I never noticed him slipping out via the service lift either."

"Oh, there's a service lift." I nodded. "I thought it would be strange for you to carry up your mops and pails through that very posh foyer."

She laughed. "Yeah, that would have got me some stares, wouldn't it? No, love, there's a service entrance round the back for the likes of us, *and* for gentlemen who want to slip out without being recognized. I can tell you one who was scared silly when I spotted him. 'Don't worry, sir,' I said. 'My lips is sealed.'"

"You're talking about a royal person?"

"Oh no. Nobody like that." She gave me a knowing wink.

"So tell me, Mrs. Preston," I said, "did you do everything for Miss Carrington? She didn't have a maid?"

"Well, she used to, didn't she? Quite fond of her, she was. They'd been together for some time and then out of the blue she goes and sacks her. Just like that. I was quite surprised and she never told me why. I can't say I was pleased either. More work for me because she's not the neatest of young ladies. She'd have that place like a pigsty if I wasn't there." A sad look came over her face. "So I suppose I'm going to be looking for work now. That's not a nice thing to face with winter coming on."

I immediately thought of Belinda. Mrs. Preston had had great experience at being discreet.

"I might know somebody who would need your services, Mrs. Preston," I said. "Not too far away, in Knightsbridge."

"Well, thank you kindly, miss," she said. "That's good of you. And I'm forgetting my manners. Would you like a cup of tea? The kettle's always on."

"Kind of you, but I have to be on my way," I said. "If I could just have those keys?"

"Oh yes. I'll fetch them for you." She bobbed out into the kitchen, reminding me of a Cockney sparrow. I had stood up when she returned.

"Thank you so much," I said. "I'll return them to Frederick and they'll let you know if they want you to go back and clean up the place after she's moved out."

"Right you are, miss," she said.

"And I'll speak to my friend about you right away," I said.

"Good of you, miss. You're a real toff," she said.

I felt awkward and had a bad taste in my mouth as I came out into the street. I had, after all, tricked her out of her keys. But then she would no longer have a job looking after Bobo Carrington, would she? And someone else would have asked for the return of the keys, less politely than I had done. And I might have a new job for her too. Thus reassured, I went around the back of the station to Buckingham Palace Road and hopped on a bus going up to Park Lane. It wasn't that I was too tired to walk. Nobody who has grown up in the Scottish Highlands, walking miles through the heather, would find it daunting to walk in London, but time was now of the essence and I wanted to cram as much as possible into my free morning.

This time I did not present myself to Frederick at the front entrance to Bobo's building. Instead I went skulking around until I found an alley leading past the dustbins to a back way in. What's more, the outer door opened without a key and I found myself in a narrow, dark hallway, facing a small service lift. Up I went and let myself into Bobo's flat without anybody seeing me. I was feeling rather proud of myself. I was going to take my gloves off, but then decided I should leave no fingerprints. I went through the sitting room, finding nothing. In the bathroom I found a syringe and what must have been some kind of drug. But then, the police knew about her habit. I expected they'd found out by now who supplied it to her. I hoped so, as that was certainly something I didn't want to look into. Dealing with drug gangs was out of my league.

I'd managed to put Darcy from my mind until I went through into the bedroom. There was that dressing gown hanging behind the door, thick navy blue wool with his initials on it. And my insides clenched themselves into knots again. Had he been visiting her all the time he'd professed he loved me? And then the second thought—had he gone to her because I had refused to sleep with him? I didn't know whether to be glad the police were now grilling him and giving him an unpleasant time, or frightened that they might really try to pin this murder on him.

I turned my back on that door and forced him out of my mind. I had to work quickly and thoroughly. There was a small modern writing desk by the window. I went through it but it contained nothing revealing. No checkbook. No personal letters. Of course the police had probably taken them away. It was silly of me really to think I could find anything of value here. I was about to walk away from the desk when I noticed the blotter. It hadn't been changed and there was the faintest imprint of writing on it. I lifted it up and carried it over to the mirror. Holding it up, I read with some difficulty:

Mary Boyle, 14 Edward Street, Deptford, London

I wasn't familiar with all parts of London but I was fairly sure that Deptford was not one of the more fashionable parts. Somewhere south of the river Thames, I thought. And I wondered who Bobo would be writing to there. The last letter she had written, presumably, unless the police had removed more recent sheets of blotting paper. Mary Boyle sounded like an Irish name to me and it occurred to me that this might be her former maid, of whom she had seemed to be fond. I wondered if she had dismissed her when she discovered she was pregnant, not wanting anyone close to her at such a time. Or maybe the Irish maid had left her when she threatened to get an abortion . . . and Bobo had written to her to tell her she had changed her mind and was going to have the child. This was all complete supposition. It could equally have been her dressmaker to whom she was sending a check. But it was all worth thinking about.

I copied down the address with a sheet of Bobo's own writing paper. Then there didn't seem anything more to be done. I knew I should get out of Bobo's flat while the going was good. As I was crossing the floor, stepping over Bobo's various piles of discarded clothing, I somehow put my hand through the strap of a brassiere that she had left hanging from her bedpost. I should I have realized that I had been accident free for longer than usual and that disaster was looming. I was jerked off balance, tripped over a dress on the floor and found myself careening across the room. The wall came rushing up to meet me, with one of Bobo's large and rather tasteless paintings directly in my path. The last thing I wanted was to put my hand through the canvas, so I grabbed at the frame. The painting fell. I tried to hold on to it, but I was still off balance and it was heavy. It slipped through my fingers and landed on the floor with an almighty thud.

"Bugger," I muttered, looking around guiltily just in case anyone had heard such an unladylike outburst. I picked it up and was relieved to see it was more or less intact. When I went to lift it, to put it back in place, I saw why Bobo had chosen to hang it here, on a wall of her bedroom where it could not properly be admired and got no real light. There was a safe behind it. With trembling fingers I tried to open it. Of course the wheels turned on the dial but it remained firmly shut. No wonder she had nothing of interest in her desk, I thought. It was all in here, and it looked very much as if the police had not yet discovered it. Now all I had to do was find a way to open it.

I had no idea where to find someone who knew how to

open a safe, but I knew someone who might. I made my way to Green Park tube station as quickly as possible and soon was heading out of town to Essex and my grandfather.

"You want a what?" he asked me after he had seated me in his warm little kitchen.

"I wondered if you knew how to open a safe."

"Blimey, ducks. You haven't taken up burglary now as a hobby, have you?" He didn't know whether to laugh or be shocked.

"No, but I'm helping the authorities in an investigation I can't tell you about, and I've just discovered a safe in someone's bedroom. So I thought if you knew how to open it . . ." I let the rest of the sentence hang.

He laughed, a trifle nervously. "My job was apprehending criminals, love. Not joining them. But come to think of it I might know someone who can help us. Willie Lightfingers Buxton. He was reputed to be the best there was. And I know he's out of the Scrubs."

"The Scrubs?"

"Wormwood Scrubs. Clink. Prison."

I wasn't sure I wanted to extend my investigation to include convicted felons.

"A convict, Granddad? I'm not sure . . ."

"Salt of the earth, old Willie. One of the old-style cons. Looked upon safecracking as his profession, just the way a surgeon looks at his. No, you'd be all right with old Willie— if he'll do it. He's as old as me and retired and has no wish to go back to the Scrubs again."

"Would you ask him anyway? I'm not planning to steal anything, just look at the contents and then shut it up again. And I do have the permission of someone really senior in the Home Office."

"I suppose I could do that for you. Where do I send him when I find him?"

Oh golly. "You probably shouldn't send him to Kensington

Palace," I said. "I don't think the royals would approve. We'll arrange where to meet when you've contacted him."

"Bob's yer uncle, ducks," he said. He was looking at me with his head to one side. "You're not doing anything dangerous, are you? Not involved in any kind of funny business?"

"No, it's not dangerous, Granddad. More trying to avoid a scandal," I said. "I'm afraid I can't give you any details. I'm sworn to silence."

"You watch yourself, my girl," he said. "You're too fond of dabbling where you shouldn't. I remember when you almost got yourself killed up on Dartmoor by poking your nose in something that should have been left to the police."

"But I found the murderer, didn't I? They didn't."

"I'd rather you stayed safe and sound," he said. "The sooner you marry that young man of yours and have some little nippers, the better, if you ask me."

"Oh, Granddad." My voice cracked and I was horribly afraid I was going to cry. "I don't think I'll be marrying Darcy after all."

"Why not?"

"I don't want to share him with other women. I want someone who loves me and me only."

He put a wizened old hand over mine. "Lots of young men, especially your sort, sow their wild oats before they marry. I suspect your Darcy is a decent bloke and once you're married he'll do the right thing."

"But what if he doesn't?" I was crying now. "What if I never know where he is or who he's been with?"

"It all comes down to trust. If you can't trust someone, then there's no basis for a marriage. Simple as that. You have to decide."

"That's just it," I said. "I don't think I can trust him anymore."

"Do you want to tell me about it?" he asked gently.

I shook my head. "I'm sorry, but I can't tell you. I can't tell anyone." I attempted to get up. "I should leave. Go now. The princess is expecting me."

He laid a firm hand on my shoulder. "It's dinnertime. Now, how about a nice bowl of stew to warm you up before you dash off again. I've just made a corker with a lamb bone from Sunday's joint. Lots of good carrots and parsnips and haricot beans."

I nodded weakly. "Thank you. Yes. That might be a good idea. And it does smell heavenly."

He ladled out a generous bowl and sat there watching me eat. Again I found myself wishing that I could live with him all the time and have him take care of me. And I could forget all about royal scandals and unfaithful men and be quite happy. But I knew that I couldn't.

Chapter 22

Life just gets more and more complicated.

I arrived back at Kensington Palace just as it was starting to rain—the hard, stinging kind of winter rain that makes walking so miserable. I was about to open the front door, anticipating a roaring fire and tea to follow when I was conscious of footsteps behind me. I turned to see a large bobby coming toward me.

"Lady Georgiana?" he asked. "DCI Pelham has requested that you come with me. He'd like to speak with you again."

"Oh really, this is too silly," I said. "I've nothing more to tell him."

"I couldn't say what it's about, my lady," he said. "I was just sent to fetch you, and I've been waiting quite some time."

"I didn't realize that I had to ask permission before I left the palace," I said testily. Actually I wasn't feeling annoyed but scared. Had they found out somehow that I had gone to Bobo's flat this morning? Perhaps someone had heard that picture crashing down and called the police. And, more worrisome still, perhaps they wanted to trap me into saying something incriminating about Darcy.

I decided that haughty indignation was my best defense, so I strode down the corridors at Scotland Yard so fast that the young constable had trouble keeping up with me. I was shown into DCI Pelham's office and approached his desk with the same belligerence as my ancestor Robert Bruce Rannoch had displayed going into battle.

"Really, this is too tiresome, Chief Inspector," I said. "What can you possibly need from me now? I thought I made it clear that I'd tell you if I came up with anything you should know about."

His eyes were focused on me like a snake's, unblinking.

"Take a seat, Lady Georgiana."

I sat. He leaned back in his big leather chair and folded his arms, never taking his eyes off me for an instant.

"I called you back here because I don't think you did quite tell me everything when we chatted last time. You kept some interesting snippets of information from me, didn't you?"

"Such as what?"

His expression didn't change. "You and Mr. O'Mara, for example. Not just a friend, is he?"

"My relationship with Mr. O'Mara has nothing to do with you," I said, keeping my haughty stare rather well, I thought.

"Oh, but I think it's most important," he said. "Most pertinent to this case."

"That's ridiculous. In what way?"

He leaned back in his chair. "A motive for killing Miss Carrington, perhaps?"

"A motive? Whose motive?"

"Yours, Lady Georgiana. Jealousy is the strongest motive I've ever come across. That and fear."

"And who is supposed to be jealous of whom?"

"You were jealous of Mr. O'Mara's relationship with Miss Carrington, obviously."

"Since I didn't find out about it until after she was dead, I would say it's hardly relevant," I said.

"That's your word."

"Surely you can't think I had anything to do with Miss Carrington's death?" The laugh sounded a trifle uneasy.

He leaned forward again now, hoping to be intimidating, I suspected. "That's exactly what I might be thinking. But the one thing I'm not sure of—was it you alone, luring her to the palace in a fit of jealousy, or had Mr. O'Mara found that he needed to get her out of the way and you helped him to do it? Because, you see, he has an alibi for the whole evening she was killed."

This time I did chuckle. "Oh, and I didn't? I think dinner at Buckingham Palace with the entire royal family is a pretty watertight alibi."

"We're not sure exactly when she was killed," he said. "It could have been earlier in the evening, given the bitter cold out there. And you were seen, you see."

"I was what?" I looked up, startled. "I was seen where?"

"In the courtyard where the body was found."

I gave another chuckle, this time of relief. "Of course I was seen. I believe I told you how I saw something and went to investigate and discovered the body lying there."

"That was when you returned from dinner, and actually I've been puzzled about your statement. It didn't make sense at the time that you thought you saw something—because from the front of the house there is no possible way you could see anything under that arch."

"I told you—I saw a glowing sort of light."

"We checked. There is no light source under that arch, or in that courtyard, apart from a couple of windows. And the time you were seen was before you went to dinner."

"Before?" I shook my head. "But I wasn't in that courtyard before we left. I came straight out with Princess Marina and got into the car. It was still raining. A footman held an umbrella over us." I glared at him. "Who says they saw me?"

"The foreign lady. The countess. Sir Jeremy had a little talk with her today because you had told him you suspected her because her coat was wet. And the interesting thing was that she claimed she had seen *you* in the courtyard, prowling around, right before you went to dinner."

"How utterly absurd," I said. "I never went near the courtyard. What does she think she's playing at? And how did she explain away her wet jacket?"

"She says she went out later. She said the food was so bad that she decided to walk down to the town and have something to eat in a café. But she said that nothing was open except pubs because it was Sunday evening, and she wasn't about to go into a common public house."

"That's interesting," I said, "because she told me that she had spent the evening in, reading. And did she explain the knife in her pocket?"

"Miss Carrington was not stabbed, Lady Georgiana. She was drugged and then suffocated. If anyone carries a knife, it seems to be irrelevant." He gave an annoying half sniff, half snort through his nostrils. "And what possible motive could a foreign lady have for killing an Englishwoman she had never met?"

"The perfect motive, Chief Inspector," I said. "She worships Princess Marina. She would do anything to protect her, and if she'd learned that Bobo Carrington had been Prince George's mistress and that he may be the father of her child, she would stop at nothing to prevent that news from becoming public."

He was staring at me as if he was digesting this information and it was beginning to make sense.

"And she was alone all evening with servants who aren't the most attentive and who would have been having their own evening meal in a kitchen where they would not have heard or seen anything."

Again I paused, letting him consider this.

I leaned forward in my chair. "Picture this, Chief Inspector. Bobo comes to the front door, demanding to see Princess Marina. Perhaps she has decided to come clean and tell Marina the truth about her and the prince. Perhaps her motive is not as pure and she wants money to stay mum about her story. But Princess Marina is not home so she tells the countess instead. And the countess decides she must not be allowed to leave. She puts Marina's sleeping drops in the coffee and then finishes Bobo off by suffocating her." I paused, then went on, "And she has all the time in the world because the servants find her disagreeable and are keeping well away."

There was a long moment of silence, punctuated only by the loud tick of his clock on the wall. Then he nodded. "As you say, it does make sense."

"While I, on the other hand, possess no Veronal and only discovered that Princess Marina uses it when the subject came up in conversation yesterday. So you have the motive, the knowledge of where to find Veronal *and* a wet jacket. I'd say that adds up to something pretty compelling. And—" I paused again. Really, I should have become a barrister. I was rather pleased with myself. "She is so rattled that you are getting near to the truth that she tries to claim she saw me in the courtyard. She is jealous of me, Chief Inspector, because I have been assigned to be the princess's companion. And as you just said, jealousy is the most compelling of motives."

Another long pause. "You do make a good case, Lady Georgiana," he said grudgingly. "And I have to admit that it seems most likely that Miss Carrington was killed after your departure for Buckingham Palace."

"And actually my maid was helping me to dress until I went down to join Princess Marina," I said. "I don't believe there was a moment when I was alone, which I'm sure the others can verify."

"Which still leaves us with Mr. O'Mara," he said. "Given his close ties to the murdered girl and the fact that he has been so devilishly hard to find. Almost as if he'd gone into hiding."

"Mr. O'Mara is always hard to find," I said. "He has no London address. He never has a forwarding address. But I'm sure you can ask Sir Jeremy. He knows more about Mr. O'Mara than I do, apparently." I stood up. "And if there is nothing else, I take it I have your permission to go now?"

"Yes, I see no reason to detain you further at this stage," he said. "After all, we know where to find you until the wedding, don't we? And if the countess divulges anything else that might be of interest to us, you will let us know, won't you?"

I laughed. "One minute I'm the prime suspect, the next I'm working undercover for the police."

It was his turn to give an uneasy chuckle. "Oh, I wouldn't go as far as prime suspect, Lady Georgiana. You were just helping us with our inquiries." He paused as I stood up. "We may need to chat again at some stage. I suspect you know more than you're saying about this Mr. O'Mara. He's definitely not off the hook yet. I think he's a bit of a slippery customer. No known means of income but he lives well enough, moves in the right circles. When we start probing a bit deeper I think it may come out that he has connections to the underworld, possibly drug trafficking. So if you want my advice, I'd say you were well rid of him, Lady Georgiana."

I wanted to tell him that I wouldn't want his advice if he was the last person on the planet, but I didn't dare open my mouth, afraid I'd let myself down. There was no way I was going to let the obnoxious chief inspector know how much Darcy had meant to me. This time I did not stride out ahead of my escorting policeman. I stumbled blindly behind him because I had realized that DCI Pelham had said something that made sense. Links to the underworld, possible drug trafficking. So that was how Darcy managed to survive. That was how Darcy was so thick with Bobo Carrington—the girl with the silver syringe. That was why he popped off so frequently to South America. He was involved in the buying and selling of drugs.

I felt physically sick. My mother and Belinda were always telling me how naïve I was. And it was true. Brought up sheltered in the wilds of Scotland, how could I possibly know how to be aware of things like drugs? It seemed that Darcy had deceived me on every possible level. Perhaps he even had killed Bobo Carrington because she was becoming a nuisance or had threatened to tell the police about his activities. As DCI Pelham had said, I was well out of it. A lucky escape. I could have been married to a dangerous criminal—a dangerous criminal who would be unfaithful to me and break my heart. I would do as Fig had suggested and try to meet a suitable member of European royalty at the wedding. Then I would live as my family expected me to, doing the right thing, producing the heir . . . but with a great empty hole in my heart.

Chapter 23

NOVEMBER 7

**Going to a gambling club this evening. Any other time I
would have been excited.**

I was not conscious of being driven home. I wanted to creep
straight up to my room, but as I came into Kensington Palace
the door to the sitting room was open and Marina and the
countess were having tea.

"Lovely hot crumpets," Marina called, waving at me.
"Come and get warm. It's horribly cold today, isn't it?"

So of course I had no option but to join them. I saw
Irmtraut studying me with a smug look on her face.

"Ah, you return at last, Georgiana. Her Highness wondered where you had gone. I hope you have had a pleasant
day?" she said.

"About as pleasant as yours, I should think," I said.

"Mine has been disagreeable," she said. "Somebody in
this place has been spying on me. What do you think of
that? And saying bad things about me."

"Surely not." I leaned over and poured myself a cup of tea.

"Then why did that man wish to talk to me? He is part of your English police, I am sure of this. Do they think I have committed a crime? He would not tell me why he asks me stupid questions."

"The English police are known to be fair. The innocent have nothing to worry about in this country," I said. "I'm sure the questions were only routine. The police are naturally concerned for Marina's safety." I managed a bright smile.

As I drank my tea I studied her. Did she look worried? Was she more uneasy than usual? With her normal grumpy glare I couldn't tell. But at least her plan to implicate me had backfired. That must have irked her.

We had an early dinner, then the major arrived to escort us to Crockford's.

"I had a word with them today, Your Highness," he said, "and they will be honored to waive their requirement that you must be the guest of a member. They look forward to your visit."

"How kind." Marina nodded graciously.

"But if you don't mind, I will not come with you tonight," he said. "The manager will be waiting for you and will make sure you are well looked after all evening. And frankly I would rather not be seen at a gambling club right now. I understand that I may be up for promotion to colonel and I don't want to do anything that could be perceived as unsoldierly." He gave an apologetic little smile.

He had dressed for dinner, of course. I couldn't help thinking how smart he looked in civilian white tie and tails, rather than his army dress uniform. A good catch for some girl. But then I remembered that he had lamented trying to live on army pay. So not such a good catch. Probably a younger son who wasn't going to inherit anything. They were the ones who were always sent into the army.

He ushered us into the motorcar and off we went. I have to confess I felt a thrill of anticipation as the car pulled up outside the white portico of the club on Curzon Street. It was the sort of place I had looked at wistfully from the outside and had only sneaked into once, when I was spying on someone. So I had never actually had the experience of gambling there, as a patron. And now I was being welcomed graciously in the presence of a princess. If I hadn't been so enveloped in misery, I should have savored this moment.

"Your Royal Highness, welcome to Crockford's." The manager, looking rather regal himself, came forward to meet us. "And Lady Georgiana. Such an honor." He gave us a warm smile and a bow before he ushered us across that grand foyer with its red carpet and chandeliers. "If you will be good enough to sign our book, please." He stopped at a table with the open book and pen on it. When it was my turn to sign I noticed that people signed with their name and address. And I remembered Belinda telling me that Bobo had been seen looking distressed as she spoke with an American at Crockford's.

"Someone told me that they had seen an American friend of mine here a few days ago," I said. "I didn't even know he was in the country. May I look and see if it really was he, and where he's staying?"

"I'm afraid not, my lady." The manager sounded shocked. "Our guest book is completely confidential. It wouldn't do to let wives check on wayward husbands, would it?" And he gave a little chuckle.

"You wouldn't happen to remember if an American gentleman was here, probably last week?"

"Again our rules of confidentiality don't allow me to reveal that, even if I knew," he said. "We get American visitors all the time, of course. Crockford's is one of the places one has to go when one is a visitor to London."

"Of course," I said and retreated with my most gracious smile.

He turned his attention to Princess Marina. "Let me give you a tour of what we have to offer and then I have arranged for some jetons to start you off, with our compliments."

We entered the main gambling salon, with its sparkling chandeliers overhead and knots of men and women clustered around roulette and card tables. We were then taken to the cashier's booth and handed a nice little stack of tokens, called in casinos by their French name of jetons—because one throws them onto the table, presumably.

"Now, feel free to try your hand at any table you choose," the manager said. "May I have a bottle of champagne opened for you?"

"Most kind," Marina said again. Actually she looked as much out of her depth as I felt as I gazed at the impossibly elegant and sophisticated men and women languidly placing piles of jetons on the roulette table. These were people to whom the loss of a hundred pounds meant nothing. I supposed my father must have been just like them. I never really got to know him well, because he spent his time in Nice and Monte Carlo and lost most of the family fortune at the tables. Luckily I had inherited the sensible side of my ancestors and was determined to make my free tokens last all evening. I was also determined to get a look at that guest book.

"What shall we play first, Georgiana?" Marina asked.

"I think most people play roulette," I said. "And it's not complicated."

"I tried it once in Monte," she said. "It's rather fun, isn't it?"

I glanced over my shoulder. I had a funny feeling that I was being observed. But then, of course there is always someone observing in a casino, to make sure that no cheating goes on. I turned back to the table and placed my bet on number six, which I've always liked for some reason. The wheel started to spin. The little ball clattered down until it fell into a slot.

"Six," the croupier called, pronouncing it in the French way, and pushed a stack of tokens toward me.

"Well done," Marina said.

"Beginner's luck." I blushed.

Glasses of champagne were brought to us.

"It's warm in here," Marina said, shifting her mink wrap to her arm.

"Would you like me to hang up our wraps in the cloak-room?" I asked.

"Good idea. Thank you." She handed hers to me. One of the employees sprang into action. "Here, let me take those for you, my lady."

"It's quite all right," I said. "I need to powder my nose anyway." And I carried the wraps out of the room, back into the foyer. The manager was nowhere to be seen, but there was a man in a rather splendid uniform waiting by the front door. He was facing outward, not toward me. I let my wrap fall over the guest book, then swept it up and walked swiftly into the ladies' room. Of course there was an attendant so I had to flee into one of the stalls before I looked at the book. About a week ago, it must have been. I leafed through the pages until I spotted Belinda's name. And Bobo Carrington's. And, a few lines above, one J. Walter Oppenheimer of Philadelphia, guest of Sir Toby Blenchley.

So Sir Toby had been there that evening, as well as this Mr. Oppenheimer, who had somehow upset Bobo. Then I glanced down the rest of the page and saw another signature— bold and black. Hon. Darcy O'Mara. Kilhenny Castle. Ireland. So Belinda *had* been going to tell me that she'd seen Darcy and Bobo together. I hurried out of the cloakroom and deposited the book back on the table without being seen.

J. Walter Oppenheimer, guest of Sir Toby, I muttered to myself, making sure I remembered the name. Right. Concentrate, Georgie. You are now going to go in there and have a good time. I came into the gaming room with my head held high and joined Marina at the table.

"Look, I've won ten pounds." Marina beamed at me. "Isn't this fun?"

I took a glass of champagne and put a pile of jetons on the board without actually bothering where. The wheel was spun again.

"*Trente-deux*," the croupier called out in French and pushed a considerable number of tokens in my direction.

"Georgiana, you are so lucky," Marina exclaimed.

"Oh yes," I said. "So lucky." And I turned away so that she couldn't see the bleak despair on my face.

It was a night of irony. I won quite consistently. The pile kept growing. Strange men hovered around me, encouraging and congratulating. It should have been a heady experience to be the life of the party at Crockford's.

"Why haven't we seen you here before, you gorgeous creature?" a smooth young man said to me.

"You're Binky's sister?" another asked. "We had no idea Binky had such a divine sister. Has he been hiding you away? You have to come to a hunt ball with us next weekend. The Bedfords are giving it."

"I'm afraid I'm helping to look after Princess Marina until her wedding," I said.

"Oh yes. The wedding. I'd forgotten that. So old George is finally getting hitched. What a riot, eh, Monty?" And the two men laughed.

"Can we take you in to supper?" one of them asked. "They do a slap-up good meal here."

"Thank you. I think I've pushed my luck enough for one night," I said. "But I think I'd better go and cash these in first."

"We'll help you." My two new suitors picked up my tokens and carried them for me to the cashier.

"Would you please keep my winnings for me until I'm ready to go?" I asked. "I'm about to have supper and I've nowhere to put money in this purse."

"Of course, my lady." His face betrayed no reaction at all.

"I should check on Princess Marina," I said. "I shouldn't leave her alone." I was trying to think of a way to have her asked to supper too, but one of them beat me to it.

"Ask her to supper too, eh, Monty?"

"Oh rather," Monty agreed. "Old George would want us to take care of his intended." And they both grinned as if this was a good joke. I suspected they had seen George at Crockford's with many different partners over the years, and I rather wished that I had had more time to examine that guest book and see exactly whose name had appeared next to his.

I went in search of the princess, who was now playing vingt-et-un, and told her we'd been invited to supper by two young men.

"How terribly sweet of them." She stood up from the table. "Frankly, I think I've tired of gambling for tonight. I don't seem to be winning recently. And supper with two nice young men does sound like fun. It might make George jealous."

Our escorts were waiting and introduced themselves formally as Monty and Whiffie. We never did find out what Whiffie's real name was but we had a merry supper. I could see why Belinda liked it here. It was a world of fantasy. And I realized I had two habitués at my fingertips, who knew the club well.

"Did you happen to meet an American man who came here with Sir Toby last week?" I asked.

"With Sir Toby? Tall, serious sort of chap, wasn't he?" Monty frowned, trying to picture him. "Didn't seem to be having fun at all."

"I heard he had some sort of argument with Bobo Carrington," I said.

"You're right, Bobo was here that evening. But I didn't see any kind of confrontation. She was only here briefly. Actually we hadn't seen her in ages, had we, Whiffie, old thing?"

"That's right," Whiffie replied. "We commented on the fact. Someone said, 'Bobo's come back into circulation, I notice,' and we had a bet as to who she'd make a beeline for. But next time we looked around, she'd gone again."

"And the American man too?"

"No, I think he stayed on. At least, Sir Toby did."

"So you haven't seen Bobo with anyone else recently?"

"Haven't seen her at all. She must have been on the Continent."

"Sir Toby went to America. Perhaps she tagged along," Whiffie said. "I know his wife stayed home." They exchanged another grin.

"Sir Toby? Was Bobo involved with him?"

"So rumor had it. Of course he was always very careful in public. Got an image to live up to, what?" The two men laughed.

"Sir Toby Blenchley?" Marina asked. "Is he not a member of Parliament here?"

"Cabinet minister, old thing—I mean, Your Highness."

Marina looked around the room, where various couples

sat together at tables. "I suppose powerful men do not always behave as they should," she said thoughtfully. I wondered if she was wondering about rumors she had heard of her future husband. Irmtraut had definitely heard them and might have spilled the beans.

Our table companions also picked up her troubled look. "Well, it's one thing to play the field before marriage," one of them said, "but when one is a cabinet minister, I mean, dash it all . . ."

I digested this new fact. Sir Toby Blenchley, he who preached the sanctity of the family, had had Bobo Carrington as his mistress. Who had more to lose than he if this fact became known?

Monty and Whiffie were good company and we laughed a lot over oysters and smoked salmon and soufflés. It was getting late by the time they brought our coffees. I tried to stifle a yawn, but Marina saw it. "We should be going," she said. "I have a busy day tomorrow. Another fitting for my dress, and then I'm meeting my parents off the boat train."

"Your parents are arriving? Where will they be staying?"

"They were invited to stay at Buckingham Palace with the king and queen, but they wanted something a little less formal, so they've opted for the Dorchester instead."

I tried to picture a life in which the Dorchester counted as less formal. I smiled. "How lovely for you to have them here."

"I'm not so sure. Mummy and my sisters will want to come shopping with me and I rather enjoy our adventures alone, don't you?"

"Yes, I do, but I think it's a mother's prerogative to help her daughter choose her trousseau."

She nodded. "I suppose so. But we'll still make time for evenings out without them. This was fun tonight." She beamed at our escorts. "Thank you both. I'm rather sad, now, that I'm getting married with such delightful company in London."

The two boys had the grace to blush. We got up to leave. Whiffie and Monty escorted us into the foyer and sent for our car.

"So you've promised we can see you again as soon as this blasted wedding business is over," Monty said to me. "You will come to a hunt ball?"

"That will be nice," I replied as he put my wrap around my shoulders.

The manager appeared. "Thank you so much for gracing us with your presence, Your Royal Highness," he said, bowing unctuously. "Allow me to escort you to your car." He ushered her out of the front door. I was about to follow when an employee tapped me on the shoulder. "I was told to remind you to collect your winnings, Lady Georgiana. They are being held for you. Please follow me."

My winnings, of course. How silly of me. It just shows what too much champagne and brandy can do to the brain. I was escorted across the gaming room.

"I was told that they were being held for you in here," he said and opened a door for me. I stepped into one of the small private gaming rooms with a baize table in its center. While I was taking this in, and looking for where my winnings might be, I heard the click of a latch as the door was closed behind me.

I spun around. Darcy was standing in front of the door.

Chapter 24

"What are you doing here?" I demanded angrily. "I thought you'd be in a dungeon in the Tower of London by now."

He grinned. "I might say the same for you."

"It was quite obvious I had done nothing wrong," I said haughtily. "Now please open this door immediately. Princess Marina is waiting for me."

He put a restraining hand on my shoulder. "The princess has been sent home without you. She has been told you have met an old friend and will be following in a separate car."

"You had no right to do this!" I tried to get past him to the door handle. "Now let me out of here or I'll scream the place down."

"I don't think you'd want to cause any unpleasantness," he said. "Think of the scandal. Your family wouldn't approve."

"This is kidnapping," I said. "I'll report you to DCI Pelham. He can add it to your other crimes."

"I rather think not." Darcy smiled now. "In fact I've been asked to keep an eye on you."

"DCI Pelham thinks you're a slippery customer. He told me so."

"DCI Pelham doesn't know very much. Luckily someone high up in the Home Office came to my rescue and had me released, or I'd still be in a cell. I couldn't tell Pelham exactly what I was doing, you see."

"With Bobo Carrington? I should think that was rather obvious."

He actually laughed then. "You are adorable, Georgie. Do you know that?"

"No. I'm naïve and stupid," I said. "I know nothing about drugs or people like Bobo Carrington. But it doesn't matter anymore. I'm going to do my duty and marry a young man of impeccable background and forget all about you."

"Georgie," he said softly. "When you asked me if I'd slept with Bobo Carrington, I was caught off guard. I did sleep with her, but that was several years ago. Long before I met you."

"Several years ago, or one year ago?" I demanded.

He shook his head. "No, I am not the father of her child, if that's what you're wondering. I believe we slept together a couple of times when I was newly arrived in London. The way one does."

The way one does. Those words rattled around in my head. How easy it seemed to be for other people. "But your dressing gown. I saw it behind her door."

"That's actually quite simply explained," he said.

"Really?" I gave him my best sarcastic look.

He nodded. "I need somewhere to stay when I'm in London. Bobo lets me use her flat sometimes, when she's out of town. I left my dressing gown behind once. She said it was cozier than hers and she was keeping it in payment for using the flat."

"Oh," I said. I couldn't think of anything else to say. Part of me was thinking that this was highly plausible and part was reminding me that Darcy was Irish and had the gift of the gab. I wanted to believe him. I was trying to believe him. "So you are trying to tell me that you haven't been near her recently?"

"I haven't been near her recently, at least not in the way you mean."

"But you were seen at Crockford's with her."

"Ah. That's true. We did bump into each other at Crockford's."

I turned to look at him, noticing that his eyes were smiling and he was so devilishly handsome. But I was going to be strong this time. I would not be swayed by Irish charm and good looks. "And the DCI thinks you're involved in drugs and the underworld. What have you got to say about that?"

"Well, he's not wrong," he said.

"Aha. I knew it. And he suspects Bobo's death might be tied to her drug use and to her dealings with drug suppliers."

"Actually I have been involved," he said. "But not in the way you think. This is to go no further, Georgie, but I've been shadowing people like Bobo because I was assigned to find the kingpin. We know who the small dealers are, but we are still not sure how cocaine is getting into this country in such large quantities."

"Oh," I said. "And you suspect that Bobo might have had something to do with it?"

"Possibly," he said. "She certainly seemed to have an apparently inexhaustible supply of cash, even when she was not with a particular man. It had to come from somewhere. I was hoping to get back into her confidence, when she was killed."

"So someone killed her to prevent her from giving away secrets to you?"

"I don't know. The timing was rather coincidental, don't you think?"

There was a long pause. I still wasn't ready to forgive him completely. "So how do you think I feel, knowing that you were in London and you didn't try to contact me, but you were going to clubs with people like Bobo Carrington?" I said. "Or am I too dull for such outings?"

"Contact you?" His voice was sharp now too. "My dear girl, as soon as I returned to England I wrote to Castle

Rannoch, asking them to forward the letter. I telephoned several times and each time I was told by your infuriating butler that Lady Georgiana was not in residence and they did not know where she was or when she would be returning home. Then I went to your London house and was told the same thing."

"Probably Fig being poisonous," I said. "But then partly my fault. I really didn't let them know where I was staying when I came back to England."

"With your mother, I presume?"

"No, I was using Belinda's mews cottage until she returned and turfed me out. Then fortunately I was invited to Kensington Palace."

"Quite a step up in the world," he said. He paused, eyeing me critically. "You look washed out. I'll get us a taxicab. If you'll permit me to escort you home, that is?"

I couldn't look at him. "I'm sorry, Darcy," I said. "I suppose I jumped to conclusions."

He looked at me then burst out laughing. "Oh, Georgie, what an idiot you can be sometimes."

I turned away. "Fine. Go ahead. Laugh. How do you think you would feel if a policeman told you that I'd been carrying on an affair behind your back? And he was enjoying telling me too."

He took my arm and turned me to face him. He was looking deadly serious now. "Georgie, we have no hope of a successful marriage if we can't trust one another."

"You're right," I said. "It's just that everyone else seems to take bed-hopping for granted. Everybody in London has slept with everybody else, except me."

He smiled at me, his eyes sparkling, and reached out a finger to stroke my cheek. "Poor little Georgie. So deprived. And now you'll never get the chance, because I'm keeping you all to myself."

"That's fine with me as long as the same rules apply to you," I said.

"Absolutely."

"You really mean that?"

"I do."

We stood there, looking at each other. Then I flung myself into his arms. "Oh, Darcy, I've been so miserable," I said.

That was the last thing I said for a long time as his lips came down to meet mine. When we broke apart we were both rather breathless and I was looking a trifle disheveled.

"I can't keep up this celibacy thing forever," Darcy muttered. "I've a good mind to rip off your clothes right here and now and make love to you on that table."

I laughed uneasily. "I wouldn't mind," I said, "but I'd hate to be interrupted, and I rather think it might not be appreciated in a place as hallowed as this."

He smoothed back my hair. "I'm so tempted to suggest we run off to Gretna Green right now and get married and to hell with everything."

"That would be fine with me too," I said. "I've always told you that I'd be happy to live anywhere, as long as it was with you. But I can't elope right now, not when the queen has charged me with looking after Princess Marina." I looked nervously toward the doorway. "Speaking of which, I'd probably better go back to the palace. She'll be wondering where I've got to."

"Nonsense. She'll understand. I think she's a romantic, isn't she?"

"I don't know. I think she's fairly realistic."

"She'll have to be, married to good old George," Darcy said.

"You don't think he'll change once he's married?"

"Probably not. Infidelity does seem to run in your family, apart from the king and queen."

"And the Yorks. They are frightfully monogamous."

"Yes, but you can't see Bertie York flirting with sundry girls, can you? Not with his stutter."

"That's not kind," I said. "He's a really nice chap. And he adores his wife. So let him be a role model for you, young man."

"I'm sure I'll be adoring and terribly domestic," Darcy

said. "But I must get you home. Oh, and some chap left an envelope for you on the table. It's your winnings, I gather."

"Oh yes. I had quite a lucky evening." It was with delight that I picked up the envelope and opened it. Then my jaw dropped open. "Crikey. There's a lot of money in here."

"How much did you think you'd won?"

"I don't know. I never thought. Probably twenty pounds."

"Twenty pounds?" He laughed. "This looks more like five hundred and twenty."

I was still speechless. "I had no idea. I know I won a lot of chips but I thought they were maybe five shillings each."

Darcy shook his head. "More like five pounds each."

"Crikey," I said again. "So that's why I was so popular tonight. I've never had young men fighting over me before. And Monty and Whiffie took me to supper and were so attentive."

"Monty Pratchett and Whiffie Anstruther?"

"I never knew their proper names."

"Both younger sons of earls and therefore penniless like me. Obviously trying to snag a young woman with a fortune."

"And they thought I was she. How screamingly funny, Darcy."

"To many people five hundred pounds is a fortune. In the East End they could live for years on that."

I became thoughtful as he opened the door and we crossed the gaming room. "You know, we really could run away to Gretna Green and set up a home on this money," I said.

"I know it's tempting, but I've told you before, I'm not having you live in a poky little place. Your family has certain expectations for you. I want to do the thing properly. I am starting to put money away, Georgie. I'm taking every job I'm offered. And I'd like you to keep that money and know you've got some put by for emergencies."

I nodded. "Anyway, I have things to do here," I said. My wrap was produced and we were ushered into a waiting taxicab. As we drove off I said in a low voice, "As well as looking after the princess, I have to find out who killed Bobo Carrington."

"Surely that's up to the police."

"You've seen DCI Pelham," I said. "Sir Jeremy is also working behind the scenes to make sure her murder stays out of the newspapers, and I've been asked to keep my ears and eyes open too. Just in case someone at Kensington saw something."

"Don't get too carried away by this, Georgie," he said. "If drugs are involved, these chaps are nasty customers."

"I'll leave that side of things to you," I said. "But the big question is, why was her body lying in a courtyard at Kensington Palace? Not the sort of place she'd meet with a drug dealer. So either she came to see somebody there and was killed because of it, or she was killed by persons unknown somewhere else and her body was dumped there to implicate the royal family and cause a scandal."

"She could have come to the palace to see Princess Marina and tell her about her relationship with Prince George," he said.

"But Marina and I were out dining at Buckingham Palace. I have my suspicions about Marina's cousin Countess Irmtraut."

He chuckled. "Countess Irmtraut. What a ghastly name."

"Equally ghastly person. Very jealous and protective of Marina. So if Bobo told her who she was, I can quite see Irmtraut killing her. But then why leave her for all to see? Why not at least try to hide the body in some bushes?"

"She was disturbed and had to beat a retreat?" he suggested.

"Anyway, I don't know how we'd get her to confess."

"You've passed on this suspicion?"

"To Sir Jeremy. He's questioned her."

"So your job is done."

"Not quite," I said. "I managed to break into Bobo's flat."

"You did what?" He sounded horrified.

"Well, actually I used a key I'd acquired from the cleaning lady."

"Georgie, that's breaking and entering. Don't do things like that, please. Leave it to the professionals."

"Only the professionals didn't discover she had a wall safe behind a painting."

"Then tell them, and don't do things like that anymore." He slipped his arm around my shoulder. "Georgie, Bobo was connected to all kinds of people who might be dangerous. You have no way of finding out her various dealings. Nor should you try."

"I am going to follow up on one thing," I said. "There was an address on her blotting paper. A Mary Boyle in Deptford. I wondered if it might be her maid. I was told she'd had a maid and dismissed her. But I was also told she was fond of her."

Darcy shook his head. "I don't remember her maid being called Mary. And what might you discover from the maid?"

"Who was the father of her child, perhaps. Surely that's one of the key factors, isn't it? Someone who has a lot to lose . . ." My thoughts went to Sir Toby. "Sir Toby Blenchley," I said. "I was told she was linked to him for a while. He'd have everything to lose if it came out that she'd had their child."

"Don't you dare try to follow up on that," he said. "Leave it to me. He's the sort of man who doesn't always play by the rules."

"So he might have killed her to keep her quiet?"

"He'd have had someone else kill her. Sir Toby wouldn't do his own dirty work. Presumably the police have established her movements on the evening she was killed—whether she had any visitors at her flat, where she may have gone in a taxicab . . ."

"There is a night doorman at her block of flats. I haven't questioned him but I expect the police have. It's hard to ask the questions if we can't tell anyone it's part of a murder investigation," I said. "They just think we're being nosy."

"I realize that." He looked up. "Oh damn. We've already reached Kensington Palace and I've wasted the whole time with you on talking."

"Where can I find you?" I asked as the taxicab driver came around to open the door.

"I know where to find you now," he said. "I'm staying here and there, but I'll bring you a telephone number." He clambered out after me. "And if there is an emergency before I see you again, telephone Sir Jeremy. Do you have his number?"

I nodded.

"Good. He can track me down."

"Good night, then." I stood there looking at him, thinking how much I loved him and wanted him.

"Remember, I'll be keeping an eye on you, so no stupid heroics about tackling drug dealers, all right?"

"I promise. No drug dealers."

"Good night," he said. Then he took me into his arms and kissed me. I reacted as a band of light fell onto us. I looked up. Irmtraut was standing at her window, holding back the curtain and staring down at us.

Chapter 25

THURSDAY, NOVEMBER 8

Rushing around, but with a smile on my face.

Miraculously Queenie had stayed up to undress me.

"Your brassiere is undone at the back," she commented. "You've been having a bit of the old how's yer father."

"Maids are not supposed to comment on their mistress's behavior," I said primly. "Your job is to help me off with my clothes."

She chuckled. "Looks like someone's already tried to do that for you."

I slept much better that night, knowing that Darcy was nearby and all was right again—at least for us. Not for Bobo Carrington.

And in the morning I was up and ready for a busy day ahead. I was going to make the most of Princess Marina being occupied with fittings and greeting her parents. I didn't wait for breakfast to be put out, but contented myself with a cup of tea and two digestive biscuits, then off I went. I didn't often move about London at this early hour and soon realized that this was the time that people went to work. The Underground was packed. Crowds streamed out of London Bridge Station ranging from city gents with bowler hats and rolled umbrellas to typists wearing a little too much makeup. I was going the other way, out of the City, so the train I took to Deptford was quite empty. We rattled through one depressing row of backyards after another with gray washing hanging limply on clotheslines, narrow grimy streets with mothers scrubbing front steps or walking skinny children to school. It was horrid to think that some people lived in such drabness and grime. I had felt hard up sometimes myself, but I had never had to endure the ugliness of this sort of life. As Darcy had said, to some people my winnings would be wealth beyond their wildest dreams. I resolved that if and when I was a lady of means, I would do all that I could to help the poor.

I alighted from the train at Deptford Station, asked for Edward Street and was given directions. I followed a long high street on which shops were now opening, greengrocers were arranging vegetables and early housewives were shopping for the evening meal with toddlers clinging onto a pram. At last I came to Edward Street, a narrow backwater with two grimy rows of identical houses facing each other, and it was only then that I realized I had thought out no good reason for visiting Mary Boyle. I could barge in, asking questions about Bobo, but I'd appear rude and inquisitive and she'd probably tell me nothing. I could perhaps say I was looking for a maid myself and Bobo had recommended her. But that wouldn't be fair if she was unemployed. I shouldn't raise her hopes falsely. I could be from a newspaper writing an article on Bobo Carrington. . . . I toyed with that idea. Since Bobo had been featured regularly in newspapers and magazines this would not seem too strange. But then again she might decide to tell me nothing out of loyalty to her former employer.

As I stood on the doorstep and knocked on the door I decided to play it as safe as possible.

"Are you Mary Boyle, by any chance?" I asked when the

door was opened. She was older than I had expected, with a fresh, distinctly Irish-looking face, and her eyes darted nervously.

"Yes, I am Mary Boyle. What might this be about?"

"It's about Bobo Carrington," I said. "I've been trying to locate her and I wondered if you might have news of her."

"Oh, and why should I do that?" she asked. Her Irish accent was still strong.

"Because I was in her flat and I saw your address on her blotting paper, so I knew she must have written to you recently."

"And why would you be wanting to find Miss Carrington?" she asked.

I smiled hopefully. "Do you think I could come in? It's awfully cold on the doorstep and I'm sure you're letting cold air into the house."

"All right. Come in if you must," she said, "but there's not much I can tell you. She moves around as she pleases. If she's out of town then she's off to stay with friends." She led me through to a cold front parlor. The fire had not been lit but it was neat and tidy enough, making me feel that it probably was only used for visitors such as myself. "Now why did you say you were looking for her?" she repeated. "You're not one of those reporters, are you?"

"Oh good heavens no." I gave my carefree little laugh. "Bobo and I used to be friends once. I've been out of the country in America so when I returned I tried to look her up. But apparently nobody's seen her."

"Nobody's seen her?"

"No. She seems to have vanished into thin air. So I'm trying anybody I can think of who might know where she is."

Even as I said this I felt terrible. If she had indeed been fond of Bobo, she'd be heartbroken to know that Bobo was lying in the morgue right this moment.

"Have you asked at her flat? The doorman would know," she said.

"I did ask him. He said he hadn't seen Miss Carrington

for the past few days. And other people told me they hadn't seen her all summer."

"Ah, well, I do happen to know she was away for a while at the end of the summer," she said.

"Oh, did she go to the Continent again? I bumped into her there a couple of years ago but friends said they hadn't seen her there recently."

"No, I think she went to the seaside. Nice healthy air."

"You know her well, do you?" I asked.

"I do."

"And you're fond of her."

"I am."

"Then I wondered, could something be wrong? I wrote to Bobo and she never answered my letter. That's not like her, is it? And we were such good friends at one time."

"She wasn't too well for a while. I can tell you that much," she said. "But now everything's fine again. And she should be out and about, and I'm sure you'll catch up with her soon enough."

I was dying to tell her that I knew about the baby. I was trying to think of a way I could ask if she knew who the father was.

"So tell me." I leaned forward. "What does she think about Prince George getting married? I mean, we all knew that she and the prince were . . . quite close . . . at some stage."

Her expression became guarded. "Are you sure you're not one of those reporters? What do you really mean, coming here and asking me all these questions? You'll get nothing more out of me."

"I meant no harm, honestly," I said. "And I'm not any kind of reporter. I was just concerned, that's all. It's not like Bobo to vanish completely from London society."

I had been looking around the room as we spoke. My gaze had focused on the mantelpiece. I decided to act. I stood up. "I won't trouble you any longer, Mrs. Boyle," I said. "But I wonder—you don't happen to have the kettle on for tea, do you? It's icy cold out there today."

"I do." She said it grudgingly. "I'll get you a cup."

The moment she left the room I made for the mantelpiece and picked up the postcard. It was a picture of the south coast. *Greetings from Worthing-on-Sea.* I turned it over and read, *Everything fine. Don't worry. Home soon. Kathleen.* And the postmark was not Worthing but Goring-by-Sea. I only just managed to return it to its place before she brought me the cup of tea. It was extremely strong and sweet, but I drank it with an expression of enjoyment, then put it down on the nearest table. "I'll be off, then. I'm so sorry to have bothered you. If you do hear from Bobo, please tell her I've been trying to get hold of her. My name's Belinda Warburton-Stoke."

"As I said, she's back in London, as far as I know. Back at her old place. You'll see her soon enough."

"And she is still trying to survive without a maid?" I said. "Why is she doing that?"

"I gather the last girl didn't prove satisfactory. And it's easier just to have someone come in and clean. Less complicated, if you know what I mean."

"Yes, I can see that." I nodded. "Well, thanks awfully, Mrs. Boyle."

I felt her watching my back as I walked down the street. Actually my head was buzzing, and I almost turned the wrong way onto the high street. She had said that Bobo had been to the seaside for the good fresh air. The postcard had come from Worthing on the south coast. And it had been important enough to Mary Boyle to keep it on her mantelpiece for two months. But it had been signed *Kathleen.* And I realized something else. As I came down the dark and narrow hallway in her house I had glimpsed something standing behind the stairs. It was a pram.

A postcard from the south coast. And I remembered the two women at the party talking about that place on the south coast where one went to take care of unfortunate occurrences. Was it just possible that Bobo Carrington's real name was Kathleen? In which case was Mary Boyle a relative and not her maid after all? Didn't she say that the last girl had proved unsatisfactory? That seemed to indicate she had never acted in that capacity herself. And she was older than I had expected. I stood on the street corner, finding it hard to breathe with excitement. Those women had speculated that Bobo wouldn't have had an abortion because she was Catholic. Was it possible that Mary Boyle was her mother? In which case that pram in the front hall might actually mean that she was looking after the baby. I was tempted to stake out the house and see if she came out later with the pram, but I knew that my time was precious and limited and I wanted to accomplish as much as possible.

Should I go to see if Granddad had located his safe-cracker yet, or—I took a deep breath at this daring thought—should I go down to Worthing myself and see if I could locate the place where Bobo had gone? I wasn't quite sure what this might accomplish, but perhaps I'd find out when she'd had the child and possibly secure details of the birth certificate. If I didn't succeed in this, then at least Sir Jeremy could see if one Kathleen Boyle had filled out a birth certificate recently and whether she had named the father.

I was brimming with excitement as I went back to the station, took the train to London Bridge and from there the Underground to Waterloo. I knew that a train to Worthing would take me an hour or more, but I did have the whole day ahead of me. I was in luck as a train to the south coast was due to leave in ten minutes. I bought my ticket, then sprinted over to the platform just as doors were slamming and the guard was shouting "all aboard." I settled myself in a ladies-only carriage and soon I was steaming southward in the company of two middle-aged matrons who gossiped nonstop about the failings of the new vicar who was too High Church for them and had even introduced incense. They got out at Horsham and I was alone for the rest of the journey.

When we reached Worthing I asked for directions to Goring-by-Sea at the ticket office.

"It's about two miles out of town, miss," the man said. "There's a bus goes once an hour."

I decided that I couldn't wait for a bus and for once would make use of my newfound wealth and take a taxicab. I told the cabdriver that I was looking for a clinic or convalescent home in Goring-by-Sea. Did he know of it? He thought he did. "Big white place, isn't it? Posh looking." That sounded like it. So off we went. In summertime and in good weather it would have been a charming drive along the seafront with its rows of white, bow-windowed guesthouses and its long pier and bandstand. But today a fierce wind whipped up a slate gray sea and the promenade was deserted. At last the town gave way to big houses set amid spacious grounds, sports fields, and on the front the occasional seaside bungalow. Then the taxicab slowed. "This is it, I believe," he said. "Yes, there you are." And a sign said, *The Larches. Convalescent Home.* We turned in through white gates, followed a drive lined with larch trees and pulled up at a portico outside a big white Georgian house. I paid the taxi driver and rang the doorbell.

I was greeted warmly by a young woman in nurse's uniform when I said that I'd come down from London and wanted to see the matron or the person in charge. I couldn't believe how smoothly this had gone so far.

"Here to see a relative, are you, dear?" she asked as she escorted me down the front hallway. "Your grandma maybe?"

We were passing a common room. The door was open and inside I saw nothing but old people, sitting in armchairs. This was clearly not the right place.

"I think I've made a mistake," I said. "I was told the clinic was in Goring-by-Sea but I was expecting a place for much younger people. Younger women."

Her expression changed to part disgust and part pity. "The clinic?" she said. "This is a convalescent home, my dear. You'll be thinking of Haseldene. It's about a mile from here along the road to Findon."

As I thanked her she followed me to the front door. "It's a good walk," she said. "Are you up to it? Should I call a taxicab for you?" And I realized then that she thought I was a potential patient, not a visitor. Also that she knew full well what went on at Haseldene.

It was not what I'd usually call a long walk. But today the wind whipped off the Channel and rain threatened, making the going unpleasant. I asked the only two people I met if they knew where I'd find a house called Haseldene and at last I came to it. It was set back in well-landscaped grounds and looked like any other white and modern seaside house with the curved lines of art deco design. The brass plaque on the white surrounding wall said *Haseldene*, but nothing else. No mention of its function.

During the train ride I had tried to think of what on earth I could possibly say. I was sure such places prided themselves on confidentiality. Should I pretend to be a patient and then see if I could slip into the office to see the records? That was too risky. If they examined me they'd know I did not need their services. I decided that the best course of action might be to come clean. I'd tell the matron who I was and that a scandal about Bobo's child was threatening the royal family. Had she named the father?

It had seemed possible as I journeyed down through Sussex. Now it seemed like frightful cheek, even if I was a royal relative. I fully expected to be thrown out on my ear. I was about to knock on the door when I noticed that it was slightly open. A new idea crept into my head. Maybe I could sneak in, undetected, and have a chance to look at their records. If I was caught, I'd say I'd come to check out the place for a friend.

I pushed open the door and stepped into a thickly carpeted foyer. The place was decidedly warm and felt more like a comfortable private house than a clinic. There was none of that disinfectant smell that lingers in hospitals. There was a vase of chrysanthemums on a polished table and a grandfather clock ticking away solemnly. Otherwise there was no sound. I stood listening and thought I detected a distant radio. I began to wonder if I'd come to the right place. I knew I had to work fast. There were several doors around that foyer, a flight of stairs leading up to a second floor, and behind them the hall narrowed and led to the back of the building.

I had no idea where to start. Surely one of the rooms at the front of the house would be the office, while rooms for more medical purposes would be upstairs. I went to the door on my left—the room with one of the bay windows—and opened it cautiously. It was a sitting room. A fire was burning in the grate and there were sofas and armchairs arranged around it. Magazines were scattered over a low table. It looked like anyone's sitting room and at first glance I had thought the room to be empty. Then I noticed that someone was curled up in one of the armchairs, facing out toward the fields and the sea. She was looking at a magazine and hadn't heard me enter. I went to back out again but as I turned my overcoat sleeve must have brushed against the table, knocking a newspaper to the floor. The girl looked up and we both gasped at the same time.

It was Belinda.

Chapter 26

NOVEMBER 8
AT A CLINIC NEAR WORTHING-ON-SEA

Belinda looked pale and somehow delicate. She was staring at me in astonishment. "Georgie, what are you doing here? How did you find me?" she demanded. "I didn't tell a soul."

"I had no idea," I stammered. "I came here checking on someone else." I went over and sat down beside her. "Belinda. Why didn't you tell me? I could see you were upset and not your normal self."

"I didn't think you'd understand," she said. "I know you don't approve of my lifestyle. You'd think I got what I deserved."

"But Belinda, I'm your friend," I said. "I'd have stood by you, no matter what."

She gave me a weak little smile. "You're a nice person, Georgie."

"So that's why you came home from America. You found out you were going to have a baby." I came over to her and perched on the arm of her chair.

She nodded. "I was such a fool, Georgie," she said. "Such

a bloody fool. There was this man, you see. He was just perfect—handsome, debonair, big motorcar, lots of money. A Hollywood producer, or so he said. You know how they talk over there. He made me think he was so successful and he knew everybody. I suppose it was being out of my own environment, but I fell for him rather hard. It was all wonderful and I actually believed he loved me. I really thought he wanted to marry me." She put her hand up to her mouth and turned away from me, taking a moment to collect herself before she continued. "Well, now that I look back on it, he didn't actually say the word 'marriage,' but he certainly implied it. Or implied that he wanted us to be together, and I believed him." She turned away again, staring out at rain that was now streaking the windows. "I've always made fun of you for being so naïve. I can't believe how stupidly naïve I was. I bloody well believed him, Georgie."

I nodded, to show that I understood.

She sighed. "I was usually so careful, you know. Took the right precautions. So good about my little bowler hat. But I suppose I let my guard down with him. And when I found out that I was—you know—I thought, 'Well, so what? He'll marry me.' So I told him."

"And what did he say?"

"He was completely offhand. He said it wasn't really his business, but since I was such a nice kid he knew of a doctor who took care of these things. Wouldn't charge me too much."

"Belinda, how horrid. So you came home."

She nodded. "I came home. I didn't know what to do. I realized I couldn't have the baby, of course. There was no way. My family would cut me off completely. So I had no alternative. I'd heard other girls talk about this place, so I made up my mind in the middle of the night, and I bolted. Didn't want to tell a soul. I thought I could take care of it and be back in London and nobody would be any the wiser."

"You came here to have an—?" I couldn't make myself say the word out loud.

She nodded. "I was supposed to have it yesterday. But

when it came to it I couldn't do it. I simply couldn't do it, Georgie."

"So what's going to happen now?" I asked. "What will you do? Where will you go?"

"I have absolutely no idea. They have been very kind here. They told me that many girls go through the same panic as I did and I should stay on for a few days and think it over. They also said that if I decide to have the baby I can come back here when it's closer to my time and they'll help with finding a family to adopt it." Her whole body shook with a huge sigh. "But I simply can't afford their prices, and I can't ask anyone for money."

"I'd ask that rat in America," I said with such vehemence that she looked up at me and actually smiled.

"No use in asking him," she said.

"There is no one in your family you can approach?" I asked. "Your grandmother is rich, isn't she?"

"My grandmother is the most correct lady in the world. She would do the whole 'do not darken my door again' routine." She sighed again. "I suppose I have come to think that an abortion is the only option."

"You could go abroad to have the baby. Lots of girls do, so I hear."

She nodded. "I suppose so. One can live cheaply in Italy. Part of me would really like to keep the baby, but that's stupid, isn't it? I can't make enough to support myself and if the family found out about it, I'd be cut off from my inheritance—which will be considerable when Granny dies."

I smiled at her. "If we were back in America, we could hire a hitman to bump her off."

She had to laugh then. "Georgie, there is a wild side to you I'd never noticed before."

"I'm just trying to think of all possibilities, Belinda. There must be something."

"No, I think you're right. Abroad it must be. I'll stick around until, you know, it starts to show and then I'll rent out my London place and retreat to a small village in the mountains or on a lake somewhere. God, it sounds pretty bleak, doesn't it?"

The words "on a lake" had triggered a thought. "I've just had a brilliant idea, Belinda. My mother. She has that villa in Nice and the new one on the lake in Lugano and she's never there. I bet she'd let you stay at either one if I asked her. She'd understand what you're going through. She's probably been through it herself, knowing the way she has lived."

"But why would your mother do anything for me?" she asked.

"Because I'd ask her to."

She turned eyes brimming with tears up to me. "Gosh, Georgie. You've given me a sliver of hope for the first time. I'm going to pack my things and go back to London." She reached out to me. "Will you write to her immediately?"

"On the train going home, I promise."

She took my hand and hugged it to her. I suppose I'd always secretly admired Belinda for the fearless and reckless way she lived. She was someone who knew how to take care of herself, who took risks, who never considered consequences. This was the first time I had ever seen a chink in her armor.

She sat up suddenly and brushed tears from her face. "I'm so sorry," she said. "What must you think of me?"

"You've had a really bad experience. You've had your heart broken. But it will all work out. You'll go away to the Continent for a few months, then you'll come back to London and get on with your life."

"I know one thing. I'm going to stay well away from men. I'm done with men forever."

"You were prepared to be rather chummy with Sir Toby Blenchley not long ago," I couldn't resist saying.

"Stupid of me. I was really flattered that a powerful man like that would want someone like me. It did cross my mind that he might set me up as his mistress and I'd be safe. But when he left I came down to earth and realized he just wanted someone for uncomplicated sex. I just happened to be willing and available. But no more, Georgie. I'm going to live like a nun from now on. In fact I may enter a convent."

This made me start to laugh. I couldn't help myself. "I'm sorry, but the thought of you in a convent, Belinda . . ."

She looked at my face and began laughing too. "I'd certainly shake the place up, wouldn't I?" she said. Then she grew solemn again. "What am I going to do with my life, Georgie? In Hollywood I really thought I'd get married and settle down. But after this, who would ever want me? I'll never shake off my reputation and I have virtually no money that any man would want."

"You'll meet a nice chap one day who won't care," I said. "And in the meantime you will hide yourself away in Mummy's villa somewhere and you'll go back to your fashion designs. You're a good designer, you know. You could return to London with a complete collection." I waved my hands as I became more enthusiastic. "Design something that Mummy would wear. She'll show it off for you and get you orders. She may even find you people who will pay up and not want things on credit."

She gave me a wet smile. "Yes, maybe that's a good idea. I have to do something. Thank you, Georgie. I'm so glad you know now. It will make things easier." Then she looked at me curiously. "So tell me. Why are you here? Who did you come to see?"

"I came to check whether Bobo Carrington was ever here," I said.

Her face lit up. "She was."

"How do you know?"

"One of the maids is rather chatty. I don't know how Bobo's name came up but she said to me, 'She was here, you know. Under another name, but I recognized her from her pictures.'"

"Brilliant," I said. "Do you think there's a chance I could talk to this maid?"

"I'll go and see if I can find her," she said. "Wait here. And if anyone asks, you've come to visit me."

"Of course." I watched her get up and walk to the door.

I was still finding her news hard to take in. I felt shivery and moved closer to the fire. I was sitting with my hands extended toward the flames when Belinda returned with a sheepish-looking redheaded girl.

"This is Maureen," Belinda said. "She's from Ireland." She turned to the girl. "This lady is a friend of Bobo Carrington's."

"Are you, miss?" she asked. "I was ever so fond of her. Of course, she didn't use her proper name when she was here."

"She was called Kathleen, wasn't she?"

"That's right, miss. That's how we got friendly. She was originally from Ireland too. We talked about it and she knew the place I'd come from. Fancy that."

"Maureen, I don't suppose the child's father came to visit, did he?"

"Oh no, miss. You rarely see a man in here."

"And did she ever let on who the father was?"

"She didn't say a word. But someone important, I know that. I got the feeling he couldn't marry her because he was already married. But she did say it was all over between them. I know she wanted to keep the baby, which most of the ladies don't. She said she'd like to buy a little house in the country and keep the baby out there. She said she'd got money saved up. Nobody need know. And you know what, miss? She suggested I might like to come and work for her—help take care of the baby."

"Did she?"

"She did. But I haven't heard from her since, so I have to think that she's found someone better. A real nursemaid, maybe."

She looked incredibly disappointed.

"Maybe someone in her family is looking after the baby," I suggested.

"That may be right, miss. I know her mum knew about it."

"Maureen, would you know where the office is? Do they keep copies of the birth certificates?"

She was looking at me strangely now. "No, miss. The birth certificates go straight to the county. We don't keep many records here . . . and you can understand why, can't you? The ladies come here because it's private."

"Yes, I suppose so." I sighed. I didn't think I had time for a trip to county hall. Nor did I think they'd be willing to release birth records to someone turning up from out of the blue with no authority. A long trip for nothing. Or at least, not for nothing, because I had found Belinda, and now had a chance to help her. Also I had found that Bobo planned to keep the baby at a little house in the country. And I'd have information to share with Sir Jeremy. Birth certificates would be up to him now.

"Thank you, Maureen. That will be all," I said.

Her face gradually lit up. "I know who you are too," she said. "I've seen your picture in the papers as well. You're the lady who's related to the royal family, aren't you? My, what an honor, Your Highness. And here was me, calling you 'miss.'"

I smiled. "My fault for not introducing myself."

She curtsied before she left. I turned to Belinda. "I have to go. But I'll come and see you as soon as you get back to London. And I'll write to Mummy immediately."

She nodded. "Thanks, Georgie."

I took her hand. "It will be all right. I promise."

She squeezed my hand fiercely. "God, I hope so. You must have enough optimism for the both of us."

Chapter 27

It was still raining hard when I arrived back in London. On the train journey home I had carefully composed my letter to Mummy. Then I had jotted down the things I wanted to tell Sir Jeremy. That Bobo was really Kathleen Boyle from Ireland and had a mother living in Deptford. That the baby had been born near Worthing but she had said she wanted to keep it in a little house in the country. That Sir Toby had signed in an American called J. Walter Oppenheimer who had seemed out of place at Crockford's and who had upset Bobo when he spoke with her. That Sir Toby was known to have been pally with Bobo. I toyed with that. So who was the American and why was she upset by him? Had he threatened her in some way?

I went to the nearest telephone box at Waterloo Station and rang Sir Jeremy's number. Again he answered in his noncommittal manner and said he was tied up at the moment but would send a car for me in an hour. This made me realize what a dangerous implement the telephone can be. Anyone manning a switchboard could theoretically listen in on a conversation. Might it be worth talking to the girls who operated the Mayfair switchboard and would have connected Bobo's calls?

I made my way back to Kensington Palace. A maid greeted me in the front hall. "There have been some messages for you, my lady," she said. "On the tray over there."

My heart gave a little leap of joy. Darcy would have left me his telephone number. The first one was a telegram and I opened it with trepidation. It was from my grandfather. It said, *Lightfingers don't want to do it. Sorry.* I looked at it and had to laugh, even though I was disappointed at not being able to crack Bobo's safe. Still, the police would surely have their own contacts among safecrackers and could take it from here.

The second message was from Noel Coward. *Have set up a little soiree on Sunday, if you and the charming princess are free. Chez moi.* And he added his address. *Shall we say cocktails at six?* I read.

What a glamorous life I was leading these days. I thought back to the time of baked beans on toast and how easily one adapts to messages from luminaries like Noel Coward saying "Cocktails at six."

But that was it. No message from Darcy. I had just gone upstairs to change my clothes, which were now rather rainsodden, when I heard my name being called. Irmtraut came stomping out of her bedroom at the end of the hall.

"Where have you been? I do not see you all day." It sounded more like an accusation than a friendly inquiry.

"I had to visit a sick friend," I said. "She's in a convalescent home on the south coast." It is so much easier when one doesn't have to lie.

"Ah so." She nodded as if she couldn't find anything to criticize in this behavior. "So you did not go to meet a man?" She glared.

"A man?"

"I saw you with a man last night," she said. "You were in an embrace with him outside the front door."

"That was my intended."

"I do not wish to hear what you intended to do," she said.

"No, I meant that I plan to marry him."

"He is suitable? Of the right social class?"

"Quite unsuitable in most ways," I said. "But yes, he's of the right social class. Son of a peer."

"A pair of what?"

"No, a peer. An aristocrat."

"Ach so. This is good."

"Not that it's any of your business," I said. I had had enough of being polite to her. "And speaking of snooping, may I ask why you told the authorities that you had seen me in the courtyard when you know that wasn't true?"

Her face went red then. "Because they try to accuse me of something and they won't say what. They keep asking me why I go to the courtyard and I tell them no, I do not go to the courtyard. And they say Lady Georgiana thinks that you did. So this is why I tell them because I find it so disagreeable."

I wanted to ask why she carried a knife in her pocket but I couldn't find a good way to do so without admitting to being in her room. But then she went straight on. "I wish that you dismiss your maid immediately."

"My maid? What has she done?" A horrid sinking feeling came into my stomach. I had thought it would be only a matter of time before Queenie created a major disaster.

"I will tell you. She has been snooping in my room." She pronounced it "schnooping."

"Oh no. Surely not." Queenie was many things, but probably the least curious person on the planet.

"*Ja.*" She nodded so violently that a hairpin came loose and clattered to the stone floor. "I had her come to my room and take my washing downstairs," she said. "I left the bundle ready to be carried. But later, when I looked in my garderobe, I saw that she had been there. I leave my shoes in neat rows on the floor of my garderobe but when I look they are in disarray. Somebody has disarranged them."

"Good heavens," I said. "When was this? Today?"

"No. A day or so ago."

Oh dear. I couldn't let Queenie take the blame for my snooping in her wardrobe, could I? But I also couldn't think of a good explanation for the shoes in disarray.

"I'm sure Queenie would never do that," I said. "Maybe something fell off a hanger and displaced your shoes."

"Nothing fell." Her face was stony.

"Was something missing?" I asked.

"No. Nothing was taken."

"Then I think we have to overlook simple curiosity, don't we?" I said. "Unless you have something to hide, that is?" I smiled at her sweetly. "You haven't got the crown jewels or a body in there, have you?"

She tossed her head proudly and another hairpin bounced to the floor. "I have nothing to hide," she said. "I do not touch your crown jewels."

I was still dying to ask about that knife in her pocket.

"That is not the only fault of your maid," she said. "Today I asked her to clean my shoes, since she has no work to do and I have no maid of my own here."

"And she didn't polish them well enough for you?" I asked as the sinking feeling returned.

"Yes. She polished them." She went ahead of me into her room and appeared with a pair of highly polished shoes. "Look at them."

"They look very nice," I said. "Queenie did a good job. Why are you unhappy with her?"

"Because they were green suede," she said. "And she has polished them with black boot polish."

Oh dear. I didn't dare laugh.

"I'm so sorry," I said. "I'm afraid I have a very simple wardrobe and Queenie has not come across green suede shoes before. She meant well."

Irmtraut snorted. "You English. You do not know how to train and discipline servants. This girl is a disgrace. Do you know what she called me?"

Oh golly. Nothing too rude, I prayed.

"She called me 'miss,' when she is told I am a countess.

Miss. Like a common shopgirl. And then she insulted me even more by telling me I had an uncle called Bob."

This time I did laugh. "She must have said 'Bob's your uncle,'" I said. "It's an expression Londoners use to mean that everything will be taken care of."

"How can 'Bob is your uncle' mean that everything will be taken care of? It makes no sense. This English language is very stupid." And she stomped back into her room and slammed the door.

I CHANGED MY clothes, wrote out the letter to Mummy, handed it to a servant to post and was just about to snatch a quick tea when the car arrived. Regretfully I put down my uneaten crumpet. I went to get my coat and hat and was soon being driven through rush-hour crowds as offices emptied out at five. I had no idea where we were going but it seemed to be in the general direction of Scotland Yard. However, we drove past the familiar black and white building and turned into a side street, stopping outside a row of Georgian houses like those on Downing Street not too far away.

The chauffeur helped me out, then led me to the front door. A bell sounded from within and the door was opened by Sir Jeremy himself.

"Welcome to my humble abode," he said.

"This is your house?" I asked, stepping into a deliciously warm entrance hall.

"One of the perks of being a civil servant," he said, smiling. "Come through to the sitting room."

This was clearly a room of a man who liked his comforts. Thick Axminster carpet with a white bearskin rug in front of a marble fireplace. There were old prints on the walls and Chinese vases on a shelf. In one corner was a drinks cabinet stacked with bottles and gleaming glasses, and a glass-topped table displayed a collection of paperweights. To my delight a low table was set with a tea tray. I realized I hadn't eaten all day (unless one counted the dry and unappetizing cheese sandwich I'd bought at Worthing Station).

"I expect you'd like some tea," Sir Jeremy said. "Do take a seat. Beastly old day, isn't it? I don't know why anyone stays in England during November."

I sat in one of the big red leather armchairs. It was so big and so soft that it was hard to sit upright and when Sir Jeremy handed me a cup of tea I had a moment's panic that I'd tip over backward and deposit the contents all over myself and the chair. I managed to put the cup down on the table and perched myself at the front of the chair to avoid future accidents. Sir Jeremy let me work my way through some smoked salmon sandwiches, a scone and a slice of Dundee cake before I realized that he was an important man and probably didn't want to waste his time watching me eat.

"I should probably tell you why I called you," I said.

"No rush. I'm expecting another visitor," he said.

Almost on cue the doorbell rang. I heard a manservant's voice say, "Good evening, sir. Sir Jeremy is in the sitting room."

And to my surprise the visitor was Darcy.

"You made it." Sir Jeremy held out his hand. "I believe you two know each other. Take a seat, O'Mara. Tea or are you ready to move on to whiskey?"

"Nothing right now, thank you, sir," Darcy said. He pulled up a padded upright chair beside me and gave me a cheeky little smile, one that said, "You didn't expect to see me here, did you?"

"Lady Georgiana, I invited O'Mara to join us as he might be able to look into some aspects of this case that would not be possible for you. He had already been observing Miss Carrington's connections to drug trafficking as part of an ongoing project for my department."

I nodded.

Sir Jeremy turned back to Darcy. "But as yet you've not found what we're looking for?"

"Not yet, sir. We know about the smaller players but we still don't know how the drugs get into the country."

"Too bad she died when she did. She needed a regular supply. She might well have led us to the big boys." He sighed, then got up, walked across to the drinks table and poured himself a generous amount of Scotch. He came back to his chair and sat down before he said, "Lady Georgiana has some news for us, I believe."

"I have," I said, and I recounted my visit to Worthing, and to Bobo's mother. I was pleased to note that both men looked impressed.

"So now you'll be able to take a look at the birth certificate and see if she listed the father," I said. "Oh, and a servant told me that she planned to keep the child at a house outside London."

"Well done," Sir Jeremy said. "I don't really know where we go from here. We're still fishing around in the dark as to how she died, aren't we? Was it the father of the child? Was it to do with her drug habit? Someone had a very good reason for killing her and dumping her body at Kensington Palace."

"And there's still Countess Irmtraut," I said.

Sir Jeremy shook his head. "She might well be capable of violence but I don't think she's capable of lying. She was most outraged and insistent and I can usually tell when someone isn't telling the truth."

"There is one more move we can make," I said. "There is a wall safe in Bobo's apartment. I discovered it."

Sir Jeremy looked at Darcy, inquiring whether he knew that I had been breaking and entering. Darcy's face remained impassive.

"My grandfather is a former London policeman," I went on. "I asked him if he could find someone who could open a safe. He thought he knew an ex-convict who was an expert with safes, but the man wouldn't do it."

Sir Jeremy put down his whiskey glass, shaking his head. "Lady Georgiana, you never fail to surprise me," he said. "You calmly talk about dead bodies and now finding an ex-convict to crack a safe. Most young ladies in your position would have swooned at the mention of such things."

"I suppose I take after my Rannoch ancestors," I said. "They were known to be fearless and reckless. And I've had my share of being involved in unpleasant matters."

"We can turn this knowledge over to DCI Pelham," Sir

Jeremy said. "I'm sure he must have access to safecrackers and I don't think he seems to be getting anywhere either. He was most annoyed when we told him he had to release O'Mara because he had been working undercover."

Darcy shifted uneasily on his chair. "If you want the safe opened without telling Pelham, I could give it a try," he said. "I've opened a couple of safes in my dubious career and I suspect that a wall safe in a woman's flat wouldn't be too complicated. But how do we get in without going past the hall porter?"

"I have a key. I obtained it from her former cleaning lady," I said. "I think it works for the servants' entrance."

Sir Jeremy rolled his eyes. "I have not heard a word of this conversation," he said, "but if you find anything of significance in that safe, I'd like to know about it."

"Of course," we said in unison, looked at each other and smiled.

Chapter 28

LATE ON NOVEMBER 8

A spot of safecracking.

It was quite dark by the time we left Sir Jeremy's and Darcy hailed a taxicab. Luckily I had Bobo's key in my purse. Darcy had the cab drop us on Park Lane rather than outside Bobo's block of flats. I felt rather proud of myself when I led Darcy around to show him the back entrance, but the pride vanished when we found the entrance locked for the night. I tried both my keys but neither worked.

"Bolted from the inside for the night. That's torn it," Darcy said. "Now we have two options. Either we go away and try during the daytime tomorrow or we bluff our way past the doorman." He looked at me and grinned. "I say the latter."

"You do the talking," I said. "That Irish blarney of yours might get us past."

"As it happens, I don't even think we'll need too much blarney," he said. "Come on, let's go and present ourselves to William."

We went around to the front of the building and Darcy

marched ahead of me through those glass swing doors and up to the doorman's cubby. A ginger-haired man started to come out when he heard us, then stopped.

"Good evening, William," Darcy said, going up to him with a jaunty stride. "It's been a long time. How are you?"

The man's face lit up. "Mr. O'Mara. How nice to see you. It has been a long time. In fact we were just talking about you the other day and saying that we had expected you to come and stay when Miss Carrington was away during the summer."

"Unfortunately I couldn't make it this time, although I always enjoy staying here," Darcy said. "I was in America, as it happens."

"America? Fancy that. Is it all that they say it is?"

"And more," Darcy said. "But a terrible depression is going on there just like here."

William nodded. "There's not a day goes by that I'm not thankful I've got a job, Mr. O'Mara. When you see all those poor wretches on street corners, don't you? And at the soup kitchens in the stations."

"You do indeed." Darcy paused for an instant. "You've been keeping well? And the family? Growing up fast?"

"Indeed they are, Mr. O'Mara," William said. "Eating us out of house and home." Then his smile faded. "But I'm afraid Miss Carrington isn't in residence, if that's who you've come to see, sir. Hasn't been home for days now." He leaned closer to Darcy. "And between ourselves, there's something funny going on. Frederick says the police were here. They didn't identify themselves as police, but you can always tell, can't you?"

"That's exactly why I'm here," Darcy said. He moved over until he and William were standing very close together. "I heard about the police, you see, and it occurred to me that I might have left some items in Miss Carrington's flat. Now, I suspect the police raid must have something to do with drugs. We all know that Miss Carrington has a nasty little habit, don't we? Well, I've never touched a drug in my life and I don't want the police putting two and two together and making five, if you get my meaning. So I thought I'd take a quick look around and make sure there's nothing of mine up in the flat. If that's all right with you, of course?"

William wrinkled his nose, deliberating. "I'm not sure about that, Mr. O'Mara."

"Did the police actually tell you nobody was to go up to the flat?"

"It was Frederick they talked to, not me. But he didn't say that."

"So then there would be no reason for me not to take a quick look, would there?" Darcy said. "If you don't feel comfortable, you can always look the other way, you know. I've still got my key, so theoretically I can let myself in whenever I want."

"So you can, Mr. O'Mara." William nodded. "Why not?" Then his gaze turned to me. "But the young lady—I don't think Miss Carrington would like that."

"This is my fiancée, William. Lady Georgiana Rannoch. The king's cousin. Quite beyond reproach."

"Blimey, so it is," William said. "Well, then, in that case . . . you ain't the first royal we've had here."

And he gave us both a knowing nod. I thought it wiser not to ask any questions, but followed Darcy over to the lift.

It wasn't until we were safely ascending that I asked, "Was it wise to tell him so much? Won't he spill the beans to DCI Pelham?"

"You heard him. The Cockney's inbred distrust of the police. And we are old friends. I've always tipped him generously."

"You amaze me sometimes," I said.

"That's good." He smiled at me. "Amazement and adoration seem like a good basis for a happy marriage."

"You mean my amazement and your adoration?" I quipped back, making him laugh.

THE LIFT DOORS opened and we crossed a deserted landing to Bobo's flat. It smelled even more musty and unpleasant than last time with the rotting food items looking quite disgusting. Darcy recoiled at the state of the place. "Well, one thing is clear," he said as he crossed the room to hastily draw the curtains. "She'd been living here and intended to come back shortly. She wouldn't have left the place like this for more than an hour or so." He looked around. "I wonder if she asked William to hail her a taxicab that evening. Or whether anyone came to call for her. We can ask on the way down." He went through into the bedroom and pulled the heavy curtains across those floor-to-ceiling windows. "Oh, there's my dressing gown," he said, turning back again.

"You can't take it," I said hurriedly. "The police will know you've been here."

"Quite right. I wonder whether I have left anything else here? No time for that now. Well, where's this safe?"

I went over to the wall and removed the painting. Darcy examined the safe and grunted. "Very modern. I don't think I've seen one just like this. So what would Bobo use as a combination? Her birthday? I know the date but not the year." He tried several with no success. He tried other combinations, then shook his head. He put his ear to the safe and turned the dial slowly. Then he said, "Let's think. She's sneaky in some ways. Inventive. But lazy. Wait a minute." He turned the dial left then right and to my amazement the safe swung open.

"How did you do that?" I asked.

He grinned. "Luck," he said. "I retraced my steps to where we began and figured she might only have moved the dial once after she closed the safe. Lazy, you see."

It was a small safe, stuffed quite full. I had expected maybe jewels but I was surprised to pull out mainly photographs and letters. Darcy whistled as he removed a large bundle of five-pound notes. "A little emergency cash," he said. "And here is where the rest goes." He held up what seemed to be a bankbook. "Swiss bank account. She plays the helpless female very well but she's as sharp as they come."

"Played," I said. "She's dead. She wasn't sharp enough to spot danger coming."

We both stood in silence for a moment. Then Darcy said, "So what about these photos and letters?"

I picked up one. "'My darling Gerald, how I've pined for you. Are you staying away deliberately, you wicked boy? I've been at the Black Cat numerous times and you've never shown up.'" I looked up at Darcy.

"A love letter," I said, then I read down to the signature. "It's signed, 'Your heartbroken Hugo.'

"It's from another man," I said. "What was Bobo doing with it?"

I picked up one of the photographs. It was of a group of men in bathing costumes, standing with arms draped around each other's shoulders. I thought some of them looked familiar. It was a small snapshot and I peered harder. "That one looks quite like Major Beauchamp-Chough," I said. "Only younger and minus the mustache."

"Probably a younger brother," Darcy said. "Although most army types tend to look the same. Eton and Sandhurst, you know." He peered at the photograph. "I don't know why she'd want snapshots of men on a beach. But look at this." He held out a picture of a woman standing with a pretty little girl of six or seven by a country cottage. On the back of the snapshot someone had written, *She looks just like you, Toby.*

"Toby?" I asked. "As in Sir Toby Blenchley? But that's not his wife?"

"Definitely not," he said. "I get the feeling we know now how Bobo made her money. I thought it might be selling drugs, but look at all this. Incriminating evidence. I'd bet the farm that Bobo was a blackmailer."

"Golly," I said. "There are a lot of items here. So any one of these people would have wanted her dead."

"I must take this lot to Sir Jeremy," he said. "I think I'd be playing with fire if I started probing too closely into Sir Toby's life without proper authority."

"But she was reputed to be his mistress," I said. "How could she be blackmailing him?"

"That may be how she worked. She became friendly with powerful men. They gave away too many secrets in the heat of passion and she threatened to expose them. Men with too much to lose."

"Like Sir Toby," I said. "The least we can do is to ascertain his movements on the evening Bobo was killed."

Darcy shook his head. "I already told you that a man like Sir Toby wouldn't do his own dirty work. He'd have hired someone."

"Could he risk hiring someone?"

"I expect he has a loyal underling who has done unpleasant jobs before and is well paid for his silence," Darcy said. "It's strange how powerful men think they are untouchable."

"I wonder why he didn't have someone try to break in here to retrieve the evidence from the safe," I said, staring down at that snapshot.

"She probably made him think the evidence was in a bank vault or somewhere equally untouchable. In that bank in Switzerland, maybe."

I leafed through other photographs and letters. I came across a picture of Bobo in a bathing suit, sitting on a yacht with Prince George. He had his arm around her shoulder and they were both holding cocktail glasses. "Surely she couldn't have tried to blackmail him?" I asked.

Darcy stared down at it. "I suppose it's possible if she was ruthless enough."

"Oh dear. That's exactly what the royal family feared," I said. "Now he'll seem to be a suspect again."

"The only thing against that is that he would never have dumped her body outside the very place where his bride-to-be was staying. Even good old George wouldn't be that stupid or that insensitive."

"That's true." I felt a little better. I liked George. I liked Marina. I didn't want this complication to blight their marriage and I certainly didn't want to believe that George could be a killer. "The person who did this wanted us to jump to the conclusion that it was Prince George and thus divert suspicion from himself," I said at last. I leafed through more photographs. Faces seemed familiar but only vaguely, the way one recognizes distant acquaintances at parties.

"We should close the safe and go," I said. "William will get suspicious if we stay up here too long."

Darcy closed it, then took out his handkerchief and wiped it free of fingerprints. "Can't be too careful," he said, grinning. He put back the picture, then looked around the room. "It seems an awful shame to waste the one time we're quite alone and won't be interrupted," he said.

"Darcy O'Mara," I replied indignantly, "if you think I'm going to allow any hanky-panky in a room where you've been with another woman, you can think again."

He chuckled. "I wasn't suggesting a full-blown roll in the hay, but a little kiss and cuddle would be nice."

"I've nothing against a kiss and a cuddle," I said, slipping my arms around his neck, "just as long as you don't get carried away."

"I'm not the only one who gets carried away," he said. "I think you can be quite a hot little piece at times, young woman. But you're wasting time talking." And he shut me up very effectively. His kisses were as wonderful as ever and I felt desire welling up in the pit of my stomach. I did want him, badly, and I think I would not only have given in, but even encouraged him at that moment, had it not been for the glimpse of his dressing gown hanging behind Bobo's door. I pushed away from him. "We should go," I said. "I don't feel comfortable here. Whatever Bobo did, however she lived, you liked her enough once to make love to her, and she didn't deserve to die."

Darcy nodded solemnly and we left the flat, closing the door behind us. In the lift on the way down, Darcy had the foresight to tuck the evidence inside his greatcoat.

"Any luck, Mr. O'Mara?" William asked. "Find anything?"

"Nothing at all, William, except for an old dressing gown," Darcy said. "Tell me, when did you see Miss Carrington last?"

"Let me see. It would have been four days ago," William said, frowning as he tried to remember. "That's right. Sunday, I think it was."

"Did she say where she was going? Did she have a suitcase with her?"

"No, the last time I saw her it was just like any other evening. She was dressed to go out, evening gown, long fur coat. I asked her if she wanted a taxicab but she said she was meeting someone, and off she went toward Park Lane. Of course, Frederick might have seen her since then."

"Thank you, William," Darcy said. "My best regards to your family."

"We hope to see you again soon, Mr. O'Mara," William said. "When this nasty old business is taken care of, whatever it turns out to be."

How sad, I thought. Nobody knew that Bobo was dead and would not be coming back to her flat. Darcy hailed a taxicab and took me back to Kensington. I invited him to join us for dinner but he said he had better get straight back to Sir Jeremy so they could put together a plan of action. I wished he might have included me, but I understood that he couldn't. And I regretted not going with him even more so when I found out that Marina was dining with her parents at the Dorchester and my dinner companion was Countess Irmtraut.

Chapter 29

It feels strange not having anything more to do with the
   investigation into Bobo's death. Darcy will show the
   letters and photographs to Sir Jeremy and they'll
   know how to look into the lives of powerful men. I
   must put the whole thing from my mind and just
   help Marina prepare for her wedding.

Queenie was in my room, waiting to undress me. "I ain't
going near that foreign lady no more," she said. "You should
have heard her shouting at me, and all because I used the
wrong polish on a pair of shoes. Blimey, miss, you'd have
thought I had just drowned her only child in a bathtub."

I sighed. "I suppose you can't be blamed for not knowing
how to treat suede. I don't possess any suede shoes. And it's
probably a good idea that you stay away from her. I really
don't want word of your behavior getting back to the

princess or the major. They'd know you weren't a suitable maid and it might even get back to the queen."

"I don't know why you think I'm so unsuitable," she said. "I take care of you all right, don't I?"

I shot her an exasperated look. "Queenie, since we've been here you've left one evening dress behind and soaked another one. Since we've been together you have burned, ironed, singed or shrunk almost everything I own. You really aren't suited to any kind of work, but you have a good heart. You mean well and actually I've grown quite fond of you. The way one does with a dog that pees on the carpet."

"I don't pee on the carpet," she said indignantly and yanked my dress over my head.

I think I was smiling as I fell asleep.

The next day it was strange not to be rushing about worrying. I had posted my letter to Mummy, but I went over to Belinda's house, stocked it with some food for her and some flowers to cheer her up before she came back to London. And when I returned to the palace that afternoon I learned that I was invited to luncheon with Marina's parents at the Dorchester the next day. So was Irmtraut, who appeared at breakfast the next morning wearing some sort of hideous national costume with silver buttons down the front. I was thankful she had chosen to dress like this, as it made my outfit look normal and even quite smart. I was a little apprehensive about meeting European royals, even if they had been deposed and exiled. But they turned out to be charming. Marina's Danish-Greek father and her Russian-born mother both had a good sense of humor and spoke perfect English, and we had a pleasant luncheon together. I was even becoming accustomed to frequenting places like the Dorchester!

Marina told her mother about our shopping expeditions, as a result of which her mother declared she didn't want to miss out on all the fun and we should all go to Bond Street before the shops closed. Her father said that wild horses couldn't drag him to go shopping with a gaggle of women and retired to the bar. But we piled into a taxicab and had a spiffing time hunting down odd trousseau items like a blue garter, white silk stockings and a deliciously sinful negligee that made Irmtraut so upset in the shop that an assistant had to bring her a glass of water.

Marina's mother came back to Kensington Palace with us for tea. Marina took her mama up to show her her suite. I followed, and we were halfway up the stairs when I spotted Queenie coming down. She was carrying an empty tea plate and cup and her mouth was liberally decorated with jam. What's more, there were crumbs down the front of her black dress.

"Whatcher, miss," she said, not batting an eyelid that she was passing two royal ladies.

"Queenie," I hissed.

To my horror, Marina's mother turned around. Oh golly. She thought I had been calling her.

"Yes, my dear?" she asked, looking puzzled. "I'm actually only a princess, not a queen."

"I'm so sorry, Your Royal Highness," I stammered. "I was speaking to a maid. Unfortunately her Christian name is Queenie."

Luckily both Marina and her mother thought this was awfully funny and an international incident was avoided. I noticed that Queenie took advantage of the laughter to escape down the stairs. I resolved to speak to her sternly next time we were alone.

While we were having tea, a footman appeared with a note on a silver salver. I half expected it to be from Darcy, but it was addressed to Princess Marina. She took it, opened it and smiled. "Oh, how kind. It is from Princess Louise. She says the aunts usually meet for Sunday luncheon at Princess Alice's apartment and they would love it if Georgiana and I were free to join them tomorrow."

"That's very nice of them," I said. "Are you free?"

She glanced at her mother. "I promised Mama and Papa that I'd go to church with them, but after that we had no plans," she said. "I think I should meet my future relatives, don't you?"

"Absolutely," her mother agreed.

"And I?" Irmtraut asked. "I am not invited?"

"I don't think they realized you were staying here. I'll send them a note back and ask that you may be included, Traudi," Marina said. "Of course you should come with us."

She was really a sweet-natured person.

"I think that perhaps you should not attend, Irmtraut," Marina's mother said. "It is to be a family occasion for Marina to meet her new aunts."

"Very well," Irmtraut said stiffly. "I should not intrude on a family occasion."

"Oh, but Mama, surely . . ." Marina began but Irmtraut interrupted.

"No, you are right. I should not attend," Irmtraut said stiffly. "I should not feel comfortable and I do not wish to seem like the poor relation."

"As you wish," Marina said and I could tell even she was becoming exasperated with Irmtraut.

She turned to me. "Now you must tell me all about these aunts so that I get it right tomorrow."

Oh crikey. I was clear enough about Princesses Louise and Beatrice, both Queen Victoria's daughters. Princess Alice, I understood, had married Prince Alexander of Teck, and was thus related to Queen Mary as well as the king. The last royal aunt, the Dowager Marchioness of Milford Haven, was a little more nebulous to me. I knew she was also a granddaughter of Queen Victoria and therefore cousin to my father, but not much else about her. It seemed that Queen Victoria had had enough children to populate the royal houses of Europe.

"But you know her, Marina," her mother said when I mentioned the name. "Her daughter Alice is your aunt. She married Daddy's brother."

"Oh yes. Of course." Marina smiled. "Then her grandson must be Philip. The blond boy."

"Such a handsome lad already," Marina's mother said. "I wonder who he will marry one day?"

"Unfortunately too young for you, Georgie," Marina said. "But you have someone else in mind, don't you?"

So we had a lovely Sunday to look forward to—luncheon with the aunts and then a glamorous soiree with Noel Coward. How easily one slips into the mode of thinking there is nothing extraordinary about this. If only Fig could see me now!

Marina was dining with her parents at Buckingham Palace so it was to be just Irmtraut and me at Kensington again. We were having sherry, prior to dining, when a maid appeared.

"Your ladyship, there is a gentleman to see you at the front door," she said. "A Mr. O'Mara."

"Thank you." I felt my cheeks turning red as I went out to meet him. He was standing in the long gallery off the front entrance, looking around with interest.

"This place could do with a coat of paint," he said. "Couldn't they have found anywhere a little less dingy to house a princess?"

"It was the only apartment that was vacant here," I said. "There are several royal aunts in residence."

"Ah yes. The Prince of Wales's Aunt Heap." Darcy smiled.

"Will you come in for sherry? I could introduce you to the dreaded Irmtraut."

He looked dubious. "I just stopped by to give you the latest news. We've found the birth certificate and no father is listed. It seems the child is already in America."

"America?"

He nodded. "Sir Jeremy went to have a chat with Sir Toby. He was told that Sir Toby arranged the adoption with a wealthy American publisher while he was over in the States. He said there was a little unpleasantness because Bobo changed her mind at the last moment and didn't want to give up her baby. But he said he made her see sense."

"So Toby Blenchley was the father?" I asked.

"Not according to him. She was just a young acquaintance, but he'd heard about her unfortunate circumstances and his mind went instantly to his friend in America whose wife was longing for a baby. So he helped arrange the adoption. End of story."

"Would you go to all that trouble for a distant acquaintance?" I asked.

"Probably not." Darcy smiled. "But Sir Toby hasn't been in government this long without learning a thing or two. I don't see any way we could prove he was the father. In fact he hinted to Sir Jeremy that everyone knew that Prince George was the child's father, but naturally, as good Englishmen, they would never express that thought in company."

"But we know she has been seen around with Sir Toby. If she wasn't his mistress, then why?"

"Another idea that I don't think we'll be able to prove," he said. "It's possible he brings in the drugs when he comes back from trade missions. It's unlikely the bags of a minister on government business would ever be searched. He might have been supplying people like Bobo."

"But you'd never get anyone to talk."

"We'll act as if we suspect nothing. Then next time he goes to New York, we'll go through every bag with a fine-toothed comb."

I nodded. Then took a deep breath. "But we're no nearer to being able to find out who killed her. If he was supplying her with drugs, wouldn't he want her alive? On the other hand, if she was blackmailing him and had recently threatened to take incriminating evidence to the newspapers . . ."

I paused. "She may have become too much of a liability," Darcy finished for me.

"Surely there is more that the police could do," I said angrily. "I'd be questioning every hobo in Kensington Gardens, any constable who patrols the gardens. Someone must have seen a motorcar driving up to the palace."

"So what? If you'd seen a big motor drive past, wouldn't you automatically think it was one of the palace occupants returning home? You wouldn't look twice, would you? And it was unpleasant weather. No late evening strollers. Everyone tucked up at home."

"I hate to think that someone is going to get away with this," I said.

"The problem is the need for secrecy," he said. "In the case of a normal murder we'd be asking the public to come forward with anything they'd seen. We'd be asking for tips from those involved in the world of drugs. But we can do none of this. Ah well." He ran his hand through those dark curls. "My money is still on Sir Toby. Maybe he'll slip up someday. Maybe someone will squeal. In the meantime go back and enjoy your sherry. I can let myself out."

"Why don't you come have dinner with us," I said, reaching out to take his hand. "Surely you can't be too busy on a Saturday evening?"

He looked around. "I have a few things that have to be done. But I'm not dressed."

"It's only Irmtraut and me," I said. "I'm sure she'll understand."

He smiled then. "All right. Why not. I've no better offer."

"I can tell how very keen you are to be with me," I said.

He laughed and put an arm around my shoulder. "Come on, then. Introduce me to the formidable countess."

I led him through to the sitting room. Irmtraut started, looking as if I'd brought a farm laborer in muddy boots into the place.

"Countess, this is my young man, the Honorable Darcy O'Mara, son of Lord Kilhenny," I said.

"How do you do." She held out a hand, giving him a "we are not amused" stare that would have rivaled one from my great-grandmother.

He took the hand and to my amazement brought it to his lips to kiss it. "*Enchanté*, Countess," he said.

After that he had her eating out of his hand and I could witness the charm that had attracted me to him in the first place. Because the princess wasn't present, the dinner was solid family food—not as bad as toad in the hole but steak and kidney pie and cabbage followed by spotted dick. Irmtraut poked at it with her fork.

"And what is this?" she demanded.

"Spotted dick," I said.

She peered at it. "Who or what is a dick and why is he spotted?"

Darcy and I stared hard at our plates to stop us from bursting out laughing.

"You certainly charmed the countess," I commented when I escorted him to the front door after coffee.

He grinned. "Occasionally I need to prove that I still have what it takes. Perhaps she'll be nicer to you from now on."

Then he gave me a suitably chaste kiss before departing.

"Your young man is charming," Irmtraut said when I returned to the drawing room. "And he is Irish, did you say?"

"Half Irish, half English," I said.

"He is Catholic, then?"

"Yes, he is."

"But surely you will not be able to marry him, I think. Does the law of England not say that members of the royal family must marry Protestants? Marina told me that she must give up her Greek Orthodox religion and convert to the Church of England when she marries George or the marriage will not be allowed."

"That's true. But I'm so far from the throne that I'd be willing to renounce my place in the line of succession."

"And if the king will not allow this?"

Oh golly. I wish she hadn't started down that path. "I'm sure he will," I said with more conviction than I felt.

She looked smug and I suspected she was pleased to have thrown another spoke into another wheel. It was probably the highlight of her day.

※

ON SUNDAY I had a lazy morning with only a slight twinge of guilt that I was not joining the others at church. I ate only a small breakfast of kippers and poached egg, knowing that the full traditional English Sunday lunch lay ahead of me. The churchgoers returned and we sat over coffee in the morning room until it was time to make our way to Princess Alice's apartment. The delicious smell of roasting beef wafted toward us as the front door was opened. We arrived at the same time as the major, who was looking absolutely splendid in his dress uniform. The four elderly ladies certainly made a fuss of him as we were led through to a charmingly furnished sitting room.

"I'm so glad you wore your uniform, Major," Princess Alice said. "I remember seeing you come home the other night when I was going to bed and thinking how distinguished you looked, walking up the path in that uniform. I'm surprised some eligible young woman hasn't snapped you up by now."

"Not many young women want to live on a soldier's pay, Your Highness," he said with a regretful smile. "I'm a second son. I'm not going to inherit anything."

"Such a stupid rule," Princess Louise said. "That concept of 'winner take all.' Most old-fashioned. And who wants to inherit a great house these days? It costs a fortune to heat it and to pay servants to run it. I count my blessings daily that I have this small establishment here and not some great drafty stately home. If you young people heed my advice you'll live in London with Harrods and Fortnum's on the doorstep."

Sherry was served, and then we went through to the dining room, overlooking the main entrance. It being Sunday, the place was closed to visitors.

"Thank God there is no tramp, tramp of people going up the stairs today," Princess Alice said.

Princess Beatrice nodded agreement. "At least your rooms are not beneath them. Some days it sounds like an invading army. My mama would have been horrified. It was her apartment once, you know." She turned to Marina. "And where shall you be living, my dear? Not still at St. James's Palace with the Prince of Wales?"

"No, we've been given a house on Belgrave Square," Marina said. "Close to Georgiana's London home. I'm looking forward to our being neighbors as I've never run my own establishment before."

"Unfortunately it's not my home any longer. It belongs to my brother and his wife these days and I'm not exactly welcome there," I said.

"How sad. Families should support one another," Princess Louise said. "We have each other for company, do we not? And a charming young woman like you, Georgiana. Who would not want you to live with them?"

"My sister-in-law, apparently," I said as a footman came to serve me with Yorkshire pudding.

It was a splendid meal. The elderly ladies and the major were good company and there was much laughter. The party didn't break up until four o'clock and we returned to find Irmtraut sitting in solitary state at tea. She was in a grumpy mood and answered Marina in monosyllables.

"We should have a rest before going to Mr. Coward's," Marina said. "Will it be formal, do you think?"

"Rather too informal, I should think," I said. "Mr. Coward's friends span all levels of society."

"How exciting." Marina gave me a pleased smile.

"I shall not be coming," Irmtraut said. "I do not wish to mingle with bohemians and actors. My parents would not approve."

"Oh, Traudi, don't be such a stick-in-the-mud," Marina said.

"I do not look like a stick," Irmtraut replied. "You are rude."

"No, that's not what I meant," Marina started to say but Irmtraut had risen to her feet and stalked from the room.

Marina looked at me. "Oh dear. I'm afraid I offended her. I don't really know why she insisted on coming. She's not having a good time."

"She's annoyed that the queen asked me to be your companion. She feels put out," I said. "And there was nothing I could do about it because one does not say no to the queen."

"Of course not." She covered my hand with hers. "Dear Georgie. I'm so glad you're here. You must come and stay with us if your sister-in-law doesn't want you."

"Thank you."

As I came out through the door I detected a movement at the top of the stairs. Irmtraut had been standing there, listening to our conversation.

Chapter 30

SUNDAY, NOVEMBER 11

Cocktails with Noel Coward. What could be more glamorous?

The motorcar came for us at six and whisked us to the house in Chelsea. We were among the first to arrive but were introduced to Noel's actress friend Gertrude Lawrence and to a couple of fellow writers and society matron Mrs. Astley-Cooper.

"You've come without your bridegroom, I see," she said and got a warning look from Noel. "Very wise. So many women think that they are only allowed out as an appendage to their spouse once they marry. Make sure you have your own life and your own friends."

"Who is talking about appendages?" one of the young men asked.

"Naughty, naughty, Hugo, my boy. Respectable young women present," Noel said, slapping his hand.

I looked at the man with interest. Hugo was not a very common name and one of the letters in Bobo's safe had been signed by him. A love letter to another man called Gerald. So Hugo was presumably another of those being black-mailed. I looked around the room. Was Gerald also here?

More and more people arrived, some that I recognized from their photographs in the picture papers. Cocktails were poured. Canapés were served. Noel sat at the piano and entertained. He was awfully witty, terribly risqué, and I was glad that Irmtraut had decided not to come. Either she wouldn't have understood his wicked innuendoes or she would have been mortally offended by them. Marina, how-ever, laughed with the rest of us.

"I think she'll do nicely for George, don't you?" I heard one of the men saying in a low voice.

"Ah, but will she take him out of circulation? That's the question."

Noel was singing another song, one he had just made up, according to him. "It's a bit risqué, what do you think?" he asked. "Dare I try it on audiences? Is the London theater ready for it?"

"You should try it out first at the Black Cat," someone called out and there was laughter.

"Is the Black Cat a nightclub?" I asked the man standing next to me.

"In a way," he replied, looking at me cautiously. "It's a place where young men of a certain persuasion go to meet other young men of similar persuasion. Very discreet or the police would shut it down."

"Oh, I see." I glanced across at Hugo, who was now chat-ting with a rather too gorgeous young man with blond curls. He had complained that Gerald no longer came to the Black Cat. I turned back to the man I had been chatting with.

"Is—uh—Gerald here tonight then?" I asked.

His eyebrows raised. "I shouldn't think so," he replied hastily. "Not his sort of thing. He wouldn't want to be associ-ated with Noel, would he? Very cautious is our Gerry boy."

So Gerald might have had more to lose. I should report that to Darcy tomorrow. I wondered how many more people there were, willing to keep paying Bobo for her silence about behavior that society would not accept. And whether one of them had decided she had to be silenced forever.

The party showed no signs of ending but at nine o'clock Princess Marina indicated that she was ready to leave and sent someone for our motor.

"I'm sorry, but I was getting a headache," she said as the car drove away. "All that smoke and noise and people one doesn't know talking to each other and only including one occasionally to be polite."

"I know, I felt rather the same," I said, realizing how very overwhelming it must be for her, having to be nice to everyone in a strange country when she would be nervous about her wedding. "They certainly like to hold forth, don't they? Each trying to outdo the other in wit."

She chuckled then. "That would be tiring in everyday friends."

We arrived back at Kensington Palace to find that Irmtraut was nowhere to be seen. But she had left a note on the front table. "I retired to bed early with headache."

"Poor Traudi, she's sulking," Marina said. "I've tried to include her as much as possible but she's not easy to please."

"Has she always been that way?"

"We hardly ever saw her branch of the family but I do remember her as a morose child who didn't want to play pranks with my sisters and me—" She put her hand up to her mouth. "Oh God," she said. "I forgot all about it."

"What?"

"My sisters and the other bridesmaids will be arriving on the overnight train from Hook of Holland. Mama suggested I should be at the station to meet them. I completely forgot to tell the chauffeur. Too many cocktails."

"What time does the boat train arrive?" I asked.

"Seven thirty at Liverpool Street Station. Can you imagine?" She looked around. "And there is no telephone and I wouldn't know who to call either."

"I suppose you could always order a taxicab or two."

"I don't think it would go down well to meet royal young ladies in a taxicab," she said. "I'd better go and find the major. He will know."

She looked completely washed out. "I'll go for you," I said. "If you have to be up that early you should go to bed now."

She gave me a big smile. "You're wonderful, Georgie. Thank you. Tell him I need the motor to be here at seven. I believe it's quite a long way to Liverpool Street Station, isn't it?"

"Yes. The other side of London. But half an hour should be sufficient." I smiled and went back out into the night. It was crisp and cold and my footsteps echoed on the path as I made my way around to the main entrance of the palace. I realized I could have taken a shortcut through the courtyard to his back door, but I didn't think it would be correct to appear at a back door unless it was an emergency. Also I was reluctant to cross that courtyard in the dark. My key admitted me to the main foyer, which was bathed in gloom. There was just one small lamp alight over the stairs and I found myself tiptoeing across the marble floor before I came to what I remembered to be the major's front door. There was a calling card in the brass card holder and I peered at it to make sure I was in the right place. I was about to knock when my hand was poised, frozen, a few inches from the door.

Major Gerald Beauchamp-Chough.

"Crikey," I whispered.

HE WAS GERALD. I knew there were plenty of other Geralds in the world, but it all made sense now. The upright major who hoped to be promoted to colonel could never risk letting anyone know that he was a homosexual. It would mean the end of his career. The only problem was that he had not been at the palace all evening. He had arrived back at the same moment as ourselves. Or rather he had said he had just arrived back. But then I remembered. Princess Alice had seen him from her bedroom window when she was going to bed.

I needed to know what time she went to bed. And it occurred to me that she could be in great danger because of that innocent remark. I tiptoed up the marble staircase and turned toward Princess Alice's apartment. I peered at my watch in the dim light. Nine thirty-five. Not horribly late to call upon someone. I tapped at her door. After a long while it was opened by a maid who had clearly put on her cap hurriedly to answer the door.

"Lady Georgiana," she said in a breathless voice. "I'm sorry, but Her Highness has retired for the night."

"Does she always go to bed this early?" I asked.

"Always. Early to bed and early to rise, she likes to say. She gets up at six and goes for a walk in the park."

"Thank you. I am sorry to have disturbed you," I said.

"Is there a message?"

"Not now. I'll deliver it myself tomorrow morning."

I came away again, not sure now what to do. I had promised to deliver a message to the major for Princess Marina. Could I deliver it now and not give away that I suspected him? Should I go and find a telephone booth and ring Sir Jeremy's number? My heart was hammering. I was surely safe for now. It was Princess Alice I worried about, going for that early walk on a misty November morning. I shook my head in disbelief. Surely he wouldn't consider killing a member of the royal family, would he?

He would if he could make it look like an accident, I thought. I'd make sure I was up and on that walk with her. The marble banister felt solid and comforting as I made my way down the stairs. I went as silently as possible. I didn't want the major to know I had been up to the princess's suite. As the stair curved around I peered down to the foyer and my heart gave a jolt as I saw a figure standing in the gloom at the bottom of the stairs. It was the major and he was watching me.

I put on my brightest smile. "Hello, Major. I was just coming to see you," I said. "I promised Princess Marina I'd deliver a message for her. She needs a motorcar early tomorrow morning. Can that be arranged?"

He came up the steps slowly, one by one. "What were

you doing upstairs, Lady Georgiana? Not taking a tour of the royal galleries at this time of night, surely?"

I laughed my best gay and carefree laugh. "No, I also promised Princess Marina that I'd deliver a message to Princess Alice for her."

"But she has already retired for the night. I overheard."

"Yes. No matter. I'll come back in the morning."

Why was he coming up the stairs toward me, step by step, slowly and methodically? He was blocking my escape route, that was what he was doing. His face was calm and composed but I was reminded that he was a trained killer. And he had killed once. After that first time, it is easy.

I was determined to keep bluffing. "Do you need something upstairs, Major? Isn't it just Princess Alice's suite and the royal galleries leading from this staircase?"

"I thought we might take a tour of the royal galleries together," he said. "Since you're here and I'm here."

"Lovely thought, but I've just been to a party and I'm awfully tired."

Wild thoughts were racing through my head. I was conscious of our voices, echoing around the foyer, of the staircase disappearing into darkness below and the feeling of being utterly isolated from the world. If I screamed, probably nobody would ever hear me. I looked around. Smooth marble, high painted ceiling above. Nothing to use as a weapon. Utterly defenseless.

"On second thought," I said brightly, "I think I will deliver that message to Princess Alice tonight. I'll write her a little note so that she gets it first thing in the morning when she wakes up."

And I turned and marched deliberately up the stairs. I could sense he was right behind me, but I wasn't going to turn around. If I could just reach her front door . . . just hammer on it . . .

But as I came to the top of the stairs he slid past, standing between me and Princess Alice's suite. "Oh no, my dear. I suggest we go downstairs again. To my place. A nice hot drink, eh?"

He was still being polite and friendly but I knew beyond any doubt that the drink would contain Veronal. A stronger dose this time to make sure he didn't actually have to suffocate me.

"You obviously think I'm completely naïve," I said. "I don't want to meet the same fate as poor Bobo. How did you know I'd figured it out?"

"I saw the way you looked at Princess Alice when she said she'd seen me coming home when she was going to bed. You sneaked a glance at me and you studied my uniform, didn't you? I realized then that you'd noticed the sequin that got caught in the braid. A big sequin from her dress. I didn't see it initially. No batman to take care of me, you see."

Of course, I thought. Something sparkling. Something that my subconscious took in as incongruous. How stupid of me.

"You were going to find out what time Princess Alice went to bed, weren't you? And when I heard her servant say she had already retired I knew you'd tell Sir Jeremy as soon as you found a telephone."

I inched away from him, still saying nothing.

"I didn't want to do any of this, you know," he said. "I had no qualms about killing her. She was a scheming little bitch. But you . . . if only I could trust you to stay silent. But I can't, can I? You have the moral fiber of your ancestors. You'd have to tell the truth. So I'm sorry. I really am. But it's my whole future, you see. Everything I've lived and worked for."

I glanced first at the major and then down the stairs. The front door was still open. If I ran fast enough down the stairs I might make it out of the door before him. But I was wearing an evening gown and dainty little slippers. He could outrun me. He could just as easily catch me in the darkness of the park.

If I went the other way—the way he wasn't expecting, into the royal galleries—I might have a chance. Plenty of places to hide, maybe a weapon of some sort with which to

defend myself. And maybe another staircase I could slip
down and out into the night. I lifted my skirt so that I could
run more easily, then I turned and fled into the darkness.
My footsteps clattered and echoed across the landing. After
the dim lighting of the foyer it was pitch-black in there. I
blundered into a glass case containing some kind of exhibit,
felt my way around it, and around a second, and through to
a second room. I heard him curse behind me as he obviously
bumped into something too. Now I was used to the dark I
could vaguely make out old furniture, a display of costumes.
I didn't hesitate another second. I jumped up and took up
position in the middle of the display among the mannequins.

Just in time. He came blundering past. His breath echoed
loudly. "You can't go on hiding, you know. I'll find you.
There's only one way out."

I stayed perfectly still among the mannequins. There was
a chance he'd think I'd gone through to the other rooms and
then I could creep down the stairs.

Rats. He was coming back. I could hear his breath,
ragged with agitation now.

"There's a light switch here somewhere," he said.

I couldn't let him get to the light switch. Was there anything here I could use as a weapon? My hand touched the
nearest mannequin's cold arm. Did it come off? I tugged
gently but it didn't move. Then I felt the parasol in her hand.
A parasol was dainty and probably not much use but it was
better than nothing. And it had a solid handle of some kind
of stone. I eased myself down from the podium and crept
toward the sound of his breathing. There he was, his back
toward me, still fumbling for the light switch. I lifted the
parasol and brought it crashing down over his head. He cried
out, staggered and reeled, but he didn't fall. Bugger.

I fled back through the doorway and out onto the landing.
He'd catch me. Of course he'd catch me, but I had to try and
run anyway. If I could make it across the landing and down
the hallway on the other side, I'd hammer on Princess
Alice's door. I'd scream. Someone would hear me. His feet
were pounding close behind me. I was halfway across the

landing when suddenly there was a gust of cold wind. It became icily cold. A shape appeared out of nowhere—a white shape that formed itself into a young woman. She swept past me, even before I realized exactly what was happening. I froze. The major had come out of the royal rooms and was advancing toward me across the foyer with a look of grim determination on his face. He stopped short at the top of the stairs as the apparition advanced on him. As she came closer she seemed to glow. The major took a step back. Still she approached.

"I don't believe in ghosts," he said loudly. "You're not real. You can't hurt me."

Then, from his other side and horribly close, came a burst of wild, maniacal laughter. It was so sudden that my heart nearly leaped out of my chest. The major reacted too. A boy had appeared, clad in green, his hair a mass of unruly curls, his face wild and excited. The major took another step backward as the boy leaped at him. It was his fatal mistake. He stepped into nothing at the top of the staircase, lost his balance and fell. I could hear the cries and thuds as he bounced down the stairs. The boy shot me a delighted look and vanished. The white woman also looked at me as she vanished into a wall. It was a look of recognition, of one family member to another.

Chapter 31

I rushed to wake up Princess Alice's servants.

"Come quickly. The major has fallen down the stairs," I shouted. Princess Alice herself appeared in her nightclothes. "Call an ambulance, Hettie," she said to her maid.

"I think that won't be necessary," I said. One of the maids had turned on the main lights in the chandelier. I could see the major's face staring up at me, his head at a strange, unnatural angle.

Suddenly I wanted to cry. It was all for the best really, wasn't it? All so stupid that people had died like this. I was taken into Princess Alice's suite and given a brandy. I told her about the ghosts and how the major had been on his nightly rounds when one of them had appeared from nowhere and so startled him that he had stepped back and lost his footing. I didn't add that he had been trying to kill me.

"A wild child who laughs?" she said. "That would be Peter, the Wild Boy. I saw him once. He was a favorite of George the First, who had him brought back from the forests of Germany. I gather he's very protective of the royal family."

And she looked at me long and hard.

Police and ambulance men came. I wanted to suggest that they summon DCI Pelham but I couldn't think of a reason to do that for what I was claiming to be a horrible accident. It was fortunate that I could say with complete honesty that I had seen Major Beauchamp-Chough at the top of the stairs when one of the ghosts had appeared from the wall. He had stepped back and lost his footing. It was terrible. So tragic. Nothing more was asked of me.

As soon as I could I slipped away, found a telephone and dialed Sir Jeremy's number. He told me to stay put. He'd come immediately. Then I rang the number Darcy had given me. Nobody answered there. I was on my way back to my own apartment, wanting nothing more than a hot drink and bed, when I heard running feet behind me. Darcy came charging up and grabbed me.

"Are you all right?" he said. "I got a garbled message from Sir Jeremy that the major had fallen down the stairs. Was anyone else involved? Was it really an accident? And why the major?"

I told him as calmly as I could. "Remember that one photograph I said looked like him, only younger and minus the mustache? It must have been him with a group of his, um, friends."

"So you put two and two together and went looking for him? At this time of night?" He was shouting now.

"No. Nothing like that," I replied. "Princess Marina asked me to deliver a message to the major. It was only when I was at his front door that I saw his card and realized his name was Gerald—the name in that love letter, remember? And the Black Cat is where . . ."

"I know what the Black Cat is," he said curtly.

"And Princess Alice had said at luncheon today that she'd seen the major coming home, looking smart in his uniform, when she was going to bed. So I went up to her apartment to find out what time she went to bed and it was early. The major assumed I knew more than I did and he was going to kill me."

"So you pushed him down the stairs?"

"No, I didn't. Two of the family ghosts made him step backward and he lost his balance. Princess Sophia and the Wild Boy."

"You're not serious!"

"Deadly serious, Darcy. I'd seen Princess Sophia before, but she was wonderful. She came right at him as if she knew she was saving me."

Darcy shook his head. "Amazing," he said. "And to think it was Beauchamp-Chough all the time. I suppose we overlooked him because we thought his one motive would have been to protect the prince. And we thought he wouldn't be stupid enough to leave an incriminating body lying around at the castle, thus implicating Prince George."

"He meant to kill her with a Veronal-laced drink," I said. "I think he drugged her, then went out to his regimental dinner to set up his alibi. He planned to come back and find her dead, having taken her own life. Only she must have had a high tolerance for drugs and alcohol, so she woke up enough to try to escape. My maid said she looked out of the window and saw something wafting about in the courtyard. I think that must have been Bobo staggering around, half doped. The major returned and caught her just in time and had to suffocate her. Then he saw our motorcar approaching and rushed back into his suite to act as if he had just come in the door when we came to find him. Obviously he didn't think we'd go to look in the courtyard that night and believed he could spirit the body away before anyone found it."

"So why did you go to look?" Darcy asked.

"I saw this greenish light glowing and I wanted to see what was causing it. It must have been the palace ghosts again because there is no light under that archway."

"I don't know." Darcy shook his head. "Why can't you ever leave well enough alone and behave like a normal young lady? Take up the pianoforte or embroidery, for God's sake. Don't always go looking for trouble. I can't spend my life worrying about you every time you're out of my sight."

"There's an answer to that," I said. "Don't let me out of your sight so often. And you'd be bored with me in five minutes if I took up embroidery."

He took my face in his hands, looked down at me and smiled. "God, Georgie. I do love you."

"I love you too," I said.

And for the next few minutes neither of us spoke at all.

A FINE OBITUARY appeared in the *Times* two days later, listing all the accomplishments of Major Beauchamp-Chough and saying what a splendid chap he was. And I had to agree. He was a splendid chap in most ways. It's funny but I don't think I've ever met a truly evil murderer. Just desperate people backed into a corner so thoroughly that killing is the only way out.

At least we could now concentrate on the final preparations for the wedding. There were dress fittings and Queen Mary's tea for the young ladies in the wedding party—at which I didn't spill or drop anything, or even knock over a vase. I wondered if I might be growing out of my clumsiness. Could it be the added self-assurance of knowing that I was loved by Darcy? That I had a future to look forward to?

Belinda returned to London and I went to greet her, making sure she had enough supplies and didn't have to go out shopping for a while. She still looked frail, not the flamboyant girl I so admired.

"You're a peach, Georgie," she said as I made her tea and crumpets. "Where will you go after the wedding?"

"I don't know. I might stay on with Binky and Fig in the London house at least until Christmas."

"You could always come here," she said. "I don't plan to hire another live-in maid. At least not until we've heard from your mother and I can start to plan for the future. So I could clear out the spare bedroom for you. Make it nice and cozy."

"Wouldn't I cramp your style?"

"I don't plan to have that kind of style, at least not for the moment. And I'd welcome the company."

"What about Queenie? I can't just abandon her."

"We could set up a camp bed in the attic. If she doesn't mind climbing a stepladder."

"Can you see Queenie climbing a ladder?" I asked and we both laughed.

"I'll make sure I'm nearby, whatever happens," I said, taking her hands in mine. "It will all work out. You'll see."

"Thank you, Georgie. You're such a good friend," she said. "I hope you live happily ever after and have oodles of children."

"I hope so too," I said.

THE GREAT DAY arrived. I decided to squander part of my casino winnings on a smart new royal blue two-piece and matching hat with a feather in it. Darcy received an invitation to sit beside me in St. Margaret's, Westminster. It was a fine, crisp day and the couple looked splendid, and happy. I hoped that their happiness would last. As Marina walked up the aisle with her train and veil flowing out behind her I couldn't help fantasizing about my own wedding. Would I someday be married in a place like this? With Darcy waiting for me up at the altar and the choir singing? I suppose it's every girl's dream, isn't it? I confess to taking an occasional glance at Darcy, sitting beside me. Once I found him looking at me and he smiled.

After the ceremony we went to Buckingham Palace for the reception. The Prince of Wales was there, looking sulky without Mrs. Simpson. She certainly would not have been welcome. When the happy couple came past him George clapped him on the shoulder. "Your turn next, old boy," he said. "Or are you going to turn into a grouchy old confirmed bachelor?"

"You know very well what I want to do," David said in

a clipped voice. "If this blasted family would stop badgering me and trying to live my life for me."

"Ah, but the big difference is that you're going to be king and the rest of us aren't," George said. "I think it's time you buckled down and did your duty, old chap."

"Talk about the pot calling the kettle black." David gave a brittle laugh. "I don't have nearly as much buckling down to do as you."

"Ah, but I'm doing it. I'm going to be a thoroughly good boy from now on, and a devoted husband."

"I'll believe it when I see it," David said. He looked around. Marina was being kissed on the cheek by some elderly Continental royal lady. "By the way, whatever happened to Bobo?"

"She's dead, old chap. Drug overdose, they say," George said.

"That was a piece of luck for you, wasn't it?" David muttered. "Not the sort of thing one would want the blushing bride to hear about."

THE HAPPY COUPLE departed and the rest of us took our leave of the king and queen.

"Your turn next, eh, young Georgie?" the king asked.

"We'll have to see, sir," I replied, trying not to sneak a glance in Darcy's direction.

Darcy and I took a taxicab back to Kensington. "It seems a pity to waste a free evening," Darcy said.

"I'd better go and change out of this new outfit into something more eveningy," I said. "And I'll hang it up myself before Queenie can ruin it."

"No, don't change. We're going out. You look just perfect for where we're headed."

"All right." I gave him an excited smile.

"I've borrowed a motorcar," he said. "Come on. What are you waiting for?"

It wasn't the ragtop Triumph he had borrowed once before but a sleek Armstrong Siddeley.

"This is rather posh," I said. "From whom did you manage to borrow a motorcar like this?"

"I have my connections," he said with a mysterious smile.

I climbed in beside him. Darkness had fallen and a mist hung over the Round Pond.

"So where are we going?" I asked.

"You'll see." He was grinning.

We drove. City lights flashed past us. Up the Edgware Road to the Finchley Road past Golders Green. City lights gave way to rows of suburban houses, little high streets with people queuing to get into picture palaces and loitering around corner pubs.

"We're going out of London?" I asked.

He nodded, still staring straight ahead.

"To a friend's place?"

"No."

"You're being annoying, Darcy O'Mara."

He grinned, still staring at the road, which was now down to the occasional streetlight overhead. I felt a knot of excitement and apprehension. Had Darcy decided we had waited long enough and was he taking me to a hotel for the night? In which case didn't people normally head south to places like Brighton or the New Forest instead of to this northern fringe of the city with only the industrial midlands ahead? It didn't seem particularly attractive, but maybe he had a special place in mind. . . . The knot in my stomach grew. Was that what I wanted? A picture of Belinda, sitting alone at that clinic on the coast, suddenly flashed into my head. And Bobo, who was forced to give up her child, and Princess Sophia, whose ghost wandered the palace looking for the child who was taken from her. It was true that my circumstance was different from theirs. I had Darcy. He wouldn't desert me. He'd marry me if the unthinkable happened. All the same . . .

"Darcy," I began. He glanced across at me. "I don't want . . . I mean, I want it to be right. The time to be right."

It was as if he read my thoughts. "It will be," he said.

"Because, you know . . ."

He took a hand off the steering wheel and covered mine with his own. "It will be," he said. "I understand."

"So where the heck are we going?" I demanded.

He didn't look at me but stared straight ahead into the night. "Gretna Green," he said.

Historical Note

To those of you who think I have besmirched the good name of the royal family, I have to tell you that this story is based on truth.

Prince George, the Duke of Kent, was known for his profligate behavior, both before and after his marriage. He had both male and female lovers, including Noel Coward, singer Jessie Matthews and reputedly even novelist Barbara Cartland.

In the Roaring Twenties he was introduced to Alice "Kiki" Preston, a London party girl who was known as the "girl with the silver syringe" because of her drug habit. Kiki and George were lovers for years.

It was known that Prince George produced a love child. Was Kiki the mother, or was it another of his mistresses, called Violet Evans? Biographers disagree. However, arrangements were made to have the child adopted by an American publishing magnate and taken back to America. His name became Michael Canfield and he achieved celebrity when he married Lee Bouvier (Jackie Kennedy's sister). But he had a troubled life marred by alcohol and pills and died on a plane flight from New York.

All the participants in this drama came to a sad end. Prince George was killed during World War II, when his plane hit a Scottish hillside. It is not known whether this was pilot error.

Kiki Preston threw herself from a fifth-floor window in New York in 1946. Violet Evans gassed herself.

Prince George's behavior was so scandalous that his papers were sealed on his death and have not been made available to the public.

In contrast his older brother Albert—later King George VI—lived an exemplary life and brought England through the dark days of World War II.

Darkest night, Thursday, November 29, 1934

In an Armstrong Siddeley motorcar with the Honorable Darcy O'Mara, heading northward.

No idea where we are going, but Darcy is beside me so that's all right.

I was in a motorcar, sitting beside Darcy, and we were driving northward, out of London. He had whisked me away earlier that day, after we had both attended Princess Marina's wedding to the Duke of Kent. I first thought I was being taken for a romantic dinner. Then, as we left the streets of London behind, I began to suspect it may not be a dinner we were going to but a hotel in a naughty place like Brighton. But we were heading north, not south, and I couldn't think of any naughty places to the north of London. Surely nobody goes to the industrial grime of the Midlands to be naughty? I suppose in a way I was relieved. Much as I wanted to spend the night with Darcy, and heaven knows we had waited long enough, there was also that element of worry about the consequences.

Darcy was being enigmatic, driving with a rather smug grin on his face and not answering my questions. Eventually I told myself that we were probably going to a house party somewhere in the country, given by one of his numerous friends, which would be quite an acceptable thing to do, if not as exciting as a night at a hotel in Brighton, signed in as Mr. and Mrs. Smith. But as the lights of London vanished and we were driving into complete darkness I couldn't stand it a minute longer.

"Darcy, where on earth are we going?" I demanded.

He was still staring straight ahead of him into the night. "Gretna Green," he replied.

"Gretna Green? Are you serious?" The words came out as squeaks. "But that's in Scotland. And it's where people go when—"

"When they elope to get married. Quite right."

I glanced at his profile. He still had that satisfied smile on his face. "I know you too well, Georgie," he replied. "You're altogether too respectable. You've inherited too much from your great-grandmother." (Who, in case you don't know, was Queen Victoria.) "You don't want to take that next step with me until there is a ring on your finger and I respect that. So I aim to remedy the situation. If we drive all night then by tomorrow you will be Mrs. Darcy O'Mara and I can take you to bed with a clear conscience."

"Golly," I replied. Not exactly the most sophisticated of answers, I know, but I was taken by surprise. I found myself grinning too. Mrs. Darcy O'Mara. Not quite as lofty as Lady Georgiana Rannoch, but infinitely more satisfying. I couldn't wait to see my sister-in-law Fig's face when I returned to London and waved my ringed finger at her. The thought of Fig led me to a more practical consideration. Darcy was a young man of no fixed abode. He had an impeccable pedigree. He had grown up, like me, in a castle. He would inherit a title one day. But, also like me, he was penniless. He lived by his wits and accepted clandestine assignments he wouldn't talk about. He slept on friends' couches or looked after their London houses while they were away on their yachts or on the Riviera. That sort of life was fine for a single man, but I could hardly share a couch at a bachelor friend's establishment, could I?

Tentatively I broached this matter. "So, Darcy, if I'm not being too inquisitive, where had you planned for us to live?"

"I hadn't," he said. "You'll go back to your brother and I'll go wherever I am offered an assignment. I'm saving any money I earn and when I have enough to establish us in a suitably proper form of residence, then we'll announce our marriage. Gretna Green is just to make sure that if anything untoward happened and you found yourself"—he paused and coughed—"in the family way, we could then wave our marriage certificate at them and all would be well and your honor would be intact."

I had to laugh at this. Actually I think I giggled, nervously, but these were such heady topics to be talking about with a man.

"So how long do you think it might take, until we can afford a place of our own?" I asked.

"Not too long, I hope." He sighed. "If only my father hadn't lost all his money and had to sell the castle and the racing stable, we could have moved into my ancestral home. You would have liked Kilhenny Castle. It's less wild and remote than Castle Rannoch. Quite civilized, in fact."

"Your father still lives in the lodge, doesn't he?"

"Yes, and he's paid to run the racing stable by the American who bought the whole shebang. He's now the hired help on an estate our family has owned for centuries. I can't go near the place. Too painful." He paused again. "Not that my father would want to see me anyway. He doesn't like me very much."

"He doesn't approve of your lifestyle?"

Darcy snorted. "He's hardly in a position not to approve, is he? I wasn't the one who sold the family heritage. No, it's simpler than that. He has never forgiven me for staying alive."

"What?" I looked up at him sharply. His mouth was set in a hard line.

"When the Spanish flu reached us in 1920 I was away at prep school in England. My mother and my two little brothers caught it and died. My school was so freezing cold and miserable that not even the flu could survive there, so I survived. My father once said, when he was in his cups, that whenever he looks at me he is reminded that my mother died and I lived."

"Hardly your fault," I said angrily.

"My father never was the most rational of men. Always had a terrible temper and always carried grudges. But let's not talk about him. We're about to embark upon an adventure and to hell with our families."

"That's right," I said, covering his hand on the steering wheel with my own. "Since they don't support us, then it's none of their business whether we get married or not."

Lights sped by us from the other direction, illuminating the interior of our car for an instant before plunging us into darkness again. I was picturing telling my family that Darcy and I had married. My brother, Binky, would be happy for me. Fig would not approve because Darcy was penniless and also a Roman Catholic and . . .

"Golly!" I said again, sitting bolt upright in my seat. Darcy turned to look at me. "I can't marry you, Darcy," I said. "I'd completely forgotten, but I'm not allowed to. I'm still in the line of succession to the throne and we're not allowed to marry a Catholic."

"I thought we agreed you could just renounce your claim to the throne and then all would be well," he said. He looked at me with a half smile on his face. "Unless, of course, you'd rather give up the chance to marry me just in case you become queen someday."

I chuckled. "Since I'm currently thirty-fifth in line it would have to be another visit of the Black Death to wipe out those between me and the throne," I said. "And who would ever want to be queen? Of course I want to marry you, but I think it has to be done officially. I have to petition the king and I believe it has to go through Parliament. So we'd better turn around and go back before we go too far."

Darcy shook his head. "I'm not turning around. We're

going to Scotland and we're going to get married. We won't tell anybody, and in due course you can approach your royal kin and ask permission to marry me. Then we can have a proper wedding at a suitable church with veil and brides-maids and nobody but us need ever know that we were married already."

"Can one do that?" I asked.

"Who is to know?"

"What if the king and queen refuse my request?"

"Why would they? And if they did, then I'd renounce my religion if it was the only way to marry you."

A lump came into my throat. "Darcy, I'd never ask you to do that. Your religion means a lot to you."

"I agree that my family did fight for it for many hundreds of years, but as I say, if it's the only way to marry you, then so be it. Becoming an Anglican wouldn't be so bad . . . just a watered-down form of being a Catholic."

I laughed now, with relief. Darcy loved me so much that he was willing to give up anything for me. I can't tell you how wonderful that felt.

We drove on. It was becoming really cold. I found a rug on the backseat and tucked it around my knees. Then it started to rain, a hard-driving sleety sort of rain that pep-pered the windscreen. Darcy swore under his breath as he peered closer, trying to see where we were going.

"We could find somewhere to spend the night if this is going to continue," I said. "It's no fun for you driving in these conditions."

"No, we'll keep going," he said. "It will pass."

But it didn't. One by one, signposts to the Midland cities came and went. We stopped for a meat pie and beer at a pub in the middle of nowhere. A big fire roared in the grate and I looked at it longingly as we rushed through the rain back to our motorcar.

By the time we reached Yorkshire the rain had turned to snow—a heavy wet snow that stuck to the windscreen wipers and started to pile up as it was pushed from side to side. No other traffic seemed to be crazy enough to be on the road.

"We should stop," I said. "This is becoming dangerous."

"It's a good solid motor," Darcy replied. "It should handle the conditions all right."

"I don't want to skid and find myself upside down in a ditch," I said.

We passed by roads leading to the cities of Leeds, then York, although no sign of them could be seen. We seemed to be driving through bleak hills with little sign of human habitation. We might have been in the middle of nowhere. Suddenly Darcy jammed on the brakes and I felt the rear of the motor sliding sideways. I think I screamed. Darcy fought to right us. We spun around. Headlights flashed crazily onto trees and snow. Then, miraculously, we stopped sliding. I opened my eyes to find us facing the wrong way.

"What was that?" I asked, my voice horribly shaky.

"A bit of a wild ride for a moment there." Darcy sounded almost as if he'd enjoyed it.

I glared at him, fear giving way to anger. "You didn't do that on purpose, did you?"

"Of course I didn't. Do you take me for an idiot?"

"Then why did you brake suddenly like that?"

"Because there is a damned-fool lorry blocking the road ahead." Even he sounded tense now. He opened the door, letting in a freezing draft and swirling snow, then stepped out into the blizzard. I wrapped the rug more firmly around me, trying to peer out through the snow to see what was happening. Darcy had vanished into the swirling whiteness. I held my breath until he returned, looking grim.

"Well, that's that for tonight," he said. "The road ahead is blocked by snow. I asked if there was another route we could take but the chap said that if the Great North Road was blocked then the smaller roads would be hopeless. His very words were, 'If it's snowing like this down here, then a right bugger of a blizzard would be howling up on the moors.'" He sighed impatiently. "We'll have to wait until someone comes to clear it tomorrow. Or the day after. . . . The chaps there didn't seem to know much, just that we can't go any further. So I'm afraid we'll have to take your suggestion and find a place to spend the night."

"We passed a pub a mile or so back," I said.

"Then we'll try that." Darcy scraped the coating of snow away from the windscreen, then dusted himself down before he climbed back in and carefully turned the motor around. "I hope they'll have some kind of accommodation. I don't want to have to go back too far." He slapped his palms against the steering wheel. "Oh, this is too frustrating, isn't it? Just when I thought I had planned everything perfectly. When I'd persuaded that hopeless maid of yours to pack a case for you. When I'd managed to borrow a suitable motorcar. And now this."

I laid my hand on his sleeve. "It's only a delay, Darcy. They'll have to clear this road pretty quickly, won't they? It's the main artery to Scotland and the north of England. What is a day or so more?"

He nodded. "You're right. Just a delay. We've waited three years. What's one more night?"

"I remember when you first met me you made a bet with my friend Belinda that you'd get me into bed within the week, or was it a month?" I gave him a quizzical stare.

He grinned. "I can't remember, but clearly I lost the bet and should pay up. I hadn't banked on your stern willpower and royal sense of propriety."

"And circumstances conspiring against us, as they are now," I said. "My mother could never believe we were taking so long about it."

Darcy gave a half laugh, half snort. "Well, your mother is hardly a good role model for chaste living, is she? How many times has she been married? Or not married, as the case may be?"

My mother had in fact bolted from my father, the Duke

of Rannoch, when I was two, and since then had been a great many things to a great many men on six of the seven continents. Antarctica had only escaped as it was too bloody cold! At this moment I could appreciate her reasoning, as my feet had turned to blocks of ice.

WE STARTED RETRACING our route southward. The pub I had remembered seeing was called the Pig and Whistle. It looked inviting in a quaint countrified sort of way, but the front door was, alas, locked and no lights shone. Darcy got out, shook and rattled the front door, then came back to the motorcar in disgust, brushing the snow from his jacket.

"Stupid licensing hours," Darcy muttered as he put the motor into gear again. "Why can't we be like France and Italy and let everyone drink all night if they want to?"

"Because we don't want half the population blind drunk and unable to work, I suppose."

He snorted at this. "Do you see them all blind drunk on the Continent?"

"I suppose they grow up used to it. And they drink wine rather than beer and whiskey. Wine is supposed to be good for you. And they don't work as hard as we do. Drive past any café in France and you'll see men sitting around with glasses of wine in the middle of the morning. They just don't take life seriously."

"How come you're always so damned rational and composed?" he snapped. "Anyone would think you didn't want to elope with me." He stopped and turned sharply to look at me. "You do want to, don't you? I never actually asked you."

The question caught me by surprise. Did I want to? Wasn't I worried about what my royal relatives would say? Hadn't I looked forward to the long white dress and veil all my life? Then I looked at Darcy. Even in the darkness of the motorcar he was so handsome, and I loved him so much. "Of course I do," I said.

"You hesitated before you answered me," he replied.

"Only because I'm too cold to make my mouth move."

"I could warm it up for you," he said. He reached behind my head and drew me toward him, kissing me long and hard. "Right," he said when we broke apart a little breathlessly. "Let's find somewhere to spend the night before we both end up frozen to death."

We drove on, hoping to see at least a village close to the road. I think we must have been almost back as far as York when we finally found any sign of human habitation, at least humans who might be still awake. This was also a pub, a little off the road and by a railway crossing. The sign, swinging in the blizzardlike wind, said *The Drowning Man* and showed a hand coming out of a pond.

"Hardly encouraging," Darcy said dryly. "But at least a light is still burning and hopefully someone is still awake."

He opened the driver's side door, letting in a great flurry of snow, then wrestled the wind to close it hurriedly before running across to the pub. I peered through the snow-clad windscreen, watching him. He knocked, waited, and to my relief the door finally opened, letting out a band of light across the snow. Darcy seemed to be having a prolonged conversation during which the other person could be seen peering at me, then he marched back to the car. For a horrible moment I thought he was going to say that they had nothing available and that we'd have to drive on. But instead he came around to my door and opened it for me.

"They appear to have rooms. Hardly the most welcoming of places, from what I can see, but it's really a case of any port in a storm." He took my hand and led me through the snow to the building. I was going to say the warmth of the building, but in truth it wasn't much warmer than the motorcar had been. One naked bulb hung in a hallway and an uncarpeted stair disappeared into darkness.

"Caught in the storm, were you?" the innkeeper asked. Now that we could see her, I noticed that she was a big-boned cart horse of a woman with little darting eyes in a pudgy, heavy-jowled face.

I shot a swift glance at Darcy, praying he wouldn't make

a facetious comment along the lines that we were actually heading for the Riviera and took a wrong turn.

"We were heading for Scotland but the road is closed," I said before he could answer.

"Aye. We heard that on the wireless," she said. "Reckon it will take days, don't they? So you'll be wanting a room, then?"

"We will," Darcy said.

"I've just the one room," she said. "The others are occupied. You are a married couple, I take it?" And she gave us a hard stare, trying to see a wedding ring through my gloves, I suspected.

"Of course," Darcy said briskly. "Mr. and Mrs. Chomondley-Fanshaw. That's spelled Featherstonehaugh, by the way."

I fought back a desire to giggle. She was still eyeing us suspiciously. "I don't care how it's spelled," she said. "We don't go for airs and graces in this part of the country. As long as good honest folk have the brass to pay, we don't care how many hyphens they have in their names."

"Right, then," Darcy said. "If you'd be good enough to show us the room?"

She didn't budge but pointed. "Turn right at the top of the stairs and it's at the end of the hall. Number thirteen."

Then she reached into a cubby and handed us a key. "Breakfast from seven to nine in the dining room. Breakfast is extra. Oh, and if you want a bath you'll have to wait till morning. Hot water is turned off between ten and six. And the bath's extra too."

Darcy gave me a look but said nothing. "I'll take you up first then go and get the bags," he said. "Come on."

I followed him up the narrow stair. An icy draft blew down at us.

"Are there fires in the rooms?" Darcy turned back to ask the landlady, who was still standing there watching us.

"No fireplace in that room," she said.

"And I suppose a cup of hot chocolate is out of the question?" There wasn't much hope in his voice.

"Kitchen closed at eight." She turned her back and walked into the darkness of the hallway.

"We don't have to stay here," Darcy whispered to me. "There must be proper hotels in York. It's not that far now."

"It's still miles away And we've no guarantee anyone else has a room," I said. "If all the roads northward are closed . . ." In truth I felt close to tears. It had been a long day, starting with helping to dress the bride at Kensington Palace, then the ceremony for Marina and Prince George at St. Margaret's Westminster, then the reception at Buckingham Palace and the long, cold, snowy drive. All I wanted to do was curl up into a little ball and go to sleep.

The floorboards creaked horribly as we tiptoed down the hall. Number thirteen was about the gloomiest room I had ever seen—and I had grown up in a Scottish castle noted for its gloominess. It was small, crowded with mismatched furniture and dominated by an enormous carved wardrobe that took up the one wall where the ceiling didn't slope. In the midst of this clutter was a narrow brass bed with a patchwork quilt on it. A naked bulb gave just enough anemic light to reveal sagging and stained curtains at the window and a small braided rug on the bare floor.

"Golly!" I let out the childish exclamation before I remembered that I had resolved to be sophisticated from now on. "It is pretty grim, isn't it?"

"It's bloody awful," Darcy said. "Sorry for swearing, but if ever a room deserved the word 'bloody,' this is it. Let's just get out of here while we can. I wouldn't be surprised if the landlady didn't kill off the guests during the night and make them into pies."

I started laughing at the thought. "Oh, Darcy. What are we doing here?"

"My lovely surprise," he said, shaking his head, but smiling too. "Oh well, if we start off life together in these surroundings it can only get better, can't it?"

I nodded. "Do you suppose there is an indoor loo or will it be at the bottom of the garden?"

We explored the hall and were relieved to find a lavatory and bathroom of sorts at the far end.

"I'll go and get the bags," Darcy said. "If you're really sure you want to stay."

"I'm not sure that I want to undress. I'd freeze." I reconsidered. "But I suppose I shouldn't crease my good outfit any more. Do you have any idea what Queenie packed for me?"

"I told her sensible outfits to travel in. And your nightclothes."

"Knowing Queenie, that will mean a dinner dress and riding boots."

However, when he returned with the bags I was pleasantly surprised to find that she had packed my sponge bag, a warm flannel nightdress and dressing gown and my tweed suit. She rose considerably in my estimation. In fact I felt quite warmly toward her. She'd be asleep right now in Kensington Palace, with fires in the rooms and hot chocolate whenever one rang a bell, while her mistress . . . I looked around the room again but words failed me. Darcy had undressed rapidly and looked ridiculously rakish in maroon silk pajamas. I felt shy about undressing in front of him, then reminded myself we were about to become Mr. and Mrs.

I turned away and unbuttoned my jacket. Then I remembered the dress had hooks down the back. I reached around but clearly they were impossible. Then a voice said, "Here, let me," and he was unhooking them for me. I was horribly conscious of his hands touching my skin. He helped me out of the dress, then put his hands on my shoulders and kissed the bare back of my neck. It was an incredibly sexy gesture and on any other occasion I would have responded. But at this moment I was cold and tired and a little frightened. I turned to him and buried my head on his shoulder.

"Oh, Darcy, what are we doing here?" I asked, half laughing, half crying.

His arms came around me. "I wanted our first night together to be very different from this," he said.

"We've spent nights together before," I reminded him. "At least parts of nights."

"I meant our first real night together," he said. "You know

what I meant. And we will certainly save that sort of thing for a better time. I bet that old bat will be listening for any creaks in the bedsprings."

That made me laugh. I finished undressing, put my robe on over my nightclothes, then climbed into bed. The sheets were stiff and icy.

"It's freezing," I said through chattering teeth.

Darcy tiptoed around to turn off the light, and when he climbed into bed beside me the springs did indeed give an ominous twang that set both of us giggling like schoolchildren.

"That certainly rules out hanky-panky of any sort," he said, still chuckling. He wrapped me in his arms. "Still freezing?" he asked.

"Better now," I whispered. "Much better."

RHYS BOWEN

"Wonderful characters . . . A delight."

—Charlaine Harris, #1 *New York Times* bestselling author

For a complete list of titles,
please visit prh.com/rhysbowen